Seventeen Gifts for Frannie and Jess

Seventeen Gifts

for
Frannie and Jess

Nasser Hashmi

Matador
9 Priory Business Park,
Wistow Road, Kibworth Beauchamp,
Leicestershire. LE8 0RX
Tel: 0116 279 2299
Email: books@troubador.co.uk
Web: www.troubador.co.uk/matador
Twitter: @matadorbooks

ISBN 978 1785892 592

British Library Cataloguing in Publication Data.
A catalogue record for this book is available from the British Library.

Printed and bound in the UK by TJ International, Padstow, Cornwall
Typeset in 11pt Palatino by Troubador Publishing Ltd, Leicester, UK

Matador is an imprint of Troubador Publishing Ltd

To friendship...

ALSO BY THE SAME AUTHOR

NOVELS

Season of Sid
Wacko Hacko
A Fistful of Dust

nasserhashmi.com
nasseronmars.com

DAY ONE

An Opening Ceremony without Donald Hartford's guiding hand feels wrong. My husband pushed me hard to become a volunteer so how can I board the train to London without him? Surely that would be traumatic with 80,000 people inside the Olympic Stadium looking at me? But Donald would tap his knuckles on the palm of his other hand and say 'Frannie, this is chance of a lifetime, don't waste it'. After all, he was there in 1948 and now kept the precious 2012 tickets in his favourite crimson dinner jacket to protect them for the big day. That big day was here now – and he wasn't. Couldn't you have waited, Donald? Just a bit longer so we could have shared this moment?

I rub a photo of Donald and my Olympic ticket together as if they will magically make my decision for me. The other ticket has no doubt ended up in the hands of someone ready to savour the event and smile all the time. I'll have to sit to next to them. Do they have a husband or wife? Children? What if they want to talk to me? Oh, Donald you are a swine for doing this to me.

I roll up the photo – of a tired-looking Donald during his service in Borneo – and slide it into his favourite Union flag mug. The same image of Donald will be beamed to the world inside the Olympic Stadium within hours. My team leader Rob Miles, who came to Donald's funeral three months ago, was adamant Donald should be remembered just like the 7/7 victims and Danny Boyle's father who had also died recently. Really Rob? Was my Donald that important? He only spent a few years in the army but then became a librarian for the rest of his life. I can't understand how he'd measure up against those people. He'd be so embarrassed about it.

I put the mug, ticket and photo on Donald's pillow and get up off the bed. It's not butterflies in my stomach but caterpillars, hundreds of them. I walk to the bathroom and imagine Donald's voice, humming to Dean Martin, drawing me inside. I walk in and it feels colder than ever, even though we're in the middle of summer. I stand in front of the mirror and imagine myself dressed in my volunteer's uniform; a purple and red pensioner nursing a bereavement and a trail of bad luck. It's a personal best for shortest amount of time spent in the bathroom. I head downstairs and turn on the TV but the story is clear: the whole event is going to be a disaster anyway so why go? Ticketing problems, recruitment issues, bad weather; I mean, even the army had been brought in so it was all going to be a catastrophe. Good old Britain messing it up again. Why would I want to be a part of that?

I think about Donald's favourite mug and connect it to the news. He never used the Union flag mug if guests came round to visit in case anyone was offended. I remember once an Indian man came round,

2

selling complicated gas deals, but Donald hid his mug away to ensure there were no awkward moments. It was silly but Donald was like that; overcompensated, planned everything, saw the traps. Me? I took what came up: volunteered at the WI, filled envelopes at the charity shop, helped make breakfasts at the care home. Not much is it? Although Mr Nash might think otherwise after he nearly choked on his boiled egg at the care home one frosty morning. I'd like to think I helped save his life – at least that's how I see it anyway.

I'm ready to make dinner and settle down to watch the ceremony on TV at about 9pm. It's so much cosier at home anyway. Since my sister Abigail – and her family – showed up at Donald's funeral, I've been feeling more like that every day: keep my head down, don't go out, stay within my boundaries. It was like the two-year training for London 2012 didn't happen at all. It'd been obliterated by Donald's stroke.

I start preparing the anchovies and olives to go into the pasta for the evening meal. It annoys me that Abigail didn't even come to the house after the funeral – but I hadn't seen her for eight years so I was grateful she at least came to the service. She lives in France now, with her architect husband and such a big family that I'd lost count. People said I shouldn't let her treat me like that but what can I do? She's always took things when she wanted them. I could never ask – and by the time I did, it was too late.

The London 2012 training did change that, of course. I spoke to people, asked questions, put on a big act – but most of the time, my body vibrated when I spoke, there was a tingling sensation round my temple and I had to swallow before starting a new sentence. Oh, and we met Sally Gunnell so that didn't help. I always liked her but meeting her rendered me completely speechless. If it wasn't for Donald, accompanying me to the training sessions – giving me encouragement and support – I'm not sure I would have made it through.

I prepare a fresh salad for dinner and glance up at a small National Trust calendar pinned on the kitchen door. Donald liked to circle important events on it or things he had to do. There is a small note saying library books need to be given back – it goes back to early June. How did I not notice that before? Because I had enough on my plate contacting our bank, our insurers and God knows who else after he died. This was so stressful I wanted to leave the country. In one call, I was kept waiting 40 minutes and couldn't speak when I finally got through to a human voice. I sobbed and put the phone down. Did they do this to our country on purpose? Did the dead not matter anymore? I quickly head up to his study to check through some of Donald's things. Everything had been left untouched; I couldn't bear to move anything. I look under the spare bed and there they are – three books, neatly stacked and heavy (he always liked the big, historical ones with plenty of pictures). I pull them out and sit on the bed. The first is a colourful history of Egyptian art. The second is on Dutch colonies in the East Indies.

The third is called *The 1948 Olympics: How London Rescued The Games* by Bob Phillips. I open it and read the foreword by Sir Roger Bannister. A yellow Post-it note pops out. I instantly recognise the writing.

> *Donald, I knew you were trying to hunt down this book (even though you read it years ago) so here it is! Our tiny library strikes again! Hope you have a great time at the Olympic Stadium.*
> *Ginny*

Ginny worked with Donald at the community library. She was leading the campaign to keep the library open which was under the threat of closure (and still is). I knew her quite well – she came to the funeral and our home afterwards – but I haven't seen her since. But it doesn't matter now – she's done her bit in persuading me that I *must* stop moping and seize the opportunity of a lifetime. I read her final sentence again: *Hope you have a great time at the Olympic Stadium*. I imagine Donald in there, proud as Punch, waving his Union flag and blurting out the national anthem even though his dry cough would spoil his naturally fine rhythm. I am next to him, trying to keep up, but getting the words of the anthem wrong. We are together once again, hand in hand, ready to spark Britain into life again. I read more of the book and feel captivated by the heartwarming stories and the achievements. How could I not want to be part of this? I close the book and get up. I go to the bathroom and quickly get changed. I go downstairs, have a quick dinner (while standing in the kitchen) and then check my Olympic ticket one last time. I walk out of the front door and head for the station to board the train to London. If it is daunting and intimidating, I can take it. I *am* a volunteer. That's my job.

I sit on the blue-covered seat of the Chiltern Railways' train where it is standing room only. A kind, young gentleman, with white earphones plugged to his lobes, offers me his seat and, then cheekily, hands me one of his earphones which blurts out an almighty racket. I smile and politely decline his second offer. Hasn't he got any Petula Clark or Lulu? I sit down and cross my hands, acknowledging the man in a beanie hat sat next to me, who's swiping a shiny device with his extremely long fingers. What did they call these things? Tablets? I had a mobile, of course (but only when Donald pushed me into getting one) and he was right: it was essential for my volunteering and Locog training – but these *Apple* things (or whatever they were called) scared me. People will stop shaking hands soon. I remember a young assistant at the charity shop doing just that when I offered my hand to her on her first day. She asked me to hold on a moment because she was in the middle of texting her boyfriend. She was very nice and apologetic after that but spent most of the rest of the day (it wasn't very busy) doing the same thing. She only lasted three weeks. But Donald said at least these devices gave people something to do with their fingers rather than smoking. Perhaps, but head down or get smoke blown in your face? It wasn't much of a choice.

I am thankful to reach Marylebone Station for the sole reason I can get off a packed train. The Tube isn't much better but at least I get a seat immediately – for both journeys; first on the Bakerloo Line to Baker Street, then on the Jubilee Line all the way to Stratford. I'm annoyed that I didn't bring anything to read. I look up and can only see the backside of man in a suit. This is why Donald never liked taking the Tube; never knew where to put your eyes. I divert mine to the map I can't see over a tall lady's head. As we get to Canary Wharf, my thoughts become scrambled and my hands begin to tremble. Did I leave my Olympic ticket at home? Inside the book given to Donald? How could I have done that after spending weeks thinking about the event? I check my purse and pockets and, after a minute or two of utter panic, I am so relieved to find the ticket in my coat pocket. My sigh is so loud it attracts the attention of the man next to me. I clutch the ticket and then, with a sense of slight embarrassment, put it back into my pocket.

'For the Opening Ceremony, yes?' says the man, moving his head closer to my ear. 'Bet you can't wait.'

'Sorry, can you speak up a bit? This train's so loud, I find it hard to think in here…'

'The ticket?' he says, moving even closer and raising his voice a little. 'Is it for the Olympic Opening Ceremony? Are you going to be in the stadium?'

'Yes, I'll be in the stadium…'

'Are you going with anyone?'

'No.'

The man nods and leans back in his seat. He looks about 35, clean-shaven, swollen cheeks, hair camouflaging the top of his ears. He's wearing a short-sleeved sky blue shirt and brown trousers. Every time he rocks back and forth, I get a strong whiff of deodorant going up my nostrils. There is a long pause and then he moves forward again.

'I hope this summer's better than last,' he says. 'The riots were dreadful, absolutely dreadful. We shamed this city. I hope the Olympics banishes all those memories. It's a got a lot to live up to.'

'I never thought of it like that,' I reply, finding it excruciatingly hard to make eye contact. 'Never really crossed my mind really: the riots. Saw them on TV – but don't think we should be dwelling on them now.'

'Dwelling!' says the man, with a laugh and a snigger. 'That's a fine word you've come up with there: a fine, fine word.'

I finally turn and look the man in the eye. I wonder if he's okay. He seems to be speaking to himself rather than addressing me.

'My name's Richard,' he says, with an abruptness that made me shudder. 'I was on duty with the Met last year when the riots started. I was caught right in the centre of the carnage. A few thugs got stuck into me. They got their time and a half. We were outnumbered. I went to hospital and was signed off indefinitely until I got better.' He smiles and looks up at me. 'I've recovered now so I start work next week. I want these Olympics to succeed so we can show a better face to the world. I know I get a bit worked up about it but it really matters. Do you see where I'm coming from?'

I sigh and shift in my seat to face the man. 'Of course, I do. I'm sorry you suffered so much but this is going to be different. We're going to be showing a different face to the world; a bolder and brighter one.'

'You say 'we', are you taking part or something?'

I hesitate and consider whether I want to take this conversation further. I don't even know the man. Donald would always ask me to be wary of men asking too many questions – and wearing too much deodorant.

'It's okay if you don't want to talk,' he says, folding his arms. 'I need to save my energy for the woman I'm trying to court. I'm meeting her this evening in Canning Town. She's got a couple of kids, but that's no problem because I've got a son of my own. Don't see him a lot though...'

'Divorced, are you?'

He nods and smiles.

'See, that made you feel better didn't it?' he says.

I almost break out into a smile but look away just in time. There is another long pause and I consider whether to tell Richard about Donald. Is it too early? Would he be interested? I judge it's too early. Strangers need to keep their distance.

'My guess would be that you're a volunteer,' he says. 'I mean, no offence, you're unlikely to be competing because of your golden years so I reckon that's what you'll be doing? Am I right?'

This time I do break out into a smile. I nod and cross my hands.

'That's great to hear,' he says. 'So many people could learn from you. A little bit of TLC to the community never did anyone harm. Good luck to you.' He pauses and looks up. 'Oh, here's my stop, I'm getting off here.' He gets up and nearly falls over as we approach Canning Town station. 'Thanks for the little chat; made me feel better.'

I nod but don't say anything. Then Richard does something unexpected. He reaches into his trouser pocket and hands me a card. It has his details and number on it.

'I've learnt to be a little more thoughtful about other people since the riots last year,' he says. 'If you need any help from me, give me a call. Even if you don't I'd love to know how you went on at the Olympics.' He walks away towards the exit doors. 'Oh and tell Usain Bolt to come down for a drink after his 100 metres win.' He smiles and waves. He leaves the Tube train and we move off again.

I look around the rest of the carriage: this time making eye contact with many more people. I pull out my Olympic Opening Ceremony ticket again – and stroke it between my palms. I may have been uncertain about coming down here before. Not now. I'm ready for a night to remember.

As soon as Bradley Wiggins enters the stage, the stadium erupts. The noise crackles through my senses, creating an out-of-body experience as though I'm about to float away from my seat. It's like Wiggins' yellow jersey has turned gold and is sprinkling dust all over the spectators. Eighty thousand people cheer and clap, waving their flags and taking pictures. The roar is so deafening I have to close my eyes for a moment because it scares me. It's as if a secret power is propelling me forward; shimmering and intoxicating, pushing me into the centre of the stadium. How will I deal with this every day? My left ear popped regularly as it was. The man next to me, who has Donald's ticket, stands up and pumps his fist. 'Go Wiggo,' he says. I imagine Donald being a little less animated. As Bradley Wiggins leaves the stage after taking the plaudits, the man next to me sits down – and then pulls his socks up.

'This'll be bigger than Beijing, don't you think?' he says, glancing at me. 'I can't believe I'm here. Did you come on your own too?'

I don't answer immediately, as another bout of cheering gives me the opportunity to divert attention away from the man's question.

'Wiggo's a bit of a hero of mine. Sorry, I got a bit carried away.'

I smile at him but find it difficult to say anything. The bright, glitzy lights of the unfolding ceremony – and Wiggins' entrance – have scrambled my emotions so much I'm not sure how to behave. How can I cheer now when I've been crying at dawn for the last few months? But then I realise I may have to spend the next few hours with this man who's taken Donald's place. Like it or not, we're stuck with each other.

Perhaps, I should be nicer to him? The problem is, I'm not seeing him as a person at all right now. Fate, death and fortune may have brought us together but all I see is a cheering ghost, a physical specimen, a man who should have been my husband but isn't. When he opens his mouth, I imagine Donald's words coming out.

A children's choir begins to sing *Jerusalem* and people dance around the maypoles in their costumes. Green fields, maids and village cricket being played. The boy's voice so sharp and golden, I have to turn away in case he plucks a tear from my soul. It's as though he's addressing me directly rather than thousands of others inside the stadium. I recover in time to see Isambard Kingdom Brunel walk out as he recites Shakespeare's *The Tempest* with Elgar playing the background.

'Kenneth Branagh that is…' says the man next to me.

'Yes I know, someone told me he was appearing…'

I regret it the moment it slips out of my mouth – but that's what *Jerusalem* and little boys do to me. The man turns and looks at me. He folds his arms and gives me a knowing smile.

'I thought this ceremony was supposed to be a secret,' he says. 'Are you one of those volunteers' relatives then? Those performers down there?' He points just in case I don't understand the question. 'They probably tweeted everyone during rehearsals.'

'No, I'm not a relative or a performer…'

I hope it's the end of the conversation – but he presses on.

'You're not his mother are you?'

'No, I'm not Kenneth Branagh's mother.' I sigh and realise there's no way out of this unless I come clean. 'I'm a volunteer – and I start work tomorrow. My team leader, who's got his ear to the ground, told me that one of the actors had dropped out a few weeks ago – and Kenneth Branagh was taking over. He knew my husband was a big admirer of Branagh so that's why he probably told me.' I glance across at the man. 'Now, can we watch the ceremony please?'

'Yes, but why isn't your husband here if he's such a big admirer?'

The man stares at me as Brunel's recital ends. I glance at the couple in the seats to my right. I'd hardly noticed them because they were almost facing each other, knees touching, holding hands and, generally looking like they were completely besotted with each other. If only nosey parker to my left would be like them.

'Because you *are...*' I say.

He nods and seems taken aback by my answer. I feel much better as it's the first time I've asserted myself since Donald and I had dinner in a Thai restaurant – and the main course didn't turn up. It doesn't affect him for long though.

'Oh here are the drums,' he says, standing up and doing a little jig to the pounding drumbeat. 'Industrial Revolution time; I'm loving this.'

He sits down after a few minutes – a bit out of

breath – and gets his phone out. He raises it in the air and starts recording as soon as the chimneys start rising from the ground. Many other people do the same. It's an awesome sight. Music and image are in such harmony that I feel the whole stadium is vibrating. Then the Suffragettes come out. Would I be here without them? No, but the old struggle feels like the same one for me. Who'll fight for me now?

'Danny Boyle's racing through this part, isn't he?' says the man, trying to cock his neck round while still trying to keep his mobile steady. 'The Beatles, Windrush, the Chelsea Pensioners, I hope to see Zeppelin soon...'

I don't answer as I'm transfixed by the momentum of the Industrial Revolution sequence. It all comes to a spectacular climax as five Olympic rings are formed in the sky – and then shower their golden light onto everyone below. I didn't expect to be so moved by it. The conversion of the harsh, heavy chimneys to the bright glow of the Olympic symbol rings is breathtaking. Oh Donald, why couldn't you be here to see this? It's euphoric and epic. You can forget your Greeks and your Egyptians.

The man shakes his head in disbelief and then switches off his phone and sits down. 'Man, that was something else; electric. Phew, Danny boy, you've given the pretenders a hell of a beating.' He looks at me and raises his palm above his head, probably thinking I didn't have a clue what he's up to. I smack his palm hard with my own.

'Whoa, you know what a high five is,' he says. 'Absolute mint.'

'There were a lot of young people at our Games training,' I say, wiping my palm after its heavy duty. 'I pick up things quickly.'

He looks at me again – and nods as though he's acknowledged a deep character trait about me.

'I'm sorry that I asked about your husband,' he says. 'That's private. I'm Marcus. I've come all the way down from Manchester for this. I think that sequence has just made it all worthwhile.'

I hesitate but realise social norms are being loosened by the second due to the spectacle unfolding in front of us.

'Francesca – and I definitely haven't come that far…'

'Where then?'

'A village in Buckinghamshire…'

'Bet it's posh isn't it? Buckinghamshire Palace and all that. Have you got maids and servants?'

I laugh for the first time in the evening. Can I do that yet? Is the mourning period over so soon? I feel guilty about not keeping myself under control.

'Speaking of which, is that James Bond going into the Palace?' he says, looking up at the big screen. 'Looks like he's got a date with the Queen.'

'I bet she prefers Sean Connery…'

Marcus laughs this time – and I'm surprised by my quick-witted response. We watch the big screen as 007 and Her Royal Highness get into a helicopter. The sequence then develops to make it look as though

15

the Queen has parachuted down into the Olympic Stadium. There are mass cheers around the stadium – but it also feels like a personal moment of reassurance. If the Queen can take part in the ceremony – be a good sport and let her hair down – then surely I can too.

The National Anthem is sung by a group of children – and then Mike Oldfield performs *Tubular Bells*.

'God, it's *The Exorcist*,' says Marcus, putting his hands over his eyes.

'No, it's Mike Oldfield...'

'Bit before my time, Francesca. I've seen that film six times. He needs to get out more. People might recognise him one day.'

I offer a mild smile but avert my gaze to the curious, but uplifting, spectacle of NHS nurses and doctors dancing in the centre of the arena. Patients too, spring out of bed and join the staff to create a heartwarming scene, as though a magic, happy virus has spread through the ward to create eternal good health. Then the announcer introduces J.K. Rowling. Marcus gets his phone out again and records the Harry Potter author's performance, a reading of *Peter Pan*. It's hard to keep up with the children's characters popping up everywhere: Voldemort, Mary Poppins, the Child Catcher. I remember hearing about *Chitty Chitty Bang Bang* being filmed in Hambleden in the late 60s (just a few miles from our village) and it's still one of my favourite films. Donald and I even visited the exact location where the car took its first drive! This pleasant memory doesn't last long, however, as the sequence ends with a giant baby in a bed which I find quite scary. Marcus laughs and ensures he's got it all on his phone. He sits down again and offers me the phone.

'Want to see that again?'

I shake my head. He puts his phone away and starts fiddling with the cables on his pixel screen. Every spectator has one of these tablet-like screens in front of them, which has nine lights and is designed to illuminate the whole stadium. I'm sceptical about them but have to admit that, in the dark, they look spectacular and very colourful. Marcus is not convinced that his is working. He misses Simon Rattle being introduced – but as soon as *Chariots of Fire* begins he looks up. The stirring melody is so beautiful that I feel I can't move. But it doesn't last long – as Mr Bean pops up, playing the synthesiser.

'We just know how to do it, don't we?' says Marcus, shaking his head as if he'd just seen Jesus himself walking into the stadium.

'What do you mean?'

'NHS, Mr Bean, chimneys; we just don't care. We just put it out there and try to get a smile on people's faces. Wit and flippancy, we're the best in the world at it.' He glances at the big screen. 'I mean, look at him!'

Mr Bean is cut into the famous scene in *Chariots of Fire* where the men are running barefoot on the beach. I find it amusing but do feel a little disappointed that we're being diverted from such glorious music. Perhaps the laughter is too soon for me after all.

'He's one of our biggest exports,' says Marcus. 'I

work for an event management company in Cheshire – and get to travel abroad sometimes. You wouldn't believe how many people have heard of Mr Bean. He doesn't even need to say anything. People around the world *know* what he's about. It's the same thing as all of us: we love to laugh and we love to be silly. I mean, what about Monty Python? I rest my case.'

'Donald didn't like them…'

'Who's Donald?'

I couldn't believe how stupid I'd been. Every time I tried to put Donald at the back of my mind – and enjoy the ceremony – he re-emerged to join the conversation. It was if he was saying: 'What are doing here, talking to this strange man? You have nothing in common'.

'Sorry Francesca, I won't pry again.'

'It's okay, it's just…'

'If you want to talk, I'll listen – but you're not half as interesting as Mr Bean over there…'

'You've made that clear already!' I pause and continue to watch the big screen as Mr Bean gets to the finishing line. 'No, let's just watch the ceremony. That's what we're here for…'

Marcus nods and starts clapping vigorously even before the sequence has come to an end. I sense I'm doing the right thing: I cannot share Donald's intimate details with a man I've known for barely an hour. I realise people share things very fast these days – in the news or on social media or whatever it's called – but there's still a time for patience and restraint; and this is one of those occasions.

The whole stadium gives Mr Bean and Simon Rattle a rapturous send-off and a few minutes later, we're into a music and cultural montage which gets Marcus excited again. Whenever a band or film are mentioned, Marcus shouts the title and then sings along to the words or quotes from the film. It becomes a bit trying after a while.

'It's The Jam!'

'It's OMD!'

'Charlie Chaplin!'

'*Gregory's Girl!*'

'The Beatles!

'The Specials!'

'*Doctor Who!*'

'Happy Mondays!'

'Prodigy!'

I hadn't heard of most of the bands mentioned. Then a performer came onto the stage who had the strangest name I'd ever heard. Couldn't he think of something more pleasant on a night like this?

'It's Dizzee Rascal!'

I am thankful when the sequence ends. Only good old Charlie – and perhaps Ray Davies of The Kinks – give me a lift. Marcus sits down again.

'Phew, I'm tired after that,' says Marcus. 'Cracking that was. Who's this fella now?'

'Invented the internet, I think.'

'Oh yeah, Tim Berners-Lee. Thought you'd have known who he was with his double-barrelled surname? Probably lives round the corner from you.'

'Not by inventing that kind of thing he doesn't. We like a bit of peace where we come from.'

Marcus smiles but doesn't respond. After Berners-Lee, there is a sequence about the 1948 Olympics as black and white images of King George, the flame being lit and an achingly young Elizabeth are shown on the big screen. I slide my hands over my face and rest them on my lips. It's like I'm frozen in time. Donald was in that stadium – and I'm in this one. If only we could be reunited again. Luckily, the montage is very short – not enough time for me to get worked up again.

But that comes a few minutes later – after a musical sequence about the 70-day torch relay and David Beckham bringing the flame to the stadium in a speedboat. The big screen beams a short pictorial tribute to friends and relatives who couldn't attend the ceremony. Donald is there, in amongst 7/7 victims, Danny Boyle's father and many others. His shy smile flashes up for a second – and then is gone forever. This time there is no restraint. My eyes fill up as the big screen becomes so dark I think I'm going blind. I feel unsteady but proud. The images are gone as quick as they came. I clear the tears with my thumb. I hope there is no more of this – or the night will become impossible.

Luckily, Marcus doesn't notice my sobbing – and thank God for that. He might try another joke. Britain likes its humour but there's a limit.

The stadium goes quiet as Emeli Sandè begins to sing *Abide With Me*. It's like they're trying to do this to me personally: batter me into submission with emotion and nostalgia. I manage to keep myself under control but then I see a dancer performing such a moving sequence that my head and eyes begin to fill up again.

'Who's that dancer?' I ask, trying to keep my voice under control.

'Akram Khan…'

Marcus doesn't have to say any more – we are both captivated. The song continues and I'm not sure I can make it to the end. I'm sobbing now and I need to do something; stand up, escape, go to the toilet, anything, because this is going to finish me off. It's coming to the end now and I think I'm going to make it in one piece. I take a tissue out of my purse and wipe my nose, cheeks and eyes. But that little boy with Akram Khan is prolonging the anguish. He's an angel, a beautiful soul, fluttering over the surface with innocence and grace. The love I feel for him right now is too much to bear. Oh Donald, if you could have seen this you would have gone to your grave a happier man. The boy hugs Akram Khan who carries him away towards the sun. *In Life in Death, O Lord, Abide With Me…* The boy reaches up and puts his arm up in the air. This time it is too much for me. The song ends and I get up from my seat, trying to keep the tears at bay. I walk past Marcus who is still clapping and whistling at the compelling performance he's just seen.

'Where are you going?' he asks.

I raise my arm to acknowledge him but say

nothing. I walk away from our seats and head for the exit. I fleetingly think about Team GB coming into the stadium or the Olympic flame being lit. Am I going to miss that? Regretfully, yes. Some things are more important, like my memories of Donald, which have been illuminated beautifully tonight. I will not make a sobbing spectacle of myself and spoil the night for everyone. I will go home with that little boy – and Donald by my side; forever.

DAY TWO

The journey to Stratford is peaceful enough; not much sign of Olympic fever here. I get to the Olympic Park and fear the whole event will be a damp squib. There's a palpable sense of trepidation and fear, although I admit it might just be me. Missing a portion of the Opening Ceremony seems to have affected me more than my colleagues. There are plenty of smiles around. I get changed into my uniform and put my hand in my trouser pocket to touch Donald's library card. It gives me a lift as I imagine having to make conversation throughout the day – from giving directions, checking tickets and smiling when I feel like hell inside. After our meeting in the control room – where we are put into groups and handed our lunch vouchers – I head out into the giant playground of the Olympic Park to prepare for the bustling intake of spectators. I know two people in my group – Sheena and Ben – but not well enough to initiate conversation. Ben spoke to me during my training and said he was a film student. He asked me about old classics and we did get onto David Lean films like *Brief Encounter* and *Great Expectations*. I recommended *This Happy Breed* to him but he'd never heard of it. I wouldn't mind Ben speaking to me – but he got extremely busy straight away, peering into a map given to him by three Croatian women, wearing national flags as capes and with their faces painted like a red and white chessboard. So much colour and enthusiasm, I thought. I didn't want to miss this opportunity to get fired up so I straightened my name badge and stepped forward, waiting for the three women to walk past. They take longer than expected. Ben gets on well with them. Finally, they part company and I get the chance to kickstart my Olympic campaign. Donald would be so proud of me.

'Going to the Basketball Arena?' I ask, unashamedly trying to show off my knowledge and develop some confidence at the same time. 'Preliminaries, isn't it? Who are you playing?'

'America, but it doesn't start till 4.45, so we're very early...'

'Very,' I say. 'Well, I suppose it gives you time to see the whole of the Olympic Park!'

'Of course, and there's hardly anyone here yet. How many events are there happening here today?'

'In the Park? Three: Basketball, Swimming and Handball. Obviously, there's many more going on elsewhere like the Cycling at The Mall and the Tennis at Wimbledon...'

'Oh, don't say Wimbledon, I'm going to faint,' says one of the women who hadn't spoken yet. 'It only means one word to me...'

'What's that?'

'GORAN!' she shouts, as she enthusiastically smacks the palm of her friend's hand extremely hard. 'You remember him? The King of Wimbledon?'

For a moment, I'm lost again. I vaguely remember a Wimbledon final which went onto a Monday afternoon and I can picture the player's languid, loping features – but for the life of me I can't remember his surname. I raise my hand quickly and hope they don't notice.

'GORAN!' I shout, together with the other three women as they strike my palm as they walk past. 'How good was he?'

'Not good. GOD!!'

The women laugh and head off into the Olympic Park. One of them mimes a tennis serve and does an exploding sound once imaginary ball hits imaginary racket. I breathe a sigh of relief and feel quite content with myself. It's like I've taken some small baby steps before things really get serious. But my right hand feels stiff so I clench my fist repeatedly to ease the pain, grimacing and gritting my teeth with each movement (it was an awkward *high five*). A few minutes later, I see Jessica, another colleague in my team, running towards me, pink foam pointer in her hand, high-visibility jacket and tied-up blonde hair smacking against her shoulders. She stops by my side – and I wonder what on earth has got into her.

'Are you all right, Francesca?' she asks, slightly out of breath.

'Of course, what's the matter?'

'Well, you looked to be in pain. I thought I'd come and ask how you were.'

'And why would you do that?'

She doesn't answer immediately. She looks over her shoulder towards Stratford Gate.

'Shouldn't you be getting back over there,' I say, crossing my hands in front of my waist. 'Few more coming in as far as I can see.'

'Well yes, but…'

'But what?'

'Nothing,' she says, touching the back of her hair. 'I'll get back up there now.' She begins to walk off.

'Wait, what the hell did you run over here for? I don't understand. Has Rob told you something he shouldn't have? I hope he hasn't because some things in this world have to stay private…'

Jessica turns and waits. She's about to speak but thinks better of it. She heads off again.

'Don't walk off when I'm talking to you…'

'I'll be over there if you need me,' she says, with a glance over her shoulder.

She runs off very fast so I decide not to say anything else as I know it's futile. A couple of minutes ago I was feeling quite euphoric but now I'm annoyed. No, I'm angry. How could Rob tell someone who I didn't know (apart from the usual pleasantries) about Donald's death without consulting me first? Isn't this wrong? Don't we have a moral code anymore? Jessica seems a nice girl but that's not the point. She shouldn't have been told. Rob has some explaining to do – and not just for spoiling my morning. I need to speak to him but I don't know where the hell he is.

'Hello, can you tell me where the Copper Box is?'

says a woman holding the hand of a young child. 'I have tickets for the Russia game.'

I look down at the child for longer than necessary. He's probably about seven; with jet black hair, huge eyes and a gaze that seems to interpret my life story in a few seconds.

'Hello Madam, are you listening?' she says, showing me her tickets. 'I asked where the Copper Box is...'

I pause again and take a deep breath. I feel so hot I have a desperate urge to run towards the Aquatics Centre and jump into one of the pools. It's like I've completely lost my bearings and don't know where I am. But I look down at the child again and he breaks out into a smile, melting away my anxiety.

'Oh yes, I'm dreadfully sorry, I didn't mean to be like that,' I say, offering a belated smile. 'Yes, the Copper Box, of course...' I look to my right and raise my arm to point the way. 'What you have to do is go down here, turn right, keep on walking for a while until you see that strange-looking brown block on your left. You can't miss it.'

'Thank you,' says the woman. 'Come on, Wasafa, let's go. Let's hope we can beat the mighty Russia today.'

The boy tries to hold his mother's hand but she eases it away. I notice the movement and she looks up and smiles at me. She shows me her hand.

'In Angola, I thought I could make the handball team but then I had to come to England,' she says, eager to show me her worn, semi-bandaged hand. 'It was an opportunity too good to miss. But it didn't stop me from playing with Wasafa in the back garden. It was in my blood. So much that my hand has blisters. See?'

I nod and smile at the woman and boy. 'Yes, and that's before you do the cooking and cleaning!'

'No, Kenneth, my husband does that. I trained him well…'

We both laugh but there is another awkward moment of silence before the woman walks off with her son towards the Copper Box. The thought occurs to me that it all seems to be about hands this morning: Goran's, mine, the Angolan lady's. I'd like to just hold Donald's again. I know that's impossible but maybe, just maybe – as I slip my hand into my pocket and touch *that* library card again – the spirit of 48 will be revived 64 years later. If not, this will be a long 16 days.

I have lunch in the canteen on my own – but don't eat much. A half-eaten tuna sandwich, a nibble on a cereal bar and a coffee is all I can manage. I'm so tired I wonder if I'll be able to get to the weekend, never mind the Closing Ceremony. Standing up for four or five hours has been more difficult than I imagined. I notice Jessica, Ben and Sheena sitting together a few tables away from me. Jessica seems to be the centre of attention. She's quite loud and boisterous and I'm glad I didn't engage with her this morning (my aching legs and the inquisitive spectators were more than enough to be going on with). Finally, I spot Rob coming into the canteen. I wave to him but have to do it twice to ensure he sees me. He walks towards me, puts his arm on my shoulder and then sits down at my table.

'So sorry, Frannie,' he says, rubbing his neck with his hand and rolling it from side to side. 'We had a little emergency outside the Aquatics Centre and I had to help out. Otherwise, I would have been with you this morning.'

'But you got Jessica to keep her beady eye on me instead…' I reply, taking another sip of coffee and regretting it immediately. 'So, what happened?'

'A bloke got ill so I had to keep his children occupied until we got more help. I bent down so much my neck got stiff. Probably, just the stress though.' He eyes up my cereal bar which has hardly been touched. 'Can I have a bite? Bit of a queue up there.'

'You'll never change,' I say, sliding the cereal bar across to him. 'Can't you get your own? Here, finish off my coffee too.'

'Sharing is my mission,' he says, picking up the cereal bar and taking a big bite. 'Hmm, in the spirit of Macca, Hey Chewed.'

'What?'

'Paul McCartney at the Opening Ceremony last night. *Hey Jude* was the last song. Which reminds me, did you enjoy the ceremony on TV? How did it look? I was in the stadium; it was electric.'

I pause and don't answer immediately. It didn't feel like yesterday at all. It felt like another time – or even another era. I had *Abide With Me* ringing in my ears all night, sung by the little boy.

'I was in the stadium,' I say, crossing my hands on the table. 'I was at the Opening Ceremony.'

'JESUS!' says Rob, spurting out some coffee from his mouth which ended up on his trousers. 'You came to the Opening Ceremony? Why? I thought you'd handed the tickets back to Locog. Who did you come down with?'

I tap my index finger in the middle of my chest.

'You came on your own?' He wipes his mouth and looks annoyed. 'Frannie, why didn't you say? I would have met up with you. Made sure you were safe. There was loads of us here on the night. We could have kept an eye on you.'

'But you've got Jessica to do that for you now. Why did you tell her about Donald?'

Rob sighs and pulls out a tissue from his pocket to wipe his trousers. He grimaces as the warm coffee stain deepens into his thigh.

'Have I not looked after you, Frannie?' he says, without looking up.

'Of course you have, but that wasn't the question I asked. I wanted to know why you told a complete stranger about my husband's death. He's only been dead three months. Even some of my distant family don't know about it.'

'Jessica's not a complete stranger; you've spoken to her a few times already...'

'In your internet world she may not be but she is in mine,' I say, wanting to get up and leave the canteen. 'I'm not ready to share everything yet.'

'We don't share *everything* on the web, Frannie, it's

just a tool to connect with more people. I don't think that's a bad thing. I got a couple of extra driving jobs simply because I discovered a few organisations that needed help. They needed to get their kids out of the classroom environment so they called me up. It's not all bad.'

Each time Rob talks about his job, I am cowed and humbled. It takes the sting out of any mild dispute or disagreement I might have with him (this is the second if I recall. The first came when he wanted to stay overnight after Donald's death to look after me. I said I was fine and won that small battle). He is a driver for a charity called *Swings in the Sky* and takes disabled children to local museums, parks, art galleries and sports events. He's been doing the same job for nearly 25 years since being made redundant in the late 80s and having his house repossessed. When I first met him at my training at the ExCeL, I couldn't believe how cheerful he was after he told me all this. I am not sure how Donald and I would have coped with such indignities. You hear about them on the news but they seem so far away.

'It was the Olympic torch montage that did it for me, yesterday,' says Rob, finishing off the cereal bar and wiping some crumbs away from the side of his mouth. 'That sequence made me well up something rotten. It might have been because a group of local kids were down there, one of ours, watching a disabled man carry the torch down the road, being cheered on by thousands. God, when I saw the look on those kids' faces...' He shakes his head repeatedly as if he's trying to purge a deeply-buried memory. 'Did you see that bit?'

'Yes – and I agree, it was emotional. But Emeli Sandè was the one for me and that other man...'

'Akram Khan...'

'Yes, him...'

There is a moment of silence between us and I sense the fatigue kicking in again (there are still a few hours of my shift to go and I need my energy).

'Did you travel down to London on your own, then?' he asks.

'Yes, it wasn't too bad.'

'When did you get home?'

'Earlier than you think. I left before the teams came out.'

'For God's sake, why?'

'I've already told you. Emeli Sandè...'

'I know some people don't like her but she's not bad...'

I shake my head and put the palms of my hands over my face.

'Oh sorry, Frannie, I get it. I can understand how it might have all got too much for you. Sorry for being so insensitive.'

'Stop apologising all the time...'

'It's the kids I spend time with. Must be catching. They're always saying sorry even though they haven't done anything. I've been trying to work on their self-esteem.'

Another long silence develops. I sometimes think I'm at some counselling clinic rather than the

Olympics. Are all the days going to be this bad? Everyone on eggshells around me all the time?

'Are you going to tell me about Jessica then or not?' I ask. 'Why did you tell her?'

Rob sighs and folds his arms. 'Because I knew I wasn't going to be around – and I wanted her to look after you, it's as simple and as complicated as that. She's a good person is Jess; if only you'd given her a chance instead of shooing her off.'

'I didn't do that. Is that what she said?'

'No, I just like using that word.' He smiles and gets up from the table. 'I've got to go and find out why a couple of volunteers didn't turn up for their shifts this morning. I know the Opening Ceremony finished late but that's no excuse.' He bends down and peers at me. 'Are you happy with your shifts for the next couple of weeks? Five days on, two off and then five and two again? I've worked hard with my Locog boss to get you that freedom. I want to make sure you can manage.'

'My legs hurt already – but I think I can manage. I know we had to tell one or two people about Donald – to ensure I could still do my job properly – but I didn't want the news splashed across the Park. You know how women talk.'

'Believe me, I do. Having five of the loudest in my house makes me escape to the sanctuary of the bedroom. It's probably why I trusted Jessica so much.' He prepares to leave and straightens the sleeve on his t-shirt. 'But point taken, Mrs Hartford. It won't happen again. Donald deserved better.'

I am surprised by Rob's contrition but believe it's utterly genuine. He looks down at the stain on his trousers and tuts. 'Might have to change these,' he says, carefully looking over his shoulder to ensure no one notices. But someone does. To my horror – Jessica walks towards the table.

'What's up captain, caught short down below?' she says, with a smile. 'Your teenage daughters are tidier than you are.'

'Course they are, but they also know who's boss...' He looks at his watch. 'And this boss says it's time for you to get back on shift.' He smiles and playfully tugs a strand of Jessica's hair which has become loose. 'Oh and don't take the megaphone out this time. You're like a lethal weapon with that around your mouth.'

He walks away and laughs. Jessica smiles too but then nervously looks over her shoulder.

'Remember to change your pants too,' she says, rather loudly for my taste.

Rob leaves the canteen and Jessica looks at me. She offers a polite smile and then sits down at the table.

'Am I the only one that hated the Queen and James Bond sequence last night?' she asks.

I am bemused and don't know what to say. So I just nod my head and hope she'll go away.

Jessica is really enjoying herself this afternoon with her foam pointer. It's like she's taking part in the Olympics herself, creating a new event called Air Hands (rhythmic) such are the twirly movements of her comically flexible arm. On another day, I might have felt she was more like a stuck-up traffic warden telling the bemused people clutching a ticket where to go but as I look at some of those faces – children with their mums and dads, teenagers in baggy t-shirts and jeans, patriots covered from head-to-toe in national colours – I can see they're responding to her well and, perhaps, I need to loosen up a bit. She only asked about my wellbeing after all. Was that so bad?

She approaches me as a lull develops in the number of spectators coming into the Olympic Park. I brace myself and nervously glance to my right, hoping that a spectator might grab me instantly and ask me where the toilets are but, alas, no luck and Jessica is onto me before I can make any excuses. She takes off her hat and runs her fingers through her hair.

'Don't you want to have a go with this?' she asks, handing me the foam pointer.

'No, my shift ends in about an hour…'

'Mo Farah can run two 10,000's in that time so you've got plenty of free minutes. Where do you live then?'

I look her up and down. Today's been like a marathon – and I'm not about to fall at the line.

'Are you always this..?'

'This what?' she says, interrupting. 'Forward, assertive, bolshy, what? It's the Olympics and we're the eyes and ears of London. Shouldn't we be engaging with our spectators? Making them happy? Giving them a good experience? I admire you for being here after all. You've shown a lot of courage but I don't understand why you're being so difficult with me. I've only been trying to help.'

'So you think I'm being difficult?'

She pauses and sighs, using the foam pointer to wipe some imaginary sweat off her forehead.

'Okay, maybe that was the wrong word: guarded might be better...'

I nod and examine her closely again. Perhaps I'd underestimated her.

'Yes, guarded – that sounds better,' I say, with a hint of relish.

There's a long silence between us. We turn to face the spectators and I can tell we're both desperate for someone, anyone, to come up to one of us and break the fog of discomfort.

'Did you see Steve Redgrave with those young Olympians last night?' says Jessica, finally breaking the shackles. 'They lit the flame together. I found it really moving.'

'I didn't see that bit. I came home in the middle of the ceremony.'

She turns and looks at me.

'I probably know the reason why...' she says, '... but I don't want you to bite my head off if I get it wrong.'

'Who told you I bite?'

'No-one,' she says, doing a high five with a young boy wearing a baseball cap. 'But if I lost a loved one so close to me...' She pauses again and then looks up at me. 'I might end up biting a few people – and not know it.'

I pause and then offer a mild smile for the first time. My moods have fluctuated so much over the past three months that any slight upturn in fortunes is to be welcomed – and seized without delay.

'How old are you?' I ask.

'24...'

'A student aren't you? Rob told me what you were studying but, for the life of me, I can't remember...'

'Sports Science at Leeds University...'

'Oh yes, good course is it?'

'To be honest, I'm not enjoying the course as much as I thought I would. Too many other distractions...'

'Like what?'

Jessica is about to answer but a man walks past us with an angry look on his face, as though we have wronged him in some manner.

'Sort those empty seats out, what are you doing?' he says, shaking his head but not making eye contact. 'You need bums on seat or these Olympics'll be destroyed. Where's Coe? Get him here and I'll take him on.'

I wonder if the man is drunk. Jessica smiles at him politely and thankfully calms him down.

'Have you just come from the Aquatics Centre, sir?' she asks.

'Yeah, how could you tell?'

'You're still sweating. Don't worry I'll get onto Seb Coe immediately and tell him about your concerns. Now sorry, I've just got to attend to that young girl behind you. She seems to have lost her ticket...'

The man looks bemused and walks off towards the exit for West Ham tube station.

'Do you know Seb Coe personally then?' I ask.

'Do I hell. My dad's got videos of him, though.'

She heads off and tries to help the young girl find her ticket. It doesn't take more than a couple of minutes – and she's back by my side.

'Talking of my dad,' she says, looking beyond me and smiling at a group of Korean spectators taking group shots with a shiny phone. 'I can see him now, sitting by the telly in Leeds with his mushroom risotto and rice, lapping up everything from the boxing to the archery.' She looks at me and rolls her eyes. 'Must have got the craziness from him.'

'What does your dad do?'

'Bit embarrassing really. Works at a bookies. But he had enough a long time ago…'

'And your mum?'

'Now who's asking the questions,' she says, with a smile. 'She's a dinnerlady in Keighley. Again, it's just a few hours a week so she fills the time by volunteering at a health clinic.' She looks at me with those piercing blue eyes. 'Heard, you've been volunteering nearly all your life. I think that's something to be proud of.'

'Maybe it is, but I've never thought of it that way.' I can see the next batch of spectators coming out of Stratford station. 'So where are you staying then? You don't get the train down from Leeds every morning do you? You'll be exhausted by the time the Athletics starts.'

'I'm bunking above a chippy in Streatham. It's

a bit rough, but it's cheap – and I get hot, vinegary chips for free!'

'Are your parents okay with that? I mean, aren't they concerned?'

'About what? I'm a big girl now, I can look after myself. A friend at uni in Leeds is actually from Clapham and she knew I was going to be involved in the Olympics so she pulled a few strings and got me in touch with this husband and wife team in Streatham who run the chippy. I was a bit sceptical at first because I had some other places I could have stayed but they were so nice I thought 'why bother looking anywhere else?' It saved me a lot of hassle.'

'It's nice to know there are still a lot of people like that out there...'

'Yes...' she says, pausing and offering me a nervous glance, '...mind if I ask you about your husband?'

'Yes, this is neither the time nor the place...'

'I understand,' she says, stroking the foam pointer with her hand as though it were fur on a cat. 'Maybe a room above a chippy might be the best place to break that particular conversation.' She looks up and smiles. 'When was the last time you had chips and gravy? Looks like you need some to bring you back in the common domain again...'

'Give me that foam pointer, you rotter!' I say, laughing freely for the first time in months. 'I'll teach you a lesson with it.'

Jessica skilfully moves away from me and waves a cheeky goodbye. She's also laughing and I try to make sense of how this situation escalated so quickly and dangerously. Shouldn't I feel guilty about laughing so soon? What would Donald think if he could see me now? Wouldn't it be shameful? Perhaps, but as I look at Jessica's sparkling eyes and feel a chink of light emerging shouldn't I allow a sliver of enjoyment to seep through? It's as though she's saying 'come with me' there's nothing to fear. But there is. The fear of tarnishing Donald's memory burns so deep I cannot push things too far yet. He would never forgive me. I cannot let 46 years of marriage disintegrate in a few hours – on the altar of cheap laughs. I must concentrate on my duty – and let the others have their carnival.

I get home and immediately take my shoes off, rubbing my toes vigorously to ease the pain and numbness. I can't believe how exhausted I am. Even the Tube and train journey back home (I got a seat both times) didn't make a difference; the feet ache like never before. Another few days of this and I won't be able to move. I lie down for an hour and then have a shower followed by a light dinner with a glass of white wine. Gradually, I begin to feel better but then realise how quiet it is at home: a crushing silence in comparison to the humming and buzzing of the Olympic Park. My ears are still ringing because I can still hear the people milling around. I listen to John Tavener's *The Protected Veil* and feel a premature tug of my bed and pillow; I *am* more tired than I think. I turn on the radio and hear that Britain (as expected) has won no gold medals on the opening day. China are racing away already with four golds and even Kazakhstan have won a gold! Are we that bad? This could be more embarrassing than I thought. Ryan Lochte is the hero in the pool, beating Michael Phelps into fourth place in the 400m individual medley. Donald did tell me he thought Phelps was the Muhammad Ali of the pool but if that was the case how come he lost on the opening day? He could have gone a few rounds (or lengths) at least. Maybe, he's preserving his energy for the events to come. Donald said the greatest competitors always played the long game.

I try to sleep but images of the Orbit tower and the silver-saucered Olympic Stadium make me restless. The Orbit tower, in particular, is giving me an unsettling, queasy feeling. If I have to look at those twisted red veins for another 15 days I may not make it to the Closing Ceremony. I get up and sit on the bed for a few minutes. I slip my feet into Donald's huge slippers and feel a warmth and intimacy that's soothing and reassuring. I get off the bed and walk downstairs in them, even though they are three sizes too big for me. I warm up a glass of milk and reach for Donald's favourite coconut cookies. I take one and dip it into my milk, savouring the gooey, mushy portion melting into my mouth. I want to put some more John Tavener on but resist it as I know how it will all end: with tears stealthily invading my top lip. I go back upstairs and walk into all three bedrooms for no other reason than to have a change of scene (Donald's specialist, Dr Latimer-Rees, said this was a good cure for insomnia). I sit down in the room Donald had turned into a study with its bookcase, computer, office chair and framed portraits of old Ashes victories by the England cricket team. It was the room Donald had his stroke. Everything remains the same. A Post-it note, with Donald's scrawled handwriting, is still stuck on the bottom of the monitor. He even used sellotape on it to ensure it stayed there. I don't need to read it – I know what it says. The campaign against the library closure had taken up a lot of Donald's time in the last couple of years. He sent out leaflets, held meetings and lobbied the local MP. One time, Donald organised a special book fair with Gillian where they were hoping to raise awareness (and funds) to keep the community library open. He was absolutely crushed when only six people turned up. He brushed it off but I could tell it affected him. He redoubled his efforts and worked even harder – until that crisp April morning where our world fell apart. I was in the kitchen making warm porridge and pancakes for breakfast when I heard a loud thud in the bedroom-turned-study (which is directly above the kitchen). Initially, I walked upstairs calmly thinking it just might be the bookcase toppling over or even the computer falling off the desk but when I walked in, I saw Donald lying on the carpet with the office chair still lodged behind his back and his face to the floor. I rushed towards him but the horror of his listless eyes, violet lips and sagging cheeks were too much to bear. I tried to get him up but his arm and right side of the face drooped like jelly. His uncontrollable saliva fell onto my hand. I said his name a few times but it was futile. I ran downstairs, nearly falling over, and called emergency. They came within 15 minutes. I went in the ambulance with him. I spent three hours in intensive care by his side. He died in the early hours of the next morning. A massive heart attack had followed his stroke. I didn't have porridge and pancakes the next day – or for 24 days afterwards.

But now I sense his presence in this room. I can hear him talking to me: 'Frannie, don't let my fate spoil the Olympics for you, volovant.' He liked to call me volovant for no other reason that I'd spent the latter part of my life volunteering in the community; it was nothing to do with food. It's something I grew to love along with our short breaks to the Lake District, the crooner albums and occasional trips to the West End for a major play. I cannot let all that become a burden. I must treasure it.

I get up and walk out of the room, glancing behind me one last time. I'm not sure I want to go in there again for a very, very long time. I walk down the corridor and feel incredibly sleepy again. I head to my bedroom but wonder how long I can stay in an empty house where there is so much darkness and silence. The rooms are bare and the walls are suffocating me. As I lie down in my bed, I'm only thinking about one person – and it's not Donald. She is probably having the sweet dreams of youth right now. Jessica.

DAY THREE

I spend most of the night having odd dreams of plucking the five Olympic rings from the Olympic Park and using them as hoops around my waist. The fantasy doesn't last long as the stiffness, when I swivel my legs out of the bed, brings its own bone-creaking reality. The sound isn't one I'd like to take to work today. I go downstairs and pick up yesterday's mail from my mat (I ignored it yesterday as I was too tired) but now I have no desire for clutter in an already packed schedule. Left for a week, I'd have pizza leaflets, quotes for new conservatories and hedge-cutting flyers clogging up my doormat so I clear them out but spot an envelope underneath with a wonky first-class stamp on it and a handwritten address. I open it immediately and unfold a neatly-typed letter, which also has a handwritten signature at the bottom. I recognise it immediately and feel annoyed I didn't open it yesterday.

Good luck for the Olympics

Dear Francesca
   I would have sent you an email but I know you haven't been reading them lately so I've written this on my father's old Compaq computer. How are

you anyway? I'm sorry I can't be down there with you as you start your adventure as volunteer at the greatest show on earth. Doesn't that sound good? Yes, and you deserve it.

As you know my father has been quite ill lately and mum has found it difficult to cope so that's why I've been up here in Harrogate trying to offer my help in the best way I can. To be honest, I feel quite lost and, sometimes think your volunteering skills would be much more useful to them than my soft-fingered experiences with reference books and inquisitive customers! My mother even said 'why don't you ask Francesca to come up here?' to which I replied 'Mum, she's starting work at the Olympics soon'. She always wants to make new friends. I suppose she's just feeling lonely.

As you know, I would have liked to sit on the sofa with you and watched the Olympic Opening Ceremony but it was not to be. I hope you'll forgive me for that. There's been so much going on since the start of the year and my father's deep brain stimulation procedure is just another examination for all of us. I really do worry about it. Yes, his Parkinson's is bad – but is that the answer? Mother thinks so but I am not so sure.

You can tell from all this that the library campaign has lost momentum since the turn of the year. It was inevitable this would happen when Donald died – but it really has been disappointing how little I've been able to give to it and also how

*little people, in general, care about their community
facilities.*

*Oh Frannie, I'll go on and rant all day if I'm
allowed! So I'll let you go and prepare for your
wonderful adventure in London – it's the least I
can do after the last few months you've suffered.*

*You should be the one getting a gold medal
round your neck.*

Cherish Forever
Gillian

I take the letter into the kitchen and reread it while
eating breakfast. Gillian has given my spirits a lift. She
has always been good to me, despite vicious rumours
circulating two years ago that she was having an affair
with Donald. I knew this was nonsense because of the
way she dealt with it. She invited the two of us to
have dinner at her house with her husband Lawrence,
and their two sons, William and Jack. She also invited
almost everyone else in the parish. At least 30 people
did turn up (they enjoyed the free food) and she put
everyone on the spot asking them why they think she
would ever threaten her 26-year marriage by having
an affair with a colleague at work. I could see the
hurt in her face. I believed her – and so did everyone
else. Donald just looked sheepish throughout the
whole curious spectacle. But why did we all have
to go through that? To humiliate ourselves in that
manner? Because it was the only way to get our point
across, adamantly and vociferously, that nothing
untoward had happened. In one way, it was chilling

and frightening because our word was no longer enough; there had to be more, a drama, a spectacle, a gathering. Luckily, it worked and no more rumours surfaced – but it had the strange effect of making me feel even more isolated, less talkative and less trusting of strangers. I didn't want to engage in conversation in case the subject came up again; it was too hurtful. I do still think about Gillian's persuasive performance that day and think she did a wonderful thing: she used grace and kindness to demolish a virulent piece of gossip. But her evening dinner also served a bigger purpose. It made me realise how much I *really* loved Donald.

I go upstairs and slip Gillian's letter into the 1948 Olympics book. I get dressed and head out to the station to catch the train to London. I have worked out in my mind what I will say to Jessica; I will apologise to her for being so abrupt yesterday. It is something I regret. I will also apologise to Rob; he was only looking out for me. People have cared for me since Donald died – and I should realise that. There is no point keeping it all locked inside. What good is privacy if the rooms are bare and the house is empty? I get to Stratford ten minutes behind schedule. The morning meeting has already started. I can see Rob but no Jessica. Maybe she's late too. I think of wild scenarios like her stomach being pumped after eating too many chips or her father turning up to ask her why on earth she was living like Albert Steptoe. The troops are ready. The purple and red brigade march out to take their positions. It's a bright, lovely day (at the least the weather has held up so far). I'm further down the Olympic Park this time, closer to the Olympic Stadium – but move around a lot as it gets busier throughout the morning. We spend most of the time helping spectators read maps and deal with ticket resale issues – but the most common question is 'Where's the Riverbank Arena' as the hockey tournament – and the women's preliminaries – get underway today. There are also questions about the Water Polo Arena and one man who queues for half an hour at the Aquatics Centre thinking the men's preliminaries would be held there. He is annoyed that he's late for the first game – and blames Sheena. We are glad when he disappears into the arena. It is much busier than yesterday, but that is expected as there are an extra three events going on in and around the Olympic Park. Sheena and I finally get a breather just before noon. I still wonder why I haven't seen Jessica and ask Sheena if she knows where she is.

'Probably got in late,' she says. 'Might have been assigned the Riverbank Arena. Lucky her.' Sheena looks at me and blows down her t-shirt as the midday sun begins to take its toll. 'Why do you ask? Thought you didn't like her?'

'Who told you that?'

'She did.'

'Well, it's not true.'

Sheena smiles and folds her arms. 'You know, my son Theo, said the exact same thing to me when he came home from school the other day: 'Mummy I don't like you'.'

'But Jessica and I didn't say that to each other…'

'I know but I'm just making the point that even when someone says that it means something completely different.'

'So what did you think your son meant?'

'That he wanted a pair of new trainers and a *Spiderman* DVD…'

'And did you get them for him?'

'I'm a volunteer not a banker! The last full-time job I did was before Theo was born. He's nine now, then Holly came along, she's six, then Joel, who's just about to start nursery. I get my husband Gary to buy all the stuff for him. I'm almost permanently wedded to the kitchen or the school gates. It's like being a maid in your own house. I sometimes think, did I get married to that man – or have those kids? For my sins, yes, but I have to keep reminding myself sometimes.' She looks up at me, perhaps feeling guilty she may have spoken for too long. 'Do you have family?'

I pause and the word vibrates in my head like a gymnast pummelling a trampoline. *Family? Do I have any?*

'Yes, I've got a sister Abigail, she lives in France. She's married to Vincent and they have two daughters and three sons. My folks have passed away, I'm afraid.'

'I mean your own family…'

'Yes…'

'Do you have children?'

I sigh and look around, desperate for intervention. I see two women, dressed in orange from head-to-toe,

49

approaching us. They look anxious and distracted, clutching their tickets.

'Riverbank down there, yes?' says one, shaking her head and pointing at the same time. 'If the Belgians have won today, I'll never forgive you, Maria.'

'No way,' says Maria. 'They won't win. But I told you a thousand times, it's not my fault we're late. We should have got the earlier flight.'

'Ladies, you do know that Holland and Belgium started about an hour and 15 minutes ago?' says Sheena, rather more abruptly than necessary. 'You've missed the earlier New Zealand/Australia match too.'

'We know that, don't rub it in,' says the first woman. 'I know we're one of the favourites to win gold, for sure, but missing this match has ruined the Olympics for me already. I wanted to see the Belgians get hurt.'

'Does your country not like them or something?' asks Sheena.

The women smile at each other, take their tickets and sprint off towards the Riverbank Arena.

'You fell into that one,' I say with a smile, quite pleased that the Dutch ladies had saved me from more potentially awkward questions.

'So do *you* know why the countries don't like each other?' she asks.

I hesitate and wonder if I should allow myself an indulgence that could be seen as arrogance. There is also the small matter of not wanting to drag Donald into the conversation again. But I can't help putting these things on the line; it's what I trained for after all.

'It's something to do with their history I think,' I say, crossing my hands in front of my stomach. 'Belgium was part of the Netherlands about two centuries ago – but then the people revolted and became independent. That's about all I know. There's a language thing as well. I think a lot of Belgian people speak Dutch – or Flemish.'

'You've been going way too far on your training?' says Sheena, with a polite smile.

'I was actually told about an athlete at the 1948 London games called Fanny Blankers-Koen, a Dutch girl who won four gold medals. I only stumbled on the Belgium / Holland information from there. I didn't read the illustrated history of the Low Countries.'

'The Low Countries, what are them? That's like double dutch to me!'

We both laugh and I'm relieved our conversation has turned away from the thorny subject of family.

'The only Dutch thing I know is a football player Theo is mad about: Van Pertwee or something...'

'Van Pertwee! Sounds like a scarecrow driving in the field...'

'Feel like a couple of scarecrows standing here. Come on, shall we move down here a little bit? Give these spectators a bit of room.'

I nod and we start walking, continuing to laugh but trying not to draw attention to ourselves.

'Team GB aren't going to win any medals so we might as well enjoy ourselves,' says Sheena.

'Early days yet, but I am getting nervous…'

Just as we stop, Sheena is approached by two young men carrying huge backpacks. She glances at me before she prepares to greet them.

'So if you don't have kids, are you married?' she asks.

After lunch, many people keep their eye on the Women's Road Race, which ends at The Mall, to see if Team GB can grab its first medal but as it's so long (over three hours) I find it hard to watch for a concerted period. Sheena is loving it though and we part ways for a while as a steady stream of spectators approach us with a variety of questions and requests. I get my photo taken with a large group of Tunisian spectators and also get asked to sign someone's hat which I find quite strange. More than an hour passes and I feel the pace again, having been on my feet for most of the day (a bigger lunch is probably also a factor in something I've come to know as 'matinee idle') but then, magically, just when I'm thinking of home again up pops Jessica, about 20 feet away, her hat swinging in her hand, walking so briskly as if there is an emergency nearby that has to be dealt with immediately. She doesn't see me. I raise my hand and call out. Nothing. Is she blanking me? Why would she do that? She walks straight past, without as much as an acknowledgment. There are lots of people between us: spectators, children, even a film crew, but I cannot believe she didn't see me. In a few minutes, she's gone; heading down towards the Aquatics Centre. I turn and try and shrug her image out of my head. I carry on with my smiles and my greetings – but I'm quite annoyed inside. But then a massive cheer erupts throughout the Olympic Park. Did we win something? Sheena comes running towards me after a couple of minutes – and raises her fist.

'Izzy, wizzy, let's get Lizzy,' she shouts, clapping her hands, smiling and then raising her fist again. 'Liz Armitstead's done it, Frannie, she's got the first medal for us. One of many!' She does a high five with three spectators in a row – and then locks arms with a couple more in an awkward jig of delight.

'Our first gold, yeeeess!' I say, trying not to draw attention to myself.

'It was a silver…'

'Oh. Still a medal though. We're on our way now.'

'I think the good old British rain helped her. It was bashing it down over there. Now, we just need Becky Adlington tonight to round off a good day for us.'

'What's she going in?'

'The 400m Freestyle. It's not her favourite but she won it in Beijing.'

'Different pressure here…'

Sheena looks at me and nods. 'I think she feels it too. Do you remember when Frankie Boyle made that cruel 'back of the spoon' joke about her?'

'Who's Frankie Boyle?'

'My husband loves him. He's got his stand-up shows on DVDs and swears he's the best comedian on the planet.'

'Still haven't heard of him.'

Sheena is about to answer but sees Jessica, again, breezing past us, about 50 feet away.

'Hey Jess!' she shouts. 'Where are you going?'

'BACK TO THE RIVERBANK.'

'Just come here for a mo, Frannie needs a word.'

'What?' I say. 'No I don't.'

'I'M BUSY, BIG GAME AGAINST JAPAN TONIGHT.'

'Oh, just for a minute you busybody. Come on…'

Jessica reluctantly looks round and then heads towards us. She stops by our side.

'Look Jess, Frannie's been asking about you all day,' says Sheena. 'She's been worried about you…'

'No I haven't.'

'She has.' She looks at Jessica. 'Just tell her what you've been doing…'

Jessica sighs and looks at her watch. 'Look, I haven't got much time to waste but because we're all feeling a bit better now after landing our first medal I'll make an exception.' She looks at me directly, making me feel more defensive than necessary. 'My two favourite events are on today: hockey and judo. I know a couple of the girls in the Team GB hockey team and I used to play regularly with them at school and then at college. I'm just dealing with some of their families today who I haven't seen for years. The match against Japan starts at seven so I'm going to be here for a while yet. It's annoying that the judo's going on at the same time but I did have a break and caught some of the semi-final before getting back to work.' She pauses and then folds her arms. 'Anything else Francesca, or can I go now?'

'Jess, stop being so rude,' says Sheena. 'Frannie cares about you, that's all.'

'About time somebody did...' She begins to walk off.

I step forward and grab Jessica's arm. 'Hey, what's wrong?' I ask. 'You seem to be having a great day – and yet you're not.'

'This isn't the time and the place. Can I go?'

'Yes. But not before you tell me what the problem is.'

Jessica tuts and takes her cap off her head. She aggressively pushes her fingers through her hair and then replaces the cap.

'The chippy where I'm staying was raided last night,' she says. 'Turns out, the room I was staying in was occupied by an illegal immigrant before me. I was asleep when these beasts, with big helmets, roared in just before dawn. They took me in but released me after a couple of hours when I told them I was a volunteer at the Olympics. Mr and Mrs Hatton are still getting a grilling.' She fiddles with her collar and looks away. 'Worse of it is, Mum and Dad want me to come home immediately. Pack it all in. Go back to Leeds.'

'You look so pale,' I say. 'What on earth did you come to work for? Couldn't Rob have given you day off?'

'I told him I wanted to come in. No-one's going to

stop me from taking part in these Games. No-one. I've been dreaming about them since July 6 2005 when we won the right to host them.'

'What about your mum and dad?' asks Sheena. 'Have you told them?'

She sighs and looks away. 'Mum kept going on about the so-called crime in London before I came down here. She went on about the knife crime and the no-go areas. She was proper paranoid to begin with – and now she's proper mad.' She shakes her head and closes her eyes while running her hand over her face. 'I understand it in a way. I didn't tell her I was staying at that chippy. I said I was kipping at a friend's house in Clapham. There was no time really. It was so chaotic building up to this event. That was probably a mistake.'

'You should have told your parents the truth, Jessica,' I say. 'They care about you deeply.'

'And you would know?'

'It's common sense. But forget about that. What about Mr and Mrs Hatton? I can't believe a confident girl like you would have been duped so easily.'

'I wasn't duped. It could have happened to anybody. I didn't have much money so I couldn't stay at the Hilton – and my friend said they were good people so I went along with it. When I met them, they looked so respectable. I can't understand why they let that man live there. He was involved in some criminal activity too.'

'They might not have known themselves,' says Sheena. 'Not everyone can do background checks. Well, at least you look okay. Must have shaken you up a bit?'

'Yes, it did but I met some of my old friends this morning so I've forgotten about it already.' She smiles and taps me on the shoulder. 'Okay, must get on. Told my parents, there's absolutely no way I'm going back up to Yorkshire just yet. Only just got here!'

I look at Jessica and imagine her playing hockey for Team GB tonight against Japan in front of a full house at the Riverbank Arena. She raises her stick and strikes the ball home. *Home*. The word almost feels meaningless to me now.

'But where are you going to stay?' I ask.

'Rob's already ringing around his mates so I don't expect any problems. If not I can kip on his sofa.'

I pause and take a deep breath. I must not hesitate any longer. What am I scared of? Fear of intimacy? Ridicule?

'My house is empty,' I say, in a low voice. 'You could stay there for a night or two if you like…'

Jessica doesn't take up my offer immediately – but will tell me by the weekend if she wants to stay. She is content to stay at Rob's house in Watford for the time being where there are other like-minded girls (Rob's daughters) to keep her company. I accept her decision but when I get home, and sit down on my cold sofa with a cup of black coffee perched on my thigh, I feel crushed. The disappointment is so overwhelming I think there must be something wrong with me. The only comfort I can take is that I must still be in mourning for Donald; it's why I've reacted to the news so badly. Yet I cannot help but think Jessica is wary of coming to my house. She has never stepped foot in Buckinghamshire before and would feel completely out of place in a parish like ours with its well-kept lawns, boutique shops and pathological green-belt champions. Has she ever lived in a place like this? A working-class girl from Leeds does not want to spend a week with an old widow while the greatest show on earth is exciting everyone in the big city. It's just the way it is. I would bore her – and I need to get over it.

But I can't. Donald used to fill the house with his considered, drawn-out voice and fourteen-stone stoop but I feel smaller by the day, as if the purple flower buds on the living room wallpaper are releasing a suffocating nectar. I used to think this was the prettiest living room I ever saw – now I think it needs a decorator. I watch TV for a while and then prepare for an early night. I am so tired I can't be bothered checking this evening's Olympic results. Someone won, someone lost, so what? I admonish myself for my cynicism but I have little else left. I am just about to get changed into my bed clothes when I hear the bell ring. I think about not answering it – but when it rings twice more, I give in and go downstairs. I wait one more time by the door – and it rings for a fourth time – so I open it.

'Hello Mrs Hartford,' says William, running his fingers through his hair as he talks. 'Mum wanted me to come round to see how you were doing. Can I come in?'

'Oh, William, er, really surprised to see you. It's a bit late…'

'I know you've probably had a long shift but I'll only be a few minutes. You need your rest, I understand that.'

'Your mum not back yet?'

'She's staying in Harrogate for a few more days...'

I move away from the door and let William come in. He also has a small bag over his shoulder, one of those fashionable bright things that young men like to carry, with a diagonal strap and hardly any storage room to speak of. He smiles and wipes his feet on the doormat.

'Thanks, I won't press you for a cuppa, don't worry.'

'And you won't get one! There's a limit to hospitality if you've been at it all day.'

He laughs and walks into the living room. He sits down on the sofa, and I feel strangely uplifted as though the living room I'd inhabited a few minutes ago has been given an injection of energy.

'I've just been watching the football,' he says. 'Team GB are playing UAE. You wouldn't believe it but they scored a goal against us. Did you see it?'

'No.'

'Sorry, I'm just getting a bit carried away. It was on in the place where I work...'

'You still at that pub in Beaconsfield? Thought you'd have got a job more in line with your abilities by now. What was your degree in again?'

'Graphic design. I've sent out loads of applications and I'm still earning so I'm still hanging in there. Might start my own business soon anyway and become a website designer. I think I can do better than what's already out there.'

'Well, I'll tell you one thing…' I say, moving away from the door and sitting on the opposite side of the sofa. 'You're too good to be working in a pub pulling pints for a pittance. And I told Gillian that too…'

'That's kind of you, Mrs Hartford.'

He pauses and swivels his bag round onto his lap. He unzips it, looks down and waits. He then looks up at me and sighs.

'What's in there, William?' I ask.

'I should have given it you before, but I held onto it…'

'What is it?'

He slowly reaches in to the bag and pulls out Donald's check-patterned trilby hat. I look at it without feeling any emotion, which surprises me.

'How did that end up in your bag?'

He pauses again and feels the trilby in his hands. He sighs and leans back on the sofa.

'Do you remember the time my father, Donald, Jack and I went to the Ashes Test at The Oval in 2005?'

'Yes, and he didn't make me want to forget it. Is that where he lost his hat?'

'Well, it was flicked off his head when someone in the crowd cheered an England boundary. It was quite raucous in there. Anyway, he tried to find it under the seats but there were so many spectators it was impossible.' He pauses and folds his arms. 'Anyway, at close of play, just as we were leaving the ground, I was at the back and someone tapped me on the shoulder. The trilby had been found and a man handed it over to me rather than Donald. I said I'd give it to him, as Donald was in conversation with my father. But for some reason, I didn't, I put it in my bag. I don't know why. It was like something had come over me. It felt like a memento, like one of the wickets that players pull out of the ground after a famous victory...'

'So you didn't give it back?'

'No. I'm ashamed to say it but I was ready to sell it on eBay. I was only 15 at the time and any easy money was welcome. But that didn't happen...'

'And there was me thinking you were a nice boy...'

'I was a stupid teenager, that's all. Anyway, the reason I didn't sell it was because the very next night I happened to be in the library and Donald recommended I should read a book about the Bodyline tour of the 30s. I agreed but then he stunned me by saying he knew I'd put the trilby in my bag. He'd seen it but hadn't said anything. He took me out back and I started crying and said sorry. He said it didn't matter and asked me if I wanted to keep it. I wasn't sure but he said I should take it home because 'golden memories' don't come round very often – and you need to treasure these moments. He said in years to come, when I looked at the hat, I'd just remember that glorious day at The Oval when England won The Ashes.' He sighs and looks up at the ceiling. 'So I did keep it and here it is. I think I should hand it back now.'

'Why on earth would you want to do that? Donald wanted you to keep it so it's yours.'

'I still feel guilty about it.'

'Don't. You've done a brave thing by coming round here and telling me this. The bottom line is, you and your family have been rocks to me in my time of need. I don't know what I would have done without you. The aftermath of the funeral nearly killed me too, what with Abigail's posturing and the stress of the Olympics schedule. I thought I might as well join Donald…' I move closer to William and put my hand on his thigh. 'But you've restored my faith in humanity, for want of a better word. I admire you for coming round here. I'm not sure many young people want to be seen at an old woman's home like mine anymore…'

'What are you on about?' he says, finally banishing his gloomy demeanour. 'You're not an old woman – and why wouldn't young people want to come here? Jack and I were round here all the time with Donald. I really don't think you should talk like that. I know you've suffered a lot but not all young people are the same.' He pauses and puts his hand on mine. 'Did someone diss you at the Olympics? If they did, tell me and I'll ensure they never do it again…'

'No, don't be silly. No-one dissed me, it's just…'

'What?'

I pause and take the trilby off William's lap. I stroke the rim of the hat with my fingers.

'It's just this girl I work with, one of the volunteers. There's something about her, a vulnerability I can relate to. She's got problems with accommodation so I asked if she wanted to stay here. She said 'no' for the time being. I don't know why but it felt like a sword going through my heart. I can't describe it. It's as though when Donald went, so did my emotional defence. I don't have one, everything fires through at a rate of knots. Rejections, in particular, spin round in my head until I feel sick.'

'You shouldn't be so hard on yourself, Mrs Hartford. You're still in the grieving process. And it's not as if this girl said 'no' permanently did she? She's probably just weighing up her options.'

'What? Live with an old lady or live with her peer group? Not much of an option is it?'

'She *will* stay here, just you wait and see. Once she feels your kindness and warmth, she'll be round here quicker than you can say Daniel Sturridge.'

'Who's he?'

'He scored a couple of goals for Team GB tonight...'

'Oh, not football again!' I say, with a smile. 'I'm going to ban all football and cricket talk in this house from now on.'

'Er football is part of the Olympics and as you're an ambassador for the Games, it kind of defeats your argument...'

'Clever clogs!' I pick up the trilby and playfully put it on William's head. 'That's why I don't let young people in the house. They think they're so superior.'

William holds his hands up and asks me to wait. He tilts the trilby on his head and lowers his head slightly the way Donald did when he spoke. I expect to be apprehensive about what William is about to do but I feel strangely calm. He does an impression of Donald and, after a couple of lines, I break out into a big smile.

'Ah, have you got any crackers in your sandwich box there, William? Nothing like the bite of a cracker with a bit of cheese at an Ashes Test match. Makes it all worthwhile. Followed by an apple and a flask of warm tea. Marvellous.'

As William speaks, the events of earlier in the day evaporate into the reenergised living room. I forget all about Jessica. I remember life again. Donald's – and I remember not to just mourn it but remember it.

DAY FOUR

The aches and pains I'd felt on my previous two shifts magically disappear on the third morning. It's like William has opened my eyes to another way of seeing, a thought process I didn't know existed, a bit of humour that I thought was insensitive. When is it okay to laugh over a loved one? Three months? Six? A year? Never? Well, we did laugh a great deal – and I didn't feel guilty at all. I am still thinking about William as I stand in the Olympic Park in the morning almost three hours into my shift. I'm not feeling the pace at all in the morning – until I talk to a man about McDonald's sponsorship of the Games. He waffles on for a long period about the 'crap' McDonald's put into their food and why they shouldn't have been given the chance to be associated with such a prestigious event. I listen politely but realise if I keep absorbing the man's endless gripes, all the gains I'd made from last night onwards (relaxation, smiles, good memories, less fatigue) might be destroyed in a few minutes. I look beyond the man and notice Ben is a few yards away trying to fix the zip on a little girl's tracksuit top.

'Sorry sir, I just have to talk to my colleague for a second...'

'So this is not important to you then?' he says,

putting his hand in his cagoule pocket. 'I guess if the SS can cover for Hitler, then you can cover for McDonald's. They're both killing machines.'

'Oh come on, that's ridiculous. You can't compare a fast food outlet to Hitler.'

'Why not? I just have. Both are responsible for mass murder.'

I examine the man closely. He has spiky blond hair and a tiny earring. His bleached jeans and polished Doc Martens boots do not fill me with confidence that we'll agree on anything, never mind on this subject. But perhaps I should be more open after my experience with William.

'So which event are you seeing today?' I ask, desperately hoping Ben will see me. 'If you're so anti-McDonald's and the Olympics, why are you here?'

'I'm not seeing any events. I've got a ticket for the Orbit tower and the Olympic Park.' He turns and points at the twisting, spiralling tower behind him. 'I'm writing a major blog about big companies like Coca-Cola and McDonald's and their sponsorship of major sporting events like the Olympics and the World Cup. They can't live without one another. So when they're not killing the planet with their planning application for big stadiums and parks, they're killing people with their shit drinks and poisonous food. That's why I'm going up the Orbit. I can get a good view of the damage done to east London.'

'You've got quite extreme views, don't you think?'

'Only to those people who haven't got any.' He turns and looks at me, his piercing light blue eyes making me feel somewhat inadequate. 'Which includes you, I guess.'

'Maybe it does…'

'Here…' he says, reaching into the pocket of his cagoule and handing me, of all things, his passport. 'Report me if you want. If you think I have extreme views, as you put it, call security and get me carted out of this glorious utopia. I won't mind. I know what I'm up against.'

I take the passport in my hand, open it up and look at the picture. The image only faintly resembles the man I see in front of me.

'Looks forged anyway…'

'It isn't. That was taken at least four years ago.'

'That was a joke,' I say, with a smile. I hand the passport back to him. 'Look, I'm not interested in calling security or anyone else. You believe in something – and that matters. Good luck with your campaign.'

'I knew you wouldn't report me,' he says, taking the passport with a mild shake of the head. 'I could see it in your gentle manner and your oh-so tired eyes. You have more humanity than you think. We all do. We just don't show it enough.'

'People are showing it all the time in this Olympic Park,' I say, beginning to move off.

'Not enough though…'

'Maybe you could show them the way then…'

'I will.'

The man walks off at a brisk pace towards the Orbit tower. The thought does occur to me that his rather extreme views might have been dealt with differently by one of my colleagues. Would they have called in the heavy lifters? I'd hope not. Ben was telling me that one of the more jobsworth volunteers (Inspector Hector we called him) had already 'stuck his nose' into a couple of disputes which ended up with spectators being ejected from the Park or from a stadium or venue. Ben did like to ham this up a bit so I didn't know how much of it was true. I dread to think what Inspector Hector, of the Purple and Red force, would do to the anti-McDonald's blogger.

Ben finally manages to fix the young girl's zip and the family are pleased with his handiwork. He taps her on the head and off she goes towards the Aquatics Centre. I stop by Ben's side and he asks me about the 'weirdo' I'd just had a conversation with. I admit, I felt uncomfortable with Ben's choice of words – but he did have a habit of getting to the point. 'If I want to be a director, I have to be direct' he said, quite regularly, which seemed to have a twisted logic to it.

'Don't tell me, he's watching the Water Polo this afternoon and smuggling a joint in with him,' he says, finally getting up from a crouched position. 'Or has he got the hots for Tom Daley? He'll get a good look at him this afternoon. It's always the weirdly dressed ones you have to look out for.'

'No, it's none of those things. He just doesn't like McDonald's…'

'Join the club.'

'Or much else by the sounds of it…'

'So he's a sort of activist then…'

'Yes, that was the word I was looking for. Why couldn't I think of that?'

'Because you've probably had too much on your mind lately…' He moves closer to me and puts his arm round me. 'Come on, let's go for our break. We've had a good couple of cameos this morning.'

'Talking of which, Sheena tells me you wanted to get Jessica into one of your short student films?'

'Yes, I wanted to but she wasn't having it. She burns up the screen, no doubt about that. Pity she burns up everything around her too. Bad luck follows her like a virus.'

'What do you mean?'

'Her place getting raided, huge debts, losing her bag on the Tube…'

'She didn't tell me about that?'

'No, she wouldn't. I'd stay well clear. She's lovely and all, but she's Miss Fortune as far as I am concerned…'

'But you still wanted her in your film?'

He smiles and looks towards me. 'Yes…' he says, with a wink. '…But directors can get very nasty when they're spurned by their leading ladies.'

'So the bad luck affected you too…'

'You could say that.' He looks over his shoulder. 'By the way, have you seen Jessica this morning?'

'No – and she won't appear in your mucky student film.'

We both laugh and head to the canteen for a welcome break.

* * *

The Olympic Park seems much busier in the afternoon, so I'm actually sad to be leaving my shift for once! I'm not tired at all. Park Live (a kind of alter ego to Henman Hill or Murray Mount at Wimbledon) has filled up nicely as Tom Daley's Diving final provides plenty of entertainment and frustration for the spectators on the big screen. It doesn't look as though Tom's going to land the first gold for Team GB. Shame, as he'd be the perfect role model to get our campaign underway. I do fear we might not get any golds at all. But I also sense a sprinkling of gold dust circulating in the atmosphere. As I watch the spectators, I notice a subtle shift in their moods and attitudes. During the first couple of days, there was a wariness and even anxiety coming from every pore of the Park (I admit, I was one of the chief worriers) but now I sense a small change in the way people are talking and interacting with each other. There are more smiles and nods of acknowledgement. People are asking me for help even if they know they don't need it. It's like the Olympic Park has been given some kind of electric jolt and, dare I say it, a fuzzy, unthreatening patriotism has taken hold. It's so nice to see the flag being raised so often and so vigorously. It's being reclaimed before my very eyes. The only downside is Donald's not here to see it.

I'm ready to leave for the end of my shift as I catch sight of a large group of children a few feet away, some of them drinking water from plastic bottles. A couple of them are having co-ordination problems as they try to get the bottle into their mouths. There are many spectators in the way so I cannot see if there is an adult with them. After a minute or so of squinting my eyes, I'm amazed to see Rob, dressed in jeans and Black Sabbath t-shirt, pop up behind them and offer his help to one of the young boys, who has spilt some water on his collar. Rob pulls out a tissue and wipes the boy's shirt. When he's finished, he pulls the boy's cheek playfully as he gets up. Rob then turns and notices me. He smiles and points at the boy to look at me, as if to say 'respect that lady in uniform'.

'I thought you were working today, what happened?' I ask, moving forward and picking up one of bottles dropped by the same boy.

'Change of plan. We're all off to North Greenwich to watch the Gymnastics later today. I got a call from the powers-that-be late last night that they needed some bums on seats over there so here I am. General Dogsbody strikes again. Always willing but never sees a shilling.' He pauses and moves towards me, putting his hand on my shoulder. 'How are you anyway, Frannie? Sorry that I haven't been able to see you for a couple of days, I've been so busy – and the athletics haven't even started yet!'

'Oh don't worry about that, I'm fine. I can see you've got your hands full with the kids. Did they come down on the train?'

'Yes, they came to London with a couple of their special needs teachers. They're already at the North Greenwich Arena right now. We're meeting them there.' He looks down at the children. 'But they were desperate to come to the Olympic Park first so I obliged. I feel so proud that I got them here in such a short space of time…'

'So it wasn't prearranged?'

'No, after I got the call from Lord Locog last night, I started making arrangements. Somehow, we got it all organised. Didn't have to come far though, only from Watford – and strangely the Tube and the trains were less jam-packed than expected even though it was a working day.'

'Maybe we're better organised than we think. We always talk ourselves down.'

'Not anymore!' says Rob, using his hand to help a boy wave a small Union flag. 'We're putting the 'Great' back in Britain again!'

'Not with that ghastly t-shirt you're not! What on earth possessed you to wear that?'

'Possessed: good word, very appropriate. No, I just didn't have any time to put on anything else, and that's the God's honest truth. They're a great band anyway, what's your problem?'

'I've never heard of them…'

'And I'd never heard of John Tavener…'

'Oh, you're so slanderous Rob, please stop,' I say, with a smile.

Rob laughs too – but he then pauses and watches me for a few seconds.

'It's so great to see you smile, Frannie, do you know that?' he says. 'You've been through so much that it fills me with a joy I can't describe…'

'It's this…' I say, looking around the Olympic Park

and raising my hands. '…and these people, and those flags and these children…' I bend down and stroke the forehead of a boy who's more interested in the big Park Live screen behind me. '…What can I say? There's something in the air…'

Rob taps me on the shoulder and starts singing Phil Collins *In the Air Tonight* in such an appalling manner that I can't wait for him to stop.

'You have such a terrible taste in music, do you know that?' I say.

'Who says I like the old Genesis mucker? The song's just appropriate for this moment. I can belt out a Black Sabbath number if you want?'

'Oh don't do that, please…'

Rob laughs and moves closer to me. He gives me a hug and then starts to move off with the children.

'I hope you enjoy yourself, have we got a chance of a medal in the gymnastics?' I ask.

'Maybe. It's Louis Smith and the boys – but who cares? The kids will remember this event forever.'

I am just about to wave goodbye but remember a niggling detail that has been hovering in the background all day.

'Have you seen Jessica today?'

'She's moving her stuff from Streatham to Watford. She *has* got the day off unlike yours truly. She'll be back tomorrow.'

'She's staying at your place then?'

'Well, she can't stay on the streets can she?'

'No, I suppose not…'

'Don't worry, she hasn't stopped talking about

73

you for the last couple of days. She'll be knocking on your door pretty soon.'

'Oh, she won't do that now. She needs to be with her own age group and her own friends.'

'Maybe but she feels a connection with you. Don't knock that, Frannie, because she could become the best friend you've ever had.'

I get home and realise I have enough energy to watch the highlights on TV. While I'm disappointed we haven't won a gold (we're in 20th place in the medal table with one silver and two bronze medals), I'm hopeful, after today's events, that something good is about to happen, particularly after seeing the Men's team in the Gymnastics perform so heroically. They win a bronze – but it could have been so much more after a protest by one of the other teams demotes them from a silver medal. But Tom Daley – and his diving partner Peter Waterfield – miss out on a medal altogether, finishing fourth in the synchronised event. This fails to puncture my inexplicable optimism, which I can only put down to the random meeting with Rob and his wonderful gang this afternoon – and, perhaps to a lesser extent, William's visit to the house last night. I hope it remains. I have experienced such wild fluctuations in mood over the last few months that I'm not holding my breath. But for now, it's even drawing me in to events I'd never watch like the weightlifting and the water polo. I even catch a bit of Great Britain's hockey match against Argentina. Even though it's the Men's tournament I wonder, somewhat irrationally, if Jessica is there. A few minutes later, the bell rings. I almost can't believe that two people would want to visit the house in two days; I'm not sure that even happened in Donald's day. I get up and answer it, still thinking about those wonderful gymnasts in the North Greenwich Arena like Louis Smith and Max Whitlock. Such well-rounded boys. I wonder if Rob and his crew got to the arena in time. I hope so, they wouldn't have wanted to miss that. I open the door and am quite shocked to see Lawrence, standing there in his suit, mobile in one hand, trilby hat in the other. He doesn't make eye contact with me.

'Hello Francesca, here you go,' he says, handing Donald's trilby hat to me. 'William should not have kept it in the first place. If I'd have known, I would have handed it back years ago.'

'Come in, Lawrence, why don't I make you a cuppa?'

'No, I've just got back from London…'

'So have I…'

'No, from work I mean, so I can't really hang around. I have a couple more reports to write this evening. It's rather hectic right now.'

I pause and don't take the trilby from Lawrence immediately. It amazes me that Lawrence has never stepped foot in this house. Of course, he was friends with Donald and they attended a few Test matches together but that was because they had a shared love for cricket. I got the impression they had little else in common. And then the rumours of Gillian's dalliance with Donald started and that widened the gap between the two men further. Lawrence always claimed to be too busy to be a 'good neighbour' but it was more that he wasn't a neighbour at all. I hardly saw him. His work for a global software company meant he caught the train at the crack of dawn and didn't return from London earlier than 9pm each night. Gillian had been going on about it for years. Yet it did give her the freedom and the resources to pursue her own passions which were obviously the library, the theatre and the local community. Perhaps they didn't step on each other's toes – and they liked it that way.

'Well, if you're not going to come in...' I say, folding my arms in a clear indication I wasn't going to take anything from him. '...I really would like to know why William can't keep the hat. Donald gave it to him – and he likes it. Can't we just let things be?'

'Look Francesca, I know you've been through a lot but I really want you to take this. William was actually wearing it this morning when he went to work in Beaconsfield, can you believe that? A part-time barman in his early 20s wearing a checked trilby hat; it looked ridiculous.'

'I thought he was full-time?'

'Full-time, part-time, who cares? It's a mind-numbing job anyway and he needs to find something that'll motivate him a bit more. Here, please take the hat?'

He hands it over again – and I keep my arms folded.

'I don't think the hat looks so bad on William,' I

say. 'He was wearing it last night in this house. He looked quite stylish, I thought.'

'Please take it...'

I am annoyed Lawrence isn't engaging with my line of argument.

'Only if you come in. The Olympics are still on. We can talk about the separate worlds of London we inhabit. You should have seen the Olympic Park today; there was so much goodwill I had to pinch myself that I was in the capital...'

He eases the hat back by his side and steps back a little.

'No, it's a gracious offer but if I waste any more minutes this evening, I won't be able to function for the rest of the week.' He sighs and looks down at his phone. 'Gillian won't be back until midweek at the earliest – and we're surviving on pizzas and takeaways right now, so that's another consideration.'

'You should cook a bit more often...'

'I do – at weekends. But I rely on Gillian throughout the week – and she's not here.' He looks down at the trilby and shakes it a couple of times as though he's trying to clear some dandruff or errant strands of hair. 'I'll see you again soon, Francesca. I hope you're enjoying your work at the Olympics. Oh, keep the Tube empty will you. I can't do with all these new spectators and visitors to London.' He offers the first smile of the evening and starts to walk away.

'Who knows, you might have to speak to them one day...'

'Hope not,' he says, raising a hand without

looking behind him. 'It's like Last Night of the Proms with all those garish flags. No thanks...'

'You should get behind the team?' I say, a bit louder.

'I only deal with winners...'

With that, Lawrence heads off down the street and I shut the door, a little more annoyed than I was a few minutes ago. But I truly will be annoyed if he doesn't give the hat back to William. What is his problem anyway? My guess is when he sees his son wearing the trilby hat, he's actually seeing Donald – and all the niggly problems they had in the later years. He might also think William was – and still is – too close to Donald; that their relationship is more like father and son than his own. This can't be too pleasant for him – but perhaps he should do more to ensure his son doesn't feel that way about his father. It does get me worked up when I see parents and children not seeing eye-to-eye. I never would have let that happen. It still pains me that I didn't have the choice.

Lawrence has put me off any more television for the evening so I go upstairs and prepare for bed. Yet his visit has also aroused a curious urge to look through some old photo albums with Donald specifically wearing the checked trilby hat. It's like I need to put it back into its rightful place. So I pull out some of the dusty albums from the bottom drawer of the cupboard in our bedroom. I sit on the bed and flick through them. I log a few of the places Donald is wearing his favourite hat: at a picnic with me in the Lake District; at a Ramblers walk through the

Chilterns, outside the Norden Farm Arts Centre in Maidenhead, outside Chelmsford cricket ground. I go through another album but on the first page, there's a reminder I don't want to see. He's wearing the hat outside Wexham Park Hospital. *At hospital – with me inside.* I feel a tiredness when I see him out there. I close the album and place it back into the cupboard. I'm not ready for this yet. Lawrence has fiddled with my emotions again. I quickly get changed and hope to put the light out as soon as possible. My mobile phone rings just as I'm about to get into bed. Who now? The Olympics has increased the numbers of conversations but not always to my benefit. It can wear me out at the wrong time.

'Hello Frannie, how are you? It's Jessica here. I'm at Rob's place in Watford watching Great Britain v Algeria in the volleyball. You weren't asleep were you?'

'It's late Jessica…'

'I know, I'm sorry about that but I needed to tell you something, I'm not sure it can wait.'

'We'll be awake again in a few hours, can't it wait till the morning?'

'No, because my Dad's coming down from Leeds. He got worried about the little problem I had in Streatham and, once he heard about the police, he decided to get down here as fast as he could. I told him not to worry but he didn't listen…'

'But what's that got to do with me?' I say, sitting up in bed and trying to get the mobile closer to my ear. 'He just sounds worried. Is that so bad?'

'It's not bad – but I'm afraid he might be coming your way first…'

'What?'

'He has your address so he might be heading down there as we speak.'

'For Lord's sake, Jessica, how did he get that? Did you give it to him? I sincerely hope not.'

'Well look, things have been very confusing for the past couple of days. I didn't know if I was coming or going, never mind where I was staying. My intention was to take up your offer of staying at your place but then Dad rang and everything got muddled up again. I gave him your address to reassure him, I didn't expect him to waltz down south and get all cranky.'

'Why didn't you give him Rob's address?'

'I tried to but he was already travelling down to London by then. His phone was either not in service or breaking up all the time. He's still got one of those old crap ones with no internet access. I just couldn't get through. Also, I knew it was very crowded at Rob's and I didn't think I'd be able to stay that long.'

'Whereas I'm living in the house that time forgot, yes?'

'I made a mistake, Frannie, I'm sorry. I just didn't expect him to get carried away like that. He still thinks I'm a little girl…'

'Hmm, maybe Ben was right about you. Bad luck follows you around…'

'Well, he should know. Only had his driving licence for eight months and he's wrote off three cars already.'

'I didn't know that…'

'There's a lot you don't know about Ben but forget him, I just wanted to make sure you were prepared if, for some reason, my father turns up your door.'

'But it's late. Why would he do that at this time of night?'

'It's still early where we're from. On days off, he's usually watching telly till about 3am.'

'I won't answer the door.'

'Fine, I just thought I'd warn you.'

There is a long silence as I think of something to say – and I decide there's no point in skirting round the issue anymore.

'Why didn't you take up my offer of staying at my place when I asked you the first time?' I say. 'Is it because I'm old and a widow? Because I will make you look bad in front of your cool young friends? Is that it Jessica? Because that's how it feels to me...'

'No, course not. I don't think that way...'

'Are you sure, Jessica? I'm sorry if I'm getting emotional and oversensitive but it's better to feel like that than to feel nothing at all. After Donald died, I felt so numb in mind and body that I feared it would never leave me – but it did. But then when you rejected my offer, the numbness came flooding back again. I know I might be overreacting but that's the truth, I can't hide it...'

'I'm so sorry, Francesca, I really am. I shouldn't have called you in the first place...'

'No, you did the right thing,' I say, lying down and resting my head on the pillow. 'Because now it means we both know where we stand. If you want to come and live here, you need to understand exactly how I've been feeling. I don't think you really grasped that before. Am I right?'

'Maybe…'

'Am I right?'

'Yes. It's true I've never lost anyone close to me like that. My grandfather did pass away – but I was only three then so I don't really have memories of it. I can't imagine what you've been through, honestly.' She pauses and sighs. 'I'll let you go now because you're probably extremely tired…'

I turn my head to the right and look at Donald's face in our framed anniversary photo lying on the bedside table.

'I'll be more tired if you don't come and stay here with me…'

'When?'

'Soon.'

'You might be seeing my Dad first…'

'Not tonight I won't. I've talked to enough people for one day.' I turn over in bed and try to get comfortable. 'Goodbye Jessica.'

'Wait, if he calls, you will let him in won't you?'

'Bye. See you tomorrow, I hope.'

I end the call abruptly and put my mobile under my pillow. I don't care if I'm on the end of a chippy-style raid in Streatham, I won't move from this bed till morning.

DAY FIVE

The distant sound of my front door being thumped wakes me up. At least I am prepared for it. I ignore it but glance over at my alarm clock and, amazingly it's 5.15am already – in other words; close to getting up time. Did I have that much unbroken sleep? How? This Olympic adventure is doing strange things to my body. I imagine what Jessica's dad looks like. His impulsiveness makes me think of people like Albert Finney, Tom Courtenay or Ted Hughes; northern men who knew their own mind and had a certain uncompromising manner about them (even it was an act). Is Jessica's dad the same? I hope not. He's got off on the wrong foot with me to begin with. I get up and head to the bathroom as the banging on the door continues. It stops after a couple of minutes. I get changed and head downstairs to eat breakfast. It's so nice to have some peace back in the house. I listen to Radio Three to get my mind back in order – and then prepare to leave the house. If Jessica's dad has gone away then it's been an excellent few hours: good sleep, good breakfast and good music; I'm ready for another marathon day in the Olympic Park. I open the front door and step out of my house – wondering if I'll get a seat on the Chiltern Railways train to Marylebone – when I notice a man sitting down on the ground a few yards away, his back against the fence, his hands in his coat pockets, collars up, sleeves slightly torn. I surprise myself by not being startled. He gets up immediately; quite athletically, with a thrust of his shoulders and smooth pivot of his lean body. I'm not surprised Jessica is so mad about sport. I can see where she got it from. He walks towards me but still doesn't say anything. I am quite intimidated because he should be making steps to compromise not the other way round. He stops just inches away, hands still in his pockets.

'A pleasure, Mrs Hartford,' he says, finally offering his hand tentatively while flitting his eyes across the front of the house. 'I'm Simon Lees, Jessica's dad. Can you get her for us? When does her shift start?'

'No, she's not here,' I reply, as he grips my hand for longer than necessary. 'I thought you knew that? She's in Watford, didn't she tell you that?'

'Sort of – but it wasn't clear...'

'How did you get here?'

'By train. I hopped on the last one from Leeds to Euston – and then a cab. I can't drive on motorways anymore. Got an injury while doing pole vault at Harriers when I was 17. I get double vision trying to keep up with the pace and the speed of the cars. Too dangerous.'

I look into his tired eyes and feel some sympathy – but not for long.

'Don't you think it's irrational to bang on a stranger's door in the early hours? I can't see how you think that's normal behaviour.'

84

'Yes, but when my daughter's involved with the police, I get involved, simple as. If I woke you up then I'm sorry but a father's got to look out for his daughter and if he doesn't he's no father at all.'

'You didn't wake me up,' I say, asking him to make way so I can get to the gate. 'We still don't do that kind of thing round here. We have a bit more respect.'

'Like the police had for Jess when they raided that shithole she was living in?'

'That was in London, I meant here – in our village...'

'Same thing.'

'Look if you'll excuse me, Mr Lees, I have to catch the train at a certain time otherwise I'll be late.'

'Can I come back for dinner tonight?'

'Sorry?' I say, with a touch of bewilderment. 'I don't know, I might be back late anyway.' I walk past him but then stop to examine him for a few seconds. 'Have you called Jessica this morning? I don't see why I should get involved in your family disputes.'

'She's not answering her calls,' he says, pulling out a packet of Lambert & Butler cigarettes from his coat pocket. 'Probably ashamed that her old man's travelled nearly 200 miles to save her from the big bad city.' He lights his cigarette with a copper-coloured Zippo lighter.

'You can't smoke here...'

'Why? Brekkie's never the same without a fag. Perks me up in the morning.'

'I said you can't smoke in my front garden. Isn't your wife a dinnerlady? I thought she might have taught you a bit about health considerations. Not to mention Jessica's sport science degree. Aren't you setting a bad example and being hypocritical?'

'What like McDonald's and Coca-Cola sponsoring the Olympics? I'm sure the athletes could run faster if they ate and drank that stuff.'

I pause and look at him and he puts his cigarettes back in his pocket.

'You're the second person to mention McDonald's to me in just a few days,' I say. 'Is this something people are getting worked up about? I hope it doesn't spoil the whole event.'

'That, and the army coming in, and the empty seats and God knows what else. These big events always bring a lot of baggage. I went to an England game at the 2010 World Cup in South Africa and the media banged on about the crime rate in the country but nothing happened. We had a ridiculously good time.'

'Oh no, not football...look I've really got to go.'

'I'm not a Three Lions obsessive, if that's what you're thinking. The tickets came through Jessie's sporting connections at university. I've been a Huddersfield Town fan for 36 years.'

'Why would you think I'd be interested in that?'

'I don't know,' he says, turning the collars of his coat down. 'Because I do care about things. And if I didn't, why the hell would I be outside your front door at 5am?'

I sigh and walk past him. 'I still haven't worked that one out.' I head to the front gate and open it, praying that he's just behind me which would indicate that he's about to leave.

'How about I totter down to London with you today?' he says. 'I'm here now so I might as well make myself useful.'

'Oh no, you'll wear me out on the train. It's out of the question.' I close the gate behind me and look at him. 'I still can't understand why you're here in the first place. I'm sure you knew Jessica wasn't here.'

He pauses and walks towards me. He stops at the gate and puts his hands on it.

'Honestly, I thought she might be here – and that's the truth. But there was another consideration. I've never been in this part of the country before and things have been tight for the family in the last few years, at least in economic terms. So when I heard Jessie might be staying in a well-to-do house like this, I thought I'd come down and see what the job situation was in this neck of the woods.'

'So this is not about Jessica at all…'

'It's all about Jessie – but we also have to keep the big picture in mind. I took her to Harriers when she was 12-years-old and Debbie and I have supported her through university. We now need to make sure her Olympic volunteering dream doesn't go belly up before it's started. We've done everything for her and if I can do more, in this part of the country, then I will.'

There is a long silence between us. I look at him and almost regret not agreeing to his request to accompany me to London.

'Close the gate behind you,' I say. 'I don't mind you coming for dinner – but I haven't time to do any shopping. It'll be just basic things like potatoes or pasta.'

'It's all we eat,' he says, turning his collars up again. 'Where's the high street in this village?'

I point the way and then leave without looking back. As I head towards the train station, the annoyance I'd felt at Simon Lees popping up at my house melts away. A certain grudging respect – and even admiration – takes hold. He'd come a long way. Would I, as a parent, have gone that far? Absolutely, but fate bundled me down a darker path.

I'm still thinking of Simon Lees during the morning team meeting – but once we get out into the less suffocating surroundings of the Olympic Park, the range and upbeat nature of spectators divert my attention. One of my conversations is with three Icelandic fans, who have national flags wrapped round their waist, and are playing Tunisia in the handball preliminaries. They are incredibly enthusiastic and keep asking me to thank Seb Coe for putting on a great Games but that I should also ask him to put his shorts back on because Team GB have been 'pants' in terms of trying to win gold medals. I said the medals would come (although I wasn't completely convinced) and then one of them did a playful magic trick with his hands and said 'Now I lift the ash cloud from the London Olympics and Great Britain will start to win golds'. We laughed and he then went on to tell us how he was stranded for 48 hours last year after the Icelandic ash cloud had grounded so many planes. I had almost forgotten about that news story. Donald was alive then. It felt like decades ago, not last year. These spectators also took a picture with me – and then went off to the Copper Box for their game. I missed them immediately.

About two hours into my shift, I finally have a chance to speak to Jessica. I'd seen her before but there were always many people round her – volunteers, spectators, team leaders – so I let her be. The perils of being popular, I suppose. She acknowledges me by raising two fingers in a curious 'peace' symbol. Or did she mean, there'd be two people staying at my house tonight: her and her father? She finally walks up to me with a shake of the head, minimal eye contact and the palm of her hand vigorously rubbing her forehead as if it needs to be shaken from its nightly trauma. I notice a cold sore has also developed on the side of her mouth. This isn't the Jessica that started the Olympics. I thought it was meant to be enjoyable?

'Go on what did he say?' she says, with a weary roll of the eyes. 'He's not staying is he?'

'Why are you ignoring his calls?'

'I'm not ignoring them, I've just been busy. In the last month, I've slept in three different places, now I'm going to be sleeping in a fourth. I would have been better off staying at home and getting the train down from Leeds.'

'So why didn't you then? A parent's home is always the best...'

'Independence, a desire to see London, meet new people...the kind of experiences most people want. Didn't you want to get away from your parents?' She pauses and makes eye contact for the first time. 'Or did the Sixties not swing for you?'

'You know you're the cheekiest girl I've ever had the misfortune to come across, but...'

'I'm funny?'

'I wouldn't go that far. I'd say you're quite perceptive in your thoughts but pretty shabby in your actions. I've got a mind to say that having you in the house would be like waiting for a nuclear bomb to go off in the country.'

'Don't exaggerate Frannie, that's for Dad to do. Did he say he wanted dinner? He always does. Food's on his mind even when there's a so-called crisis going on...'

'Now you ask, he did talk about dinner...'

'Chippies are never enough for us northerners you see...'

'Yes, that's why the police ended up in your Streatham palace...'

I am pleased that I've been able to get a bit of my own back on Jessica. She's not the only one who can crack a joke. Yet I also have to admit I'm having second thoughts of one, never mind, two of them being at my house this evening. They've got this forthright, almost formidable, streak about them that makes me nervous. They could do things I'll regret. But there's also something else about them I can't deny: a life-affirming vigour that had all but disappeared from my life.

'Your father said he helped you financially through university, he seems to be under a bit of pressure,' I say, smiling at each spectator as they walk by.

'Mum did too – but it's still not enough. He took a loan out I think and I don't know if he's paid it back. None of our family have ever been to university so it's a big thing for them. Didn't really feel like it to me because all my friends are going anyway.'

'Used to be special that, going to university. Donald had his dreams of going after he'd come home from Borneo but it never worked out for him. Now, it feels as common as going to the supermarket.'

'Who are you calling 'common'?'

'Well, this is the 'Common Domain'. If we were special, we'd be in the Olympic Stadium helping with the starting blocks or in the Aquatics Centre watching great swimmers, like Michael Phelps, jump into the pool.'

'Yes, but I wanted to do this…'

I look at her with a bewildered expression.

'What? You had the chance to be a specialist but you preferred staying out here in the Olympic Park?'

'Yes, because I want to engage with people – not with athletes or dignitaries, there's a big difference. I was all set to be one of the meet and greet volunteers with the Australian national team but decided against it. I wanted to be out here, where all the action is.'

'And Locog gave you that choice?'

'Rob did. He then told me about you and it was a two birds with one stone, kind of thing. See if I could look after you too. I haven't regretted if for a single day. I'm loving it.'

91

I pause and nod for a few seconds, wondering how this girl keeps surprising me. I'm thinking about putting on a bigger, better dinner tonight when a tall man with his face painted red, white and green walks towards us. I try and work out which country he's from but fail to do so. He doesn't speak but shows Jessica his ticket. Jessica points him in the direction of the Copper Box.

'Ask him where he's from?' I whisper to Jessica. 'It's nagging me now.'

'I think its Hungary,' says Jessica. 'They're playing South Korea in the handball this morning...'

I shake my head, annoyed that Jessica has trumped me again.

'How did you know that? Have you been to Budapest or something?'

She pauses and smiles at me.

'No, it says it on the ticket,' she says, starting to laugh. 'South Korea versus HUNGARY!'

I am astonished at my gullibility and Jessica throws her arms round me, still unable to curb her laughter. I cannot help but submit to her infectious smile and warm embrace.

Jessica spends most of the time with the police in the afternoon after she reports a man for trying to sell fake tickets for the Swimming finals. Her suspicions are aroused when she sees the tout – who is actually wearing a shirt, a very loose tie and a leather jacket – handing out folded tickets from his wallet and then waiting until the spectator slips him a note. Jessica takes the initiative and approaches him but then a minor dispute ensues and, eventually, Locog officials and the police are called to take the man in. I do admire Jessica's courage for challenging the ticket tout – but I am glad to watch from afar, uninvolved and, therefore, free from intimidation or anxiety. I still sense I'm some way off, in terms of taking the lead or reporting suspicious activity. Greeting spectators is enough. So Jessica's actions indirectly lead to Eric Bramwell, one of our most experienced volunteers, coming to say hello to me in the afternoon to see how I was faring. All this love and concern for me; it felt quite overwhelming. Eric felt I might have been alarmed that a ticket tout was operating just a few yards away from me but I told him I was fine. I had never spoken to Eric before, although I had seen him in around the Olympic Park and the canteen. He is so tall and wiry I feel he may keel over any second – but he uses that height to arch over people in a genial, gentle way, crossing his hands almost permanently while flicking his thumbs together. He speaks about his 45 years of volunteering across a range of groups, organisations and institutions. It makes me feel inadequate – as though I've never helped anyone in my life.

'I remember seeing one of my mother's friend's round at our place, sometime in 67 I think it was, and she was in tears,' he says, shaking his head. 'Her son had been in London for three days and not returned. She said he'd got into music and drugs and terrible things like that – and there was no-one to look after her now. She was adamant she needed to see a doctor because of her 'mental problems'. It was weird listening to all this in my front room. It rang a bell in me that I must help this woman because there was no-one else she could turn to. I felt that was wrong – and still do.'

'So what did you call the group?'

'*Community Road*. I know it's a silly name – but when I got married, which was very young, my wife came up with the name *Rings of Life* and that worked better. We branched out and started helping women with family planning advice and things like that, because they were very isolated. She still does that but I got into other things like helping young people with domestic problems, abuse, that kind of thing. Not very pleasant but who else did they have to turn to?'

'I admire you for doing that. I love helping – and seeing the deep acknowledgment on people's faces – but I find it hard to listen to the difficult stuff.'

'Well, someone's got to do it…'

I nod and there is a period of silence between us.

'So how many groups are you part of now?' I ask.

'Too many, particularly for my age. Probably about 30 or more. Everything from youth action to giving carers for the elderly a break in the sun. I've lost count. I still find time to play the harmonica though. I need it after listening to all that.'

'Where is it? Have you got it with you?'

'It's at home. Why, are you interested? Do you play an instrument?'

'Oh no, couldn't do that. It's just I've been listening to a lot of music lately, classical, really and it's got me thinking about how wonderful melodies and harmonies are and, you know, the contours and texture of music.' I pause and wonder if I should say any more – but can't resist. 'There's been a lot of silence in my house lately so the music seems to reach deeper, if you know what I mean. It's a strange feeling.'

'Rob told me about Donald, do you want to talk about it? It's not as though I haven't listened to these things before.'

I am taken aback by Eric's direct approach – but curiously uplifted that someone closer to my own age is broaching the subject.

'I'm not sure if I want to talk about it right here, Eric...' I say, turning away and watching the criss-crossing spectators, casual and carefree, as if suspended from the rigours and pressures of normal life. '...but since the Opening Ceremony, and these first few days of the Olympics, there's been an urge inside to talk about Donald and let it all come out. I don't know how that's happened but it's happened so fast it's almost frightening.'

'Don't fight it, Frannie, one day you'll have to talk about these things...so why not now?'

I look at my watch and check how long I've got on shift.

'Do you want to come home for dinner tonight? I'm cooking for two people already: Jessica and his dad. Why not make it a full house?'

Eric smiles but looks quite embarrassed. 'Well, I'm grateful for the offer, Frannie, but I can't tonight, I've meeting the wife and I think we're catching a film at the cinema.'

'Sorry, I shouldn't have asked,' I say, suddenly having the startling realisation that a widow had asked a married man to come and have dinner at her house. How could I have been so stupid?

'I will come,' says Eric, putting his hand on my shoulder and amending his voice slightly to offer a calm, reassuring tone. 'Probably when the Olympics end. Absolutely. You deserve nothing less.'

I pause and feel better, touching Eric's hand on my shoulder.

'Don't turn me into one of your subjects, will you?' I say. 'We're supposed to be helpers not victims.'

Eric sighs and grips my hand tight.

'Sometimes we're both,' he says.

It is odd to be going home on the train with Jessica. She doesn't talk as much as I expect. Perhaps, she's got her father on her mind? She sits on the Tube, constantly taking her music earphones on and off, picking out Denise Lewis's autobiography *Personal Best* from her bag and then putting it back again and also checking her phone from time to time for text messages. The few snatches of conversation we do have are about Team GB winning silver in the Equestrian event and about Zara Phillips, in particular. We talk about why the media are obsessed with certain members of the Royal Family and not others. The conversation inevitably leads to Princess Diana and why she became such an icon – and so much trouble for the Royal Family. We don't have any answers apart from Jessica saying she was a 'looker' and that the tabloids are 'sex mad'. I didn't think this line of argument had too much depth about it but maybe it was an indication of how Jessica was feeling. We did, however, get onto the music heard at Diana's funeral and I mentioned John Tavener's *Song For Athene* which is the only piece I never liked of his. Jessica said she actually loved Elton John's *Candle in the Wind* but not after that day, which made a sort of irrational sense, I suppose. Luckily, there are no delays on the Tube or the Chiltern Line and we get home within a couple of hours after leaving Stratford. Jessica isn't as bewildered by my home village as I expect. She claims there are many parts of Yorkshire with similar traits: boutique shops, leafy hedges and pocketbook houses. She is more concerned her father hasn't smuggled himself into my house. He hasn't and we walk in quite relieved that we can wind down a little after a hard day's work. Jessica turns the TV on almost immediately and says she is looking forward to seeing if Michael Phelps can become the greatest Olympian by going for his 19th medal in the pool. I talk to her for a few minutes and then go upstairs to the bathroom to wash my feet, as they've been pounded quite badly today. The warm water reaches deep into the pores of my toes and brings a soothing, ecstatic boost to my head. I put on my slippers but just as I am about to leave, I stop right in front of the mirror, in the exact place Donald liked to hum his Dean Martin songs. I look at my reflection for a few seconds. The house will have its first overnight guest since Donald died. Am I doing the right thing? Is too early? No, I feel good about Jessica. Her spark and vigour has reenergised me. I hastily raise my stiff arms and imagine I'm a youthful gymnast landing after an acrobatic performance. I hold the pose and, for the first time in months, savour the silence; a beautiful silence which only ends when the deafening applause erupts. I'm part of a team again. An old woman seeing chinks of light in her house once more. A few minutes later, I'm back downstairs and see Jessica stretched out on the sofa, trainers off, flicking through the TV channels with the remote control. I ask her if she wants to call her father on her mobile, as I don't know how many places to set for dinner (besides how much food to make). She says she's not hungry and I shouldn't put myself out for her.

'I'm going to say sorry in advance for my father,' she says, picking up a copy of the *Radio Times* but then putting it down again. 'He has a habit of drifting off and not quite remembering what he'd promised a few hours ago. I knew he wouldn't be here. Did he not give you a time?'

'I didn't ask to be honest. I was in a hurry to catch the train to London. He wanted to come with me.'

'You didn't tell me that…'

'I don't tell you everything, Miss Lees. Now, what do you want for your dinner? I haven't had time to do the shopping so it'll just be basic stuff like pasta or lasagne…'

She looks at me and then springs up from the sofa. She walks towards me and puts her arm on my shoulder.

'Sit down, calm down and let's watch the swimming finals,' she says, ushering me over to the sofa. She sits me down on the side Donald used to prefer. 'The swimming's very intimate on TV, there's something about those heads bobbing up and down in the water. I can almost feel the splashes on my face never mind theirs.'

'But who's going to make the dinner? Your dad might be here at any moment.'

'Forget him,' she says, sitting down next to me. 'He's probably grabbed a bag of crisps and a pint from the village pub. He might not come anyway.'

'Why do you say that, Jessica, I don't understand? His daughter's here and he's come all this way, so why would he not want to see you now after all that trouble?'

Jessica sighs and crosses her legs on the sofa. 'Did he talk about his job?'

'Not really…'

'I'm not surprised, who'd want to say you worked in a bookies?'

'Is that why you fell out? I sense you're a bit ashamed of where he works. Maybe he has to do it to make ends meet?'

She pauses and picks up a cushion, hugging it to her chest. 'I remember going in there once; I must have been about 11, I think. Absolutely grimy and filthy it was, full of old men with fags in their mouths and papers tucked under their arms or cocky lads showing their mates how good they were on fruit machines. One of these lads even asked me out: I don't think he'd seen a girl before.' Jessica looks up at me. 'I'm sure you're not surprised to hear that I couldn't wait to get out of there...'

'..And you blame your father for that experience?'

'No, but each day he continues to work there, it keeps the memory fresh.' She gets up off the sofa and starts heading towards the kitchen. 'Enough of this, I'm going to make dinner for you this evening. It's the least I can do after all you've done for us. Can I put Bat for Lashes on?'

'What? I thought we were going to watch the swimming?'

'Who cares about that? Phelps will get his 19th medal. He's great, get over it.'

I shake my head and get up off the sofa. 'I never know if I'm coming or going with you...'

'Well, come this way to the kitchen so you can show me where all the pots and pans are. We're going to have a lovely night, irrespective of whether my father turns up or not.'

'Calm down, girl, I'm coming...and what the hell is Bat for Lashes? Is that an eyeliner or something?'

'It's a band led by the lovely Natasha Khan, I've got a CD in my bag. So can I put it on or not?'

'Is she related to Akram Khan? If she is, I might give her a go. I still can't get that opening ceremony out of my head.'

'They're not related...'

The bell rings just as I get up and walk to the kitchen.

'There he is,' I say. 'I told you he'd be here. Every parent wants to see their child.'

She rolls her eyes impatiently and I sense a slight dip in her jovial mood.

'Do you want me to answer it?' she asks, folding her arms.

'Yes please, I'll just get the ingredients ready for evening dinner.'

She walks off briskly and answers the door. As I potter around the kitchen, pulling salad bags out of the fridge and opening packets of pasta by popping them with sharp knives, I feel pleased that Jessica and her father will be having dinner in my home tonight. It gives me a sense of satisfaction that a family will be back together within these four walls; chatting, eating and drinking; even if it isn't mine.

Jessica walks into the kitchen within a couple of minutes. I turn and look who is standing by her side. I am surprised to see Gillian. She walks up to me and hugs me immediately while I balance a jar of pasta sauce in my hand. I am taken aback and have to put the jar down – and then embrace her properly. I can see she is crying.

'Oh Frannie,' says Gillian, lowering her head on my shoulder. 'I'm sorry about this, I can't help it. Seeing my father like that, not knowing where he is, not recognising me, I can't take it anymore.' She eases her head off my shoulder and wipes away her tears. 'This is so embarrassing, Frannie, I hope you can forgive me. But a dad's a dad and I don't know what I'll do without him, I really don't.'

DAY SIX

I've never believed in the 'two come at once' theory because the first one is always the problem for me. It never arrives. But I am forced to change my outlook when Simon Lees turns up, yet again, at just gone 5am, banging on the door, looking worse for wear and with his leather jacket tied round his waist like a jumper. Amazingly, Jessica is fast asleep while this banging is going on and I am forced to deal with him once more. On this occasion, however, I feel much calmer and more accommodating which can only be put down to the fact that Gillian had stayed late the night before – and had talked in depth about her father's illness. It had been a sobering, emotional evening in which Jessica had also offered support to Gillian. It was by far the most heartwarming evening in my house since Donald had died – and I wouldn't let Simon do anything to spoil it. So I brought him in and made him breakfast – pancakes, soft-boiled eggs and black coffee – which he was initially enthusiastic about but hardly touched (he ended up taking two soluble paracetamol pills for his headache). He didn't ask about Jessica at all – so I had to press him on why he hadn't turned up for dinner the previous evening, after virtually twisting my arm to be invited.

'I left my job two months ago,' he says, abruptly

without looking up at me. 'Since then, I've done some temping at warehouses, packing and all that stuff, but the shifts are all over the place. Some of them start at six in the morning.' He looks up at me and smiles for the first time. 'It's probably why my body stirs into action at five-ish. I am sorry Frannie...'

'Francesca, you don't know me that well yet.'

'Okay, Francesca. Look, I know Jessica's sleeping upstairs but please don't tell her about this job situation yet. She's got enough on her plate right now. Only Debbie and you know at the moment and it's better she gets through these Olympics without any more traumas...'

'Are you sure it's her suffering the traumas and not you? Seems to me, the real troubled soul is sitting at the kitchen table, a few feet away from me. What did you do during the day? Where did you go? I didn't think you knew this area well at all.'

He fiddles with the pill-stained empty glass, rubbing it with his fingers.

'Did you go down to the betting shop all day?' I ask. 'At least there's one of those round every corner.'

'Yes, but I only went in for about half an hour to see how it's run. I spent most of time walking round the shops in the morning and then watched the Olympics for most of the rest of the day...'

'In a pub?'

'Not all the time. I did go out for a bite to eat in a restaurant.'

'But why didn't you come here? Jessica and I were expecting you.'

He pauses and then gets up from the table. He puts the glass in the sink and looks out of the window.

'You're not going to believe it if I tell you…'

'Try me. A lot of things have happened to me in 2012.'

He sighs and then swivels round to face me.

'I met another Huddersfield Town fan in the pub. He must be the only one in this county. We got talking and knocked down a few. Before we knew it, last orders kicked in – and then he invited me back to his place…'

'For a few more?'

'Well no, that wasn't the intention but, yes, that's what happened. He said he had some amazing Huddersfield memorabilia from the 1920s, when Town were top dogs, which included shirts, boots and socks. I didn't believe him but he was adamant I come home with him to have a look.'

'So you went to a stranger's house at almost midnight?'

'He wasn't a stranger. Mike's a top bloke – and we exchanged numbers. He's been down in this neck of the woods since he got a job as a production editor on the local newspaper. He was with the Huddersfield Examiner before that. I had a good night with him.'

'Better than you would have had with your daughter?'

He doesn't answer and moves away from the sink. 'Look, are you going to wake her up so I can see her. I need to see those lovely eyes today or I'm going to feel worse than I already do.'

'Well, you shouldn't have spent the whole of yesterday drinking then should you?'

'I didn't. I did a lot of walking and sightseeing too, sampling the green fields of the village with its pretty lawns and huge drives. But it *is* too quiet for me, I can't deny that.' He glances at me and walks to the door. 'Which bedroom is she in? I'll wake her up myself. If you don't push her, she'll never get out of bed.'

'No, I'll do that. She's had a calm night; I don't want her getting all worked up this morning.'

'She's my daughter, Francesca...'

I walk towards the door and brush past Simon.

'Yes, but she's sleeping in *my* Donald's study...'

I give Simon and Jessica time in the bedroom together so they can talk to each other. But after half an hour, I have to go upstairs and knock at the door to ask them to get a move on. It'll be my fifth shift in a row at the Olympics today. An overwhelming tiredness is kicking in stealthily this morning and I have to ensure I have enough time to get to Stratford without being late. I cannot wait to have two days off after this shift to recuperate. I knock again on the bedroom door after getting no response. I decide to walk in, almost out of habit as that is what I'd been doing when Donald wanted a cup of tea or a bowl of apricots and cream. I sense a good atmosphere in the room. Simon is gently swivelling round on Donald's dicky office chair and Jessica is sat on the edge of the bed, facing him, hands crossed on her lap, looking directly at him. They both smile as I stop at the door.

'Sorry Frannie, we're nearly done,' says Jessica, looking at her watch. 'Still got a few minutes haven't we? Train's not for a while yet...'

'You know I like to take the early one, Jessica,' I say, looking at Simon but imagining Donald swaying from side to side in his chair. 'Gives me time to get organised and get my thoughts arranged for the rest of the day.'

Simon stops swaying in the chair. He gets up and walks towards me. He puts his hand on my shoulder which surprises me.

'I'd like to come to London with you and Jess, today,' he says, looking down at me with a sincerity I didn't think he possessed. 'But only if you agree to it. Otherwise, I'll just go back home and do a few more temporary shifts at the warehouse than expected. The recruitment agency'll be delighted to see me.'

'Why do you want to come to London?'

He smiles and looks at Jessica. 'Who else is going to fill those empty seats we keep seeing on TV? Wembley Arena, Earls Court, Greenwich Park, someone's got to nip in there and get it sorted.' He pauses and glances at me. 'I've called some of my mates down so we can muck in and make a difference.'

'But most of the seats have been filled now. Locog, the organising committee, have got onto it and sorted out the problem.'

'There's still a few issues, Frannie,' says Jessica, with a rather abrupt interruption. 'I was speaking to Rob yesterday and some venues are still suffering. Lack of drinking water's a bit of a problem too.'

I feel confused about this sudden thaw in father/

daughter relations. It's as if the friction, frustration and downright hostility Jessica seemed to feel for her father had magically evaporated during one brief conversation in my Donald's bedroom. I need them both to come clean – otherwise there's no chance of any happy families coming down to London with me. I need my moments of peace and reflection.

'You haven't been telling the truth about your job, have you Simon?' I say, groaning as I sit down on the edge of the bed. 'Don't you think it's fair that if you come into a widow's house, and that's what I am now, you have a duty to tell her the truth and not be evasive? I mean, you've been sitting in Donald's chair for Lord's sake. Where's your dignity?'

Simon glances at Jessica and sits back down on the chair. He stretches his arms out and then crosses his legs. He finally looks at me directly – and I sense a lack of flippancy for the first time since I set eyes on him.

'I was about to made redundant from my job at the bookies but I walked first,' says Simon, with a mild shake of the head and minimal eye contact. 'It was a painful decision because I had a mortgage to pay and Jess's massive student fees to think about – but I had to do it, there was no option.' He pauses and shifts forward in his seat. 'In recent years the industry's changed so much I don't recognise it anymore. They've brought these fixed-odd betting machines into the shops and they've brought in a different kind of clientele: younger, rougher and much more aggressive. The old mob with their nicotine fingers, betting slips and whisky breath are still around but they're simply dying out, that's the reality. Anyway, sometimes I'm behind the counter on my own dealing with these new kind of people. If you ask for ID, they can go off the rails, if you say I don't have that kind of change they can abuse you so it's been hard over the last few years. A couple of months ago, though, things got out of hand on a late shift when a young lad in a hoodie that was too big for him kept throwing coins onto the glass covering of the counter just in front of where I was sat. I ignored it at first but then his mates joined in and threw more coins. Then they started banging on the counter saying they were going to kill me. I called the police but they took so long in coming that I could hardly speak when they did. And they only made one arrest, saying they couldn't identify the culprits. That was the last straw for me, so I told my bosses I was packing it in. They'd have made me redundant by Christmas anyway. They don't care about their employees at the coalface; it's all gone online now. That and fixed odd betting terminals, they're the only games in town for them. Everything else is expendable.'

I sigh and look at Jessica, who has her head down.

'Why didn't you tell me this before, Simon?' I ask. 'You could have told me twice but you went off with your football friend instead? I don't like being messed around in my house.'

'I wanted to wait until I could see Jess face to face, that's all. Then I would have told you immediately. A man walking out on his job, no matter how shit it is, is a big deal where we're from Francesca. There isn't much else around; particularly for people like me.'

Jessica reaches over and touches her father's hand.

'Okay, I understand I think,' I say, with a mild nod of the head. 'You probably thought it was the ideal time to come down and see Jessica because she'd been through her own ordeal? So it would make your own revelation easier for her to stomach?'

'Sort of, yes,' he says. 'I thought we could talk things through, away from home, and also…'

'Yes…'

'Talk about a new business idea I'd had…'

'Oh not now, Dad,' says Jessica, getting up from bed. 'Come on, Frannie let's go downstairs and have a cuppa before another big day. He's always had these harebrained ideas and I've told him I'm not listening to anything until the Olympics is over.'

'I think Jessie and I could be a good team. She's got her sports science background and I've got the sports betting so I've got this idea for a new app that would combine the two…'

'No, Dad, Frannie doesn't want to hear it. We'll see you downstairs…'

Simon gets up from the chair and folds his arms. 'And this is the sympathy I get,' he says, with a mild smile. 'I suffer dog's abuse for years and finally take a stand – and what do I get? A walkout.'

'Too right…' says Jessica, opening the door.

'So am I coming to London or not?' he says. 'I'll be the best good luck charm you've ever had. Team GB could do with some. If they don't win a gold today there'll be a riot.'

'No, you'll be a bad luck charm,' says Jessica. 'But it's up to Frannie, it's her decision.'

'Says the living, breathing voodoo doll who's only away from Yorkshire for a couple of days and ends up in a cell in the big city!'

'It's in the blood, darling.' Jessica looks at me. 'Frannie, it's your call. I'll respect whatever you say. I know you don't like to talk too much on the train or the Tube. If you take him, you might regret it…'

'Oi!' says Simon, clenching a playful fist.

Jessica puts two fists up by her chest in defence. I pause and hold the door open.

'I don't mind you coming, Simon,' I say. 'You've sat in Donald's chair so what's left? And besides, you were brave and absolutely right to walk out of your job after all that abuse. No-one should have to take that…'

As soon as we get to Stratford, Simon disappears into the Westfield shopping centre because he wanted to 'compare it to the mini-beasts of Meadowhall and the Trafford Centre'. He says he'll see us later in the morning but I'm not completely convinced he'll turn up, judging by his performances during the last couple of days. Yet Jessica is convinced and I detect a huge change in the nature of their relationship. As we walk into the Olympic Park, Jessica tells me Simon has asked her to come back to Leeds for a couple of days. She says she is considering it (as her rota was quite flexible) because he'd sacrificed quite a lot for the whole family and 'mum must be quite worried'. I find it quite touching, when I look into Jessica's eyes, that she is now thinking that way. However, I also have a palpable sense of anxiety that she might not come to stay at my house again. Her presence has been so comforting it's as though she's been living there for years.

I think about Jessica's predicament throughout our team meeting. I almost take no notice of what is being said or who is saying it. There's a lot of talk of keeping spectators' spirits up because Team GB still haven't won any gold medals. I feel my own spirits need a lift now. Oh Donald, why these sudden changes in mood? I really do get sick of them. It's as though that pleasant morning in your study, barely a couple of hours ago, never happened. After our team meeting, we are split up again and Jessica ends up outside the Aquatics Centre with Sheena while I'm with Ben near Stratford Gate. I feel so tired after the first couple of hours mainly because Ben doesn't stop talking about his Olympic Diary project – and his drastic decision to abort the 30-minute student project because Team GB's performance has been so disappointing. He thinks no-one will watch the documentary (or a 'series of interviews with his mates', as he calls it in his most cynical moments) so there's no point wasting any more time on it. The only thing he feels guilty about is 'blagging' equipment from people and using their front rooms for shooting scenes because a lot of them wanted to be in the final cut. As I listen to Ben's rabbitting on,

I do wonder if he's been influenced by this morning's team meeting. Does he really think Team GB will win no golds? That's impossible, I say, but he comes up with a long list of reasons why it *could* happen, including our big hopes like Jessica Ennis, Chris Hoy and Ben Ainslie being served a dodgy McDonald's quarter pounder in the Olympic Village and ending up getting food poisoning for the duration of the event. When pressed on why such athletes would be eating this kind of food, he laughs and says 'that'd be a film I'd want to watch because it'd be funny'. I'm not sure I would. But Ben's morning gloom does make me think. Why is it that Ben, Jessica – and for that matter, most of the young people I've met since the Olympics started – seem to be less optimistic than me (even if we consider what I've just been through)? Are their money worries, standard of living and relationships with loved ones getting them down? I had similar concerns when I married Donald in 65, not a penny in my purse or a house of our own to live in, but we got through it because there was a certain hope that things would get better and that we'd be fine at the end of the day. Does that exist now? I don't see it when I look deep into the young people's eyes. They seem to be restless and distracted, eager to move on or look for the next person or project to engage in. Of course, I could be wrong as Ben had recently written off three cars – and that could be a reason for his relentlessly downbeat demeanour. After a few moments of thinking about whether it is appropriate to bring this up, I take the plunge.

'Good myth that, Frannie,' he says, folding his

arms and looking at me. 'Truth is, I was involved in two big accidents quite close together: one on the M40 which was a six-car pile-up and one in Northampton where the brakes on my crappy Cavalier failed. I suppose the Northampton one could be deemed as my fault but what could I do? I plunged into the back of someone because my foot went right down through the pedal. The M40 one was about the posh bloke in the Ferrari behind me not spotting there were lane closures ahead and going too fast. He eventually whacked the back of my car and I ended up hitting a few more because I couldn't stop. His fault...'

'And the third?'

'There wasn't a third. I was eating breakfast one morning and the car that had crashed on the M40, but was still drivable, was parked outside my front door and a bunch of joyriders smacked into it just like that. I nearly choked on my Weetabix. If it wasn't written off before then they did the job for me.'

'...And you said Jessica was unlucky.'

'I don't see unlucky people getting a juicy insurance payout do you? Nearly five figures, I'll have you know. Lots of money for paupers like us.'

I shook my head and wondered if I'd ever really understood Ben since the first day I'd spoke to him.

'So why do you seem so down then? I don't understand.'

'Because I don't want to stand here anymore handing out fake smiles and dodgy handshakes; it's wearing me out. I need to be making films, writing, painting, anything but this. It was a mistake for me to volunteer in the first place. It's not for me. I haven't got the temperament for it. I only applied because my Mum's part of the Locog team. She thought it might do me good...'

'I didn't know your mother was part of the Locog team...'

'It's better to keep that kind of thing quiet, because people then think you might be getting the better shifts.'

'That didn't work then,' I say, with a smile.

'She's always been a slave-driver, the old girl. Look Frannie, don't get me wrong, I admire everything you are doing – and all the rest of the volunteers too – but some people can do this kind of work and some can't. I'm in the latter category.'

'It's only for a couple of weeks, for Lord's sake, can't you show some patience? The Olympics won't be coming to London again in my lifetime and it might not in yours too. Stop being so precious with your arty credentials. Who knows it might fire off some fresh creative ideas in your head?'

'Already has...'

'So why stop making that Olympic Diary? It's early days yet and I bet Team GB do better than you think.'

'Because I thought of something better; something more worthy to burn my insurance payout on. It's going to be a short film about Mum's pressurised work with Locog and how she juggles it with looking after a big family.'

'So you have a lot of brothers and sisters?'

'Six – and I'm the oldest. This will be a better piece of work. It'll concentrate more on the sacrifices women have to make…'

I examine Ben closely after that last comment. Perhaps, I'd got him wrong completely – and my generic assessment of young people was way off the mark. He has surprised me with his sensitive thoughts on family and work.

'So this new piece of work you're thinking about…' I say. 'Will you able to film your mum? Do Locog allow that?'

'I'll have to find out, but it could be a challenge. As you know, they don't even allow us to communicate on social media for the duration of the event so they might be a bit jumpy about what I've got in mind.' He looks at me and smiles. 'You do know what social media is, don't you Frannie?'

'You cheeky bleeder. I'm Auntie Media, don't forget, I'm all seeing and all knowing. I don't need to see it on a computer screen.'

He laughs and walks towards me, giving me an awkward hug. 'Oh Frannie, I'm going to miss you…'

'What?'

Before he can answer, a massive cheer erupts in the Olympic Park. I knew the women's pair of Helen Glover and Heather Stanning were going for a medal in the rowing at Eton Dorney this morning but my conversation with Ben made me forget all about it. Now, I realise with the amount of cheering in the Park, the flags suddenly beginning to wave, the shouting and, even the hugging, that Team GB has won its first gold medal. I feel a wave of joy seeping through my body and turn to look at Ben. He smacks my palm with a horrendously heavy high five.

'See I told you,' I say, 'Oh ye of little faith…'

'Shit,' he says, looking confused for the first time during our conversation. 'I might have to make that Olympic Diary doc after all…'

I end up staying in the Olympic Park well past the end of my shift – and feel rewarded when Bradley Wiggins wins Team GB's second gold of the day in the Cycling time trial. Ben has some comedy sideburns handy and sticks them onto his face, doing a jig and a manic pedalling routine to entertain a small, euphoric crowd that has gathered round him. The mood was already good but I sense it has raised another notch with more smiles, high fives and flags fluttering in children's hands. I wanted to savour some of this; why should I go home? I haven't seen Jessica or Simon all day but don't care about them now. If they want to head back home they do so with my blessing. Ben finally finishes his 'Wiggo' routine by singing The Jam's *Going Underground* and it brings me back to reality as I fear I may get caught up in rush hour if I don't get a move on soon. But again, why should I? The atmosphere is electric. Two gold medals! No-one can really believe it. A young boy, in a Chelsea replica shirt, approaches Ben and asks him to do the routine all over again. Ben feigns exhaustion and puts the sideburns on the little boy's cheek only for them to keep falling off. I watch Ben and wonder why he has decided this is his last shift today when he still has so much to offer (he told me during lunch that he couldn't take another 10 days of this and that it was better to bail out without causing a major incident). I told him bluntly (but jovially) that he was chickening out and he not only agreed but, positively endorsed my conclusion, saying there were only a few people who could volunteer in this world and he wasn't one of them. He craved expression, not sacrifice. At least he was doing that now. The young boy and Ben end up dancing like Red Indians around an imaginary campfire made up of Union flags. I do wonder why Ben has chosen to be Indian. *You see, he's different.* After this surreal scene, the small group of spectators stream away and I say goodbye to Ben. He hugs me tight and wishes me all the best for the remaining days at the Olympics. He finally touches on the subject that has dominated my life for the last three months – but which he has found hard to broach.

'Donald was a lucky man, Frannie,' he says, kissing me on the cheek. 'I hope you've found some peace lately.'

'There, you see, that wasn't too difficult was it?'

'You don't know the half of it,' he says, with a smile.

He lets go of me and then starts to sprint, in his huge size 13 shoes towards the Olympic Stadium where he says he's having a commemorative picture taken before he leaves. I watch him drift off and then look round the Park one last time before I, too, have to call it a day. It's been simply glorious, there's no other way to describe it. Jessica or not, I think I'll sleep better tonight.

On the journey home, I feel a sense of relief that I have the next two days off. No early starts, hasty dressing or rushing to the station. I look forward to a long lie-in, a lazy breakfast and a soothing dose of classical radio melodies. The shifts have been tough, but rewarding, although there is a touch of guilt that I'll be away from the action just when Team GB are getting their act together. I hope the euphoric atmosphere I felt later today will be even better when I get back to work on Saturday. I've got the front door key in my hand as I head towards my front garden, thinking about whether I have the stamina to cook anything substantial. I do feel like treating myself – a sort of 'well done for getting this far' kind of thing – but realise my body is giving me signals that it's already about to shut down for the evening. I unlock the gate and walk down the garden path, still with my head down, deep in thought about the suitability of chilli con carne and salad on a night of mild celebration and national pride. I look up and am startled to see Jessica and Simon sitting on the doorstep with at least five shopping carrier bags by their side. Jessica gets up and rushes towards me. She puts her arm round me and almost drags me into my own house.

'Are you hungry, Frannie?' she says. 'Sorry, we didn't see you today. Dad was at Wembley Arena –

and I had a hectic day once we landed that first gold. It was wild…'

I put my hand on my heart. 'Well, I don't know what to say, you gave me a shock. You shouldn't do that to an old woman.'

'It was Dad's idea to do it this way. I wanted to call you on your mobile but he wanted to surprise you.' She waits by the doorstep and picks up two of the carrier bags. 'So come on, let us in. We're going to make you an Olympic dinner. You deserve gold too after doing your five-day marathon.'

I breathe deeply and look down at Simon who is still sitting down.

'Could have known you'd have put her up to this,' I say, looking at the bulging carrier bags and actually starting to feel hungry. 'Can you cook then?'

'No,' he says, springing up from the doorstep. 'But I'd never been to the Olympics either. You wait years for an experience and then two come at once!'

'I don't believe in that theory. Now shift out, so I can get the front door open. I'm tired and I need a shower.'

I use my keys to open the door and then turn around to look at Jessica and Simon as they struggle with the heavy carrier bags in their hands. I smile and put the keys into my pocket.

'What if I was to shut this door now?' I say, gently easing the door to and fro with my hand. 'Long way back to Yorkshire, isn't it?'

'You can shut it but you won't,' says Simon, stepping forward.

'It's just I don't like these kind of surprises. They make me nervous. I was feeling very relaxed when I came home tonight – and you've spoilt it.'

Jessica steps forward and gently eases my hand off the door and pushes it open. I don't resist, probably because it's been a day full of smiles, unity and togetherness.

'…And you'll feel relaxed again in a couple of hours, Frannie,' she says, walking into the house. 'Let us cook up something wonderful for you. It's our way of saying thank you for everything you've done for us. I'll never forget it…'

Simon nods as he walks in too. I let them both go into the hallway and then look outside one last time before gently shutting the door. There is something special happening since I started work at the Olympics, I just don't know what it is.

I sense the 'two cooks' are wary of being too extravagant. They know it has only been a few months since Donald died and it isn't really time for a banquet or cases of champagne. I am happy to take whatever they serve up (mostly because it allows me to relax on the sofa all evening and relive some of the day's memorable action on TV). Jessica comes in with the starter; a fresh salad with nuts, seeds and olives. She lays the bowl on the table and says the main course, which will consist of white rice, lamb, roast potatoes and gravy, will be ready in 10 minutes. After 20 minutes, nothing has arrived but then Simon walks in wearing an apron and something distinctly odd on his face, which I can't work out because he is too far away. He comes closer and lays the main course down on the table. I am stunned to see that he has a Harold Wilson mask on his face. What on earth is he playing at? He reaches into his pocket and sticks a toy pipe into the rubbery mouth of the mask.

'Now, you do know I'm one of Huddersfield's famous sons, don't you my lady?' he says, taking the pipe out of his mouth and dabbing the food like a health inspector. 'I have a statue outside the train station. Have you been lately?'

I shake my head and break out into a smile.

'What, no Yorkshire Pudding?' he says, now aggressively prodding the lamb with the pipe. 'I'll have to get the cabinet onto that. You must sample some of that heavenly crust. Salt of the earth, that is, or is it earth of the salt?'

I shake my head again.

'Whatever, it's a grand sight better than the food served up at these Olympic Games. Where are they being held again?'

I shake my head – but this time break out into uncontrollable laughter. Simon then suddenly whips off his mask and wipes the sweat off his brow.

'Phew, it was hot in there,' he says, straightening his hair. 'Couldn't keep that on any longer.'

'Looks like you've got a hidden talent there?'

'Not really. I remember a robbery at the bookies about 16 years ago and one of the guys was wearing a John Major mask. I know it sounds ridiculous but it did happen. So I got the idea from there, really.'

'And you chose Wilson because he's from your county?'

'Sort of – and the fact he's from your era: pipe and slippers and all that.'

'Hey, don't forget whose house you're in! I'm not that old. I preferred Macmillan anyway…'

'Who? Never heard of him…'

I playfully try to smack Simon on the shoulder but he ducks out of the way. He escapes to the kitchen and I finally look down at my food: steaming hot and generously-portioned. I know I'll never get through it but I start tucking in anyway. As I start eating my food, I think about the way I used to serve Donald dinner in the evening and how he used to wave his hand over the steam coming from the dish like some magician showing off his latest trick. He felt steam had magical powers and it was good for his hands. I thought it was a bit cranky at first but did find it endearing after a while. Now I miss it, oh how God I miss it. I glance into the kitchen at Jessica and Simon making fun of each other and it fills me with pride that a family – another family – is united in my home. I raise my hand over the steaming white rice and close my eyes. If only you were here Donald, you could see that I've managed despite all the mourning and the crying and anguish. I'm okay my love. I know you've found peace. I've nearly found some too.

DAY SEVEN

I wake at 5am, annoyed that my body clock is still set to Olympic time. I think about Jessica and Simon and why they didn't stay the night. One of Simon's friends, Jim Unsworth, was so happy he got to see an Olympic event yesterday, he was adamant he would drive them all the way back to Yorkshire (he lived in Barnsley) and take them out at the weekend for good measure. It was an offer too good to refuse but Jessica baulked at the 'weekend party' saying she had to come back to London for her next shift on Saturday. As she got into Jim's car, Jessica promised me she would stay at my house for the final week, if I wanted it. Did I? Of course, but I realised her mother Debbie perhaps needed to see her more than me. It was something I didn't like thinking about too much. Only a mother knew her daughter's intimate thoughts.

I try to turn over and get back to sleep – but as soon as the left side of my head touches the pillow, I feel a vicious, almighty pain in my lower back. It's excruciating in its intensity; firing up further as I try to turn and lie on my back. My eyes begin to water and I fear I may have slipped a disc or got arthritis. I lie absolutely still for a few minutes and, thankfully, mercifully, the pain begins to subside. I reduce the severity of the diagnosis: it must be the five punishing shifts in the Olympic Park; standing for hours on end, chatting, smiling, shaking hands. It's too much for an old woman like me – and now I'm paying the price. A few more minutes pass and I feel less pain and stiffness – and more energy swarming around my body. I eventually get out of bed and get dressed. I head to the bathroom and feel relieved that the pain is now almost gone. I do some light stretches but am wary of pushing too hard. I go downstairs and have breakfast; eggs, toasted rolls and black coffee. I feel refreshed – and so relieved I don't have to go into work today. I start to clear up and put the dishes in the sink. I turn on Radio Three and start the washing-up. I turn on the tap – and the pain rips into my lower back yet again. I grab my back and have to go down and sit at the kitchen table. I take a deep breath and wonder if I should call someone: the doctor? Gillian? I give it a few minutes and the pain calms down again. This can't go on, it's ridiculous. During the morning, I move a bit better but each time I bend down or reach over for something, the pain is there again. There is no option, I have to call Doctor Adamson. I finally get through to the surgery (after 15 minutes of an engaged tone) and his secretary says there is an appointment available tomorrow morning so I agree to book it. At the end of the short conversation, the secretary recognises my voice (after I have to give my name, date of birth and address).

'Er, Mrs Hartford, there may be some cancellations this afternoon, there always are,' she says. 'Do you want me to call you if we have an appointment available?'

'Yes, that would be helpful...'

'Do you want to tell me a bit about your problem so I can give Dr Adamson a head start?'

'Not really, I'd rather speak to the doctor...'

'Very well, Mrs Hartford. I realise you've been through a difficult time. I will call you if there's a cancellation.'

The line is cut off before I get a chance to say goodbye. Dr Adamson did help me quite a lot when Donald died and the surgery as a whole were also very supportive: advice on support groups, paperwork, funeral arrangements and a few other things. The doctor didn't actually know Donald that well (perhaps because Donald had never been to the doctor in 35 years) but they met through the appointments I had to attend and, subsequently developed a respectful, if distant, relationship.

I make lunch and turn on the TV. I was adamant I'd resist the Olympics for the whole day today but can't help it: the infectious sound of chattering spectators still lingers, their patriotic tentacles continue to draw me in. I watch some rowing – the men's lightweight coxless fours – and Team GB put up another sterling show to win a silver medal. The noise and atmosphere keep me watching for longer than I should. I keep the TV on, eat lunch and then return to watch Andy Murray playing in his quarter-final at Wimbledon. It's strange to see so much colour at the All-England club. There's seems to be a casual, relaxed atmosphere amongst the players and spectators. Maybe it will help Murray win a gold medal after losing to Roger Federer earlier in the summer? It could be the turning point for him.

The phone rings and I think about not answering it: the tennis and the mild pain in my back seemed to be good enough reasons to stay put. But it rings again, on four occasions, so I get up and walk into the hallway to answer it. Gillian's voice gives me a soothing, unexpected lift. I feel guilty about not answering her call before.

'Oh you were probably resting after all your hard work,' says Gillian, speaking much quicker than usual. 'I think you deserve a day off! Look, I'm just preparing a late lunch for myself as I've been at the library all morning; I wondered if you wanted to come round to join me?'

'Thanks for the offer, Gillian, but I've just had lunch,' I say, looking over my shoulder and wondering if Andy Murray has won the latest rally. 'And besides I don't think I could even make the short walk to your place. I feel very stiff this morning. Back trouble, I think. Had to call the doctors so they've booked me in for an appointment tomorrow.'

'Oh you poor thing. Do you want me to come round immediately? I can be there in five minutes…'

'No, there's no need for that. I think I can manage for now. I just hope…'

'Yes…'

'I hope that I haven't done any damage to my back. I've still got another five shifts to do next week.

I don't want to miss out on all that. It's all happening for Team GB now. Those flags are like magic wands for me.'

'Health first, Frannie, the medals come later. Look, I'll be round in five minutes...'

'No honest, you don't need to come round...'

'I do. I really don't like to see you alone, Frannie. I think about you so much I wish I could move in with you to keep you company. But, obviously, circumstances won't allow and I have to make do with Larry-come-lately. I'm leaving now, so see you soon...'

She hangs up before I can answer. I put the phone down and walk back to the living room where I see Andy Murray hitting an effortless winner. He doesn't seem to feel the pressure and is enjoying the adulation of the crowd. He doesn't seem to have the weight of the world on his shoulders anymore. Just as I was beginning to feel the same, I'm forced to clutch my back again to absorb the searing pain.

The phone rings again and I think it must be Gillian – but the doorbell rings at almost the same time so I realise it can't be her. I answer the door first and she comes scuttling in with a book under her arm and a small pharmacy bag which seems to have a few bottles of pills in it. The phone is still ringing and she walks over to pick it up.

'No, it's okay Gillian, I'll get it,' I say, trying to show I'm in decent fettle by bending down to pick up the receiver.

'Are you sure?'

'Yes,' I say, with a polite wave of the hand to usher her into the living room.

She nods and walks off, tapping her fingers on the specific bottle of pills she thinks I need to ease the pain in my back. I answer the phone. It's Dr Adamson's secretary.

'Hello, Mrs Hartford?'

'Yes…'

'There is a cancellation this afternoon and I could get you in to see Dr Adamson at 2.40pm. Would that be suitable for you?'

'Oh er, yes, I wasn't expecting that. I've got a visitor now so I'm not sure.' I pause and think about what Gillian is doing in the living room. Is she watching the tennis? 'When do you need to know by?'

'Well, immediately really as it's only a couple of hours away. I'd need an answer now to book you in, otherwise there are many other people waiting.'

I rub my back and then straighten it a couple of times. The pain has lessened but it's so stiff I'm not sure I can sit down comfortably.

'Okay, that's fine, I'll take that appointment please; 2.40 is it?'

'Yes, Dr Adamson will see you then…'

The secretary hangs up and I put the receiver down and walk back into the living room. Gillian isn't there; she has walked through to the kitchen and is preparing a couple of soluble pills to be thrown into a glass of water. I walk towards her and she looks up at me and smiles.

'Anyone important?' she asks, watching the pills dissolve into the water. 'Dad's been through all the painkillers in the world. It's what makes me an expert. Get this inside you and you won't feel a thing for a few hours, at least.'

'It was the surgery. They've had a cancellation so I can get an appointment today...'

'No problem,' she says, looking up and handing me the fizzing glass. 'I'll drive you down there.'

'But I can walk, it's only 10 minutes away...'

'Maybe you can, but is it worth it? You might aggravate things further and that's the last thing you want right now.' She pauses and puts her hand on my shoulder. 'Isn't it Frannie?'

I nod and reluctantly take the glass.

'Get it down you, it'll ease the pain away for a while,' she says. 'Then I'll drive you down to the surgery and make you some cupcakes this afternoon, how about that?' She turns and picks up the book she'd brought with her. 'Also bought you this. It's something very personal to me but I would like you to read it.'

I take the book and wipe the dust away from its slightly amateurish cover. It's called *A Dad Shivers, A Daughter Weeps*. There is an image of a father playing hopscotch with his small daughter in the back garden. The author is Gillian Bernhard. I look at Gillian and feel a strange, fuzzy elation.

'Did you write this?'

'Yes, just published it myself, only 50 copies or so. But I wanted to get my Dad's story out there. He was diagnosed so early that he's had to live with the condition for nearly 30 years already. I need to show people what that can do to a person – and to a family.'

I feel the cover in my hands and then hold the book to my chest. 'You should be proud of yourself, Gillian. Has your father read it yet?'

'He doesn't know about it. He can still read but his hands shake when he has to hold a book. He also forgets what he's just read.' She pauses and urges me to drink the glass of pill-soaked water. 'Come on, Frannie, drink it before it loses its kick.'

I move my lips towards the glass but then pause. 'Did Donald know about this book? I'm sure he'd have encouraged you if he did.'

'He knew I wrote a few things but he didn't know about the book.' She reaches forward and eases her hand onto the bottom of the glass, tipping it towards my mouth. 'Sometimes, it's easier to put these things in print rather than talk about them in the open.'

Gillian and I walk into Dr Adamson's consultation room. He is tapping a keyboard on his computer. He sees us and swivels round in his giant chair, taking his glasses off and offering a handshake to both of us. We both sit down and Dr Adamson swivels round to his computer again, tapping some more keys before a final click of the mouse. He then turns and gives us his full attention.

'Mrs Hartford, it's nice to see you looking well,' he says. 'Have you caught a bit of the sun? Looks like it?'

'Er no, I don't think so. I have been standing outside a lot, that's true, but the sun hasn't been out that much so I'm not sure...' I turn to look at Gillian. 'I haven't changed that much have I, Gill?'

Gillian shakes her head but is clearly annoyed by Dr Adamson's opening question.

'It must be all those Olympic smiles then,' says Dr Adamson. 'Anyway, what I can do for you?'

'It's my back,' I say, awkwardly putting my arm behind me to locate the pain. 'When I woke up this morning, I was in so much pain I thought I'd never move again. It was excruciating. It's just down here, low down...'

Dr Adamson moves forward in his seat. 'Right, let's have a look. Pull your cardigan up...'

I pull my cardigan and blouse up and feel an immediate draught wafting across my body, the lower back bearing the brunt of the cold air. He presses his fingers into the lower end of my spine and then onto my fleshy bits in the same region. I don't feel anything for a couple of minutes as he continues to probe, his scalpel-like fingers almost causing as much irritation as the pain itself. He then reaches a sensitive spot and I jump in my seat.

'Ow, yes right there,' I say, as I close my eyes and let out a mild shriek of pain. 'Just there. That's very painful. Feels like I'm completely paralysed when you push down there.'

'You're not paralysed, Mrs Hartford...' he says, moving back and looking at his computer again. He types into the computer. 'Are you enjoying your work at the Olympics? My secretary sees you coming back into the village sometimes, still wearing your violet and pink volunteers' uniform.'

'It's purple and red,' says Gillian.

'Okay, purple and red,' he says, glancing up at Gillian. He turns back towards me. 'How many days have you just worked, Mrs Hartford?'

'Five…'

'Consecutive days?'

'Yes…'

'And that would be how many hours roughly?'

'I don't know, added up, maybe 40 or so.'

'When was the last time you worked 40 hours in a week?'

I look at Gillian and smile. 'I did more than that when Donald was around, particularly at home with the housework and all that.'

'I mean outside, paid work, that kind of thing…'

'Well, I suppose 20 or even 25 hours is the most I've ever done in my volunteering – but you have to remember someone had to run the house. That's a full-time job in itself.'

'I understand that Mrs Hartford but you have to put all this in context,' he says, looking at me and folding his arms. 'If you've done 40 hours this week – and I feel you're probably underplaying this because going in and out London is another 10 or 12 hours – the likelihood is that your body simply cannot cope with that kind of strain and pressure after so many years of, let's say, less rigorous work.'

'Volunteering can be very rigorous,' says Gillian,

interrupting again. 'Frannie has been working part-time for more than 25 years. Try changing some sheets when someone's defecated; I'd say that's pretty rigorous.'

'Er sorry, I haven't had the pleasure…'

'Gillian Bernhard. I work at the library. I thought I'd come down with Frannie today because she's barely been able to walk.'

'Oh yes, Mrs Bernhard, I think I read about a campaign of yours in the local paper. Also, don't you have a son?'

'Two. The younger's one regularly here clogging up your surgery. He gets a lot of sinus infections.'

'Thank you, Mrs Bernhard, now let's get back to the issue in hand,' he says, politely but with a pause that's longer than necessary. 'So Mrs Hartford, it's clear to me that your body has responded badly to the little breather you've had after a five-day stint of intense shifts. I would also mention the fact, although I realise it might be sensitive, that your husband only passed away a few months ago. This kind of psychological strain can also have a negative effect on the body. I'm not saying it has, but it could be a factor.'

'But the pain's physical, it's got nothing to do with Donald…'

'I get that – I'm just saying you've had a traumatic few months and then when you add in your whole Olympic experience, it's a lot to take…'

'…For an old woman?' says Gillian.

'You said that not me…'

133

'So you're not going to do any scans?' asks Gillian.

'Not immediately. We'll see how the pain develops. Hopefully, it will subside after a period of rest.' He turns and looks at me. 'I wouldn't worry, Mrs Hartford, I think you're going to be fine. It's just that your body is so stiff because it's not used to that kind of intensity. That is why you're getting some difficult symptoms. I'll prescribe you some painkillers...'

'That won't be necessary.'

'Are you sure? I take it you have more shifts next week. They may help you get over the line.'

'Like you said I'll just have to rest for these couple of days...'

'Yes,' he says, breaking out into a smile for the first time. 'You know I run a clinic here at the surgery, two evenings a week, which tries to get people to change their lifestyle habits and get their bodies back in some sort of health. We are absolutely overwhelmed with diabetes patients, smokers and many more who, with just a little bit of adjustment, could get their lives back on track. I mention this because yesterday something strange happened. I usually get about 20 or 30 people turning up every week – but yesterday almost 200 people turned up. We couldn't fit them all in. I could only put it to one thing...'

'Which is?' says Gillian.

'The Olympics, and in particular, Team GB's success yesterday. I can think of no other reason for the phenomenal response. More people want to get active and are inspired to do something with their lives, particularly those with health problems. They're willing to open up and share things.'

'It's true, Frannie,' says Gillian, turning towards me. 'I've seen subtle changes at the library too. One man mentioned Lizzie Armitstead to me – and I wondered who he was talking about! I know you don't see a lot of this because you're actually there, at the coalface, but it is quite strange to see the Union flag in people's windows in the village. It's not the kind of thing we usually do round here.'

I nod and notice Dr Adamson is actually enjoying listening to Gillian now. He reaches over to shake my hand and does likewise with Gillian.

'Great to see we're back on the same page,' he says. 'Now, Mrs Hartford, do come back to me if the pain gets worse. My guess is you'll be back throwing yourself through the Olympic rings next week without too much trouble.'

'Thank you doctor,' I say, getting up from my seat.

'Hmm, bit of a wasted visit, I'd say,' says Gillian.

'As I say come back to me if matters deteriorate,' says Dr Adamson.

'Don't worry, we will,' says Gillian.

'I meant Mrs Hartford...'

'Her too...'

I smile at Gillian's slightly aggressive tone. I suppose she's looking out for me. She's driven me to the surgery, given me a pill for my back pain and prepared cupcakes for me this afternoon. All the doctor has done is provided me with a nice anecdote.

'You can't trust them,' whispers Gillian, opening

135

the door as we both head out of the surgery. 'Same with the county council and their library closures. They all have too much power and none of them are really accountable.'

'I kind of trust him. He was quite nice. He did right by Donald.'

'Maybe, but you have to ask yourself a simple question: are you stressed or are you in pain? Which is it? Because as far as I can tell, you've had the happiest five days since Donald died.'

I look at Gillian as we reach the exit. I didn't have an answer and felt a twinge in my back again.

The cupcakes and custard Gillian makes are so delicious I find it hard to resist eating more. But I know I have to resist as my taste buds might cause more trouble for my back. Gillian does go on about the connection between food and joint pain – but doesn't seem to mind serving me more of her lethal, but perfect, concoctions! I browse through her book while she's fascinated by what's happening at the Olympics, particularly in the Velodrome which seems to be at fever pitch. She tells me Team GB are having a great day already – Peter Wilson wins gold in the shooting, Gemma Gibbons wins silver in the judo and there's another gold and silver in the canoe slalom (she tells me their names too but I literally can't keep up) – so obviously I'm delighted but there is a slight sadness that I'm not in the Olympic Park soaking up the atmosphere after these wonderful feats. I can only put this feeling down to the strong, soothing pills

Gillian has given me. They've taken the pain away and made me feel stronger and more energetic than I probably am.

Gillian is sitting on the sofa, shoes off, feet up, curled up with a mug of coffee in one hand and a tiny cupcake in the other. She is watching Victoria Pendleton and Jess Varnish in the women's team sprint and I put the book down temporarily to see if they can get to the final and ultimately give us three gold medals in a day. We gawp at the screen as the blistering action unfolds. The Velodrome is like a Roman colosseum, a wall of noise; a thudding rollercoaster of emotion. The dizzying wheels spin furiously in the middle while a stampeding chorus develops all around them. It feels quite frightening, at times, but it finishes so quickly I have no time to get anxious. Our team is through to the final! Gillian cheers while trying to control the crumbs from falling out of her mouth. But a few minutes later, our hopes are dashed when Pendleton and Varnish are disqualified for an illegal changeover. Team GB will not make the final. I watch Victoria Pendleton's face and the anguish is written on her face. I try to look down at my book again but her face is so compelling I'm forced to look up again. Gillian doesn't say anything for minutes. She finishes off her cake (but not her coffee) and puts both down on the table.

'Oh well, there's still Chris Hoy to come,' she says. 'We'll still probably get another gold today. Feel sorry for Vicky though…'

'Strange we call her Vicky. It's as though we know her…'

'We sort of do though, don't we?' She looks across at me and notices I've got the book open again. 'So what do you think so far?'

'I've read about four chapters already. It's wonderful, Gillian. All I can say is...'

'Yes?'

I pause again and close the book with my finger still on the relevant page. 'When a man you love unconditionally goes from your life it's a void that's never filled. I know your father's not gone yet, of course, but I hope you know what I mean.'

'Course I do, Frannie. And you're right. Father is still with me but in a different guise. He just isn't that man anymore – and I'm finding that adjustment difficult.'

I nod and there is a long silence between us.

'You know I haven't read a book for quite a long time,' I say, thankful to break the silence. 'I've forgotten how wonderful words can be. How they can get to things we can't seem to say face to face...'

Gillian nods and turns towards me. 'I agree so let me ask you this...' She pauses again and looks down at the book she'd written. 'Why don't you join the campaign against the library closure after you've done your work at the Olympics? It'll keep you occupied and help you meet new people. Get you out of the house too. You've enjoyed these few days so much that I think you could carry it on.'

'Maybe I could – but I don't feel as strongly about it as you do.'

'Donald did...'

'But he's not here now.'

She raises her hand. 'Sorry Frannie, I hope I'm not being pushy. All I'll say is, we've got a public meeting planned for next week and we're hoping for a good turnout. I've got Jack and William roped in too and some of their friends so I hope to have a good mix of young and old people. And with this Olympic madness too, who knows we might even get a bumper crowd?'

'No, they'll be glued to their TVs…'

We both laugh and Gillian gets up to clear the table.

'Oh come on, you've done enough for me,' I say. 'I'll sort that out later. Please don't start the washing-up too.'

Before she can answer, her mobile phone rings. She puts the mug back down and immediately answers it. She's about to walk into the kitchen for some privacy but chooses to stay put once she realises who it is.

'How come you're back home so early?' she asks, talking into the phone while rolling her eyes. 'There's some sandwiches in the fridge if you're hungry. I'll make you something when I get back.'

She waits for an answer and then sighs when it's rather long. She puts her hand over the phone and looks at me.

'Did you hear that, Frannie? Lawrence's boss is obsessed with Chris Hoy and he's in the Velodrome this evening. That's why he's let them go early so they can watch the race – and maybe even see him on screen.' Gillian talks into the phone again. 'I take it he'll be back slaving you into the ground by tomorrow?'

As I listen to Gillian speaking to Lawrence, I am rather shocked by how the conversation is developing. Are things that bad between them, that Gillian wanted me to listen in to her displeasure and annoyance at her husband? I feel like leaving the room as Gillian's tone becomes defensive and agitated.

'I had to see my father, Lawrence, when will you understand that?' she says, starting to pace around. 'That's non-negotiable. I've always been there for you, all those years, and now when it's my time of need, you are as hard-headed as ever. Well, I'm not going to take it anymore. You haven't said a single word about Daddy's health. It's not acceptable.'

I decide it *is* better to leave the room as I can't listen to this. Gillian tries to stop me but I breeze past with the book in my hand. I go into the kitchen and turn on the radio. I think about the few disputes or arguments I had with Donald during our 46-year marriage: stupid things over choice of dinner, political views or not being smartly dressed. But nothing compared to this. I place the book on top of the radio and imagine Donald being by my side giving me advice. 'What are you waiting for?' he'd say. 'Tell Gillian, you'll be there. After all you'll have nothing to do after the Olympics.' He is right but do I really want to be part of something that may arouse conflict, dispute and disagreement when there is so much joy, togetherness and unity around because of London 2012? We've worked hard to create this mood, I don't want to destroy it in a few hours. Gillian comes into the kitchen having ended the call.

'It's settled then,' she says, slipping the phone into her pocket.

'Yes, I'm not sure about the library thing, Gillian. I don't think I've got the stomach for the fight.'

'Oh that,' says Gillian, looking confused. 'No I meant between Lawrence and me. We're getting a divorce.'

DAY EIGHT

A text on my mobile finally wakes me up just before 11am. I feel relieved I've managed to sleep for so long; it will reenergise me for the heavy week to come. I glance at the phone but head to the bathroom before reading it. There is a strange dream still recurring in my head – and I hope some water will quell its potency. I stand static in front of the mirror, trying to open my saggy, puffed-up eyes. The image is clear: I'm carrying a bunch of flowers to Donald's grave while wearing my Olympic volunteers' uniform. It's both frightening and exhilarating. In reality, I've already visited Donald's grave eight times after his death but this would be the definitive journey: me in my special outfit, Donald watching from below, proud I was at the centre of a national event. I needed to do this again, I was being told. I would make my ninth visit – but not before I'd done my duty to the people and the nation. Then I could look back on my achievements – and share them with Donald.

I have a wash and come back to the bedroom. I check the text on my mobile; it's Jessica. She's coming back today after a 'special' couple of days at home. She's in Watford already, chatting to one of Rob's daughters who she has become friends with, but she'll be heading my way by early afternoon. I cannot wait to see her. I start tidying up immediately and only have breakfast when I'm satisfied the house is in good order and smells nice (getting rid of the cupcake smell which still lingers after yesterday's cooking is a challenge). For a moment, I think of Gillian and her possible divorce from Lawrence but it's too depressing so I put it out of my mind. I'm much happier with Gillian's medication though; the pain in my back has completely gone. I hope I haven't transferred my suffering to her. It sometimes does feel like that.

It's nearly 1pm by the time I'm happy with how everything is arranged. Jessica is likely to be staying for the whole week so getting the spare bedroom absolutely sparkling is worth the effort. I settle down for a cup of coffee and prepare to see how Team GB are faring, after having missed the whole morning. Five gold medals yesterday and up to fifth place in the table! I'm quite excited there will be even more thrills today. My mobile phone rings and I answer it immediately for once.

'Afternoon, Frannie,' says Rob, in a relentless cheery voice. 'How are you this lovely day? Not missing the Athletics are you? Got to tell you, that Jessica Ennis and company have lit up the Olympic Stadium already. There's 80,000 packed in there. And the Olympic Park, phew, it's been a sight to behold. Pure joy and colour. Absolutely stunning.' He finally pauses for breath. 'So what have you been doing on your days off?'

'Did Jessica Ennis win her heats then?'

'Not only win, she broke the British record in the 100 metre hurdles. Did you not watch it on TV?'

'I was asleep…'

'Heavy night last night was it?'

'Haven't you got work to do if there's so many people there?'

'Finally got a break, Frannie. I'm in the canteen putting my feet up.'

I roll my eyes and then walk to the TV to turn it on. 'Have we won any more golds then?' I ask.

'This morning? Yes, Kath Grainger and Anna Watkins in the rowing. That's six golds now.'

'Oh go away Rob, I'm annoyed that I've missed it…'

'Don't be. There'll be plenty more treasure later today. There's Becky Adlington and the cyclists in the Velodrome. We could have seven or eight by the end of today.'

'More than that, I hope. Anyway, Jessica's coming round today, did she tell you?'

He pauses and seems slightly confused at the switch in conversation.

'No, I thought she was back in Leeds – and she was going to travel from there every morning. I know it's a trek but this girl's been to the Himalayas so nothing's too much for her.'

'Don't know much do you? She's been at your house this morning with your daughter. No doubt playing loud music and eating all the food like students do.'

'Okay I admit it, you got me there Frannie. I had

no idea what she or my daughter were up to. But they've become quite close friends so, when that happens, old fuddy-duddy dad who drives a van and likes the true metal is no good to them. So what did Jessica say? That she'd be staying at yours for the duration of the Olympics now? I hope you're charging her rent.'

'No. She's welcome to stay her for as long as she likes without paying a penny. I like having her around. Even her dad's quite a fun character. He dressed up as Harold Wilson the other day...'

'She always told me she was ashamed of him...'

'Not now.'

'Harold Wilson eh? Probably the last politician who would have genuinely cared about the jobs we did. Now, they're just interested in careers and buffoonery. I mean look at Boris Johnson; he gets caught on a tripwire and the polls go up! He's like a circus act.'

'Oh please Rob, no politics today, I want to relax...'

'I agree, so let me give you something more palatable. Are you looking forward to your shift tomorrow?'

'Yes...'

'Will you be prepared to stay on a while longer in the afternoon? Don't worry it won't be part of your shift. We've got something in mind for you.'

'Which is?'

'That'd be telling wouldn't it? So will you stay on for a while? It'll be a great day, packed to the rafters with all the athletics going on.'

I pause and sigh, looking at the TV as a presenter and pundit talk in the studio.

'If I've got the energy, of course I'll stay,' I say. 'I didn't want to even leave on Wednesday when it was getting so exciting. But you do too much scheming, Rob, I don't know how your wife and family cope with you.'

'They don't,' he says, with a chuckle. 'See you tomorrow, Frannie, and hope you and Jessica have a wonderful day today.'

He ends the call and I sit back to watch some more events on TV. What's he got in store for me tomorrow? Is it something to do with my birthday? I hope not because I've done everything I can to keep that quiet after Donald's passing. It'd be wrong to give the date any significance, never mind have a celebration. And besides, today is the date of my birthday not tomorrow. If somebody wanted to bring it up, when better than on my day off? No, it must be something else. But in a strange way, I am looking forward to it, whatever it is – and that's worth a mild celebration in itself.

Jessica walks into the house and gives me a tight, lingering hug. She's carrying a huge Puma bag on her shoulder, a smart-looking bottle of water and a battered copy of *Runner's World* magazine. She straightens her wristband after it's been thrust out of position by our embrace.

'The world has changed since we spoke last,' she says. 'Britain is on the march! Even the ticket collector spoke to me on the way down. When I told him I was working at the Olympics, he banged on about Lynn Davies!'

'You do remember who he is?'

'Course I do, what do you take me for?'

'I was just concerned you might not remember him…'

She smiles and playfully walks back towards the front door. 'Do you want me to go back home now?' she says. 'Because I can do that, no probs, it's been a long journey.'

'No, no come in, I'm not that silly to let you go now.'

She takes her baseball cap off and hangs it on the coat hook. She walks into the living room, with me behind her, and throws her shoulder bag onto the corner of the sofa. She then stretches out onto the sofa using the bulging bag to rest her head.

'Do you want a proper pillow?' I ask, wondering how active Jessica is going to be for the rest of the day if she's slumping already. 'Donald hated cushions. He never kept any in the house.'

'Why?'

'He thought they were the most uncomfortable things he'd ever come across. He always fidgeted and fussed if he ever had to use one. Generally, he liked to throw them across the room if ever he had the misfortune to feel one on his back…'

'…Or his bottom?'

'Let's not go there shall we?' I say, walking towards the kitchen. 'Now, can I get you a cuppa – or do you want a soft drink?'

'No, I don't want anything,' she says, suddenly springing up from the sofa. 'I had one of those crappy sandwiches from the train station and it's done strange things to me.'

'Shall I put the telly on for you, then? Rob says Team GB are doing well again today.'

'Did you speak to him?'

'Yes, earlier on today. Says he's got a surprise for me tomorrow. You haven't got your mitts all over it too have you?'

'Would I do such a thing?'

'Wouldn't put it past you...' I walk across the living room towards the stairs. 'Do you want to see the bedroom you'll be sleeping in for the next week or so?'

Jessica pauses and then looks at me for rather longer than necessary. She then gets up and walks towards me, putting her hand on my shoulder.

'Stop fretting Frannie, all in good time.'

'I'm not fretting, I'm just taking care of you...'

Jessica smiles and looks beyond me at the framed picture of Donald at a jazz and swing evening in Beaconsfield. He has a microphone in his hand and is doing a classic Dean Martin impersonation.

'He's probably the same age as my Dad in that picture,' she says.

'A bit younger, I think. Seems like another lifetime anyway.'

Jessica nods and puts her arm round me. 'You know, Keeley said she couldn't understand why I had such a bad relationship with my father...'

'Keeley?'

'Rob's daughter. She's so close to her father and it's the same with the other girls. They get on so well I almost felt jealous. It was so relaxed in that household when I stayed over. I just wasn't like that with my own father...'

'But now you are?'

'It's taken a few weird events to bring us together but, yes, it's like we're starting all over again.'

'I'm so happy for you Jessica but it shouldn't take him walking out on his job to bring you back together again.'

'You're right – but it was a job I hated. I hated the thought of him working there and people asking about it, simple as that. Now he doesn't, and that's a result.'

'He also might have hated you coming down to London, staying above a chip shop and then getting arrested...'

'Course he did, that's why he came down on his horse and chariot to save me! I'm grateful to him but there's also something else...' She walks out of the living room and takes the baseball cap off the hook. She walks back in and places it on my head. It feels ever so strange on my head as if I've turned into a child again. 'It's not just Keeley and Rob and the girls and my mother and my father...' She smiles and turns the baseball cap round so that the peak is at the back. 'It's also the conversations and time I've spent with you. I honestly believe that's been the major factor in making me wake up and think about my relationship with my family. It made me think about all the things Dad and Mum were doing for me that I didn't see or simply didn't want to see. I realise now I was wrong about most of it. They've just been looking out for me that's all – and so have you.'

I feel quite tearful but the baseball cap's suffocating head grip seems to be stopping any emotion from surfacing.

'Maybe you've been good for me too,' I say. 'Have you ever thought about that?'

'Yes, and now you can tell me all about Donald because I want to hear everything about his life. He sounds like a wonderful man.'

I take the baseball cap off and put it back on Jessica's head.

'Let me show you your room first,' I say, opening the door. 'Then you can ask me anything about Donald. Absolutely anything.'

It isn't as painful as expected. The old photo albums, a neat pile of maps, a shoebox of Test cricket stubs and a small collection of vintage LPs. There is more but I feel this is enough for Jessica to be going on with. The photo albums have so many searing memories in them that I try to turn over the page quickly, even when Jessica wants to linger or highlight a certain image. Everything is covered from a weekend coach trip to Brighton in the late Sixties to a visit to the Thame Country Show as recently as 2011. Where did all that time go? The country show is Donald at his best, with a falcon on his arm and a smile for the camera. He loved it so much, it became an annual event for us. That was our 12th visit. The pile of maps, mainly from South East Asia are next, and Jessica is intrigued by some of the countries' old names, like Ceylon and Malaya. I tell her that Donald had a difficult time in Indonesia in the early 60s, serving his country, and he felt nostalgic about collecting these ancient maps. They gave him pride and reassurance – something he felt the country had lost. The shoebox of Test cricket stubs – the oldest from a game at Headingley in 1959 – doesn't interest her as she thinks cricket is the most boring game on earth. But I can see the spark back in her eyes as she goes through Donald's LP collection. It's dominated by swing and jazz but there are also albums from Dusty Springfield, The Supremes and Vaughan Williams. I point out to her that some of those were my choices. I'm thankful (and exhausted) when Jessica finally puts the final LP to the side (The Supremes *Where Did Our Love Go*) and slumps against the bedroom wall, feet outstretched, hands crossed on her lap.

'Who was *The Supremes* fan then?' she asks. 'I only know one of their songs.'

I don't answer immediately and she begins a rendition of *Baby Love*, using her hands to mimic the iconic group's moves. The sound is like a knife through my heart. She continues to sing and I keep control for about two minutes but then can't hold back any longer as her words and expressions make me burst into tears; an unexpected, almost violent, outpouring that comes deep from my soul. The anguish is crippling and painful and I bend over to try and quell the torrent. Jessica stops singing and rushes towards me on the bed.

'What's the matter, Frannie?' she says. 'Are you ill? Shall I call someone?'

'No, it's just you singing that song makes me think of things I shouldn't…'

'Like what?'

I look at her and wonder if there's any point in holding back now. Was Jessica too young to understand? Gillian knew but, as it was so long ago, we hardly mentioned it.

'I had two miscarriages and a stillborn child in the space of four years,' I say, wiping away the tears and suddenly feeling brave and defiant. 'Donald and I tried for a long time after that but nothing happened. People thought we didn't want children. It wasn't true.' I pause and put my hand on Jessica's thigh. 'I think my body was cursed. It always felt flimsy and fragile. I felt sorry for Donald because people thought there was something wrong with him. We didn't talk about these things much in those days.'

'Oh Frannie, I'm sorry, that must have been so hard for you.'

I get up and walk towards the LP collection again. I pull out Dusty Springfield's *The Look of Love* and wipe away the swathes of dust from its front cover. I turn to look at Jessica and show her the LP. 'I played this so much after my first couple of miscarriages, because I felt she was speaking to me. We shared an inner pain only we could describe. But I vowed not to play it again because I was determined to have a baby. But when I got pregnant again – and Clarissa came out stillborn at six months or so – I couldn't help but be drawn to it again...'

Jessica gets up and walks towards me. She puts her arm round me and kisses me on the cheek.

'Anything you want, I'm here for you. If you want to talk about those days, I'm all ears, if you don't, that's absolutely fine too.' She lowers her head onto my shoulder. 'Makes me think how lucky I am with Mum and Dad. I've been so stupid the way I've treated them, particularly Dad.'

'You're young, that's all. You'll learn that the bond between parent and child is the most powerful thing in the world. I can still feel Clarissa in every pore of my body.'

Jessica wipes her cheek. 'Oh don't, you're nearly setting me off now.' She smiles and looks at me. 'We've still got the emotion of all those gold medals for Team GB to go through yet!'

I nod and look down at the Dusty Springfield album. I grab Jessica's hand, as tightly as I've ever held it, and ask her to leave the room.

'Where are we going?'

'This way...'

We walk out of the room and down the landing towards Donald's study. We walk in and Jessica waits by the door while I walk towards the record player. I take the album and place it down onto the record player, easing the needle onto its velvet black surface. I step back and take Jessica's hand, asking her to come into the middle of the room. I gently put my arms over her shoulder and close my eyes as the sound of Dusty Springfield's voice soothes me one more time, perhaps for the last time. Jessica holds me tight – but I'm dreaming of another girl in my arms.

Jessica keeps shouting to me (I am in the kitchen, preparing dinner) about the gripping Roger Federer and Juan Martin Del Potro match she's watching on TV. It's 18-17 to Federer in the final set and Jessica keeps saying it will be wonderful for Andy Murray because the 'Swiss legend' (her words) will be very tired in the final. I caution that Murray has his own semi-final to play but with the exploits of Del Potro and Federer, they might never get onto court in the first place. Finally, the match ends and Federer wins. I'm thankful that it's over because at least it stops Jessica talking so much! The bell rings a couple of minutes later and I ask Jessica to answer it as my hands are drenched in lettuce juice. She returns a few minutes later with William standing next to her by the door, hands in his coat pockets, already looking quite sheepish and apologetic. Jessica smiles at me and then heads back to the living room to watch the tennis.

'Hello Mrs Hartford,' says William, almost afraid to step foot in the kitchen. 'Mum seems to have lost her purse and she wonders if she might have dropped it in your house yesterday.'

'Er I'm not sure, William, I haven't seen anything,' I say, wiping my hands on a tea towel. 'I can have a good look now if you want. She was here in the kitchen most of the time so I'd have probably seen it if she'd dropped it…'

'Well, that's all right then,' he says, already starting to move back towards the front door. 'I've got work in a couple of hours so I'm in a bit of a rush. Mum just thought you might have picked it up that's all. No problem anyway. I'll let myself out.'

'Hold on Will, I haven't had a proper look yet,' I say, starting to check behind the fridge, the cupboards and the bins. 'I've been upstairs for half of the day today. Do you want to wait five minutes? I'll make you a cup of tea.'

He sighs and scratches his head. He then checks his phone. 'Okay, I've got a couple of minutes.'

'Why don't you go in the living room and sit down with Jessica for a few minutes while I have a proper look?'

He lowers his voice and looks quite nervous. 'Who is she, anyway?'

'She's a volunteer like me. We work together in the Olympic Park. She's nice, she won't bite.'

He nods and then walks slowly into the living room. I watch him amble in and then scour the kitchen to see if I can find Gillian's purse. Her book is still there on top of the radio but I don't think she left anything else behind. After ten minutes of awkward searching (my back felt stiff again after going into areas I shouldn't) I give up and head into the living room. William and Jessica are chatting about how a gluten free diet might help Novak Djokovic play better tennis. They seem to be getting on well. I sit down, because I feel so exhausted, and lean back on the sofa.

'Phew, that tired me out a bit,' I say, blowing quite hard and looking up at the ceiling. 'The back of that fridge is murder.' I finally lean forward and look at William. 'It's not there, Will. I would have found it if it was. Say sorry to your mother but I have looked everywhere. I hope she finds it soon. Was there a lot in there?'

William is about to answer but Jessica suddenly looks interested in the conversation.

'What have you been looking for Frannie?' she asks.

'It's Gillian's purse. She was making cupcakes here yesterday. She thinks she dropped it here…'

'A purse? Oh, God yes, I saw it up in the bathroom by the sink and I was going to tell you about it but we had quite an emotional afternoon so I just forgot all about it. It was near the hairbrush and soap. Is it dark green?'

'Yeah, Mum's got a habit of leaving things in the bathroom. She takes hours in there sometimes.' William gets up from the sofa. 'Great, can I go and have a look, Mrs Hartford?'

'Do you want me to go?' I say, more out of politeness than pragmatism.

'No, I'll be fine. I won't nick any of your beauty products, honest!'

'Those are Jessica's…'

He looks at Jessica and smiles. For less than 10

minutes together, they seemed to have developed a good rapport. He walks out of the living room and heads upstairs. Jessica turns to look at me.

'He's quite a nice guy,' she says, rubbing her hand down the back of her hair. 'He wants me to come out for a drink.'

'What? Isn't that a bit fast?'

'Well no, not in that way. He's asking everyone to come to a special evening at the pub where he works. They've slashed prices for the weekend because the pub's losing punters. Don't you want to go?'

'No, it's been a long day and I need an early night. But you can go if you want.' I smile and think of Simon. 'As long as you're not like your father and waltzing in at 5am then I can take that.'

'Luckily, I haven't got a bad habit like that. It's 4am with me…'

We both laugh but then I hear noises upstairs and hope that William is okay.

'Sorry I didn't tell you about the purse,' says Jessica. 'My brain's turned to mush today with all the travelling and all the heavy stuff we've been through. It's like I've lost my bearings.'

'Doesn't matter now, shall we see what Will's getting up to?'

'I'll go, you have a rest…'

She gets up and walks to the door.

'Don't steal all their money, will you?'

'Maybe I already did,' she says, with a wicked smile.

She leaves the room and I settle down to watch

TV, trying to use the red button for a range of Olympic events but then getting irritated and deciding to stick to one; the tennis. A couple of minutes later, Will and Jessica come back into the room.

'He couldn't find it at first,' she says, looking at William with almost motherly concern. 'He was looking in the cabinet above the sink and then near the towel rack. I had to point it out to him.'

'I would have found it eventually,' says William, checking inside the purse to see if everything was there. 'Do you want to come for a drink this evening then? You're invited too, Mrs Hartford.'

Jessica comes back to sit on the sofa. 'I'm not sure, it's up to Frannie. I'd rather stay with her this evening. If she wants to go out, I'll come, otherwise, no.'

'You don't need to worry about me, Jessica,' I say. 'I'll be fine. I'm over it now.'

'Over what, Mrs Hartford?' asks William, slipping the purse into his trouser pocket. 'Sorry, maybe I shouldn't have asked.'

'No William, you don't need to know,' says Jessica. 'I'm sure you've got enough issues to deal with yourself right now. Hope you can sort them out.'

'What do you mean?'

'Well, your mum and dad's divorce?'

'What?'

I feel a shudder as soon as Jessica says the words. Her voice gets lower and she looks embarrassed.

'Doesn't William know?' she says, in almost a whisper to me. 'Fuck, I hope I haven't put my foot in it.'

I shake my head and look up at William. Before I can speak, he finally finds some fluency.

'Are you saying Mum and Dad are going to get divorced because it's the first I've heard of it? Did Mum tell you this because she's got a habit of saying things and then not going through with them? I know she's had it hard but Dad's done a lot of good things for us too. And anyway why didn't she tell me or Jack if she was thinking of such a big move? I don't believe it.'

'Will, please accept my apologies for that news coming out to you like that,' I say, getting up and walking towards him. 'It was my fault not Jessica's. I told her earlier today that your mum was considering this course of action. It was wrong of me to do that. It's been a difficult time for me too, it was just an error, I hope you won't keep it in your heart that Francesca talks about you and your mum behind your back because I don't do that.' I put my hand on his shoulder. 'Sorry again, I'm just not myself since Donald died, I'm just not.'

He pauses and I wonder how he's going to react – but then he touches my hand with his and looks down at me.

'It was only yesterday so the news would have come out soon enough,' he says. 'She likes spending time here so I can understand you talk about these kind of things. Don't worry about it, there'll never be any problem between us.' He embraces me and then looks across at Jessica. 'But as for madam over there. I'm not sure I can forgive her unless she downs eight bevies tonight at the pub so she can keep us afloat.'

'Eight? That's nothing, you should be talking about a dirty dozen.'

'Come on then, get your coat…'

'Too warm, don't need it.'

Jessica looks at me and I shake my head.

'I'm too tired, Jessica, you go…'

'Not without you.'

William looks at me. 'When was the last time you had a drink in a pub?'

'Must be at least 15 years ago. It was one of Donald's friends in Amersham. It was a quiz night, I think. After that we only went out occasionally to restaurants or the theatre.'

'Come on then, it'll do you good. I don't start work for a couple of hours so if you want to come back home immediately I'll drop you off. You don't have to stay long.'

I look at Jessica and I can tell she's desperate for me to say 'yes'. Have they got something going on that I should know about?

'Okay, just a quick one then,' I say, walking towards the TV to switch it off. 'We've got work tomorrow so we need to keep things in check.'

'Don't worry, I'll make sure I keep an eye on both of your fitness levels with my barman's beady eye app.'

'WHAT!' says Jessica. 'Sounds pervy!'

'No, it's an idea I've got for an app: barman's beady eye. You have built-in sensors so you can smell where the areas of high toxicity are. You can step in before things get ugly. I suppose it's like having a policeman patrolling the heavy drinkers in the pub.'

'Good luck with that,' says Jessica. 'I'll stick with my favourites…'

I walk towards the cabinet and take out my purse.

'Don't worry about that, Frannie,' says William, tapping his bulging trouser pocket. 'It's Mum's round…'

The Beaconsfield pub fills up steadily throughout the evening. I take an eternity to get through a single glass of vodka and blackcurrant. Jessica is on her third bottle of Stella Artois. Two big screens are positioned either side of the bar area – and a huge Union flag is draped right across the top, hanging down so much that, at times, it flicks the top of the bald landlord's head. He doesn't seem to mind though as the drinks are flowing and the mood is upbeat. The action from the Velodrome is creating a raucous atmosphere in the pub which, strangely, I do not find threatening or intimidating. It's celebratory rather than aggressive. This may be down to Victoria Pendleton winning gold (after her disqualification yesterday) which has created the sort of emotional hush in a pub I've never seen before. Andy Murray also wins and reaches the final where he'll meet Roger Federer. Can he get his revenge for the defeat at Wimbledon? Jessica is convinced he will because Federer's 'knackered' after his epic semi-final (she's told me this four times today already). William joins us before starting his shift. He has a huge glass of lemonade in his hand and sits down next to Jessica.

'Do you want me to pour some Stella into your glass?' she says, lifting her bottle towards William's glass. 'Might help you get through your shift?'

'Don't be silly,' he says, putting his hand over the glass. 'Duty calls and all that. I've only got 15 minutes until I start.'

'What's your boss like?'

'Bryan? Bit of a worrier really. If it's not the takings he's worried about, it's the stock or the temperature of the drinks. He does care about the staff though. He likes taking us on free trips to breweries or beer festivals but we don't always take them up. It's the way he drives in his Proton that really concerns us. He's a maniac.'

Jessica strokes her beer bottle with her finger. 'I really am sorry for mentioning that thing with your parents. I know how hard that can be. All that aggravation.'

'I've put it out of my mind really. Mum'll tell me soon enough, I'm sure.' He turns to me and smiles. 'So how are you enjoying it, Frannie? Not complete monsters in here, are we?'

'No. I don't know what I expected really. Maybe I thought more people would look at me and notice me because of my age – and because I'm with a young girl – but it hasn't happened.'

'You're not the only one who likes young girls in here, believe me!'

We all laugh and thoroughly enjoy the few

minutes we spend together. William then sees Bryan ushering him over from the bar area and he's forced to get up.

'That's my cue, ladies,' he says, finishing off his lemonade and picking up his empty glass. 'Oh, I nearly forgot, Frannie, do you want to go home or stay a while longer?' he asks. 'I think you should stay because you're enjoying yourself.'

I look at Jessica and glance around the pub. The pleasant ambience has a soothing effect: the sliding glasses, the criss-cross conversations, the low-level muttering. The pub is packed, with many standing, but I only spot two families, one of them has a toddler in a high chair – and she is feeding him extremely slurpy baby food.

'Frannie, did you hear me?' asks William, putting his hand on my shoulder. 'I've got to start soon but I can order you a taxi anytime you want to go home?'

'No, William,' I say, taking another sip of my ancient vodka and blackcurrant. 'I'll stay a while longer.'

He smiles, puts his glass down and mimics putting a medal round my neck with his hands. Then he claps – and so does Jessica.

'Give over,' I say. 'So when are you two getting serious then?'

They both stop clapping immediately – and look extremely embarrassed. It is nice, sometimes, when you can hold your own in a place like this.

DAY NINE

The morning goes so fast, I don't have the time to breathe. The Olympic Park doesn't get any better than this. Swarms of people glide across the giant playground with their rucksacks, hats, bottles of water and pantomime flags. A mild euphoria seeps through the atmosphere, infecting everyone in its path, elbowing out cynics, drowning out dissenters. It's like the gloom of the pre-Olympics cloud has been shattered so comprehensively that there's no way back for it now; a geniality and generosity of spirit have won the day. I only see Jessica once throughout the morning – and she says she's still disappointed Rebecca Adlington didn't win gold yesterday. But she quickly lightens up again when news of another gold in the rowing – in the Men's four – filters through. We also mention William and his offer to take her out next week. Jessica is still flattered (I can tell by her cheeks turning crimson in an instant when his name is mentioned) but she's not sure that he's 'her type', whatever that means. If only these youngsters knew what courting was like back in my day they wouldn't be so choosy. I can still remember Donald approaching me for the first time at a village fundraising event for wounded soldiers. My parents were also there (probably to keep their eye on me) but it was fascinating how Donald spoke about our small, sleepy village of a few thousand people and compared it with the vast, expansive battlefields of South East Asia. He made everyone in the hall feel part of something bigger, something global. Of course we knew about Empire and the problems of the last few years but he didn't hold back in his criticism of past and serving Prime Ministers. It drew me to him. Eight months later, we were married. Will Jessica and William last that long if they start going out? I hope so, because for some unknown reason, their brief flirtation or companionship has made me incredibly happy so far.

Unfortunately, someone who won't be happy is Rob as there's no chance of me hanging around for his 'surprise' later in the day. I'm too tired as I sit down for lunch and his surprise is probably something crude and impenetrable anyway so I'd rather nip out through the crowd before he can get hold of me. I get talking to Eric instead. He is in great spirits – his daughter has just got married and she's also agreed to live at home for the time being as a new house is out of the couple's reach – but he still finds room for a note of caution. Perhaps it's a symptom of our advancing age.

'I'm worried what will happen when all this is over,' he says, taking off his cap and rubbing his head vigorously. 'I know it's a silly thing to say on a day like this with its extraordinary atmosphere but what happens when it's all gone? When the crowd and athletes go home? Who's going to care about the volunteers then?'

'Come on Eric, what's brought this on?' I ask, drinking my black coffee rather too quickly to keep in tune with the pace of morning. 'Let's just enjoy this, we can think about all that later.'

'Well, I mention it because our local youth club had to close down a couple of days ago,' he replies, frowning as he picks away at a small cyst on the back of his head. 'There just aren't enough volunteers to keep it open. Valerie Dean, who runs it, was in tears down the phone saying she'll miss her 'young family' so much. It's like there are two parallel operations running at the moment: seventy thousand volunteers at the carnival, having the times of their lives, and the rest of the volunteers in the country, struggling along at the bottom, cobbling together a few funds to keep their services running.'

'It was always like that though, wasn't it Eric? It was the same when we started: lack of funds, lack of interest, people taking us for granted…'

'True,' he says, finally putting his hat back on his head. 'But it's worse now – because the community spirit isn't there. Apathy rules – and once you're infected by that, it's hard to rally any troops.'

'I think there's something else wrong, Eric,' I say, folding my arms. 'This is so unlike you. Your daughter's wedding made you proud and happy so what's happened?'

He pauses and looks at me for longer than necessary. He sighs and moves his chair closer, perhaps to dampen the chatty, buoyant atmosphere in the canteen.

'Of course, I was the happiest man in the world when Laura got married,' he says, raising his voice slightly and crossing his hands. 'And when she said she wanted to stay in the family home, it was even better, because I'd still get to see her beautiful smile every day...' He pauses again and eases the peak of his cap down over his forehead. 'But Jean wasn't happy with this arrangement because she wanted us to enjoy our retirement in our own home; to finally get some freedom. We fell out over it and, truth be told, I'm not used to it. It's hurt me quite badly. I'm not good at conflict, Frannie. We haven't had a big quarrel in 51 years of marriage – and I don't want to start now.'

'Oh I'm so sorry, Eric, I had no idea. I avoid conflict as much as I can too: it feels like poison at our age. Do you want me to speak to Jean?'

'No, no I wouldn't want you to do that. I just needed to tell someone that's all. It's been eating me up inside.'

'And there's me thinking you were enjoying yourself more than anyone else at the Olympics!' I say, with a shake of the head.

'I am – it's when I go home the problems start.'

'So what are you going to do about it? I can see Jean's point in a way. Laura's how old? 36, 37? She's probably thinking she'll never get the freedom of her own home. And your son-in-law? He's a solicitor isn't he? I'm sure they could afford a mortgage soon.'

'Not in our area – and Christopher's still a trainee solicitor so he's not on the greasy pole yet.'

'At his age?'

'He didn't do well at school but got into university as a mature student. So he's been playing catch up.'

'...Playing catch up? Greasy poles? Relieved I stayed away from that life.'

'...And became a volunteer?'

I look around the canteen at the lively purple and red army: eating, drinking and chatting. I imagine them as the sixth sense of the Olympics, jumping and diving through the sixth conjoined hoop, putting out fires and greeting strangers.

'I'm happy I did,' I say, rubbing the emblem on my shirt. 'I wouldn't have seen an Olympic Games otherwise...'

I glance up and notice Rob coming towards our table. He playfully turns Eric's cap to its side and straightens his name tag.

'Sorry Rob, I can't come this evening, I'm too tired,' I say.

'You don't know what I've got in store for you yet,' he says, sitting down and checking my coffee cup. 'Do you want me to finish this off? You know I haven't got time to queue up.'

'Be my guest,' I say, easing the cup towards him. 'So what *have* you got in store for me? You should be looking after an old woman, not giving her more anxiety.'

'Hey listen, I heard Jessica and this William bloke have hit it off, is that true?'

'Who told you that?'

'Jessica and my daughter are quite close friends,

as you know. They speak all the time. What's he like then, this William fella? Works in a pub doesn't he?'

I look at Eric and smile. 'And this is our dear leader Eric. The biggest gossip of them all. You should have been called Roberta!'

'Careful Frannie, that's not PC these days,' he says, finishing off my coffee. 'The Locog spies would have you for sexist innuendo.'

'It's not me interested in the prurient details of Jessica and William,' I say, looking at my watch. 'For your information, they're just friends for now...'

'Were you with them at the pub yesterday?'

'It's nearly time for me to get back on shift again,' I say, preparing to get up from my seat. 'You know it takes me 10 minutes to get off my chair because of my creaking bones.'

'I was told you stayed close to midnight...'

'Maybe I did, it was my day off, what's your point?'

'Good stamina there, Frannie, that's all. Just do another one tonight, I promise you won't regret it. Might even give you Sunday off, who knows.'

'But what is it, this big surprise? It's getting more tedious by the minute.'

Rob smiles and hands Eric the empty coffee cup. He gets up from his chair and puts his hands on his hips.

'Ask Eric, he knows,' he says. 'I'll see you at about five-ish Frannie. You'll thank me for it one day.'

He walks away from the table. I look at Eric who shrugs.

'Does everyone know about this, apart from me?' I ask.

Eric puts his hand on my shoulder. 'Ageism, pure and simple, that's what it is – and we're victims of it. He may have talked about sexism but I know his game. I think he's got it in for us old people because I haven't got a clue what he's talking about.'

I look at Eric and realise he's being deadly serious about the ageism conspiracy. He doesn't know Rob well enough. The man simply can't help playing around – he's just a big kid – and the middle Saturday of the Olympics is when he can be the biggest kid of them all.

Sheena makes me start thinking about the Paralympics for the first time. She mentions Oscar Pistorius going in the 400m heats against the world's best athletes and says it was one of the most amazing things she's ever seen. She wonders how a human being can be so driven to go against the able-bodied elite despite all the odds stacked against them. She feels the level of dedication is incredible but also a bit scary. We don't have much time to talk, as we are pulled this way and that across the Olympic Park, but the snatches of conversation we do have end up being quite funny – or even ridiculous. I definitely believe this is something to do with the overall mood of volunteers and spectators on an expectant weekend. In one of these conversations, Ben's name is mentioned and I ask how he's doing.

'He's left the country,' says Sheena. 'He's gone to some retreat in Istanbul…'

'Sounds like a proper tortured artist…'

She smiles. 'It's what he likes to think he is.'

Later in the afternoon, we end up outside the Riverbank Arena which gets very packed, mainly because of the Great Britain v China game in the women's preliminaries. This is the first time I have a small sense of regret that I won't be in the stadium watching the action rather than out here amongst the spectators, giving them directions, checking their tickets and generally talking to them about how wonderful London 2012 is. It was entirely my choice to work the middle Saturday – but now the roars are so loud from all parts of the Olympic Park, including the Olympic Stadium, that I wonder if I have missed out by being *out* here rather *in* there. Sheena doesn't let me dwell too much on this minor irritation.

'Gary wants to me to stop working in the middle of this week,' she says, just after a young Chinese man has his photo taken with her. 'He's got his hands full at the garage he runs and he can't cope with the kids. He keeps saying two was okay but he can't manage three – but there's no way I'm going back yet. I'm staying till the end. I've got tickets for the Closing Ceremony.'

'I think he's forgot how much of a blessing they are.'

'Too right. He's also forgotten about me. For the last nine years or so, I've hardly been anywhere apart from the house, supermarket or the doctor's and now that I'm in the middle of this event that everyone's talking about it's got him worked up. Theo also mentioned that I was about to meet Usain Bolt so that didn't go down well either.'

'Are you?'

'You must be joking. The active imagination of a primary school kid I'm afraid.'

A spectator asks Sheena to tie his Union flag round his waist (which has become loose) as his hands are full with food and drink. She moves towards him and bends down slightly, putting her name tag into her mouth so it doesn't get in the way. She ties it quite tightly around his portly waist. Once she's done, she cheekily takes a sip of the man's drink through the straw while he's looking away. The man thanks her and heads into the Riverbank Arena.

'Lucky he asked you to bend down not me,' I say, with a smile.

'That's five babies I've had to deal with today. Four at home and him! Nice drink though.' She laughs and moves back by my side. 'You got any plans this evening then?' she asks. 'Or are you just going home and relaxing after such a long day? Honestly, I could sleep in the Olympic Park tonight. I don't want to leave. The buzz is electric today. I've never felt anything like that.'

'…And we haven't even won anything in the Athletics yet. What if Jessica Ennis wins? I'm not sure my ears could take it.'

'The roof'll come off the Olympic Stadium. Do you wish you were in there?'

'We're commoners,' I say, with a smile. 'We're not allowed.'

'But you *were* at the Opening Ceremony. You've already sampled that kind of noise. What was it like?'

I turn and look at the Olympic Stadium; imagining hundreds of athletes sprinting, throwing and jumping within the steel bowl while hordes of spectators gasp, cheer and applaud.

'Like a joy I can't describe…'

'Oh God, I want to go in now,' says Sheena.

For the first time, since London 2012 started, I feel the same.

My shift is over and I'm not as exhausted as I expected. Perhaps the exuberance of the spectators – and Team GB's continuing medal success – has carried me through. Before I can even think about getting changed or worry about delays on the Jubilee Line, Rob appears in the changing room to whisk me away in an instant. He takes me to the canteen where I grab a sandwich and a coffee, one of the most pleasurable breaks I've had, as it allows me to think deeply about a satisfying and fulfilling day's work. He eats fast and frantically, looking up at me all the while, wearily trying to bat away my predictable questions.

'I understand you've had a hard day, Frannie,' he says, wiping away a touch of mayonnaise from his lip. 'But just bear with us a bit longer. I've got a special feeling about this evening.'

'I'm not bothered now to be honest,' I say, finishing off my sandwich. 'I've had a great day already and nothing can take that away from me.'

'You must be out on your feet though?'

'Not really, just being out there in amongst the spectators gives you a lift. It's like some happy virus has been sprinkled right across the Olympic Park.'

'Oh look, here's Jess,' he says, looking over his shoulder. 'Blimey she looks knackered.'

Jessica walks to the table and sits down.

'A man asked me out this morning near Stratford Gate,' she says, looking incredulous. 'Can you believe that? He found me again this afternoon, I don't know how, and popped the question again. He wouldn't take no for answer. Dressed all funny too, in sunglasses, shorts and long-sleeved t-shirt. Thankfully, I just saw him leave.'

'So that's two blokes after you now,' says Rob. 'I wonder what William would think...'

'I've known William for about 24 hours now. Even in our advanced Bronte-inspired county that's not enough time for a proper romance.' She looks at Rob and straightens his crooked name tag. 'So come on, tell Frannie what you've got in store for her. She's tired of your games.'

'You're not tired are you Frannie?' he asks, looking at me.

'No, but I will be if you don't get a move on.'

'Can I not finish my sandwich?'

Jessica gets up and puts her arm on Rob's shoulder. 'No, you can't.'

'But you've only just got here...'

'It's best for me to move around. That bloke might come back and be watching me right now. Who knows, he could be one of the staff in the canteen.'

'You wish...'

'Come on, get up.'

Rob is forced to get up while chewing a mouthful of bread.

'Okay ladies I get the message, no need for army measures.' He swallows his food and pinches his throat as if a piece has got stuck. 'Do you realise it's the only meal I've had today?'

'Call that a meal?' says Jessica. 'I wouldn't have fed it to the pest at Stratford Gate...'

About an hour later, I am stunned and bewildered by what is happening. I am inside the Olympic Stadium, at ground level, huddled with 50 or so other volunteers watching the semi-finals of the Women's 400m. Jessica is standing next to me but Rob has disappeared into the bowels of the stadium. The stands are jam-packed, light bulbs flashing, a crackling sense of expectation as the spectators roar and then offer mild applause. My eyes are fixed on the lush orange track as the athletes come round for the home straight. What am I doing here? I'm supposed be in the Common Domain, not in the prime venue of the Olympic Games. I'm a generalist not a specialist. I'm not supposed to have access to these venues because I don't have the specific skills. But this doesn't worry Jessica as she relishes every moment, chatting enthusiastically to the other volunteers about Christine Ohuruogu's chances if she makes the final (which she does). About 15 minutes later, Rob appears and walks towards our group with a smile on his face. Sheena is by his side carrying what looks like a small cake with candles. Eric is also there with a card in his hand. My heart starts to race faster as if I've just heard the starter gun. All the volunteers turn around and look at me. Jessica also turns but looks bewildered. She shakes her head at me as if she doesn't know what's going on. Sheena brings the cake towards me, it's filled with so many small blue candles that I cannot be in denial any longer. It's for me. Some of the candles have already been blown out; the wafts of air around the stadium are too strong for the tiny flames. All the volunteers start singing and look at me. The song can hardly be heard in amongst the cheering spectators and the constant announcements.

'Happy Birthday to you, Happy Birthday to you, Happy Birthday Dear Frannie, Happy Birthday to you...'

The volunteers cheer and clap and look at me, expecting me to blow out the candles but I hardly have any strength left. I bend down and try my best but have nothing left after three pathetic efforts. Jessica comes to help finish off the job. She puts her arm round me as we look at the writing on the cake: 'A True Olympian'; there are also two gold medals on either side. Sheena hands me a card, which I'm relieved to deal with as it's much easier than the cake. I open it and it says: 'To Frannie: For doing your duty through difficult times'. It nearly brings tears to my eyes. Rob comes over to hug me and then bends down to kiss me on the cheek.

'You've been a tower of strength to us all, Frannie, and I mean that,' he says. 'This is your night. Enjoy it.'

'But my birthday was yesterday...'

'I know,' said Rob. 'But you were off work. I wanted

your colleagues here to show their appreciation. We couldn't have done that yesterday.'

'I don't know what to say…I'm just overwhelmed really…' I look at Jessica. 'Did you know about this?'

She shakes her head. 'I didn't even know it was your birthday yesterday.'

I nod and look at Rob. 'Genuinely Rob, I know you get carried away sometimes but this is wonderful, I really mean that.'

He smiles and gives me another hug. Then he looks at his watch and eyes up the cake (still in Sheena's hand).

'Right, we've got to pack up this mini-celebration quickly or else Locog will sack us all by midnight,' he says. 'Sheena do you want to just a cut a piece of cake for Frannie and then we'll be done? There's a big night of Athletics to come, we don't want to be carted out of the stadium for causing a distraction.'

Sheena pulls a small knife out of her pocket and cuts the cake. I notice a few spectators, to our left, are peering over their seats wondering what the hell's going on. The sweet smell of the cake may have got up their nostrils. She offers me a small, crumbly slice and I pop it into my mouth, closing my eyes as the cream and jam arouse my taste buds.

'Can you cut some more?' says Rob. 'I'm bloody starving.'

'Wait on, I'm going to give Eric and Jess a piece…'

'Oh for God's sake, am I not going to get any food tonight?'

'Why do you want food when we're getting so many medals?' says Sheena.

Rob rolls his eyes and starts to walk away.

'Here Rob, you can have some of mine, I can't finish it,' I say.

He comes back reluctantly and finishes off the cake. Looking a bit happier, he folds his arms and looks out into the Olympic Stadium.

'You might see something special tonight, you might not,' he says, glancing across at me. 'But one thing's for sure: Donald would have been proud that you were still here, fronting up, helping people and making their visit more memorable.'

'Oh, you're getting carried away Rob, I'm just doing my job…'

'Maybe, but after all this is over, the London 2012 volunteers will be getting a lot of plaudits. I can feel the momentum building already: politicians and the media are already praising us. They'll need their heroes and heroines – and you'll be one of them.'

'Heroin?' I say, with a smile. 'Isn't that the white stuff that supposed to give you a lift? Feels like there was some in that cake.'

'No, that was cream. But if Jess Ennis or Mo Farah come through for Team GB tonight you'll have the mother of all overdoses.'

We both laugh before Rob steals another piece of cake that is meant for Eric.

* * *

The wall of noise round the stadium is deafening as Jessica Ennis comes into the home straight in the 800 metres. Buoyant spectators clap the athletes round the track – and I join in as the stadium seems to develop a beat and rhythm of its own. Union flags wave vigorously as she kicks for home. She still trails two athletes but breezes past them with less than 100 metres to go. I cannot believe I'm here to see this. The spectacular noise is exhilarating but too much for my tender ears. She comes up to the line and flings her arms up in the air. A cry of joy written on an unbearably emotional face. The cheers sizzle round the stadium and she bends down, hands on knees, gasping for breath. Then she falls to the floor in tears, flat on her back, body pumping, hands on her face. She's finally given a bottle of water by a colleague. She sits up, still in tears, and takes a sip. She gets up and acknowledges the crowd, arms up in the air; elation and emotion wrapped up in one. She runs to the crowd and wraps a Union flag round her shoulders. It's a glorious sight and I try and contain myself. I look away at my fellow volunteers, some cheering, some chatting, one or two in tears. I wonder where Rob is; I must thank him for this. Jessica is just a few feet ahead of me, chatting to Sheena. She moved closer to the action as the climax got closer. She turns and walks back towards me.

'You see I always told you Jessica is a great name!' she says, stopping by my side. 'Jess means blessed, simple as that.'

'This place is blessed that's for sure. I've never seen anything like that.'

'I agree,' she says, nodding her head. 'Something's happened to our country. We're allowed to wave our flags properly for once.'

'Careful,' I say, with a smile. 'Rob might have his PC brigade out again soon.'

'Hope so because they'll get swept up in it too.' She turns and looks beyond the track at the long jump event. 'And we might have another gold soon. Greg Rutherford's already jumped 8.31. He's got two jumps left.'

There is so much euphoria in the stadium I don't know where to look: at Jessica Ennis with a flag round her shoulders? At the incredible spectators or at the long jump event which is creating an excitement of its own? A few minutes later, the decision is made for me as Greg Rutherford prepares for his penultimate jump. The rhythmic hand clap begins again, a rising, urgent call to arms for an athlete ready to put his body on the line for his country. He runs up and takes off, a huge leap, as though he's suspended in the night sky above the stadium. He lands and an almighty roar circulates around the stadium. I look for the white flag. I always look for the white flag when a British athlete is competing. It's white – and the length of the jump eventually flashes up on the scoreboard. He doesn't extend his lead – but before I can dream of another gold for Team GB, another wild cheer erupts in the stadium as Mo Farah sets off in the 10,000m final. Oh where to look? They go round and round and round almost making me dizzy before Jessica tells me to watch the long jump again. I'll need glasses after this (and not the celebratory ones). American Will Claye is the only man who can stop Greg Rutherford getting a gold and he takes off, for the last time. It's not his best jump – and Rutherford puts his arms up in the air as ear-splitting cheers cascade around the stadium. He's Olympic Champion! Two golds in a few minutes! Astonishing – and that's five in one day now. Could it get any better than this? Donald didn't see a single gold for Great Britain at the 1948 games. All eyes are now on Mo Farah as he hears the bell for the last lap. The sound in the stadium now is almost unbearable; a panoramic, ferocious noise engulfing every being in the giant silver bowl. It tingles and swarms all over my body making me feel as if I could join Mo and the gang, taking every stride, pumping ever arm, taking every breath. He's in the lead with 200 metres to go and I can't help but raise my hands above my head to cheer him home. I've never been as excited as this. My purple and red-uniformed colleagues are doing the same: jumping up, cheering, pumping their fists. Mo comes into the home straight. He's going to do it. Bedlam and pandemonium in the stadium. He hits the line – and it's gold for Britain once again! Mass cheering and hysteria all around me. An exhausted Mo hugs his training partner and then slumps down on the track and kisses the floor, to give thanks for his incredible victory. He taps his head repeatedly as the tears gush out. The unrelenting din of the stadium heightening his emotions. He raises his arms in the air and rushes to the crowd, a Union flag is thrown to him. He drapes it over his shoulders and starts doing a strange thing with his hands, putting them on top of his shaved head and then tapping them repeatedly.

'What's he doing?' I ask, having to shout at Jessica because of the noise in the stadium.

'It's the Mobot,' she says, moving her mouth as close to my ear without nibbling it. 'He said he'd do it if he won – and he has.'

'But what does it mean?'

'Can't hear you, sorry,' she says, 'I'll tell you later, just enjoy this…'

I nod and look out into the stadium, captivated and exhilarated. Mo Farah is posing for the mass of photographers but then his pregnant wife and daughter come down onto the track. His daughter jumps onto him as he tries to keep hold of her and the Union flag. It's too much for me. The tears plunge into my cheeks – and I can barely see the track after a few seconds. An unbreakable bond between parent and daughter. A family united. Mo's country. Jessica sees me crying and wipes away a tear with a tissue. It's a night of dreams; a golden spectacle that will linger long in the memory. A magical party peppered with red white and blue. Happy birthday to me – even if I didn't believe in them anymore.

DAY TEN

I spend the whole morning rewatching last night's tumultuous events. Jessica, luckily for me, had remembered to record most of the action and I sit, with a coffee and an edition of the *Sunday Telegraph*, to relive some of the incredible things I witnessed. I keep using the remote control to rewind to pivotal moments: Jessica Ennis in the 800, Greg Rutherford's winning jump and, of course, Mo Farah's thrilling pursuit of 10,000m glory. But I keep pausing it again and again at Mo's embrace with his daughter; the Union flag stuck in between them, it's an image seared into my consciousness. I cannot say how wonderful it makes me feel. If the tears are an indication, then I must be in dreamland. There is also the small matter of all the other gold medals to catch up on from yesterday: two in the rowing and one in the Velodrome. It's the best day for Britain for 104 years. We now have 14 golds and 29 medals in total, sitting third in the medal table. Seeing all those smiling British faces on the podium again and again feels like a trick of the mind. Are we that good? Maybe we're not as bad as we think.

After this wonderful, lazy morning (and I don't feel any stiffness either after yesterday's marathon stint), I go upstairs and tidy what is now Jessica's bedroom. She is working this morning and, perhaps as she had to rush to London to beat the Sunday transport restrictions, her bedroom is what she likes to call a lot of things: a tip. So I begin picking up the clothes strewn on her bed as well as the odd magazine, a summer dress, socks and an empty bottle of water. I wonder if she's always this disorganised or the mitigation of our frequent London trips – at unsociable hours – should be taken into consideration. The neatly-placed picture of her mother and father that she's placed on the bedside table makes me think the latter. After a few minutes, the bedroom looks how I want it but I cannot help go through some of things Jessica and I trawled through yesterday. The old photo album and the shoebox of Test cricket stubs bring a smile to my face. I didn't expect them to do that. Donald looks so pleased in some those pictures that I imagine him standing on a podium, with a gold medal round his neck! For some reason, I'm drawn to the happier photos today rather than the ones I tended to highlight when I was with Jessica yesterday. I enjoy going through the shoebox with the Test cricket stubs. On the back of the stubs is a single word describing the day he spent at the cricket ground: 'frustrating', 'enthralling', 'captivating'. It was Donald through and through: patience and analysis; it was why he managed to stay in the army for so long. I leave the bedroom and head back downstairs, in the kind of uplifted mood I'd never thought I'd experience again in this house. I start making lunch and think of how Gillian must be coping with cooking Sunday lunch for Lawrence, William and Jack. I dread to think how Lawrence will react if Gillian tells him she wants a divorce. Dishes may fly. It also reminds me that I must finish Gillian's book, which is still lying on top of the radio. I'll be doing a disservice to her if I don't. She's in her time of need. She did the same for me when Donald died. After peeling the potatoes and shelling some disappointingly small peas, I hear the phone ring. I quickly rinse my hands under the tap, wipe my hands on the tea towel and walk out into the hallway.

'Hello, is that Mrs Hartford?'

'Yes…'

'This is Debbie Lees, Jessica's mum…'

'Oh yes, hello, how are you. Nice to finally hear your voice.'

'Well yes, I thought I'd give you a call because Jessica gave us this number and I just wondered how she was getting on. Is she there today? Because I've called her mobile and it's switched off.'

'No, I thought you knew; she's working today…'

'Oh I didn't know. I just assumed she'd be off today.'

'Well, we've both been a bit up and down with our shifts so that might be the reason you didn't know. We started off with quite a structured shift pattern but a lot of things have happened since then as you know…'

'Yeah I know, tell me about it. Simon's even got a job with a sports firm who sell advertising online. Wonders never cease.'

'That's good to hear. Is that what you wanted to talk to Jessica about?'

'Sort of but now we're on, can you tell me

honestly how Jessica has been around the house? Has she been pulling her weight? I don't want her taking the piss, if you'll excuse my language, because I know you've been through a difficult time yourself.'

I think of the bedroom 'tip' I just cleared and smile. 'No, she's been absolutely fine in the house with me. To be honest, I needed someone like her to keep me company. It's been a blessing really…'

'That's so good to hear. You don't know how much that means to me.' She pauses and I sense she's about to say goodbye – but she switches tack. 'Did you see the athletics last night? Amazing wasn't it? I know you and Jessica were on the early shift so did you watch it on TV?'

'We were in the stadium. It's a long story. But, yes, I don't have any words for it, really. It was a bit too emotional for me.'

'I can imagine. And Jessica was in there too?'

'Running every metre…'

'We recorded most of the evening's action because we went out to celebrate Simon's job in a restaurant. Unfortunately for us, a huge roar went round when Jessica Ennis won her gold medal so we knew exactly what was happening. I think they were watching in the kitchen because there was no TV screen in the main restaurant. Still a great atmosphere though.'

'She's from Yorkshire isn't she?'

'Yes, Sheffield. One of the staff actually came out later and said he went to school with Jessica Ennis. No-one believed him but it was still entertaining!'

'I do think these Olympics have made people a bit mad at times…'

'But it's fun isn't it? I would say 60 per cent of our street have red, white and blue flags in their windows. What's it like down there?'

'In our village, I'd say the ratio is a bit less because we don't like to show our true feelings that much. But in my particular street, I have noticed a few more flags, a few more smiles and, even people coming round to knock on my door more often than they did before.'

'Yes, it's the shared experience, we crave it so much. I can see it every lunchtime when I'm serving dinners at the local primary school. The buzz and joy I get from watching the kids eat and interact with each other is wonderful. They even had a themed Olympic lunch the other day with things like Usain Bolt burgers on the menu! It's nice to be working in that atmosphere, although there are downsides…'

'Like what?'

'Well, there's this one girl I see every weekday. She's dressed quite poorly, her uniform's all over the place and she doesn't seem to have any friends. I developed a relationship with her and she tells me her mother 'puts powder up her nose' all the time. I was shocked at how easily this nine-year-old girl told me about this. I didn't report it because I didn't want to hurt her anymore. It's not my job. But you can see that this girl just needs guidance, a bit of love and a bit of direction. She just isn't getting it – and that's heartbreaking.'

'Very sorry to hear that. Is that a big problem in your area? Drugs?'

'I wouldn't say that. Simon's had his alcohol and fag issues but he seems to be getting a handle on them now. The rest of the community are probably the same as anywhere else. I bet London's even worse than us.'

'Probably is,' I say, with a wry smile. 'Lucky I'm only there for the Olympics!'

'Or unlucky if you've got Jessica in your house. I'm praying she comes back in one piece.'

'She will, although I think she'll come back a changed girl; wiser and more mature.'

'I know that – and I can't thank you enough for taking her in.'

'It's really nothing, honestly. I was on my own anyway. She's even getting on well with people in the neighbourhood...'

'Like who?'

I hesitate and wonder whether I should have brought this up at all. There seems a slight loosening of the rules in terms of the boundaries of conversation. In the past week, I've noticed people – including me – saying things they should have never said, being too open and blurting out intimate information to complete strangers. It's not like me at all. But this is Jessica's mum we're talking about here – and I like her already. It can't do any harm to talk a bit more on this warm and fuzzy Sunday.

'He's called William...'

* * *

I try to get things done, like tend to the garden or clean the bathroom, but the Olympic coverage keeps getting in the way. Andy Murray and Roger Federer are playing in the men's tennis final and the sheer exuberance of the event draws me in; the wild, cheering crowd, the colour distinction when compared to the all-white of Wimbledon and the beautiful athleticism of the two players. I try to leave my sofa but I can't. Another shot leads to another blistering wall of sound as Murray seems to be getting the upper hand. It's as if the cap of stuffy regulation that dominates Wimbledon has been blown off, creating a near-hysterical, but harmonious crowd, who seem to be more to Murray's liking. He looks completely at ease on Centre Court. That hasn't always been the case. He wins the first set 6-2 and I go to the kitchen to make a cup of coffee. When I return, I'm convinced it will be Andy's day as Federer looks tired and off his game. Perhaps Jessica was right that his epic semi-final has taken its toll. He takes the second set 6-1 and is 5-4 up in the third and I'm already imagining him winning the gold medal; purging all that pent-up disappointment and beaming at his mother while the crowd go wild. He has match point on his serve but it still feels surreal: Murray in navy blue, Federer in red, surrounded by purple with hardly a tinge of white to be seen. He's 40-15 up and has match point. The crowd hold their breath – and I feel like I'm not breathing at all. He prepares to serve and – he serves an ace right down the middle. He's won the gold medal! Centre Court erupts to create a sound that's almost too much for my living room. He kneels down and puts his hands over his face. He walks to the net and shakes Federer's hand and then the two men embrace, something that always gives me goosebumps. He walks to his seat and puts his racket down. He turns, closes his eyes and points his fingers up the sky. I try to contain myself but the tiny gesture is a gateway into my soul, just like Mo and his daughter wrapping themselves in the Union flag. The tears rush down my cheeks again. Andy Murray, Olympic Champion. Thank you for this glorious, epic moment. The momentum is with us now: the past can no longer weigh us down.

I read Gillian's book in the back garden after tea and biscuits. It's a lovely day so I decide to sit out there for the first time since Donald passed away. A low-flying blackbird and a lime green butterfly are the only things to distract me from the book as I find it hard to put down. Gillian describes her relationship with her father in intimate detail, calling the early years 'extremely loving and stable'. It's clear she thinks of him as a hero and cites one particular instance when he helped clear the whole neighbourhood of debris after a nasty flood. But then his body and mind start to fail him – and Gillian finds it hard to relate to her father in the same way. The blank, distant expressions on his gaunt face, the lack of eye contact, the marathon pauses between speaking were too much for her. She continues to visit regularly but they inevitably begin to drift apart because Gillian repeats a single word again and again: helplessness. There is no way out for her and her family. They simply have to watch on as this fit, strong and able man turns into a shivering wreck with a pill-rolling tremor and an arm that pulls to the floor. 'He is not my father anymore' writes Gillian. 'That man is dead'. I think of Donald as I read those brutal words. Is it better to die or live with conditions like Dementia or Parkinson's? What if Donald had lived after his stroke? It could have happened. Would he have been disabled? Would his memory work properly? Would I have had to care for him? To wash him and bathe him? Reading Gillian's book makes me rethink these questions. They are not as clear cut as I once thought. I am so absorbed in the book that I completely ignore the distant sound of the front door opening and closing as I know it's Jessica back home after her shift (she has been using Donald's spare front door key). I carry onto to the end of Chapter 6 (there are only 8 in total) when Jessica finally walks through the house to the back garden.

'Had a much lighter day than yesterday, thank God,' she says, sitting down on the plastic white chair by my side. 'Still a bit crazy though with Andy Murray winning; did you see that?'

'Yes, the noise at Wimbledon was frightening. It felt like a different country.'

'You mean it was more rock and roll than Last Night of the Proms? I know which I prefer…'

'John Tavener…'

'Bat for Lashes, even though she's not rock and roll.'

191

'Don't think we'll ever see eye to eye on them,' I say, with a smile. 'But do remember that John Tavener's music was played at Princess Diana's funeral, a huge national event. It wasn't my favourite piece of his but a lot of people still play it. Actually, I think the mood of the nation has got similarities to that day in 1997; the flags, the shared experience but it's all about joy rather than despair...'

'Hmm, this is quite deep for early evening, Frannie,' she says, looking at Gillian's book in my hand. 'What are you reading there?'

'It's about Gillian's dad. She's published this book herself, it's about his struggles with Parkinson's Disease and how their relationship has changed.'

'I hope it's not going to send you on a downer for the rest of the evening. We've had a ridiculous couple of days. We need to enjoy the moment.'

'It won't change how I'm feeling right now,' I say, turning the book over in my hands and looking at the anorexic blurb on the back. 'Nothing will have an impact on that. But this book's got me into reading again, something I haven't really done seriously for years. Donald always loved books, obviously because he ended up working in the library, but I was always less enthusiastic; I seemed to like classical music, TV dramas and theatre a bit more. But reading this...' I look up at Jessica and curiously make a knocking gesture on the book, '...has made me appreciate what books can do. I'd forgotten how truthful and intimate they can be.'

'Agree with that. Give me a sports bio any day.

I can lap those up in a couple of weeks. I've just finished Denise Lewis's *Personal Best* and I'm tackling Mia Hamm's *Go For The Goal* next.'

'Mia Hamm, who's she?'

'American soccer player. Even Dad had heard of her...'

'Speaking of which, one of your parents did call today. Who do you think it was?'

'Dad...'

'No, it was your mother...'

She rolls her eyes. 'I did tell her I was working but you know what mother's are like.'

I smile and almost break into a laugh. 'I don't as it happens.'

'Sorry, didn't mean that but I told her not to pester you if I'm not here...'

'She didn't pester, in fact, we had a nice chat...'

'Did Dad get that sports job at that ad firm, then?'

'You already knew?'

'He hinted at it, but it wasn't confirmed...'

'I'll let your mum talk to you about that. I don't want to say anything out of turn.'

She gets up off the chair. 'Sorry, not in the mood for too much family ding-dong right now, I'm knackered. I'm going to start preparing dinner if that's all right...'

'It's okay, I've already done some prep; we've still got a bit of time.'

She heads towards the kitchen door and turns, putting her hand on her forehead.

'Oh, I nearly forgot, I've invited William to come

round this evening so I hope that's okay. We wanted to watch Usain Bolt in the 100 metres together...'

'But it'll be over in ten seconds,' I say, with a smile. 'What are you going to do for the rest of the time?'

'We'll think of something. He wants to get a takeaway too, maybe a pizza. I said I'd ask you first.'

'But we'll be having dinner, what do you want a takeaway for?'

'He usually has dinner *and* a takeaway late at night. As you can see he's rather a well-built boy.'

'We've got work tomorrow – and I'm not sure my body could take another late night.'

She opens the door and smiles. 'Don't worry I'll tuck you up with some cocoa while we polish off the pepperoni pizza at midnight.'

'What if I want some takeaway pizza? I've never had any you know...'

'NEVER?' She shouts so loud my ears hurt. 'You've never eaten takeaway pizza?'

'Of course, I've had pizza in restaurants and all that, homemade too, but no, I've never paid anyone else to send one to my house. You don't know what grubby things they put in them.'

Jessica winks. 'Well, tonight's the night Frannie. You'll be able to taste the mucky magic on your lips. What do you say?'

'I can't wait...'

'I'll give William a call now so he knows we're on...'

She's about to leave but I can't help getting in the last word, particularly after the way this conversation has developed.

'Oh, by the way, William's name did pop up in my conversation with your mother. I don't know how it happened but it did. She might ask you about him next time.'

'Oh Frannie, you didn't?'

'Whether I did or didn't is academic now it's just a case of what *you* do. After all, you did forget to tell me about Gillian's purse being left here and I did have to look silly for a while. I'd say we're one-one now, what do you think?'

'I'll take a draw as I'm playing away from home. As long as you didn't tell Mum about my untidy bedroom I'll let it go...'

'Would I do that?'

She shakes her head and smiles. She finally leaves the garden and I settle down to try and finish Gillian's short book, feeling even better than before. I'm looking forward to this evening with William, Jessica, Usain Bolt and a slice of pizza. But more importantly, I also feel like helping Gillian later in the week with her public meeting about the library campaign. Of course, Donald would want me to do that, but this time it will be my decision. The book in my hands has seen to that.

The two boxes of pizza lying on the table in the living room created an almighty stink but what could I do? A mouldy, tomato-scented smell dominated – and would take days to clear. Surely this was a mistake? Eating out of a cardboard box just felt wrong; even when I brought in plates, knives and forks to give the pizza some credibility. Jessica and William ignored the cutlery and ate with their hands, picking up the curved, lumpy slices and gobbling them up as if they'd never had a meal in their lives. I used my plate, knife and fork but found it hard to cut the damned thing as the cheese kept sticking to the plate. William and Jessica enjoyed this spectacle as much as the Olympic events that were taking place on TV. The 100 metres was about to begin – and I decided to give up on the soggy pepperoni and pineapple monstrosity on my plate. I put it back on the table and put my feet up on the sofa.

'Come on, Mrs Hartford,' says William, licking his fingers as he devoured another huge slice. 'You don't know what you're missing.'

'Oh I do Will and that's fine by me.' I glance at him and, in particular, his striking red, yellow and green wristband. 'Isn't that in Jamaican colours?' I ask.

'You're not going to believe this, but it's actually my Dad's. He's started packing a few things away, as a precaution, and this old wristband popped up from when he was a bit of a reggae fan in the late 70s...'

'Lawrence was into reggae music? You're right, I don't believe it.'

'It's true though, but I don't want to talk about that now. I'd rather Mum and Dad stay together rather than think of the past...'

'So what was Lawrence's reaction when Gillian told her?'

'Sorry, Mrs Hartford but they don't tell me anything. I just hear voices, things moving around, a bit of packing, that kind of thing. I don't know if they've made up or if they're splitting up. I think they tell Jack more than me.'

'Come on, can we concentrate on the race now, it's nearly starting?' says Jessica, sitting cross-legged on the sofa with a particularly bare slice of pizza in her hand. 'We've got time to talk about crap things later.'

'It's not crap Jessica, it's quite serious,' I say, folding my arms and leaning back on the sofa. 'No-one wants a family to break up…'

'Agreed. But talking about divorce while the fastest man on earth, a legend already, is about to race isn't my idea of a memorable evening.'

William smiles and looks at me. He stretches out his slightly greasy hand, making it into a fist. 'Call it quits for now?' he says. 'Or she might not buy me any pizza ever again.'

I make my own, somewhat hasty fist, and let him touch it.

'I can't imagine divorcing her,' he says, with a wink.

Jessica doesn't even register William's latest quip. She's deep in concentration with her eyes fixed on the TV screen. Usain Bolt is in lane six while his training partner, Johan Blake, is lane four. Jason Gatlin is sandwiched between the two. Bolt puts his finger on his lips as they prepare to take their marks. Bolt bends down and crosses himself before pointing a finger up into the sky. A deathly hush goes round the stadium. William takes another bite of pizza which annoys me a little. It feels so loud in the circumstances. All eight athletes have their heads down, eyes on the track, fingers pressed behind the white line. '*Set...*' The starter gun goes off and the crowd roar into life. Jessica screams at the top of her voice, as Bolt is left behind in the first 40 metres. But then he starts to power through and Jessica's anxiety begins to melt away. She shouts for joy as he breezes through the last 20 metres and rushes for the line. He beats Blake into second place as Gatlin gets third. The time is 9.64 and Jessica is clapping and screaming as if she is part of the Bolt team or even his own family. But I feel exhilarated as well. The shortness of the race always seems to create the highest anxiety. There is no time to mess up. No time for mistakes. All gone in a flash. Four years of build-up obliterated in ten seconds. Jessica keeps on cheering and takes William's wristband off his wrist. She starts waving it in the air and singing a weird song which I can't make head or tail of. Something about 'karmacoma' and 'Jamaica'.

'It's a Massive Attack song,' says William, as if that's going to make me understand things better. 'It was the first song she heard when she first went into the bookies to see her dad.'

'Lord, the little girl must have been frightened to death!'

Jessica wags her finger at me as if to say she was far from a frightened little bunny.

'So it was nice was it?' I ask. 'Going into a smoke-filled room with all those men clutching their betting slips. I can think of better places.'

Jessica smiles and stops singing. She sits down

and drinks a glass of water. 'Phew, I'm tired now.' She rubs her throat and looks up at me.

'I do love Usain Bolt,' she says. 'He's keeping the sport alive, basically…'

'Because everyone else is on drugs you mean?' says William, with a wicked smile.

Jessica playfully punches him on the shoulder. 'No, because he's a superstar – and people outside athletics can relate to him. It brings more people into the sport.' She looks at the TV, as Bolt wraps a Jamaican flag round his shoulders like a cape. 'I mean, look at him. That's a real superhero, not these weedy ones you see at the pictures.'

William moves up to Jessica. 'And me? Am I strong enough for you?'

'Can you run the hundred inside ten?'

William looks doubtful. 'Thirteen seconds maybe…'

'Unlucky brother…'

William tries to grab hold of Jessica but she elusively springs up off the sofa. She starts to run around the room as William chases her.

'Not fast enough, little boy,' she says, dodging his grasp. She points to the screen. 'Learn off the master!'

'Oi children, please calm down,' I say, with a mixture of bewilderment and pleasure. 'I don't want any furniture broken. The pizza odours and reggae wristbands are enough for my blood pressure, thank you.'

'Sorry, Mrs Hartford,' says William, suddenly seeming to realise whose house he's in and sitting down again. 'We had a couple before we came so I think it's got us going a bit.'

I look at William closely. 'I could smell it on you, Will, but I didn't want to say anything. Are you sure everything's all right at home?'

'I work in a pub, Mrs Hartford, of course I'll have a whiff of the nectar on me.' He pauses and settles down on the sofa. He glances at the TV and straightens his wristband. 'No, but it's true that Mum's stressed out all the time. She's got grandad to think about, the possible divorce and now this public meeting she's trying to organise for the library campaign. She's sent out leaflets and everything but it doesn't look like many people'll turn up. She can't find enough volunteers either. She's worried the village hall'll be empty.'

'I'm surprised by that, Will, I thought more people would be pulling together, you know, with this Olympic thing going on...'

'I think they are – but not for things like that. Success brings them all out of the woodwork; the library shutting down just isn't the same.' He pauses and looks at Jessica. 'And besides all you volunteers are down at the Olympics, there's none left in the rest of the country to help my Mum!'

'You know that's not true, Will. There are still thousands of good volunteers helping people round the country. It's just that we're getting noticed and they're not. They're in the shadows a bit and I almost feel guilty about it.'

There is a moment of silence as all three of us

feel complicit in revelling in some kind of party atmosphere while some people, like Gillian, continue to struggle to find volunteers for a worthy cause.

'So have you read your mother's book yet, Will?' I ask.

'Her book?'

'She's written one, about her relationship with your grandad?'

'She hasn't told me. Wrote it herself did she? Who published it? I didn't know she could write.'

'So no-one in your family knows about it?'

'It's the first I've heard…'

I look at Jessica who gestures that she's as much in the dark as Will, even though she'd already seen it round the house.

'I think she's done a fine job,' I say. 'Whatever happens, you should be proud of your mother.'

'I am – but if I don't know half the things she does, how can I be proud of her?'

'We've all got secrets, Will, just don't be too hard on her.'

William hesitates and then nods. He then uses his thumb to point at Jessica. 'What about her, has she got secrets too?'

'Too many to mention…'

'Name one…'

'Careful Frannie,' says Jessica. 'I have the best contacts in the Olympic Park. A rumour can spread in seconds.'

I pause and look at the TV, as Usain Bolt and Johan Blake are interviewed.

'She has plans to invite you up to the Yorkshire Dales for a weekend this autumn.'

'No, Frannie don't tell him that!' says Jessica, looking annoyed.

William looks at Jessica. 'Can't wait, but I haven't got many holidays left to take from work this year. Would have to ask the boss.'

Jessica's face turns beetroot red and she rushes towards me. I get up and try to head for the kitchen.

'Now, we'll see who's queen in the 40-yard dash,' she says, with a weird blend of laughter and anger.

'False start,' I say, trying to get my stiff legs moving. 'Go back to your blocks.'

Jessica reaches me within seconds. She grabs me in a playful hug and then lets go, doing a classic Usain 'Lightning' Bolt pose in a final flourish; arms outstretched, index fingers drawn. She nearly falls over as she stretches low for authenticity. I'm sure she's had more to drink (like William) than she's letting on. Eventually, she starts laughing so much that she does fall over. She crawls over to the sofa and leans her back against it, nearly touching William's leg.

'Do you think there's a chance we could move to Yorkshire permanently,' asks William. 'My family here are driving me crazy.'

Jessica stops laughing – and offers me the first serious look of the day.

DAY ELEVEN

I take a closer look at the man's waistcoat. He has a glittering row of Olympic pins tied to his waistcoat, one from each of the last eight Olympic Games. He keeps touching the tip of his Panama hat and is particularly keen to show me one of the Los Angeles games of 1984. I glance at Jessica who is a few feet away. She smiles as I nearly fall over while bending down to get a proper look. The pin shows a bird (is it an eagle or a duck?) with a stars and stripes top hat on with the words 'Canon' underneath. The camera firm's name clicks in my mind to provide a snapshot from 28 years ago. Donald and I at his parents' house watching Zola Budd and Mary Decker battle it out in the 1500 metres on a National Panasonic TV. Donald's mother so vehemently against Zola Budd running for Britain that she wanted her to trip up rather than Mary Decker. I loved his parents, more than my own, because of their freedom and independent thinking. I remember a lot of laughs on that day, even though it was highly controversial. The man with the pins pats me on the shoulder.

'Are you still with us, down there?' he says, talking a bit too loud for my liking.

'Yes, the Los Angeles one just brought back a few memories. Were you there, then?'

'No, I got that one online. But I was in Barcelona in 92...'

'So you weren't at all these Games?'

'No, but in a way, we're all at every Games aren't we?' he says, putting his hand into his waistcoat and checking his Olympic ticket. 'Television and the internet have seen to that.' He starts walking away.

'What event are you attending?'

'It's not here but it's at the ExCeL later today. I just wanted to wander the Olympic Park for a while.'

'The event?'

'Greco-Roman Wrestling,' he says, touching the peak of his Panama and then walking off.

I can see Jessica laughing and she walks towards me.

'Bit of a fruitcake wasn't he?' she says.

'Not really,' I say, looking at her with a smile. 'Seemed to make perfect sense to me.'

I keep watching him as he heads out of the Olympic Park, head bobbing up and down as if he's in tune with the acoustics of the Olympic Stadium. Applause, hush, applause again. No roars this morning in the athletics.

'I think you're just feeling nostalgic,' she says, trying to get my distracted attention. 'Anyway look, let's get on to more important matters. William *really* does want to come up to Yorkshire immediately after the Games have finished. He's deadly serious about looking at places together, even moving in together if we get a chance. He's been looking at local papers up there already, as well as property websites, and thinks the cheaper prices will be perfect for us. It's all going a bit too fast, Frannie. Maybe this wasn't such a good idea after all.'

'How serious is it? I mean you've only known him for a few days...'

'As you say how serious can it be after a few days?'

'Are you intimate?'

'I'm not sure this is the time or the place,' she says, looking around.

'Have you kissed?'

'Yes, for God's sake...'

'So it *will* get serious. I think you do have to be careful because he's quite vulnerable right now. Parents breaking up can make children do reckless things.'

'So what do you suggest? You know the family much better than me.'

'My advice might be a bit old-fashioned...'

'Yes, but I'd still like to hear it.'

'You sure?'

'Course...'

I pause and see the man with the Panama hat disappear into the station.

'Marry him.'

Eric and I are having lunch in the canteen. He tells me about the brass band he plays in – and whether it will still be going when he returns. He asks me if I want to join but I've never played an instrument and

I'm not sure I have the co-ordination and patience to start now. I know there will be little groups and organisations formed once the Olympics ends as it's a natural reaction for everyone to want to preserve and treasure their memories. I expect there'll be choirs, bands, online groups, volunteer evenings, everything under the east London sun, but I'm not sure I'll have the capacity to talk about London 2012 with any degree of eloquence. Could I deal with an interview request? I know this has already happened to many volunteers already. I'm not sure I would want any of that kind of publicity. Sharing is important – but you can take a good thing too far.

Eric tells me he watched Saturday's action on the big screen at Park Live, the big spectator area within the Olympic Park which was heaving with fans throughout the day. He said his tinnitus was so bad on Sunday morning that he considered calling the out of hours emergency line to get his ears checked out. He ended up not calling because his ears felt even worse with the phone pressed against them (he tried both sides). It's clear to me that the earth did not move for him on Saturday evening like it did for everyone else. He seems to have found it taxing and wearying, the blistering noise becoming a weight on his shoulders rather than a fillip; the flag-waving and chanting a burden to be tolerated rather than shared with joy and relish. When I ask him why he felt so cowed, he responds that he'd never been to a football ground, or any other sports-related event, in his life so this was a scary, almost savage, experience for him rather than an uplifting one. I find it strange that two people with almost similar, zero-related sports stadium experience can have wildly different experiences. Perhaps, because I was inside the stadium – and he was outside – is the simple answer to this anomaly. He doesn't think so. He shows me his forearm, which he'd kept curiously close to his body today, as though the two parts were tied together. I notice a big bruise just above his wrist.

'Someone barged into me when Jessica Ennis won her gold,' he says. 'It was an accident – and it was just exuberance really – but I think he was drunk and his funny bone caught me on the arm. I'm still in pain now. To be honest, my ears, arm and legs are aching so bad I'm not sure I'll make it to the end. The finishing line is still a long way away and I'm spent already.'

'But why didn't you tell Rob?' I ask.

'Pride, I suppose. I'm part of more than 30 voluntary groups and organisations. How can I back out of the biggest operation of them all: the Olympics? I've only worked seven days in total so far; it's nothing compared to the shifts I used to do at the textile mill.'

'But you're not that young anymore, Eric…'

'No, but a lot of these people you work with make you feel that way, don't they? You feel like you've got to keep up with them a bit or you just fade away…'

I sigh and watch Eric rub his arm vigorously.

'We don't have to keep up with them, Eric, we just have to understand them.'

'And you understand Jessica do you? You do spend a lot of time with her.'

'I think so…'

He smiles and blows onto his arm. 'If only I had that kind of luck with young people.'

The rest of my lunch break is spent telling Eric (who really wants to know) how I've managed to get Jessica living in my house and the two of us, ending up as 'friends'. We're about to get up and start our shifts again, when Rob comes into the canteen and gestures to us, from at least 20 metres away, not to get up yet. He stops to talk to about a dozen people before he gets to my table.

'Come on, sit down again, we're not going anywhere yet,' he says. 'But you can go if you want, Eric. I know you're enjoying it so much out there. How's your arm anyway?'

'Fine,' he says, getting up. 'A spectator from China did some massage on it this morning, so it's better than it was on Saturday evening.'

'Out in the Olympic Park?'

'Yes, he said he was a specialist in Tai Chi so I let him give me a few tips. Seems to have improved me no end.'

'Good man, I'll see you out there this afternoon.'

Eric waves at me and then leaves the canteen, still walking a little groggily.

'Hope he can get through to the end, he deserves it, the old mucker,' says Rob, watching Eric disappear out of the canteen. He turns back towards me. 'Now, Frannie, first of all did you enjoy Saturday night? I'm sorry I had to be so secretive about it but it wouldn't have worked otherwise.'

'I was so relieved on the Friday because I thought I was in the clear; no-one had remembered my birthday or even mentioned it. Should have known better with you around. I think you're the only person around here that knew when it was.'

'You wanted to forget because there was nothing to celebrate?'

'Yes…'

'There is now, wouldn't you agree?'

'Too much in a way. I'm not sure I've absorbed everything that's happened. But it was a wonderful night I can't deny that.'

'Agree with that, I must say you're a different person in a week.' He pauses and lowers his voice. 'Now listen, I saw Jessica this morning and she doesn't seem to be her bubbly self. She's got a face like thunder and spent a lot of time in the toilets before lunch. Has she got boyfriend trouble or something?'

'No, I don't think so. She's just got a lot on her mind…'

'Did you say she should get married to this lad or something?'

'Oh for God's sake, did she tell you that?'

'As you know, all my troops tell me everything…'

'It was a joke, Rob, I was just comparing her situation with mine all those years ago. It wasn't really a serious suggestion.'

'Is that the first joke you've told since…'

'…Since Donald died? Yes, probably.'

'Hmm, can't be that then,' says Rob, deliberately stroking his chin as if he's in deep thought. 'She mentioned someone else's name: a Lawrence. Do you know anyone called Lawrence?'

'Well, yes, he's my neighbour's husband. What about him? What did she say?'

'She said she got a text message from him saying that he was coming to the Olympic Park this afternoon to 'sort things out with her' or something. She's been quite spooked by it. I've never seen her so nervous.'

'I can't believe Lawrence would do such a thing,' I say, feeling genuinely shocked at this turn of events. 'He does work nearby, that's true, at Canary Wharf so he's not that far away but why come to the Olympic Park rather than talk to her back at my house? He only lives a few doors down.'

'Maybe he doesn't want to see you. He probably thinks he can strong-arm a young girl.'

'I need to call Gillian now...'

'No, no don't do that. You just go out onto shift now – and I'll see if I can find Jessica. Maybe this Lawrence bloke genuinely does want to talk? Let's see how it goes and not cause an incident, shall we?'

'Gillian said he hated the Olympics so I wonder how he got a ticket...'

'Works in the city, you say?'

'Sort of, not sure what he does really...'

'That mob can get anything – even lunch with the Prime Minister.'

It's late, late afternoon and Jessica and I are relieved that our shifts are coming to an end. Lawrence and William are mentioned very early after lunch and then forgotten about. Instead, we talk about Britain's showjumping gold at Greenwich Park (I'm a fan of Nick Skelton) and the fact that the Olympic Park is still a joyous place to be after the momentous events of the weekend. The most heated debate comes when Jessica mentions Nicola Adams in the women's boxing and I stress that I can't watch the sport with men going toe-to-toe with each other so seeing women raise their fists is impossible for me to stomach. Jessica then asks me whether I would watch Nicola Adams if she got to the final and was about to land another gold medal for Britain. I do not answer immediately but when Jessica says Adams was born in the same home city as her (Leeds), I tentatively agree to make an exception. I regret it immediately as the thought of women with head guards knocking lumps out of each other is not my idea of a pleasant afternoon's viewing.

A man wearing a Mo Farah mask, and with a Union flag tied round his head like a pirate, is having his picture taken a few feet away from us. He is doing that strange 'Mobot' ritual and spots us looking at him. He eventually approaches us with his phone and wants to take a picture each with the two of us. Jessica takes the phone first and I pose with this odd-looking Mo, who whispers in my ear, that he'll win gold in the 5,000 metres too. For a moment, I begin to think it is actually him. Jessica then hands me the phone and I have a moment of trepidation because modern phones seem to have all their buttons in different places. But Jessica points the way and I happily raise the phone, steady my hand and press the button for a snapshot of Jessica and masked Mo with their arm round each other. Jessica does try to take his mask off so we can see his true identity but he wags his finger and walks off. We have a good laugh about this – but a couple of minutes later the smiles are wiped off our faces. Behind us (we don't even spot him) is Lawrence, tapping Jessica on the shoulder and looking at us with that penetrating, lowered gaze of his. I'm astonished that he's actually here; loosened tie, two buttons undone on shirt, dark trousers and brown leather shoes. He smiles and tries to shake Jessica's hand, to which she eventually submits.

'So this is the famous Jessica,' he says, looking at both of us with flitting, dancing eyes. 'I thought there was only one – and we saw her on Saturday.'

'I'm surprised you're here, Lawrence,' I say. 'We *are* still working you know…'

'So am I Francesca, I'm on an extremely late lunch break. We do have to work for our money, you know.'

'Are you watching an event or have you just got an Olympic Park ticket?'

'Tickets?' he says, rather abruptly. 'I've got those coming out of my arse. I'm not here for tickets or to watch any events, I want to know why this girl has twisted my boy's thoughts so much that he wants to leave home and move to sheep shagger land up north. That's what I want to know.'

'Have you been drinking, Lawrence?'

'Like father like son,' he says, looking at Jessica. 'Now are you going to answer my question or am I going to have to come down to Frannie's house and have it out there? It's your choice. Not only do I have to deal with Gillian's impossible demands now I have my own son telling me I'm the cause of the family's woes. What the hell have you been saying to him you arrogant girl?'

'Now, Lawrence you've got to stop this. We can't talk about this here. If you want to come to my house tonight, you're very welcome. Jessica will be there and we can discuss this like reasonable adults.'

'Living with you now, isn't she? Seems to have got you all round her little finger. Do you know William is even saving up a deposit to put down on a house up there? The poor lad hasn't got a pot to piss in – I must have poured nearly 20 grand into his education – and now he's thinking of buying a house! Fucking charming. Thanks, old man.' He pauses and wipes the side of his mouth. 'How much are you putting in then, Jessica, on your wages? Got a job have you?'

'I'm still a student.'

'Ah, once the bloodsuckers of the state, now the destroyers of parents...'

'Well, you paid for William's education, you didn't have to...'

'I did because I thought the lazy bastard would get off his arse and get a proper job, make something of himself, get a career, not live at home like a spiv and drain the little resources we had left.'

'I don't think you should be calling your son a bastard, Lawrence,' I say.

'Why not? He's my son I can call the little fucker what I want.'

'I think you should treat your children better…'

'What like you did? At least I've got a couple.'

'Right, that's enough,' says Jessica, putting her hand on Lawrence's shoulder. 'Come on this way, sir…'

'Don't fucking touch me, you're the cause of all this trouble anyway, not Francesca.'

'I'll call security if you don't come this way…'

'THEN FUCKING CALL THEM, I DON'T CARE! IT'S A PITY AL QAIDA DIDN'T COME AND BLOW THIS SHITHOLE APART AT THE BEGINNING!'

'Lawrence, please don't make a scene,' I say. 'Please come to the house tonight and we can talk about it.'

'Not with this bitch there, you must be joking…'

'I'm not a bitch…'

'Well, that's what William called you…'

'He wouldn't do that.'

'You sure he wouldn't have other girlfriends either? He's got about three on the go right now, you're just the sauce so don't get too hopeful.'

'Come on this way…'

'NO!' he says, shrugging Jessica off.

I put my hand on my forehead and pray matters don't escalate. I see Eric and Sheena in the distance coming towards us, obviously concerned about what's going on. Eric stops by my side and puts his hand on my shoulder.

'Is everything okay here?' says Eric. 'Jessica? Is this man causing you trouble?'

'No, he's just about to leave,' says Jessica.

214

Lawrence looks at me – and then glances at each volunteer in turn. Eric and Sheena fold their arms and look at him to make their feelings clear. The four of us have encircled him, but not in a deliberately intimidating way.

'A volunteer army eh?' he says, with a sarcastic laugh. 'Pity you shoot blanks.' He fastens his two top buttons and pulls his tie up. 'I'm going, but this is a family matter and you extras sticking your oar in won't do you any good. This is between Jessica and me. She needs to answer some serious questions – and those won't go away.' He nods and eases his finger right across his lips. He then slowly begins to trudge off. Without looking back he sticks two fingers up over his shoulder.

'Charming,' says Sheena. 'Bloody hell, Jessica, what did you do to him? Kill his son or something?'

Jessica smiles and looks at me. 'That's one way of putting it...'

Jessica apologises to me during dinner but I say it isn't necessary. She spends most of the rest of the evening up in the bedroom, listening to music (not too loud) and ironing her washed clothes. I can tell the incident with Lawrence has shaken her up. She's not initiating or prolonging conversations and I judge it's better to let her have some peace for the evening. I go downstairs and catch up on some Olympic highlights. There's another gold for Britain in the Velodrome (Jason Kenny in the Men's Sprint) and there's also a bronze for gymnast Beth Tweddle who makes my heart melt as soon as she smiles. Dai Greene can't quite get into the medal positions in the 400 metre hurdles and Usain Bolt finally stands on the podium for the gold medal he won in the 100 metres final. I don't think Jessica's quite in the mood to be dancing around the living room like she was last night. After the highlights, I realise I have a bit of a sore throat (probably from the stress of having to raise my voice this afternoon) and make myself a glass of warm milk with honey. I take it back into the living room and then pick up Gillian's book again in an effort to finish it. About an hour later, I close the back cover and look up at the ceiling. What a wonderfully told story; evocative, truthful and utterly heartbreaking. I'd like to call Gillian immediately and tell her how good her book is but realise Jessica and I may have got too involved already. But why hasn't she been back to the house since she told me about the divorce? William's been here repeatedly and we've even seen Lawrence but no Gillian. Does she blame me (and Jessica) for escalating an already delicate situation? Have we destroyed any remote hope of reconciliation? It is strange how these negative thoughts come tumbling out after the kind of day we've had. Super Saturday suddenly seems a long time ago. I decide on an early night and go upstairs to my bedroom. On the landing, I can hear Jessica on the phone to someone. Is that the sound of crying or is she sniffing her nose? She does have a mild form of allergic rhinitis so it's hard to tell sometimes. I walk past and head into my bedroom. I start getting changed but then I hear footsteps down the landing. There's a knock on my bedroom door and then the door opens.

'It's Dad, he wants to speak to you?' she says, handing me the mobile. 'I can get him to call you tomorrow if you're tired.'

'No, I'll take it,' I say, taking the phone in my hand. 'I think this is the earliest we've gone to bed since the Olympics started.'

She nods and walks out of the room. 'I've started packing already…'

'What?'

She leaves the room without responding. I ease the phone to my ear in a state of utter confusion.

'Hello Simon…'

'Yes, Frannie look, Jessica's told me all about today. Do you want me to come down there and sort this Lawrence fella out? I've dealt with more than enough pissed-up blokes at the bookies to know I can handle an over-the-hill city boy with plenty to spare. I can be down tomorrow morning, no problem.'

'Oh Simon, no, absolutely not, I don't think that's a good idea. Yes it's true, we had a rough few minutes with Lawrence at the Olympic Park but I know their family well and I don't want things to get out of hand.'

'I understand but he shouldn't have talked to my daughter like that. She's so upset about it that she wants to come home. She's packing already even though I've asked her to take a deep breath and reconsider. She's got good people around her like you and that Rob fella so I've told her to take stock for a while and don't do anything hasty.'

'I can't believe she's thinking of leaving, Simon, it's not like her...'

'She just thinks they've got the wrong end of the stick and if it's causing too much aggro for you then it's better she comes back home. She thinks she's letting you down. She's petrified of hurting you.'

'She's not hurting me,' I say, trying to keep my head clear as the pace of events threaten to overwhelm me. 'You need to talk her out of it. I want her to stay here and see our Olympic duty through, it's our job. We can't give in to thuggish behaviour.'

He sighs and hesitates. 'I suppose I've been doing quite a lot of persuading in the last few days. Did Debbie tell you I got a new job? She said she spoke to you on the phone.'

'Yes, some kind of sports firm online...'

'It's mainly advertising space I'm trying to sell. Lots of bullshitting and persuading people. Not sure I'll last till the end of the year. But as least I'm pulling my weight. So what about this lad William? Would he pull his weight if he ever got a chance to see Jessica seriously?'

'So they're not actually seeing each other seriously yet?'

'Not according to Jessica. She says they're just friends.'

'Hmm, look, I'll talk to her and calm her down a bit. She's just got worried about Lawrence that's all. I know him a bit better than that. Him and Donald go back a long way. I know the type of flare-ups he has. He'll probably come round and say sorry in a few days.'

'Can't handle the booze then? Is that his problem?'

'Life in general, I think…'

'Okay, I'll leave it in your safe hands for now. If anything further develops then I want you to call me instantly. I do want her to stay there. She's learning so much from you that she'd be a fool to leave now.'

'Okay, I'm going into her bedroom now,' I say, walking to the door. 'Speak to you soon then. Bye.'

'Hope you bring her some good luck. Goodbye, Frannie…'

I walk straight into Jessica's bedroom, without knocking, and hand the mobile back to her. She is standing over her bed, filling her bag with clothes, with little method or enthusiasm.

'Don't you think this is a touch dramatic?' I ask. 'You've never been one to walk away so I don't understand what's brought this on.'

'I've caused enough shit round here as it is. I don't want to cause anymore.'

'If Lawrence has made you act this way, then you should reconsider immediately. It's his way. I mean, why do you think Gillian wants to divorce him? He has these problems from time to time.'

She glances up at me for the first time but doesn't say anything immediately. She then stops packing and sits down on the bed, arms folded, eyes on the floor. 'I just saw your face when he was swearing,' she says. 'I don't ever want to see it like that again. It hurt me to see it that way, that's all.'

'I can take it, I've been on this earth a long time. I've seen a lot of things.'

She nods. 'Maybe you can, but I can't.' She pauses

and gets up again, to do more packing. 'I remember going round to my Grandmother's once in her council flat and she had a neighbour who liked having the music on so loud that it went through the walls into her house. She went round to complain and I tried to act as peacemaker but the neighbour was overly aggressive and the fear in my Gran's eyes is still something that's with me now. I understand people can have disputes and fights and all that – but when it comes to old people being put under pressure like that, something really hurts inside me. I just want to run away.'

I walk towards Jessica and sit down by her side. I put my arm round her and tilt my head so it rests on her shoulder.

'So you think I'm old do you?'

She looks across at me and there is a long silence between us. She then breaks into laughter and shakes her head.

'How can I leave this?' she says, putting her arm round me. 'You're a match for anybody.'

'Not you, of course...'

She stops laughing and looks at me.

'Just promise me one thing...'

'Yes...'

'That'll you'll meet my Gran one day.'

'As long as you stop making hasty decisions. I'm not sure my heart can take any more dramas during the Olympics.'

'Done.'

She raises her hand for a high five. I smack her palm – and wonder what all the fuss was about.

DAY TWELVE

If there is a medal for Olympic mood swings, then I win with no silver or bronze in sight. I must have had a million fluctuations in less than a fortnight: from despair and bereavement to outright joy and sheer elation. And here is another one. I am standing with Jessica looking over the crowd watching the Park Live screen as the Brownlee brothers – Alistair and Jonathan – take part in the triathlon in Hyde Park. Jessica is a huge fan of the siblings (they are from Yorkshire after all) and she is cheering them on like one of the spectators. She tells me about the women's triathlon that took place on Super Saturday and ended up in a dead heat. She points out, in metronomic detail, what they had to do and it makes me tired just listening to it: a 1500m swim, then a 40km bike ride and, finally, a 10km run; can they breathe after that? Yes, says Jessica, but they are shattered, which is not surprising. And all that just to end up in a dead heat? The two girls must have wanted to wring each other's neck (if they had the power, that is). Jessica isn't so amused by my conclusion. She takes this race very seriously.

Yet, as I watch the Brownlees come out of the water in their lime green swimming caps and get onto their bikes for their punishing bike ride, I have to admit

I am fascinated and intrigued. I had never watched a second's action of triathlon before yet here I was getting drawn into this curiously compelling, almost masochistic, event which seemed to revel in pushing humans to the limits of endurance. It was almost as if the organisers wanted to see if they could break an athlete's will, torture them so much that they'll beg to stop. No-one does, of course, and I imagine that some competitors wouldn't mind if more segments were added to the event: like flying a plane, riding a speedboat or skydiving; they seem to be able to take anything.

As the race develops, the ridiculously large crowd in Hyde Park wave so many flags I keep thinking of strawberry and blueberry tarts with cream for some reason, as if our gluttonous, patriotic appetite needs constant supplies after years of hunger. But the Brownlees are doing well, right up with the leaders, although news filters through that Jonathan Brownlee may have suffered a 15-second penalty for mounting his bike too early after the swim. It doesn't matter as the brothers, along with Spaniard Javier Gomez, break clear of the pack. But then Jonathan Brownlee has to take his 15-second penalty (standing still in a penalty box while the time is counted down) which allows his brother and Gomez to contest the lead. I watch these leaders in awe – how are they still standing after going through all that? Alistair Brownlee then breaks clear and is in the lead on his own. It looks like he's going to bring in another gold for Britain. After one and three quarter hours of brutal competition, he looks over his shoulder and then grabs a Union flag from a cheering spectator. He comes into the home straight and puts it over his shoulders; the flag fluttering in the strong breeze. The joy on his face is remarkable; pleasure and pain wrapped up in one, an anguished elation that makes me proud but also giddily fatigued. He gets to the line and starts walking, touching the tape with his chest. He is Olympic champion! He falls to the floor in utter exhaustion. Jessica cheers and puts her arm round me. Gomez is second and Jonathan Brownlee third. As the cheers ring out in the Olympic Park, I still cannot believe what I have watched. It felt like an epic, biblical experience. A near-death event tackled by competitors who may as well be going out for a picnic. It's too much for me – but it's also had a completely unexpected effect: it's made me into a convert. I can't wait for the next triathlon. All life and death is here; no other event has made me feel this way.

Jessica is in much better spirits as we have lunch together in the canteen. It's strange what an event completely unconnected to your life can do. She apologises to me (again) about her hasty decision to start packing last night. She repeats that it was actually nothing to do with Lawrence at all – but for my welfare. I tell her that she doesn't need to go over what she'd already apologised for but I can tell she's quite keyed up and talkative after the Brownlees' brilliant performance this morning. She tells me about the history of triathlon and that it only became an Olympic event in the 2000 Games in Sydney. She also says that, along with hockey, it was an event that she did train for, vigorously, when she was a teenager. The real problem was trying to balance her studies with trying to keep up an intense sporting schedule. Something had to give – and it was the sport, although she says she has no regrets because high-level competition and stress is not for her. I find all this highly stimulating because I'm still trying to work Jessica out: her moods, her aspirations and, even, her family background. I feel I'm gradually beginning to understand her although her habit of surprising me from time to time is still a bit of a problem. This unpredictability feels unstable – yet it is precisely that which has brought me a modicum of peace and pleasure since the Olympics started.

Jessica continues to talk about where the Brownlees will compete next. I'd prefer it if she got back to domestic things and, in particular, her future with William. Does she have one? Or is that over? I try to wait for the right moment to pounce but, just when she takes a break from pouring out the sentences to take a drink of her orange juice, a man in uniform, with a hat under his arm, appears at the table. I'm so shocked I nearly spill my coffee with a nervous, stray hand.

'Hello ladies, I'm from the Met police,' he says, taking out a notebook and reading off it. 'Are you Francesca Hartford and Jessica Lees?'

'Yes, that's us, is there a problem?'

'Do you mind if I sit down?'

'No, we don't mind.'

He pulls up a chair and places his hat on the table. 'I'll be brief as I know it's quite busy here today. I'm just making very informal inquiries about an incident that took place yesterday…' He looks at his notebook. '…At 4.49pm. It's been reported that a man was acting quite aggressively towards a Miss Lees – and also may have been under the influence. I take it you both recall the incident?'

'Er yes,' I say, looking astonished and glancing at Jessica. 'But it was nothing really, just a small disagreement. Who reported it? I can't believe anyone thought it was a police matter.'

'At this stage, it's not important who reported it, Mrs Hartford, I just need to know whether it's worth pursuing further…'

'Must have been Eric…' says Jessica, whispering under her breath.

The policeman gives Jessica a sharp look. He reads off his notebook again. 'So did any of you know this man, Lawrence Bernhard? We've been told he was a neighbour of yours, Mrs Hartford…'

'Yes, he is my neighbour. Look, do we have to take this further? There's really nothing to get worked up about on anyone's side. Nothing happened.'

'Was he threatening and abusive?'

'Yes, a little…'

'Drunk?'

'I can't say – but he had been drinking.'

'Hmm,' he says, starting to write in his notebook. 'You know I was at Westfield Shopping Centre this morning and a shoplifter started being abusive to a member of staff when he was rumbled. The member of staff is still locked away in the toilets trying to recover. I'm going back there this afternoon after I've dealt with this matter.' He looks up at me. 'You see what I'm saying, Mrs Hartford? Abuse and threats can be very hurtful. They can damage lives. Now, can you start from the beginning and go through, exactly what happened?'

I sigh and look at Jessica who shrugs. Is she deliberately trying to stay quiet because she's already had dealings with the Met once before (with the immigration issues)? What about William and Gillian, do I mention them? After a jubilant morning, I feel in somewhat of a pickle again. Competing in a triathlon would be easier than this.

Jessica is trying to fix the body armour of a man dressed as Richard the Lionheart near a kiosk while I try and offer advice. The man continually apologises to us about 'wasting our time', waving his sword and raising his shield at bewildered spectators, but Jessica keeps telling him that Richard wouldn't have been called Lionheart if he'd kept apologising all the time. This seems to have the desired effect on the man and he starts shouting about the Crusades and how no-one should come near him if they didn't want a fight till the death. As Jessica continues to struggle to fix the shoulder area of the body armour – it has become loose and therefore won't stay on the man's body, slipping continually – I look up and see Rob sprinting towards us as if Usain Bolt himself has trained him for a few hours. He stops by my side, out of breath, hands on his knees, looking down at Jessica and the Richard the Lionheart impersonator.

'Heard the coppers were in town, what the hell for?' asks Rob, looking at me. 'Not for that Lawrence business was it? What happened anyway? I've been so busy with other things, I forgot all about it. Did he come here yesterday then?'

'Did Sheena or Eric not tell you?'

'No, like I said, I had another emergency to deal with. An athlete escaped from the Olympic Village and there was a search for him last night. So what did this copper want then?'

'Someone reported Lawrence to the police. They said he was being abusive, which I suppose he was. He was drunk too…'

'The bastard. Did he have a go at Jess?'

'A little but it was nothing really. We defused the situation really quickly. I couldn't believe it when the policeman came into the canteen at lunchtime.'

'Surely, Old Bill have got better things to do,' he said, shaking his head. 'Never mind, looks like Jessica's got over it pretty quickly with her new knight in shining armour. Watch it Jess, or that Lawrence might be down here again asking why you're seeing another bloke other than William. Are you sure you can fix that? Do you want a hand?'

Jessica glances at Rob and offers a deeply sarcastic look. Rob bends down and takes hold of the body armour. It falls even further apart and Jessica breaks out into wild laughter.

'Not having a good 24 hours are you, Rob?' says Jessica. 'You warn us about Lawrence and then disappear. The police come and you haven't got the foggiest they're here. And then you destroy Richard the Lionheart's body armour. What next? The lights go out in the Velodrome?'

Rob doesn't answer and is seriously engaged in trying to fix the man's armour. There is a clip out of position that Rob tries to fasten again but it's so awkward that his fingernail nearly breaks after another aborted attempt.

'Fuck that shit,' says Rob, dropping the body armour on the ground and getting up. 'Let big Richard sort out his own heart of darkness. If he's screwed up enough to put it on then he can sure as hell fix it himself.'

The man looks slightly annoyed at Rob as he takes the body armour back in his hands. He puts it over his body with the left shoulder area still completely unfastened. It almost falls off him as soon as he slips it on.

'We were doing fine before you came along,' said the man, picking up his sword and shield and then putting his helmet on. 'You're no Saladin.'

'Don't want to be either, mate. You two caused a lot of pain to a lot of people. We're a bigger family here; all nations, all tribes. If it was up to you and Saladin, we'd never have the Olympics in the first place.'

The man raises his sword towards Rob. 'This re-enactment begins with a magical spell that I've decided to put onto you, oh poisonous one…'

Jessica and I chuckle in the background as Rob rolls his eyes.

'Go on then, Rich,' says Rob. 'Let's see what you've got.'

Suddenly a roar goes up in the Olympic Park.

'I hear the sound of another British medal,' says Jessica. 'Looks like Richard has got magical powers, hey Rob?'

Rob doesn't look amused and shoos the man away, who responds by doing a headbutting motion with his helmet.

'Now Frannie, let's get back onto serious matters,' says Rob, putting both hands on my shoulders. 'Do you want me to come round to yours this evening just in case Lawrence tries to cause more trouble?'

I tell Rob it isn't necessary for him to protect me from Lawrence. As for Jessica, I'm less certain. Yet both us still feel it would serve no purpose for Rob to stay at my house this evening. We are on the Tube, on our way home after our shift, discussing these events when a man sitting to my right checks his Hugo Boss carrier bag for the price tags on his new clothes and then starts talking to me even though he knows I'm deep in conversation with Jessica. He looks quite smart with lightly-permed hair and white-rimmed glasses and it's perhaps because we're still in our uniforms that he wants to engage with us (Rob talked to us for so long after our shift, about police procedure, Locog procedure and every other procedure under the sun that we decided not to change to ensure we weren't late getting home). He leans forward to acknowledge Jessica just to ensure he's not accused of being rude.

'Olympic volunteers, yeah?' he says, putting his carrier bag down by his feet. 'Since Saturday, you wouldn't believe the number of people who want to talk to me about the Olympics. I work for a fashion and lifestyle mag and suddenly every man, woman or dog is a big fan of Coe's carnival. Last issue, nothing; this issue, they're all crawling out of the woodwork.' He touches his glasses and peers at me. 'Any of you interested in a shoot after the Games are over?'

'A shoot?'

'A magazine spread – or a feature – after the Games are done. If you don't mind me saying, you look like you've got years of experience. We like to be distinctive in our mag of who we feature.'

I blush and look at Jessica. 'I think she's the one you should be interested in…'

'Both of you. Do you want my number so you can call me if you're interested?'

'Bit fast, aren't you?' says Jessica.

He's already fishing in his pocket for a card. He hands one to me but I glance at Jessica so she can take it. He then takes out his phone and prepares to tap in the number.

'It'll probably get destroyed in the wash so can I take your number?' he says, looking at both of us as if we'd offend him if we didn't comply.

'I heard your magazine group was in administration,' says Jessica, flicking the card over in her hand. 'Your circulation's been crap for a number of years.'

The man is taken aback by Jessica's reply – but seems to take it in good heart.

'Is she always like this?' he asks, looking at me and slipping his phone back into his pocket.

'I don't know, I haven't known her long enough...'

He laughs and leans back in his seat, crossing his hands.

'First it was the newspapers who stole our ideas with their mag supplements and now it's the internet,' he says. 'We might be extinct in 20 years but at least we've recorded some of the great British trends over the last 40 years from punk to Kate Moss and Euro 96 to Britpop. Now, we're doing the same on the Olympics. When it goes down in our country, we've had our finger on the pulse.'

'Sorry, I can't hear you...' says Jessica, cupping her ear as the Tube train pulls into Bakerloo Station.

The man shakes his head and, this time, looks rather more annoyed than before.

'Nor can anyone else anymore...'

I realise we are late getting home but I'm looking forward to a cuppa, some soothing John Tavener melodies and a nice early night. Jessica is a few yards ahead of me but she looks over my shoulder as she can tell there is someone at my front door. As we get towards the garden path, I can see Gillian and an elderly man, who I don't recognise immediately, walking away from my door. They look like they are about to leave but then Gillian finally spots Jessica and waits by the front gate. Jessica politely waits for me to catch up and we eventually join Gillian and the man. I am shocked to realise the man next to Gillian is actually her father. I'd never seen or met him before but there is a picture of him in Gillian's book and his long, gaunt face and shock of silver hair is unmistakable. Gillian puts her hand on her father's shoulder and ushers him away from a small ditch outside our front gate. She looks up at us and smiles.

'We were just about to leave, Frannie,' says Gillian. 'Looks like you've had a long shift today. Who cares when it's Rule Brittania, hey?'

'Sorry Gillian, have you been waiting long?' I say, opening the gate and walking towards the front door. 'We did have a marathon shift – but Rob held us up even longer.'

'Think he wants it to go on forever. Look, I brought my father along with me because I thought you might want to meet him. He's been staying down here since yesterday. I wanted to give mother a rest from her caring duties so I suggested father come and stay with our family for a while.' Gillian looks at her father. 'Daddy, this is Frannie Hartford, you know the great friend I told you about. She's working at the Olympics. She's one of the heroines of the day; doing her duty and ensuring everyone else has a smile on her face.'

I smile at her father but he doesn't respond; his

wide, unblinking eyes fixed on me as though they can see right into my soul. He also has a slight tremor in his jaw which serves as the only indication he might have registered what I said.

'So good to meet you,' I say, to complete the formalities. I take my key out to open the front door. 'Come on, let's have a nice sit down and a strong cup of coffee. I think we all need one.' I look behind me. 'Oh Gillian, you have met Jessica before haven't you?'

'No, I don't think so,' she says, shaking Jessica's hand. 'So this is the girl William won't stop talking about. If only you knew the wild, romantic ideas he has about you. Have you discussed all this moving to Yorkshire stuff, then? As you know, Daddy's family is from Harrogate so it isn't such a big deal for me as it is for Lawrence.'

'Can we talk about this later?' I say, relieved to be getting into my house. 'Talking about Lawrence isn't going to help my fatigue. I need a hot drink first...'

'Of course, Frannie,' says Gillian, ushering her father through the front door. 'Mentioning his name can bring out the worst in people!'

'Didn't think it would have escalated so far though...' says Jessica, talking to Gillian for the first time.

'What do you mean?'

'The police getting involved...'

'Don't know what you're talking about...'

'Lawrence coming to the Olympic Park and abusing us. You didn't know?'

There is a long silence behind my back. I don't

want to look – and close my eyes in case Gillian gets annoyed.

'I didn't know,' she says, wiping a touch of saliva from the side of her father's lips. 'If only I could go back to stroking Daddy's face all day everything would be all right again...'

The four of us sit in the living room enjoying hot buttered scones and coffee – but it feels awkward and uncomfortable as Gillian doesn't say anything for at least half an hour. Jessica then turns the TV on and even Laura's Trott victory in the Women's Omnium isn't enough to change the mood. It's only when Victoria Pendleton starts competing in the Women's Sprint – and is penalised for the second time at these Olympics – that Gillian starts to regain her poise and composure. Pendleton wins the silver medal but her tearful, emotional interview seems to release the tension in the house.

'Women...' she says, shaking her head and picking up another scone, '...always the silver medallists in the world of humans. Relegated, disqualified, dismissed...' She turns and looks at me. 'So what did gold meddler Lawrence say to you at the Olympic Park? I can't apologise for him anymore. It's gone beyond that.'

'He was drunk, Gillian,' I say. 'But it was nothing really. I can handle him. He was a bit more abusive to Jessica – and that was a bit harder to take.'

Gillian looks at Jessica. 'I hope you gave as good as you got...'

'Wasn't worth it,' says Jessica, with her eyes fixed on the TV. 'He was drunk so I didn't want things to escalate.'

'What kind of things did he say?'

Jessica hesitates and glances at me. She wonders if it's right to talk about these delicate matters. I nod because I sincerely believe Gillian has a right to know.

'It was mainly about William and me,' she says. 'William seems to like me a bit and has asked me out a couple of times. He's also been talking about moving up with me to Yorkshire as you know. I've told him he's moving things too fast but he just ploughs on. That's got Lawrence's back up. He thinks I'm a bad influence.'

'I can't believe I've missed all this,' says Gillian, catching the crumbs from her scone on a saucer after she takes a bite. 'But when you've got to drive 200 miles to pick up your father and drive him back, I suppose you miss quite a lot of things on your own doorstep.' She pauses and rubs her fingers to wipe the crumbs off her hands. 'But how on earth did the police get involved? Did he get physical?'

'No, he just barged my shoulder a bit,' says Jessica. 'I play hockey, it was hardly anything to get worked up about.'

'Why call the police then?'

'We didn't, somebody else did. We're not sure who it was.'

Gillian picks up her tea and takes a sip. 'I hope he didn't hurt you Frannie. I'll never forgive him if he did that.'

'He didn't Gillian. I think he realised that we go back a long way…'

'Hmm, so Jessica, how much do you like my son?' asks Gillian, rather abruptly. 'Do you see a future with him?'

'Er I don't know. I do like him – but he seems to have a lot on his plate at the moment. Family issues, work problems…'

'But you've got those too…'

'Not really, not anymore. I did at the start of the Olympics but I'm in better shape now.'

'What about money problems? You've lived in three places already since London 2012 started. Don't you think Frannie's been exceptionally kind by letting you live here rent free?'

'Gillian, it's okay,' I say, with a firm interruption. 'Jessica can live here for as long as she likes. Can we talk about other things please?'

Gillian looks at me and puts her hand on her forehead. 'Sorry about that Frannie, maybe I'm getting a bit carried away. There's a bit of strain at the moment, as you can imagine, with Daddy's problems, the public meeting coming up, Lawrence's aggressive behaviour and William acting rather impetuously. If it wasn't for steady Jack, the whole family would be going insane!'

'You don't have to apologise to me, Gillian. I've read your book, it's wonderful. Well done, on a lovely piece of writing.'

Gillian suddenly lights up and puts her cup of tea down on the table. 'You finished it! Oh Frannie, you don't know how much that means to me. It's almost as if everything's all right in the world again, I mean everything. Thank you so much.' She pauses and picks up her cup again. 'Do you think I should print a few more copies then?'

I hesitate and notice her father, who has been sitting quietly in the armchair, shaking his head.

'Did you see that Gillian?' I say, with a smile. 'Your father said 'no'. I don't think he wants any more copies to go out there.'

Gillian whisks her head round to look at her father. 'Oh Daddy, you wouldn't want that would you? You'd want people to know about your life. Otherwise, how would anyone be remembered?'

This time, her father keeps his head still. Gillian laughs.

'He's always been playing games with me,' she says. 'He's not going to stop now.' She looks at me and her smile turns into an expression of defiance. 'It's what gets Lawrence worked up. He just doesn't like the fact that we're ultra close and understand each other. It's worse when Daddy comes to stay. Maybe that's why Lawrence had that drunken escapade. He'd just been told my father was staying in his home for a couple of nights. He hates it. And then there was the fact I didn't tell him about the book...'

'He didn't know?'

'No, because he would have said I shouldn't publish. His parents have both passed away so I can understand it a little but I had to explore this devastating illness and it's affect on our family. I just had to do it.'

'I think you did the right thing,' I say. 'So have you put it in your local library yet?'

'Erm no, you're the only person to have read it so far. I wanted to get your views first because I trust you. Now I can go on with a bit more confidence.' She nervously looks at Jessica and then at me. I can see something else is troubling her. 'Speaking of books, I have got something to ask you, Frannie. It's about the public meeting on Thursday with regard to the library campaign. We're having real problems attracting numbers and I fear it could all be a damp squib, which would be a disaster. I sent out flyers last week but the response hasn't been great because I've been asking people to email so I can get some ideas about turnout and attendance. There's an issue with volunteers too. I think you've stolen them all for the Olympics! I need a couple more to put out some chairs and help with the snacks at the village hall. I just cannot do everything with all the dramas I'm dealing with at home.' She pauses and glances at her father. 'It was so much easier when Donald was around. He drove things forward so well, got people interested…so I wanted to ask you something…'

'Yes…'

'I'm not sure it's the right time yet – so if you want to say no I'll totally understand…'

'What is it?'

'Well, I'd like to send flyers out this evening – I actually have a lot of them prepared already – with Donald's picture on them saying 'In Loving Memory' and underneath there will be the usual text about the cuts to the library and how Donald cared so much about his community library. I will use his exact words, if you allow me, and this might help us get more attention and rally people to the cause. I know it's been difficult to talk about Donald at all over the past few months, never mind use his image or words, but I think this could make a big difference and it could become a fitting legacy to him. But I'll only do this if you agree to it.'

I sigh and look at Jessica. She nods and crosses her hands in front of her body.

'I don't know Gillian,' I say. 'I'd obviously need to know what it looks like first but it sounds okay...'

Gillian instantly reaches into her handbag and pulls out a thick bundle of flyers wrapped in an elastic band. She hands one over to me – and I look down at it. A huge colour photo of Donald jumps off the page. His eyes meet mine again – and make me dream for a few seconds. An instant tear falls onto the tip of my nose.

'Of course, Gillian,' I say, handing the flyer back and beginning to sob uncontrollably. 'You can't believe how happy I feel seeing that...'

I get up and leave the room, needing the sink immediately to cradle my tears.

DAY THIRTEEN

After the team meeting in the morning, it suddenly dawns on me that I only have two working shifts left: today and Saturday. Even the Saturday is a bonus as I've twisted Rob's arm to let me work because I want to sample the closing weekend rather than be sat at home. I still have the energy so why not? But this slightly chilling emotion – that it will be over by this weekend – makes my imagination run riot during a morning that's quiet by Olympic standards. I start noticing the buildings and the venues more: the Riverbank Arena, the Olympic Stadium, the Aquatics Centre; how will they cope without the tingling mass of spectators? Will the giant playground of the Olympic Park become a desert? Empty and unloved? A wasteland of fleeting memories and nostalgic joy? Luckily for me, a couple of male spectators dressed in red leotards start talking to me and I snap out of my temporary wistfulness. We talk in general about the wild nature of some of the fancy dress costumes we've seen during the event. We compare the best and the worst. The men say it has to be a Sikh man dressed as the Queen with a crown perched precariously on his red, white and blue turban. I nominate a woman who, somehow, had five hoops rotating round her body all at the same time: one on her waist, two on her arms, one on her neck and one on her foot. I remember the look of breathless elation on her face and never forgot it. The men in the leotards agree that is a good choice but still feel their Royal Sikh gentleman should get the gold. We finally agree they should both get the top prize. It's an amicable compromise. When the men in leotards leave me and head to the venue, I realise I have been talking to them for much, much longer than I thought. This trend has been more prevalent since Super Saturday: an extra sentence, an extra conversation, an enthusiastic desire to share information with complete strangers. Jessica even said she wanted to make a campfire here at the weekend so she could stay all night and all morning because she was loving it so much. I sense so many people roaming around the Park today feel the same.

As the camaraderie continues with spectators during the morning, I also sense people are treating us differently than they were a week ago: there is more reverence, more recognition that we'd done a good job, more engagement in our volunteering roles outside the Olympics. I find this quiet flattering and some people are even treating us as some kind of semi-heroic figures, always there to help, always there with a smile. I'm not as comfortable with those descriptions, nice though they are. We're just doing our job; the success of Team GB is probably the main reason for our elevation.

Yet one spectator continues to labour the point – and even elaborates on our mythic status. She says she imagines all volunteers as athletes: inside the Olympic

Stadium, running on the track, throwing the javelin, doing the relays. A purple and red army called Team GM (GamesMaker) making the nation proud. I laugh at all this but can't help but join in: Jessica doing the 10,000m, me doing the discus, Eric doing the 100m hurdles, Sheena doing shot putt, Rob doing the heptathlon. All in our Team GM shorts and t-shirts, waving at the crowd and absorbing the adulation. We are kings and queens for a fortnight. In the end, it's the spectator who has to stop *me* from getting carried away as I do like the thought of Rob doing the heptathlon. Even seven events aren't enough for him.

These heartwarming encounters with spectators take me up to lunch where, even though I'm eating with Sheena, I start thinking about Donald's picture on *that* flyer. I wonder how it will be received when it pops through those letterboxes in our village. Will people ignore it or will they absorb his message and try to do something about it? I imagine the gold-coloured letterbox that has sprung up in Sheffield to pay tribute to Jessica Ennis – and hope a similar one pops up in the village, its sheen rubbing off magically on the villagers, persuading them to join the campaign to save the library. I'm not hopeful – and I'm even a bit frightened that someone will contact me and say this is a shameful move to put Donald at the heart of the campaign.

After lunch, I see Jessica near the Riverbank Arena. She's looking forward to a big semi-final this evening between GB and Argentina in the women's hockey. She's desperate for Great Britain to reach the final and wants me to promise I won't change channels this evening so she can watch the match in its entirety. I agree (I'll probably have an early night again) and try not to let on that I do find hockey a bit boring anyway. The penalty corners are exciting but that's about it. But she also has other things on her mind. Unfortunately, it's something that raises my anxiety levels again.

'Saturday is the last day for both of us,' she says, turning towards me having pointed a New Zealand fan to the relevant seating block inside the Riverbank Arena. 'I've been thinking about doing something for Sunday…'

'Doing something?'

'Having a sort of leaving party…' She corrects herself almost immediately. 'Well, not a party as such because I know it's the wrong word to be using and that to have something like that in your house is just plain wrong – but I think we should mark the end of something that we've all been part of, something that we'll remember for our whole lives. I don't want all that to just end in a damp squib on Sunday. It should end on a high, I think. I don't want to be eating a packet of crisps and watching *Songs of Praise*…'

'Nothing wrong with that,' I say, with a smile. 'I think Donald even did that a couple of times…'

'He liked crisps?'

'Not really, but he did bring those tubed ones from the supermarket once. I think William suggested them to him and he gave them a try.'

'*Pringles*, were they?'

'I think so, but he ended up using the tube as storage for his paper clips and elastic bands.'

'If only I was so resourceful!' She looks at me and hesitates. She bites her bottom lip, always a signal there is something else bubbling underneath the surface. 'Would you go ape if I already started making plans, you know, asked a few people round to the house? There's only a few days left after all.'

'No I wouldn't go 'ape' as you put it but it'd be nice to know who you've already asked. I mean, I'd rather not have Richard the Lionheart turn up at my house or those men in leotards I met this morning.'

'No, no I wouldn't invite those kind of people, course not. It's people like Sheena really – and maybe her family, if they want to come. Eric too might be interested. My parents could come down…'

'Good lord, how many people have you got in mind? I couldn't cook for all of them!'

'You wouldn't have to do a thing. There'd be enough of us to sort that side of things out. Honestly, the bottom line for this get together would be to say a big thank you for all the things you've done for me and, of course, remember the wonderful days we've spent together. Most of the people I've spoke to already are very positive about it as well. They want to pay tribute to the way you've handled these couple of weeks.'

I pause and look away from Jessica. The crowds are streaming into the Riverbank Arena, mainly New Zealand and Netherlands fans who are preparing for the first semi-final. I am almost blinded by the all-orange costumes of six Dutch fans – but they provide a lift too.

'Well, I'm a bit taken aback by people wanting to show their gratitude and all that, Jessica,' I say, rubbing my eyes. 'But I'm not sure my house could take all those people. I mean, where would they sit?'

'It's a big house, Frannie, there's oceans of room.'

'I'm not sure, Jessica, I'm really not. After all our shifts, we'll be exhausted by Sunday and might want a break from it all. Who knows I might want to watch the Closing Ceremony with a quiet cuppa and a biscuit…'

'But not a packet of crisps?'

'No, unless I can find Donald's tube of *Pringles* and throw all his paper clips out,' I say, with a smile.

'Promise you'll think about it though…'

'I will,' I say, with a sigh. 'But my house has been silent for so long the walls might crumble with so many bodies around.'

There are a few surprises waiting for me when I get home: eight, to be specific. Three letters, four emails and one phone call; all from people who want to come to the public meeting after seeing Donald's picture in the flyer. The emails – I only opened an account just before my London 2012 training – were all from people I knew in the village. Most of them feel they can now talk openly about my loss and not have to ask awkward questions about how I'm coping or whether to visit my house. The phone call is from the local greengrocer who says he nearly dropped a wooden box of cauliflower when he saw the flyer because he remembered Donald patrolling the village in his trilby hat and a couple of books tucked under his arm. Funny that, because Donald never had books under his arm; he always used a shoulder bag. We were all getting a bit carried away, I suppose. This intense period of dealing with people I thought I might never speak to again (I pledged not to speak to a soul again when Donald died but obviously this now seems silly in hindsight) goes on till early evening when Jessica is gripped by the hockey and I'm making an extremely late dinner. As I put the finishing touches to the salad, the bell rings and I ask Jessica to answer it. She shouts that she's watching the hockey but then reluctantly gets up and goes to the front door. A couple of minutes later, a woman in a long flowery dress and sandals, probably a few years younger than me, lurks at the kitchen door. I do not know who she is and wonder why on earth Jessica, who has gone back to watch the hockey, let her into my house. Surely there has to be a limit to this Olympic spirit business?

'Mrs Hartford, I wouldn't normally do this as I know you need time to yourself but I felt I had to show you this.' She pulls out a thick pile of flyers wrapped in an elastic band. 'I think these were undelivered by one of the young men Gillian hired to post them in the village. I saw him dump them on the corner of the street. Look at the top one.'

I wipe my hands on the tea towel and take the pile in my hand.

'You see what some of these young rascals are like in our village?' she says. 'No respect at all for anyone. A couple of them even broke a window at the community centre the other evening.'

I look down at the picture of Donald. It has been defaced with a red marker. He now has a beard, glasses, red hair and speech bubble saying 'I'm a wanker'. I look up at the woman and wonder about her motivation.

'Was it really necessary for you to show me this picture?' I ask. 'Does it make you feel better?'

'No, I simply thought that if these flyers are being dumped around the village and not even being delivered...'

'But they *are* being delivered,' I say, with a firm interruption. 'Many people have already contacted me today to say it's precisely what Donald would have wanted: to keep the library open, and this is a good way of highlighting that cause.'

'I'm not sure how defacing a dead man with graffiti helps anyone's cause at all...'

'Sorry, I don't know your name...'

'Agnes Vaughan. I work at the antique shop in the high street but I also hope to be elected for a parish council seat in the next couple of years. I've seen you a couple of times walking back home in your Olympic uniform so I just thought I'd come and meet you...'

'So it's not really to do with the graffiti at all but the Olympics...'

'Both. When I saw your husband's image covered in marker I wondered why the glow of the Olympics hasn't permeated through to the young people in the village.'

'Oh I think it has. This was probably just a young boy getting carried away...'

She pauses and examines me in depth for the first time. 'You've got a wonderful naivety haven't you Mrs Hartford? It's very endearing. All I'd say is that when a man's image, particularly a deceased one, starts coming through people's letterboxes it can bring a negative reaction as well as the positive one you've outlined. I've spoken to Gillian about this already...'

'You know her?'

'Of course, I've seen her working in the library over the years but I don't know her as such. That changed a couple of hours ago when I spoke to her about this...'

'About this specific image?' I say, holding up Donald's tarnished picture.

'No, I wouldn't be that insensitive. We talked about the boy she hired to deliver the flyers – and the wider campaign to keep the library open. We do need to keep it open but, I'm afraid, if there's not enough money coming in from central government big decisions have to be made.'

'Spoken like a true politician. Now is there anything else?'

'No, that was it, really. I've asked Gillian to cut down on her ambitious posting schedule. There have already been a few complaints about people not wanting to pestered.'

'Of course, I'm sure they prefer the junk mail of the pizza leaflets, taxi cards and gardening services landing on their doormat.' I look down at the flyer again. 'I'll hang this up on my wall, shall I?'

'You don't seem to be taking any of this seriously.'

'I am – but over the past couple of weeks I've learnt to see the good in people rather than the bad.'

Agnes sniffs and rolls her eyes. 'You do know it'll be over on Sunday – and good old Blighty will be back to its predictable ways yes? Errant youths, no respect for the elderly, a lack of community spirit? You talk as if the Olympics will go on forever.'

'I wish it would…'

Agnes laughs and heads for the door. 'Call me if you reconsider about having your husband's picture on the front. I know Gillian is sending more out tomorrow. We don't want any more residents getting riled.'

'I don't believe there have been any complaints…'

'What?' she says, turning round again.

'I think you made that up because you have an agenda. You want to join the parish council so you have to stir the pot a little and raise an issue or two. I understand that but I'd rather not have my husband dragged down with it. He was desperate to keep the library open and would do anything to promote the cause, including using his image. I'm not saying sorry for it or withdrawing it. In fact, I want Gillian to step up the campaign tomorrow because, on today's evidence, it's been a roaring success.'

Agnes looks flustered and is about to reply when Jessica walks in from the living room.

'Are you all right, Frannie?' she asks. 'I just heard raised voices. I thought you knew this woman; that's why I let her in.'

'Yes, I *do* know her now. She's just about to leave.'

There is a long silence between the three of us – and I'm surprised Agnes hasn't left yet. She looks down at the carpet and I sense she feels apologetic about how this conversation has developed.

'Will you be at the public meeting tomorrow, Mrs Hartford?' she asks, finally breaking the silence. Her tone is more polite and measured. 'I'll be there so I hope this hasn't got us off on the wrong foot.'

'I do intend to go, yes, but I am also very tired as you can imagine…'

'Yes, all that travelling to London for early starts must be punishing…'

Another moment of silence. I'm beginning to wonder if Agnes Vaughan is playing games with us.

'It's just that there was another reason for me highlighting that flyer with your husband's image on it…'

'Yes?'

Silence again. This time, with added fidgeting from Agnes and reduced eye contact.

'Well, I did lose a brother 14 years ago after he'd had a seizure,' she says, finally looking up at me. 'He ran a tree surgery business deep in the Chilterns countryside but one extremely hot day he just fell about 30 feet and his head hit the ground. He began to shake violently and died before the ambulance got to him. The doctors said it might have been epilepsy but they never gave a firm diagnosis. His picture then appeared in all the local papers and TV because he'd once been a promising rugby player. I didn't mind at first but then when they set up a local charity in his name I found it harder to relate to the brother I knew. He was no longer mine; he'd become someone else's property...' She pauses and sighs. 'Do you see where I'm coming from? Donald is going into so many people's homes right now. They might think they know him because his face and words are leaping out at them. Only you do...'

I look at Jessica and acknowledge that we might have misjudged Agnes Vaughan a little, although she didn't help herself when she came bounding in. Perhaps, she uses that slight arrogance and pomposity to camouflage her vulnerabilities?

'I'm very sorry about your brother, Agnes, and I'm happy you brought him up. I feel that's the real reason you came. Is it?'

'The other reasons are valid too – but I felt we shared something. Donald's picture brought it all back again...'

I nod and there is another long silence. She didn't know Donald and I didn't know her brother so what *is* there to say?

'Well, I'll be going now?' she says. 'I'll see you tomorrow at the public meeting if you can make it. I'll see myself out...'

'Goodbye Agnes...'

She walks down the hallway, opens the front door and leaves the house. I breathe an almighty sigh of relief.

'At times, I felt I was on trial there,' I say, looking at Jessica. 'I feel for her but I'm not sure I want to talk to her too much tomorrow...'

'What's that in your hand?'

'Oh this,' I say, almost forgetting the defaced picture of Donald. 'Some young idiot decided to give Donald a makeover.'

'Let's see...' Jessica walks towards me and grabs hold of the flyer. She looks down at it and instantly takes a pen out of her tracksuit bottoms. She crosses out the word 'Wanker' and changes it to 'Lawrence'. She smiles and hands it to me. 'There, that's better isn't it? Much more of a resemblance.'

We both start laughing – and wonder what exactly has happened to Lawrence since the 'incident' in the Olympic Park.

'He could use the glasses and beard as a disguise,' says Jessica. 'Add one of our uniforms and they'd never catch him...'

'He'd have to wash it first!'

We laugh a bit more until Jessica realises she's missing the hockey.

I am in my bedroom, ironing some fresh clothes in preparation for tomorrow's public meeting. That's been the only drawback of these weeks: no desire to wear anything remotely smart or elegant; too much chopping and changing. It's been tiring enough as it is. They should have given us overtime for washing and changing our clothes so often! There's a lot of rubbish in my trouser pocket: receipts, old ticket stubs and sweet wrappers (not mine, picked up from the Olympic Park) and even a couple of earrings from a spectator who said she found them in the Aquatics Centre (I never did hand them in; I must remember to do that). But there is also a card from a gentleman I'd completely forgotten about: Richard Krystal of the Met Police; the man I met on the Tube on the day of the Opening Ceremony. It seemed so long ago it felt like another era. I look at the contact details on the card – and there is a work number, a mobile and an email address. I sit down on the bed and flick the card on my thigh for a few moments. Should I call Richard and ask him if he knows anything about Lawrence and the 'incident' at the Olympic Park? Has Lawrence been arrested? Who reported it anyway? I realised the Met was a massive organisation and it's unlikely he knew anything about it but maybe he could point me in the right direction? Surely he'd be happy to hear from me? He did say any time. Just as I'm considering calling him (even though it's late), I hear a shout from downstairs: one of annoyance and despair. It's Jessica and I guess it's probably the hockey coming to a conclusion. She's been shouting at the TV all evening and I sense Great Britain have finally lost the semi-final to Argentina. A few minutes later, Jessica comes up the stairs with a glass of orange juice in her hand.

'I promised myself I wouldn't get involved,' says Jessica, almost downing the whole glass in one go.

'But once it starts, I can't help it. I sometimes think I'm as bad as a football fan...'

'You are...'

'I don't get involved in punch-ups though.' She finishes off the drink and smiles. 'Although Agnes could have pushed me in that direction, I suppose.' She wipes the side of her mouth with her finger and sits down beside me on the bed. 'What's that you've got in your hand?'

'It's from a policeman I met a few hours before the Opening Ceremony. He just started talking to me on the Tube about a few things; like the riots last year...'

'He was involved in those?'

'Yes, he got injured and had to take sick leave...'

'So why do you want to call him now?'

I pause and take the empty glass off Jessica, putting it on the dressing table.

'Don't you want to know about Lawrence?' I ask.

'Lawrence? No, not really. They've probably closed the matter already. It's hardly a big deal now.'

'I wonder if he's going to be arrested...'

'No, Miss Marple, he's not,' says Jessica, getting up from the bed. 'What's got into you? Thought you agreed with me that it was a nothing incident – and now you want to dig a bit further. What happened? Has Agnes put a spell on you or something?'

'No, but there's something I didn't tell you about earlier in the evening,' I say, slipping the card into my pocket. 'One of the people who called me about the library leaflets said there was a rumour going around the village that Lawrence wanted to be at the public meeting tomorrow night, to give Gillian his support, but that he's actually been asked to report to a police station in London for questioning. I don't know if it true and that's why I didn't tell you immediately.'

'Well I can call William now,' says Jessica, pulling out her mobile phone. 'He'll clear it up.'

'No don't do that. He might not know about it in the first place. I don't want to cause even more trouble.'

'I don't understand why Lawrence would want to come to the public meeting in the first place. I thought he wasn't supporting Gillian in anything he did. Sounds like your rumour-monger might be getting carried away.'

'Maybe he's realised he was in the wrong the other night and wants to make up for it…'

'Doesn't look like the sort to me. Stubborn as fuck.'

'Do you have to swear?'

'Yes, Great Britain lost to the Argies, what do you expect?'

'You *are* a closet hooligan aren't you?'

'If I was, Lawrence wouldn't have got away from the Olympic Park, scot free. I'd have called the hockey girls from the Olympic Park and we'd have sorted him there and then with a few hockey sticks. There'd have been no need to get the police involved.'

I offer Jessica a look of disapproval. 'I sometimes do wonder about you people from the north. You do seem to enjoy the rough and tumble.'

'What else is there in life!' She sits down again

on the bed. 'What about Gillian? You're seeing her tomorrow so you might as well ask her then. No point in worrying about it tonight.' She looks at the time on her mobile. 'Some of us are unlucky to be working tomorrow so I better get a move on…'

'What if he gets charged? And we have to face him in court?'

'Frannie, what the hell are you on about? That's not going to happen. He hardly touched us.'

I nod and cross my hands. 'I know, but I keep thinking of Gillian. She's got her sick father to think about, the divorce, the library campaign and God knows what else. If Lawrence were to end up in jail, I shudder to think what will happen to her. She works so hard.'

Jessica puts her hand on my thigh. 'You'll be the one locked up if you keep thinking like that.'

'Maybe, but I've felt locked up for long enough for now,' I say putting my hand on top of hers. 'At least I'm thinking freely now.'

DAY FOURTEEN

I think of calling Richard Krystal throughout the morning but wonder how he'll react. Will he even remember me? Does he still work for the Met? I remember the riots of last summer and compare them to this year and wonder if that was another country altogether. I didn't recognise it for sure. I think he'll be pleased the way these Olympics have gone. They might help banish some of the dark memories he experienced last year (although I admit if I'd been in the middle of that carnage I'm not sure I'd forget it for the rest of my life). I decide I'll call him after lunch because the morning is taken up going through some of the souvenirs Locog have rewarded us with to thank us for our hard work during the Olympics. These include a series of pins and a souvenir relay baton to go along with a small London 2012 bag, an umbrella and Games Maker watch that were given to us at the start of the Games. Out of these, I really do like the baton as it's the perfect symbol for the glorious fortnight we've had so far: a purple and red relay army obsessed with teamwork and togetherness. I fiddle with these items for longer than necessary and realise I may be experiencing the first signs of withdrawal symptoms in terms of not being at the Olympic Park, smiling at spectators, greeting them and pointing them in the right direction. I have only one shift left (on Saturday). What am I going to do after that? It's as though the din of noise and melodic patter of the spectators will forever be in my head even though I won't physically be part of that experience anymore. I fear the 18th day could be one of the most difficult of my life.

I have lunch and still put off calling Richard Krystal. I turn on the TV and see Charlotte Dujardin winning gold for Britain in the Dressage. Oh Lord, she hugs her mother and it's one of those moments again. I am them and they are me. I'm nearly as emotional as I was on Super Saturday. I feel uplifted so I prepare to call Richard. I get his card out and decide to try his work number first. But just as I am about to tap in the keys, my own phone rings.

'Hello Frannie,' says Gillian. 'When are you coming down? Have you had lunch yet? If not, we've got plenty of sandwiches down in here in the village hall. We could have a picnic out in the garden.'

'No, I'm okay for food, Gillian, I've just had lunch. Er, I'm not sure when I'm coming down. How are you doing for arrangements? Did you get enough people to get everything ready for the meeting this evening?'

'Yes, we're way ahead of schedule now, hence the picnic! We've had an incredible response to the leafleting campaign and so many new people, who we don't even know, have said they'll turn up. It's been wonderful, although I do know we've had the odd problem...'

'...Like the boy who dumped his leaflets on the street corner?'

'Craig Wilson, yes I've spoken to his mother. You can't imagine how sorry I am about that Frannie. I apologise from the bottom of my heart that you had to see that picture of Donald. Agnes told me all about it.'

'Is she there already?'

'No, she's coming after shutting her antique shop. I think she'll be good for us in this campaign. She gets people worked up...'

'Good at that isn't she? She did a fine job turning up at my house with Donald looking like a deformed pirate. She seemed too eager to broadcast what she was doing.'

'She wants to get on that's all. I hope she wasn't insensitive. Did she tell you about her brother?'

'Yes, but only at the end when we were nearly sick of the sight of each other!'

'I know Frannie, you've got to be a bit patient with her. She does have her peculiarities but I think her heart's in the right place. She wants to make a difference.'

I pause and look down at Richard Krystal's card in my hand, flicking it over nervously.

'Are any of your family coming to the meeting?' I ask. 'What about your father, is he still with you?'

'Jack and William say they're too busy but Lawrence said he was coming. My father's here with me now.'

'Is he okay?'

'Yes, he's just sat down at a table eating his lunch. I'll take him for a walk this afternoon…'

'Isn't this putting a strain on you?'

'No, I like him by my side that's all. He'll give me strength when I have to make a speech this evening. And besides we've got plenty of volunteers to help now. All because of Donald and you, it's as simple as that.'

'You don't need to flatter me, Gillian, it's really you and Donald that have kept the library afloat. I'm just a latecomer.' I pause and take a deep breath. 'You said Lawrence was coming, did he tell you that?'

'Yes, last night. Why?'

'Well, I'm not sure this is the best time to discuss this…'

'It's as good a time as any – as I'm going to be ridiculously busy for the next ten hours or so. Has he spoken to you? He hasn't threatened Jessica again, has he? I'll swing for him if does that.'

'No, it's nothing like that, it's just that one of the people who called me yesterday said he might have to report to the police station rather than be at the meeting…'

'To be arrested? He never told me.'

'I don't know: questioned, cautioned, I'm not sure how it really works. So he hasn't told you anything then?'

'Nothing. He said he was leaving work an hour early and he'd be at the village hall at about eight, half an hour after we start. Honestly, Frannie if this is true it's the last straw. I cannot put up with it any longer.

He has humiliated me often enough and, if he's lying about this, then I think I will leave tomorrow. I cannot take it anymore. I'll drive Daddy back to Harrogate and we'll take it from there.'

'Don't overreact Gillian, it might not even be true. And besides, if you left who's going to save the library? I am sorry for bringing it up but I thought it was necessary because I don't want you to get a shock later. This might help you to cushion it a bit if it's true.'

'I am grateful to you, Frannie, absolutely. If it's only a rumour than I can't see any harm done as it might actually make Lawrence behave better because people are gossiping about him. But if it's true, why hide it from me? From what you've told me, it's unlikely they'll charge him so why keep it from us? I just don't understand.'

'I think I know the reason…'

'Please say because I've given up on how his mind works…'

I pause and sigh. 'He abused a widow of a friend he knows well. And he was drunk in a public place full of joy and enthusiasm. I think he feels so ashamed he wants to bury it.'

'And I'll bury him…'

'No don't do that – because you'll end up at the police station.'

'TAKE ME AWAY NOW!'

Gillian laughs and I'm so relieved our call ends on a jovial note. We agree on a time of 6.30pm for me to come to the village hall (she wants me to come much earlier but this is a day off for me and I'd rather relax my aching limbs at home). After our call, I consider calling Richard Krystal again but the Olympic action on TV draws me in once more. I pick up my souvenir relay baton and grip it tight. I wonder what Lawrence could have done with one of these in his hands on that crazy afternoon in the Olympic Park.

* * *

I use a bit of Blu-Tack to stick the defaced picture of Donald onto the fridge door. There's something curiously uplifting about him having a beard, glasses and hippy-style long hair. As if that was the life he could have led had he not been in the army. I look at it for a few minutes and don't feel insulted anymore. It's as if Jessica's follow-up graffiti – scrawling Lawrence's name above Donald's head – has made it into a twisted memento, something I want to keep and preserve. The two men did spend a lot of time together watching endless, boring games of cricket so I wonder if Lawrence's current indiscretions are linked to Donald's absence. Did Lawrence miss going to the match with Donald? If he were back would Lawrence's behaviour be better? I may be getting carried away but one thing is certain: the leaflet is a symbol of Lawrence's mind – and that's why I'd like it to stay hung up until he cleans up his act.

I call Richard Krystal on his work number after staring too long at the fridge. I get through to voicemail but don't leave a message. I call his mobile and, again, it goes through to voicemail. This time I leave a hesitant message as I don't want to call him again. Almost immediately, my phone rings and I answer it.

'Hello did you just call my mobile?' says a muffled voice, from a busy, noisy place which sounds like a main road.

'Yes, it's Francesca Hartford…'

'Who?'

'Francesca Hartford. I met you on the Tube just before the Olympics. You gave me your card. You said I could call you any time.'

He pauses and shouts instructions to another person. He doesn't sound too happy. 'I TOLD YOU TO MOVE YOUR VEHICLE ONTO THE GRASS VERGE. WEREN'T YOU LISTENING?'

'Look, shall I call later,' I say. 'I can tell you're busy.'

'That depends Francesca, is it important?' He laughs. 'Has someone planted a bomb at the Orbit tower or something?'

'No, no it's nothing like that. I just wanted to ask about a man that may be about to be arrested…'

'May? That doesn't really exist in our vocabulary, Francesca. We do things. What did he do anyway? Do you know him?'

'He's a neighbour called Lawrence Bernhard. He came to the Olympic Park and got a bit aggressive towards me and my fellow volunteer Jessica.'

'Why?'

'It's a long story…'

'They always are. So was it investigated? Did someone come down to ask you a few questions, take statements?'

'Yes, while I was at work, in the canteen actually…'

'Did you get the officer's name?'

'Er no, I can't really remember, I think he gave it to us before he left but I'm not sure…'

He sighs and pauses, shouting over his shoulder again. This time, it's at least two minutes before he speaks to me again.

'Okay, Francesca look, there isn't much to go on there. Our departments are rather big so who knows which of my colleagues spoke to you that day? But I'll ask around a bit and see if we have a file for him already. Did he actually physically attack you then? If he did that, particularly at your age, he definitely does need locking up.'

'No he didn't do that. He was drunk though. Which reminds me did that date of yours go well in Canning Town?'

'From being drunk to Canning Town, how does that work? But to answer your question, yes, everything is going better than expected. I'm seeing Melissa regularly now. We're going out tonight, in fact. Funnily enough since I saw you that day, my luck's completely changed. Back at work, new girlfriend and I even saw my son at the weekend going bananas while watching Mo Farah. He even says he packing football in because he's obsessed with all these new sports. I don't believe him though.'

'Oh that's nice to hear, Richard. I hope you've changed that deodorant though, it was terrible.'

'What was wrong with it? Got me into Melissa's arms didn't it? She didn't say anything…'

'We never do. Anyway, I'll let you go because I know you're busy. I've only got one more shift at the Olympics by the way, on Saturday, so I hope we've all done a good job.'

'You volunteers are going to be knighted, what are you on about? We'd take generations to get that kind of attention. You've done it in two weeks.'

'I sense a bit of jealousy…'

'No, just an acknowledgment of our thankless task. A policeman's lot is ingratitude writ large.'

'You better watch it or they'll sign you off again. All that gloomy talk…'

'No, August 2011 was rock bottom, I'll never be in that place again. Things are looking up now…'

I pause and clear my throat. 'Which reminds me, are you doing anything this Sunday?'

'Why?'

'Well, we've organised this sort of end of the Olympics party and I thought you might be interested. You could bring your girlfriend and, perhaps, son too…'

'At your house?'

'Yes…'

'I didn't see you as the party sort,' he says, with a smile. 'Can you still get those creaking limbs moving then?'

'Jessica, my colleague, wanted this to go ahead, not me, but I'm kind of warming to it now.'

'You don't want the Olympics to end do you? You're enjoying it so much...'

'I suppose you're right there.'

'No suppose about it: the whole event been ridiculously good for the country. Look, just on this Lawrence Bernhard fella, do you know who reported it initially?'

'No, there were a lot of people in the Olympic Park at the time. It was a bit confusing.'

'But why attack you though, what motive did he have?'

'As I said, it's rather convoluted...'

'I've got a couple of minutes. Give me a summary...'

I sigh and wipe some sweat from my brow, trying not to remember Lawrence's scowling face on that day.

'To begin with I'm his friend's widow, I think he misses him...'

I did say to Jessica that I would never watch women's boxing and I'll apologise to her when she gets home. But what can I do? Nicola Adams is going for gold against Chinese fighter Ren Cancan and the frenetic noise from the TV is sucking me in like circus entertainment does to a child. But the commentators and producers do have a lot to answer for: their wide-eyed patriotism and infectious enthusiasm has almost become standard fare but it's those sweeping musical excerpts and shots of joyous spectators that really tug at the heartstrings. I cannot help but get drawn in. Yet it's still strange to see two women in head guards beating the life out of each other. My mind also wanders to yesterday when Saudi Arabian athlete Sarah Attar ran in the 800m heats and got a standing ovation even though she finished last. Her head was covered too and I wonder how far women around the globe have come since I was a child? Are women more respected now than we were? Is there less sexism? Are we more equal? I'd say we have more opportunities, definitely, but we'll never be equal. Donald did his share but he still expected me to do the bulk of the housework and cleaning. Lawrence, according to Gillian, is even worse. Yet perhaps William and Jessica will be different if they get together. Will they share all the duties 50/50? It'd be nice to think so but I still think it's impossible. Some minor niggle always gets in the way.

Adams wins gold and it's another glorious moment for Team GB! I feel particularly happy for Jessica as it's another huge success story for her county. But a few minutes later, I start to feel guilty that I'll spend all day in front of the TV so I start preparing for the evening meeting at the village hall. I have an early tea and get dressed into one of my colourful summer frocks, one of Donald's favourites which had tiny flowers draped across it in a diagonal pattern. I step out of the house and start walking down to the village hall, which is only about 10 minutes walk, close to the library and the post office. As I reach the end of my street, I'm surprised to see William walking towards me in a brisk and breezy manner. I hope he won't keep me too long as I don't want to keep his mother waiting at the village hall.

'Hello Mrs Hartford, is Jessica back yet?' he says, looking quite pleased with himself. 'Got some good news.'

'No, probably in about half an hour. I'm just going to your mother's public meeting, Aren't you going?'

'Er no, I'm just up to my neck in it at the moment...'

'So what's the good news?'

'Got a job offer in Leeds. At the same chain of pubs I already work in. I called them last week and they said they're always short staffed so I told them I was available and they offered me a job immediately! Weird that because they're always struggling for punters down here.'

'You're serious about leaving then?'

He nods and looks away from me. 'Dad just called. He's just going into a police station in London now to be questioned. I've had enough of him. He can go to hell as far as I'm concerned. He told me about what happened in the Olympic Park but it's too late now. I want to spend the rest of my life with Jessica.'

'Are you sure you've really thought this through?'

'Yes,' he says, hesitating and looking down at me. 'Hasn't Jessica been good for you too?'

'Well if you put it like that, of course, but moving hundreds of miles away from your family and friends is a big step to take.'

'Grandad's family is in Harrogate so they're close by. I'll find new friends up there. Once you get a job, the friends flow from there. No problem at all.' He puts his hands in his pockets. 'I've spoken to Simon too and he's helping me out a bit. He even says we can stay at his if we can't find a decent place to rent. A mortgage is beyond our means right now.'

'Does your mum know about this?'

'No and please don't tell her yet. I need to tell Jessica first.'

'You really should come to the public meeting…'

'Not my crowd, sorry.'

'Well, what are you going to do now then? I have to get to the village hall and there's no-one in the house.'

'I'm not going back home,' he says, abruptly. 'Prison's got a better atmosphere.'

I pause and sigh. 'Do you want my keys then? You can wait inside. Make yourself a nice cuppa?'

'No, I'd rather sit on your doorstep if that's all right…'

'Why?'

'Because I want to see Jessica walk down the street. I just can't believe I've been lucky enough to hook up with a girl like that. She's incredible and I want her to know that I'll sit on the doorstep night and day if need be. I don't think I'll ever let her go…'

I count the number of Union flags in the village hall. Seven in total. I thought I'd never tire of them but having feasted on so many in the Olympic Park and, practically everywhere else, in the shops, in train stations and in people's bedrooms I'm now a touch weary about seeing the red white and blue symbol of pride. They're beginning to hurt my eyes (I think it's the bright colour and spider-like design; a bit like the London 2012 logo). I am sat on one of the corner seats, about five rows back, in a packed hall which is listening to a volunteer speaking about their experience of reading to blind residents at a care home. There is total silence in the hall, about 300 people are captivated, listening intently to this moving tale of two people connecting through a third voice: the book. I didn't know it'd be like this. If I did, I wouldn't have prevaricated at home for so long. About half an hour later, Gillian gets up and starts talking about the leafleting campaign, the Government cuts and the future of the community library. She says if the community don't come out and fight the plans then it will become solely a volunteer-run library with reduced opening hours and patchy book selection. Gillian speaks eloquently with the microphone in her hand and keeps looking in the front row at her father, as if she is trying to get inspiration from him, a secret message between the two: keep going and never give in. I expect her to mention her own book. She doesn't – and I'm surprised by that. Wouldn't it raise her profile even more? Perhaps people know about it already. She ends by talking about Donald – and she eventually makes eye contact with me. Some people turn to look at me. I am slightly embarrassed but they seem to mean well.

'Does anyone remember this event?' she says, holding up the 1948 Olympics book that Donald had kept for so long – and cherished. 'Some of you are old enough for sure...'

There are a few laughs in the hall and, eventually, several hands go up.

'My late colleague Donald Hartford attended the last London Olympics and he never forgot it. Do you think we'll remember London 2012 in the same way?'

A loud shout of 'yes' goes up in the hall, almost in unison.

'But without this book, how much of it would we have remembered?' says Gillian. 'We would have documentary footage, of course, pictures, yes, newspapers articles, definitely, but how much of the whole story would we have captured? I'd say not enough. A book gets into the heart of the story and wrings out the truth. It is intimate and personal. It creates a fresh set of experiences for everyone. It unlocks the imagination in a way nothing else can. So I say to everyone in this hall tonight, this is what will be lost if we don't come together and fight these plans. The imagination will wither way and we, as a result will be diminished.' Gillian glances at me again. 'Will there be a book about 2012? Hundreds, I expect but I believe there should be one about the true heroes and heroines of London 2012: the Games Makers. I'd like to invite Francesca Hartford, who I'm sure you've all seen walking around the village in her snappy Olympic uniform, up onto the stage for a short address...'

Applause rings out and everyone is looking at me. Oh Gillian, you are a beast. I reluctantly get up and

271

awkwardly make my way up to the front, my sore, shuffling feet acting up as if they've been tied together for the past fortnight. I get to the front and Gillian shakes my hand. She leads me to the microphone stand and ushers me across as if I'll *have* to say something, not her. It's a horrifying, gut-wrenching prospect. She lowers the microphone stand for me and I stand behind it, looking at the expectant faces in the hall, all staring at me silently, waiting for me to offer up my first word. I look at Gillian and shake my head. I can't go through with this. She walks up to me and lowers her head, whispering into my ear.

'Just tell them about the crimson dinner jacket...' she says.

I look at her and wonder what the hell she's talking about – but then I remember the London 2012 tickets Donald kept in his inside pocket. I turn to the people in the hall and take a deep breath. Treat it as just another performance. I've been doing the same for spectators in the Olympic Park.

'If it wasn't for Donald Alfred Hartford...' I say, with an almighty sigh of relief after I've said his name, '...then I wouldn't have attended London 2012 at all. He supported me and inspired me. He took me and brought me back. He kept my spirits up when I couldn't tell my Copper Box from my Aquatics Centre or my Waterloo from my Bakerloo and gave me confidence that my volunteering skills would be valued in such a challenging environment. So he did all those things for me but there was also something he so desperately wanted to do for himself...'

I tell the audience about the way Donald ironed his crimson dinner jacket in preparation for wearing it at the Opening Ceremony. The way he took the tickets out of his inside pocket, checked them and slipped them back in when the jacket was hung up; warm and freshly pressed. It was his father's jacket. He had worn it in Wembley Stadium in 1948, when Donald was a little boy watching by his side as Harrison Dillard broke the tape to win the 100 metres. It's what Donald felt the Olympics was all about: colour and effervescence. He pledged to wear the same jacket to London 2012. It didn't happen, of course, and I tried to do my duty for the both of us. It's the least I could do.

A small round of applause breaks out when I finish speaking about Donald's relationship to the Olympics. I feel some momentum and go on to talk about his role at the library and how desperate he was to preserve it for the community. I feel less certain about this subject and, therefore, try to brief. I simply don't know enough about books or the wider issues of local authorities or budget cuts. All I know is that if an author writes a book about the volunteers of 2012, I want to be able to come to my local library and get a copy (or reserve one). Is that too much to ask? I look at Gillian when I finish and she claps as she walks up to me. Yes, she annoyed me greatly by asking me to speak but, now, with the adrenaline rushing round my body and the murmuring warmth of the audience tingling my senses, I feel somewhat grateful. She raises the microphone stand once again and puts her hand on my shoulder.

'Thanks so much for that, Frannie,' she says, in a low voice. 'I don't think they'll ever forget that.'

I smile and prepare to head back to my seat. 'Oh wait,' I say, suddenly remembering something. 'Do you want to know where Lawrence and William are?'

'No. You've made up for them. And besides I know where Lawrence is anyway: at the police station...'

'How did you know?'

She stretches out her arm towards the people in the hall as if to say 'there's enough people here to tell me'.

'I spoke to my solicitor on the phone earlier so the divorce is happening,' she says. 'I could stay with my father up in Harrogate for a while if things get messy...'

'Maybe William could join you. He's on my doorstep right now.'

'What?'

'Romeo waiting for his Juliet...' I say, walking back to my seat.

Gillian smiles and introduces her next speaker.

The meeting is about to wrap up and I see Jessica and William walking into the hall. William has a phone in his hands and both of them have their eyes fixed on the screen while shuffling forward; a skill I've noticed young people seem to be adept at these days. They sit down a few rows behind me as Gillian makes her final, persuasive plea for unity to save the library. It's a rousing end to a heartwarming evening. It's almost as if I can feel Donald's presence in the hall.

The meeting is over and, after a round of applause for Gillian, people start to leave and head home. A few stay behind to talk to Gillian. A nice couple who run the dry cleaning store in the high street even want to talk to me! Agnes, who I'd completely forgotten about, also seeks me out to say she was touched by the story of the crimson dinner jacket – and I begin to see her in a different light. She's not that bad after all. Perhaps she hasn't got over the death of her brother. The hall is nearly empty when Jessica finally approaches me, without William in tow. He's still sitting at the back of the hall, eyes down on his phone, as if a bomb wouldn't even disturb him.

'We've been watching Usain Bolt in the 200 metres, sorry,' she says, sitting down my side. 'There's just something about him that we don't want to miss. There was David Rudisha before that in the 800. It's been electric in the Olympic Stadium tonight. Did we miss much in here?'

'Only a Churchill-like speech from me,' I say, straightening the creases on my frock and trying not to break out into a smile. 'And a call to arms from Gillian. I still can't believe how many people turned up. It's been overwhelming really…'

'So the image of Donald worked then? It's weird how people relate to a picture more than anything else.'

'Maybe it did, but I think Gillian's sheer will and determination persuaded more people to come out…'

'Talking of pictures, do you remember that magazine journalist we met on the Tube? Well, he wants to come round on Sunday, with his photographer, and do an article on me and the Olympics in general.'

'Thought you weren't too keen on him?'

'I'm not – but I am on the article. It'd help with my CV, help me get noticed. Might help me get a job.'

'Is that how it works these days? Get your face on TV or magazines – and then you get a job?'

'No,' she says, with a smile. 'There aren't any around. But you have to get a profile, yes, a media profile is even better. So, will you let this man in your house if he comes around?'

'I don't know Jessica, it's rather a big thing letting a journalist prowl round your house. If you'd been here earlier you'd have seen that things are still quite emotional for me.'

She puts her hand on my thigh. 'Double sorry, I should have been here.' She pauses and looks over her shoulder at William. 'But I did have my hands full after a long shift and old Will Shakey Head there sitting on your doorstep. The shock almost made me walk on, thinking that I'd come to someone else's house. He is serious though and he might travel back up to Yorkshire with us on Sunday night.'

'With your parents?'

'That's what he wants.'

'I think he's getting carried away…'

She looks over her shoulder again and ushers William towards her with a wave of the hand.

'I prefer men who get carried away than those who don't,' she says. 'I seem to handle them better.'

William walks towards us – and sits down next

to me. He finally takes his eyes away from the screen and looks at me.

'Jess has got me hooked I'm afraid,' he says, sheepishly putting the phone in his pocket. 'Jade Jones in the Taekwondo tonight. I don't even know what that event is.'

'Nor do I? Jess?'

'They get points for landing kicks and blows in the target areas.' She smiles and looks at William. 'Just like I did when I tried to kick you away from the doorstep.'

'You won't get rid of me that easy.'

His mobile rings – and Jessica shakes her head.

'You better watch it or your mum'll throw you out if that keeps ringing.'

'Don't care. I'm toast already.'

He gets up and walks away a few feet to answer the call. He then stops and turns, looking at me in horror as he speaks into the phone.

'Yes, Dad I know,' he says, speaking quite aggressively. 'But what can I do about that? You have to sort it out with Mum. She's here now; you can speak to her if you want.'

There's another pause as William's expression turns to one of deep concern.

'You want to speak to Frannie? Why?'

William looks at me and shakes his head.

'She is here but do you think it's wise to speak to her now after what happened last time. It's great that you haven't been arrested but I think we all need a bit of calm and some time to think.'

'He hasn't been arrested,' whispers Jessica to me. 'Thank fuck for that.'

I tut as Jessica swears but quickly refocus on William's conversation with his father. What on earth does Lawrence want to say to me now? He won't speak to his wife but he wants to speak to me? If only he'd been here to see her drive everyone forward with her warmth and persistence. He might have even been proud of her.

'Okay look Dad, I'm going to give Frannie the phone. I don't know if she'll speak to you or not...'

William walks towards me but I raise my hands.

'Sorry Dad, she doesn't want to speak to you right now. She's had a heavy night. When are you coming home anyway? At least I can tell Mum so she doesn't stay up all night for you.'

Another long pause as William digests the information.

'No, I'm leaving this weekend Dad. That's final. I've got a job and accommodation won't be a problem. It's nothing to do with Jessica at all. It's my decision.'

I hope William will end the call quickly as I can see Gillian walking towards our seats from the front of the hall. She goes towards William first and kisses him on the cheek while he still speaks into the phone.

'Who is it?' asks Gillian, in a low voice, looking at Jessica and me.

'Lawrence,' I say.

Gillian raises her hand and walks off immediately towards the front of the hall again.

'But he hasn't been arrested,' I say, a bit louder.

'Tell me when their conversation is over,' she says, not turning around and still with her hand in the air.

'But he's free, Gillian,' I say, maintaining my loud pitch.

'But I'm not. Tell William to come into the tea room after he's finished talking. I'll see him there...'

Gillian disappears through a small door at the side of the hall, the surrounding wall covered in plaques, calendars and framed paintings of village history. William ends the call a couple of minutes later – and sits down next to me again.

'He's very ashamed of what he did,' says William. 'It tore him up so much that he actually handed himself in. The police were going to drop the case anyway but he wanted to show how bad he felt about it, so he went there voluntarily.'

'I said it was nothing all along,' I say. 'I'm not surprised the police won't be taking it further but I am surprised that your father...'

'What? Has a heart?'

'Well, yes, that he's gone to all that trouble to show that it was all a ghastly mistake. I think Donald's got something to do with it, I really do. He misses him and probably thinks he's tarnished his memory. That's why he wants to say sorry too.'

'I miss him too,' says William. 'Dad was a different person when he was around. So was I.'

I put my hand on William's arm. 'He's still around, Will. He's in this hall, he's at home, he's in the Olympic Park, he's everywhere.'

'Steady, Frannie,' says Jessica. 'They'll make

you head of the spiritualists convention if you keep talking like that.'

'I don't care, when I was up on that stage tonight, he was with me – cajoling me, inspiring me and teasing me – if that sounds mad then it's a small price to pay to connect with so many more people. I see a future now because of that. This campaign means something to me now. I want to be part of it after the Olympics is over. I want to make a contribution.'

'If only Dad could be so thoughtful...' says William.

'He will be again,' I say, easing my hand towards William and holding it tight. 'I'll speak to him in my own time – and then I'm sure he'll come round to the Lawrence I once knew.'

DAY FIFTEEN

I go to Waitrose in the morning to ensure I have enough fruit, drink and snacks for Sunday. Two people recognise me from last night's meeting and stop to talk by the checkout till. They chat about the Olympics, the library campaign and Donald's time in the army. The conversation is rather intimate for this time in the morning but they are extremely enthusiastic so I offer up more than expected, including the time Donald got so angry his hero Dean Martin had appeared in *The Cannonball Run* movies that he nearly broke the TV with a coffee mug. I instantly regret telling that story but they enjoy it so much my guilt ebbs away with every snort and laugh. It seems that people are being more open than usual. I get home just before noon and start preparing lunch. I turn on Radio Three and think of the weekend: tomorrow is my last day in the Olympic Park and by Sunday it'll all be over. What then? Yes, there is the library work but what else? Is that enough for me? How will I cope with an empty house again? Perhaps I could ask Jessica to stay for longer. I eat lunch and start the washing-up. The phone rings as I dry off the last plate. I quickly put the kettle on – and walk down the hallway to answer it.

'Hiya Francesca? It's Richard Krystal from the Met…'

'Oh hello, how are you this morning?'

'Decent because I'm back into the swing of things. My fourth shift now, so doing good after all that time off. Look that man you were asking about, I did ask around…'

'You don't need to worry,' I said, interrupting him rather firmly. 'He's been released without charge. He actually handed himself in. I don't think the police ever arrested him at all.'

'…Which is exactly what I was about to say. Nice work, sleuth. How did you get that info? Do you know any other coppers?'

'No, Lawrence actually called his son direct last night while we were at this public meeting. He told him everything that had happened. He was quite apologetic and he wanted to speak to me but I wasn't really in the mood at that stage…'

'Too right, you shouldn't let him off the hook that easily. Aggressive males, particularly those fuelled up by liqueur, tend not to change their behaviour.'

'That's a bit reductive isn't it?'

'In my line of work, Francesca, it pays to be reductive. Respect, yes, but getting too close? No. You have to keep your distance or you'll get your fingers burned.'

'Not sure I want you at my house now…'

'Course you do – and as it happens, I am free this Sunday and so is Melissa. Are we still invited then?'

'I suppose you are – but you're not going to spy on us are you?'

'Melissa can do that. She works for the Government...'

'Oh, what does she do?'

'She's a press officer for the Department for Transport. Getting a lot of heat about HS2 right now. That's been big news in your county, hasn't it?'

'Yes, but I haven't really been keeping up to be honest. Hope it doesn't slice its way through the Chilterns though. We've got a lot of lovely countryside here.'

'But it'll create lots of jobs for people – and new businesses.'

'Maybe it will but I'm sceptical. My husband did some work for the National Trust after he left the army so we're a bit fond of our heritage, if you know what I mean.'

'I am too but not at the expense of progress. But anyway look, I'm happy this Lawrence fella's come to his senses and that unpleasant saga is now over. I've got to get on with investigating a criminal damage incident at a warehouse this morning so if we don't talk again how about Melissa and I pop down to sleepy old Bucks at about two on Sunday? Pop us your address in an email and we'll make sure we've got the best bottle of wine ready for your final shindig.'

'Shindig? I'm beginning to think this is a terrible idea now...'

'You won't. We have to savour every single moment before it's gone. This time last year, almost to the day, I was caught in the middle of a firestorm;

a vortex of savagery I'll never forget. I don't think the scars of the riots will ever heal but this is another big step for me. A Londoner taking pride in his city again – and representing its true face to the world.'

The sound of the doorbell jolts me from my afternoon nap. I had been dreaming of William's marriage with Jessica in a huge manor house in Yorkshire; Donald and I watching on as the young couple ride off on a horse for their honeymoon. It's gone as soon as I put my feet in my slippers. I rush downstairs and open the door. I am shocked to see Lawrence in front of me; his rasping stare and restless eyes almost making me topple over. He has some kind of big album or scrapbook under his arm. He doesn't say anything immediately which annoys me greatly. Is he drunk again? I try to play the same game – but fail after about 30 seconds of a terrifyingly uncomfortable silence. It's like I'm the guest not the other way round. I think about shutting the door but instead offer a mild sigh and a tone of reconciliation.

'I thought you'd be at work, Lawrence,' I say, still holding the door quite tight as a precaution. 'Did you get off early?'

'Rang in sick this morning. They understood. Were you at Gillian's meeting yesterday?'

'Yes, we had a huge turnout. Why didn't you go?'

'You know the reason so why ask? Are you trying to humiliate me more than I already have been?'

'No, but she was expecting you.'

'She expects too much.' He sighs and looks down at his scrapbook. 'Can I come in then or not?'

'I don't know if you should Lawrence,' I say, rubbing my eyes. 'I've just had a nap. I'm not at my best.'

'Don't you want to look at these?' he says, holding up the scrapbook.

'What is it?'

'An old treasure that I'd forgotten about. It's made me think a lot over the last few days about how I've been behaving to those I love.'

'Including me?'

'Yes, you and Donald. Because I've interfered in the grieving process in such a shameful manner that I can't look you in the eye again.'

'You're making a good job of it so far...'

'I stare a lot when I've got a lot to be apologetic about. So can I come in? Why don't you rest while I make you some coffee?'

'Have you spoken to Gillian and William yet?'

'Don't need to. I know their intentions. Gillian is going ahead with the divorce and William wants to marry Jessica. One in, one out eh?'

'I'm not sure they want to marry yet but I know what you mean. So you're not going to stop William from moving up to Yorkshire with Jessica?'

'I can try and stop it but whether he'll listen is another matter.'

'Maybe it's because you haven't been setting a good example...'

'Maybe...'

I sigh again and ease my hand off the door.

'I need a pledge that you are going to apologise to Jessica because you were much harder on her than you were on me.'

'She's a tough girl. I'm sure she doesn't need any more words from me…'

'Well, I'm afraid you can't come in then…'

'That's not worthy of you, Francesca. Where is she anyway? Work?'

'Yes, her penultimate day. My last day is tomorrow.'

'I think you've both done a fine job.' He looks away from me for the first time. 'Makes me think my daily speculation on whether rival software companies are hot or not is a bit inadequate. You get the praise, we get indifference. I think I'm in the wrong job sometimes.'

'Maybe you are but at least you make money…'

'It's not everything…'

I have never heard Lawrence talk like that before. He usually claimed he was 'vital' to the sustainability of Britain's economy and that the country would fall apart if it wasn't for people like him. Had he really changed or was he just trying to get back in my good books so he could influence William and Jessica?

'How do I know if I let you in, you won't get angry with me again?'

'I wasn't angry with you, Francesca, it was more everything else, really: Jessica, William, Gillian, her dad, take your pick. Just give me this chance and you can boot me out if you don't like what you hear. I can take it; I mean I spent yesterday being interviewed by this rough-looking police sergeant.'

'You must apologise to Jessica…'

'But I'll have left by then…'

'That's the deal…'

He sighs and knocks on the scrapbook with his knuckles.

'Of course, I'll apologise to her,' he says, after a long delay. 'But that still doesn't mean I want her as a future daughter-in-law…'

I nod and finally release the door from my sweaty hands.

* * *

Lawrence is sat at the garden table looking at the faded, hand-drawn wickets on our side wall. I place a bowl of blueberries, a plate of cookies and two cups of coffee – all neatly balanced on a large tray – onto the table. I ease the scrapbook out of the way, and eventually sit down opposite him. He doesn't say anything for a long time – and then, as if he's come out of a deep sleep or a trance, he turns to me and points at the wall.

'Didn't Donald paint them for William when he used to come round to play?' he asks. 'You can hardly see them now.'

'It's not paint, they were drawn with chalk. It comes off quite easily but I decided to leave them there.' I pause and pick up a blueberry, placing it into my mouth carefully. I recall the defacement of

Donald's picture in the campaign leaflet. 'I suppose this is a form of graffiti too.'

'No it isn't. But Gillian did tell me about that bastard who spoiled Donald's picture in that leaflet. You should have called the police.'

I almost choke on my blueberry. 'Well, you were down there, why didn't you report it?'

'It's for Chiltern's finest to deal with it not the Met. Mine could have become an international incident because it happened in the Olympic Park.' He picks up a cookie and hastily takes a bigger bite than necessary. He opens the scrapbook and some of the crumbs land on the pages. He swats them away with his fingers. 'I wanted to show you this, Francesca, because there's probably a lot of pictures in here you haven't seen. I used to take my camera with me to matches even though it annoyed Donald. I don't regret it for a moment though. We caught some wonderful moments.' He eases the book towards me.

'Why are you showing this to me now, Lawrence? I'm sure you've had it for a while.'

'Yes, but I'd completely forgotten about it. William found it in the attic a couple of days ago when he was going through some of his own stuff because he wants to leave home. It was on the same day of the incident at the Olympic Park. He showed it to me and, after I'd looked through them for a couple of hours, I realised how stupid I'd been. It was one of the reasons I later handed myself to police. I felt guilty about treating you so badly after everything you'd been through. I had to make amends.'

I don't reply and start working my way through the scrapbook instead. On the first page, there is a glorious, striking picture of Donald and Lawrence bending down with their arm round a very young William outside Edgbaston cricket ground. There are literally hundreds of people around them, waiting to go into the ground, including a sizeable number of West Indian fans. The colour and vivaciousness of this picture makes me feel that I am almost there, hearing the musical instruments and sensing the lush grass about to be graced by a red cricket ball. I turn the page and it's a grubby-looking scorecard from the same match, followed by a newspaper article. Gradually, I become attuned to the scrapbook's rhythms. Plenty of scorecards, stadium memorabilia and media articles – but it's the pictures of Donald that draw me in. One of Donald, arm in arm with an elderly umpire, another with him in the member's enclosure watching the white-kitted cricketers walking out onto the field and a third showing a delirious Donald and William playing their own shortened game in a completely empty stadium as the rain lashes down. I focus in on Donald's face; he seems so happy in that moment that I wonder if he ever felt the same way anywhere else.

'How did you get that picture?' I ask. 'The place is deserted. You're the only ones there.'

'It had been raining for two days on the run. So we went on the third hoping we'd see some play but that was rained off too. Everybody went home but we got our bat and ball out and got as close as we could get to the middle. We wouldn't even get to the boundary these days. A goon in a high-visibility jacket would stop us immediately.'

I go through to the end of the scrapbook and close it. I sigh and eat some more blueberries. I savour their tangy juices on my tongue. I lean back in my chair and look at Lawrence.

'Can I keep this?' I ask. 'It's the least you can do after everything that has happened.'

'Well, it's not really yours is it?'

'Maybe it isn't. But you admit you'd completely forgotten about it until William fished it out.'

'True, but that doesn't mean it isn't special to me...'

'...Have a funny way of showing it.'

He finishes off his cookie and licks his lips. He closes his eyes and enjoys the taste. 'Lord God, that's wonderful Francesca. I wish Gillian could still make delicacies like this.'

'She can, she's just got other things on her mind.'

'Don't tell me: the library campaign,' he says, picking up his cup of coffee and taking a sip. 'It's destroyed our marriage. It's not her dad, William or her constant whingeing about my hours, it all comes down to the books. She's always loved them more than me...'

'Donald was a bit like that too...'

'No, no, they were part of his life but not the be all and end all. He did like his stats though; the cricket scorecards, the innings totals, a batsman's average. I think he picked all that up from the army; a sense of order, a sense of team play, a feeling for the numbers around you...'

'Thanks for filling me in on Donald's character,' I say, with a smile. 'I only lived with him for 46 years!'

'Much obliged,' he replies, raising his coffee cup. 'Men can only properly understand each other in a truly sporting context.'

'So sport is a great unifier then? Like the Olympics?'

'I wouldn't go that far. Cricket has a unique heartbeat and it'll be here long after the Olympic roadshow has left town. I still find those sports hard to get into. Of course, I'm proud of the British success but it'll all be forgotten by next month.'

'I don't think so. This is different.'

'You're in the loop so I can understand you think that way but the rest of us will quickly be locked into the whirlpool of work again – and it will just become a nice, but distant, memory.'

'Why do you keep on working in a place you obviously don't like?'

He sighs and takes a long, lingering drink of his coffee.

'Because I'm trapped, that's why. I've been there for more than 21 years now and if I leave where am I going to go? I can't retrain as anything now, not at my age, so I've just got to get my head down and get on with it. I've also seen the age of our employees come down dramatically and a lot of them end up in senior positions. I feel I have to act up sometimes just to keep up with them.'

I pause and dip a cookie into my coffee, glancing up at him as I take a bite of the soaked biscuit. 'You need Donald back so you can go down to the cricket with him.'

'Maybe that's what I miss, I don't know. I have no friends in London, only colleagues because I don't socialise or attend any events there. Here, I know a few people but I'm not interested in their small-time jam-making sessions or parish meetings about the latest planning application.'

I shake my head and sigh. 'I think you're lost, Lawrence. You're family's breaking up and you're taking out your frustration on everything around you. I think you should take a long, hard look at what you still have and cherish it.'

'Jack...'

'What?'

'Jack. He's the only one who understands his father. As you know, he does marketing and PR for a private healthcare firm in north London, and has just bought a new flat there. He earns money, respects me and we speak regularly on the phone, sometimes two or three times a week. He'll be visiting us on Sunday.'

'Hmm, Sunday? I haven't seen him for a while...'

'Why have you got something planned?'

'Sort of, it's the last day of the Olympics. But why do you think Jack understands you better than Gillian or William do? Or is it because you've helped him with the flat in terms of the rent and the furniture? I know it's expensive around there.'

'I'll pretend I didn't hear the second part of the question. I'm here to apologise so I must bite my lip.' He finishes off his coffee and wipes the side of his mouth with a serviette. 'Generally, I'd say, he's entered a similar kind of workplace that I have;

pressurised, intense and highly competitive, so that's why he can relate to the things I've sacrificed for the family. He even visited me in Docklands on a couple of occasions. We had lunch together. They were the best hours I've spent together with any family member in the last decade.'

'Even Gillian?'

'Our relationship has been non-existent for the past decade...'

'So what now? Is the divorce final? Can no heads be banged together at this late stage?'

He rolls his index finger around the empty cup of coffee. 'It's up to Gillian. I want the family to stay together. I want William to remain in our home. But it's up to her. She wants a divorce so bad that I think she might be having an affair...'

'Oh for God's sake Lawrence,' I say, nearly spilling the plate of cookies onto the floor with a brush of my arm. 'Not that old chestnut again. She is not having an affair. You really must get that poisonous thought out of your head. It was the same when all that disgusting stuff came up with Donald when he'd just started at the library; that she was seeing him and that she liked former army types and all that rubbish. It was and still is very distressing, don't you understand that?'

He crosses his hands abruptly and looks up at me. 'I understand that utterly and comprehensively but you, too, have to understand that if Gillian leaves me it is akin to what happened to you when Donald passed away. A bereavement, simple as that. She will be gone forever and I'm not sure I can take that. I just can't...'

Three hours later, Lawrence and I are still in the garden as Jessica finally comes home. She is shocked to see Lawrence sitting by my side and ambles towards us with uncharacteristic hesitation. She stands by our side and then reaches down to pick up a blueberry from the bowl.

'The fruits probably gone off now,' I say. 'We've been here for a while. How was the shift today? Not too taxing, I hope.'

'Finished on a high,' she says, picking up two more blueberries. 'The women's hockey team won a bronze by beating the Kiwis 3-1 this afternoon so I'm well chuffed for the girls. I've texted a couple of them already.'

'Shouldn't they have won gold?' asks Lawrence, looking up at Jessica. 'Home crowd and all that. William said they lost to Argentina or something in the semis. Did the pressure get to them?'

'I don't think so,' says Jessica, finally pulling up a chair and sitting down. 'Argentina just scored more goals.'

Lawrence laughs and shakes his head. 'Oh so glib, Jessica. Is that what you do for a living?'

Jessica looks at me and I raise my hand slightly to suggest any response to Lawrence on this occasion will be futile.

'Lawrence came round today to apologise to the both of us, didn't you Lawrence?' I look at him and he shifts in his seat. 'He's already spoken to me at length and I've accepted his apology. He did wrong and he's acknowledged it. Now you must do the same with Jessica.'

Lawrence does not reply immediately – and instead fixes his eyes on Jessica. She reaches for the scrapbook on the table.

'What's that?' she asks, picking it up and flicking through the pages. 'Looks ancient…'

'It's not that old,' says Lawrence.

'Old enough.' She keeps flicking through the pages and reaches one that makes her smile. 'Jesus, look at the picture of William in there! He looks like a Smurf.'

'So subtle as usual,' says Lawrence.

'Like you were…' she says, peering up from the scrapbook, '…when you nearly beat us up in the Olympic Park?'

Lawrence gets up and pulls back his chair which ends up about four feet away near a wall. 'If it wasn't for people like me you wouldn't have a fucking Olympics!'

'Okay, come on, calm down please,' I say, raising both hands and trying to mediate. 'You're in my house now so I won't stand for any of this nonsense. Jessica, please give Lawrence a chance. He did come here in good faith and we should let him apologise in a civil manner. I don't want these wonderful two weeks to be spoilt by petty things this late in the day.' I look at Jessica. 'Please let him say what he wants.'

'I'm not stopping him. He's got the cob on, not

me. If he doesn't like his son chasing after me then what can I do?'

'You're an arrogant so and so aren't you,' says Lawrence, with his hands on his hips. 'Where is he anyway? I haven't seen him since breakfast.'

'Gone to look at our new flat in Leeds, I think. He went up on the train this morning. Said he'd be back by seven but could be some delays, I don't know.'

Lawrence puts his hand on his forehead and starts to pace around the garden. 'For fuck's sake,' he says, more to himself than to anyone else. 'When is this shit going to end?'

'Now, if you let it,' I say, getting up and walking towards Lawrence. I put my hand on his shoulder and ease him back to the table. He is hesitant at first but then lets me take control. He sits back down and folds his arms, looking down at the ground. I sit down by his side and watch him as he stews. A couple of minutes pass in complete silence and then, without prompting, he looks up at Jessica.

'I'm genuinely sorry for putting my hands on you in an aggressive manner that day, Jessica. It was wrong. I shouldn't have been drunk and I shouldn't have been frustrated. There are no excuses for that kind of behaviour. You two were enjoying a good day at the Olympics. I spoiled that in a big way. It shouldn't have happened and I'll probably regret it for the rest of my life because I've never had dealings with the police before. It's why I went to them almost immediately. I hope you can forgive me.'

I feel almost elated that Lawrence has apologised

to Jessica in such a singular manner, with no excuses or caveats. I look at Jessica and she puts down the scrapbook. She reaches over the table and offers her hand. Lawrence hesitates but then looks up and shakes Jessica's hand vigorously.

'Genuinely sorry,' he says, finally breaking out into a smile.

'So am I if there have been any misunderstandings,' says Jessica. 'Particularly where my relationship with William is concerned.'

'…And how deep does that relationship go?'

'We'll probably be living together in Leeds by next week. Is that deep enough for you?'

Lawrence lets go of Jessica's hand and looks at me. His prolonged stare makes me feel, for the first time ever perhaps, that I understand what's he's thinking at this precise moment.

'Sometimes you have to learn to let go,' he says. 'Francesca's done that. Maybe I need to do the same with William.'

DAY SIXTEEN

Rob raises his fist in the air and shouts 'Ka-yakkety-yak!' as he celebrates Ed McKeever's gold medal at Eton Dorney. He asks a group of gathered spectators to join him and repeat this strangely seductive mantra which quickly descends into laughter and horseplay. Eventually, about 40 people end up shouting 'Ka-yakkety-yak!' with Rob as their conductor, prancing around like some Pink Panther figure who knows exactly which buttons to press. Then he flashes his fingers to denote how many gold medals Team GB have won. Twenty five! Then they all sing: 'Twenty Five, Ka-yakkety-yak!' There are people nearly falling about, unable to contain their laughter. I admire the way Rob engages with a crowd. I still can't do that – even after this sumptuous fortnight. Perhaps, I'll get a chance on Sunday with all those people coming to my house? Watching Rob makes me feel curiously upbeat about the prospect.

When the spectators have melted away, Rob walks towards me, out of breath and sweating. He stops by my side and uses my shoulder as a leaning mechanism.

'Jesus, that was more tiring than I thought,' he says, using his name badge to wipe some sweat from his brow. 'Now, I know why all those conductors went mad, you know, Mozart and the like.'

'But they were geniuses too,' I say, with a smile.

'If you say so.' He takes his forearm off my shoulder. 'What's this I hear about a party at your place on Sunday? You sure that's a good idea?'

'Did Jessica tell you about it?'

'Not only that but she threatened to cuff me to a post if I didn't come.'

'It's not a party really,' I say, folding my arms. 'It's just a way of saying thank you to some of the volunteers. I wasn't enthusiastic, at first, but Jessica's won me round.'

His expression turns serious for the first time. He moves a bit closer and bends down to ensure contact.

'Are you sure about this Frannie? Two weeks ago, you were at rock bottom, almost unable to speak. You wanted to be alone in the house, quite understandably.' He pauses and puts his hand on my arm. 'But now you want loads of people there? If that's what you want, great, but I just want to make sure it is completely your decision and your arm hasn't been twisted by the blonde bombshell. She does have a habit of getting what she wants.'

'She hasn't twisted my arm. I think she just wants to preserve some memories, that's all.' I pause and offer a polite, reassuring smile. 'I do too.'

Rob breaks out into a smile and steps back. 'Like this memory?' He raises his fist and shouts: 'Ka-yakkety-yak! Come on, Frannie, after three, you can do it too...'

'But I don't want to,' I say, hoping that no other spectators are watching this grisly spectacle. 'And besides I don't even know which event Ed McKeever won? All your yakking makes no sense to me.'

Rob falls to the ground, laughing so hard I think he's going to be ill. He does a motion with an oar.

'Some form of rowing?' I say.

'No, it was the men's 200 kilometres...' he says, almost in hysterics by now and holding his stomach to quell the laughter. 'In Ka-yakkety-yak!'

'I've got it: Kayak!'

He is unable to speak but nods his head in sheer, intense delight. As I look at him, rolling about on the ground, I do wonder if this is appropriate behaviour for a team leader. But when a young boy in a baseball cap, clutching a notebook and pen, asks for his autograph, I realise Rob has helped make these Games what they are: fun-loving, free-spirited and quietly inclusive. Letting oneself go has been the mantra (despite what the Ka-yakkety-yaks say).

* * *

After lunch, I go to the toilet and notice Sheena coming out of the cubicle in tears. Her face is as bright as our t-shirts and I wonder if I should approach her in this state. It might be something serious; I think back to my own circumstances when the Olympics started. I wait by the sink and mimic drying my hands just to give me some time. She acknowledges me with a resigned, weary smile and I realise I mustn't hold back. Silence is the enemy in this environment. I walk towards Sheena and put my arm around her.

'Hey love, what's the matter?' I ask, wiping away a tear from her cheek with my finger. 'Come on, let's go back into the canteen and have a chat about it.'

She shakes her head and continues to sob. 'No, I need some air. I'm going out in the Park…'

I give her a tissue and we both head out into the Olympic Park. A few minutes later we are standing by a kiosk where a man is selling some kind of mini-newspaper or fanzine to spectators for a pound each. He is wearing a flat-cap, wellies, a waistcoat and a dicky-bow tie. He makes Sheena smile with his rasping sales pitch, as if Del Boy had morphed into a rag and bone man.

'Get your Tom Daily here, get your Tom Daily, a pound for your paper. Read all about him. Read all about him. Going for diving gold today. Britain's golden boy. Read all about him…'

Sheena shakes her head and smiles, wiping away her tears as if they were an aberration. The man hands her a paper but she refuses.

'Sorry we're on duty,' she says. 'Are you allowed to do this round here?'

'No-one stopping us, love. Don't you want to know about Tom's existential relationship with the water? When he dives in, it's as though he's plunging into another universe. Here, this article, on page 6, explores that very issue.'

'Thanks, but I'll pass. Like I said, I've got work to do.'

'No problem. What about your friend here?'

'Me too,' I say, rather abruptly in the hope that the man will go away so I can speak to Sheena.

'Well, make sure you don't work too hard or you'll miss Major Tom getting on board later today.' He walks away and continues to talk and sell as he moves through the spectators. 'Read all about him. Get your Tom Daily…'

'Oh God, did I need that!' says Sheena, straightening her name badge which is almost over her shoulder. 'He's cured me in seconds…'

'Of what?'

She hesitates and looks at me. 'It's silly, Frannie, it's nothing…'

'Maybe it is, but it might make you feel better if we share it. After all, that's what this place is about isn't it?'

She sighs and looks away from me towards the Orbit tower. 'I'm just blubbing like a little girl because I can't bear the thought of going back home after the ridiculous high of these two weeks. Gary spoke to me this morning to say he had a backlog of stuff for me to do when I got home: piles of washing, kids' shopping and even their homework, it made feel down again, that's all. It felt like the rollercoaster has crashed – and I'd been ejected. I'm sorry Frannie, compared to what you've been through, it hardly registers.'

'It does register, Sheena, of course it does because I have similar feelings. I'm sure all 70,000 Games Makers will feel like that too. But as you know, nothing lasts forever…'

302

'No, but when I woke up this morning, I had this strange sensation that we'd carry the feelings of hope, generosity and community spirit right through with us so that when we got back home or to work, people would be the same.' She pauses and looks away from me. 'Maybe I was being optimistic...'

'No, you weren't because I see that all around me; in our village, in the streets, in the shops. People have been wonderful – and I have faith that they'll carry it on.'

'Maybe in your village,' she says, with a smile. 'You don't know Gary and the mates he hangs around with. One call and he's gone. I think he's just waiting for me to get back in the door and he'll be off down the watering hole necking his bevies again.'

'I'll know him on Sunday, though, won't I? Is he coming?'

'I'll be there, but I don't know about him. He says there's some football on so he might be busy. Community Shield or something?'

'Sounds like something volunteers would get for a heroic act like saving someone's life. Which team does he support?'

'Chelsea...'

'Only thing I know about them is Sir Richard Attenborough is a big fan...'

'The one who made Gandhi?'

'Yes...'

'I tried to watch that film once and Gary turned it off after half an hour because he said he was bored.'

'Donald saw that four times. It was the same with

Chaplin, he watched that on numerous occasions too. He liked those kind of films, about famous historical figures. He felt we didn't really make those kind of films anymore. Oh *Shadowlands* too, about CS Lewis, that was another favourite.'

'The Narnia author?'

'Yes…'

'Now that's something Gary does like: the Narnia books. He's even kept a few of them.' She laughs and folds her arms. 'He's the Lion and you know the rest…'

'A bulging wardrobe: the bane of our lives!'

'I'd love to turn into a witch for a day and sort him out.'

She's about to say something else but a couple of spectators approach us asking us if we know the exact times Mo Farah and Usain Bolt will be competing tonight in the Olympic Stadium. We provide an estimated schedule and then they ask us about the relays. We provide that information too and then one spectator talks about the relays at length and claims that Britain's persistent baton infringements, particularly in the men's team (dropping it, not handing it over in time etc…) is akin to the England football team's dire performances at successive World Cups. They do not practice hard enough, he says. Baton infringements and penalty shoot-outs are part of the same problem: a lack of technique and temperament. When he's finished, Sheena and I are none the wiser. Our lack of football knowledge has been well established but we do get his point on the baton issues. It's a pity because the relays, when in full flow, are one of the most wonderful sights at the Olympics. I always look forward to them.

Sheena nudges my arm to say there's someone right behind me. I turn and am startled to see Jessica inches away from me. I put my hand on my chest and roll my eyes.

'What are trying to do to me? Give me a heart attack?'

'It's about Lawrence,' she says, without delay. 'William called me at lunchtime and said he didn't come home last night and that Gillian is really concerned about him. No-one knows where he is.'

'So you're telling me he's missing?'

'I don't know,' she says, rubbing her palm on her forehead. 'I told William that he left your house at about seven and we don't know anything after that. To be honest, William isn't taking it very seriously; it's Gillian that's worried.'

'Have you spoken to her?'

'No, I've done enough damage for a fortnight don't you think?'

I nod in mild agreement, although it's tinged with flippancy rather than conviction.

'I need to speak to Gillian,' I say, looking at my watch. 'But I'm going to do it after our shift has ended.'

'Who are you talking about here?' asks Sheena. 'Is it that man who came to the Olympic Park, all drunk and unruly? If it is, I say good riddance.'

Jessica tuts. 'Sheena, you don't know anything about him...'

'Well, he nearly had you out for the count with a right hook, didn't he?' She folds her arms and looks at Jessica. 'I don't think you can ever indulge these kind of blokes. They will always revert to aggressive behaviour if they don't get their way. I remember a friend of Gary's knocked his wife around after a perfectly good night out with the lads. He was just frustrated for no reason at all and lashed out even though he'd had the best time of his life a few hours back. I don't trust them; that's my twopenny's worth...'

'Maybe you haven't known enough of them then,' says Jessica. 'There's plenty of decent blokes at my university. We talk, go out, play sport, everything; you can't just make assumptions based on a few numbers.'

'No, but I can make assumptions on what I saw of Lawrence – and it was ugly. If he's going to be your father-in-law, I'd think deeply about the kind of family you'll be marrying into...'

'Who said I'm getting married?'

Sheena looks at me and smiles.

'I never said anything...'

There is a long silence as Jessica looks at me too.

'Okay, I did,' I say, rather annoyed that we're veering away from the subject in hand. 'But it was just a passing remark.' I turn towards Jessica. 'Forget about that now. What about Sunday? Shall we cancel it now with all this going on? I think it might be in bad taste.'

Jessica looks astonished. 'No way is that going to happen. My Mum and Dad are coming down and there's too many others we'd let down if we didn't go ahead. We deserve to go out on a high. If Lawrence is still missing then, tough, it's nothing to do with us.'

'That's the spirit, girl,' says Sheena, putting her hand up for a high five which Jessica doesn't reciprocate.

'Oh I don't know Jessica,' I say. 'I'm having big doubts about all this now…'

'Don't,' says Jessica, putting her hand on my shoulder. 'William thinks his dad is doing this for attention anyway. He doesn't want us to leave home and live somewhere else. That's natural. He'll probably be back at the house for Sunday lunch.'

'And if he isn't? Are you and William still leaving for the north?'

'Yes, because we want to spend more time together. We've hardly seen each other through the Olympics. I've been too busy.'

'Do you want to do a swap?' says Sheena. 'You go back to my house and make bacon and eggs for Gary in the morning while I parade around the Yorkshire Moors with William Lover Boy dreaming of wild romance and exotic landscapes. Deal?'

'Er no,' says Jessica. 'You can keep your full English.' Jessica turns to me and suddenly looks quite worried. 'I'm not concerned about my relationship with William at all; we're big and tough enough to deal with it. But I *am* concerned that I might spoil it all for you right at the finishing line. We've had an incredible two weeks, I just don't want Lawrence destroying it all for us right at the death.'

Jessica's final word rings in my head for a few seconds. Why if Lawrence is dead? Why if the prospect of divorce and everything else has led him to suicide? I banish these stupid thoughts immediately. I know they have circulated because of Donald.

'He's not going to spoil anything for us,' I say, smiling at Jessica. 'And besides we've got a policeman coming so if there are any issues, he can deal with them.'

'A copper? Who?' asks Jessica.

'Oh, someone I met on the Tube on the day of the Opening Ceremony. He was involved in the riots last year. He thinks this summer has been the best ever…'

'The riots eh?' says Sheena, with a laugh. 'If this Lawrence bloke turns up on Sunday, there might be a riot at your house, Frannie.'

'We already spoke to him, yesterday, Sheena,' says Jessica. 'He apologised to us so that's not going to happen.'

I nod in agreement but imagine Lawrence turning up just before the Closing Ceremony and demanding that William stays at home. William disagrees with his father and a fight breaks out. Richard Krystal intervenes but is caught up in the melee too. Again, I can't believe I'm thinking such outlandish thoughts. But there's a happy ending to this: Donald walks down the stairs in his soldier's uniform and calms everyone down, making the peace and serving tea. As long as he's with me, I'm unbreakable – and no-one, I say, no-one – can lay a finger on me in my own house.

I realise my time in the Olympic Park is coming to an end. I watch Jessica, Sheena and Eric having their photo taken with a group of children and wonder if I will ever feel this way again. The glow of warmth, joy and intimacy, particularly since Super Saturday, has been inexplicable as well as incredible; a buzzing happy virus that has infected everyone in its vicinity. I look around and absorb the sights. I'll miss most of them but not all! The wildflower meadows, the wetland tress and the lawns surrounding the Olympic Park all look gorgeous on a sunny day and I wonder how I will do without them when I wake up in my own bed on Monday. The London 2012 megastore, the mascots Wenlock and Mandeville, the BBC commentary box perched on a stack of colourful shipping containers and those wonderful blue and red high chairs used by volunteers which, unfortunately, I never sat in. The McDonald's restaurant and the corporate sponsors who erected their temporary pavilions across the site: BP, Coca-Cola, Panasonic, BMW, Samsung and the rest. Will I miss them? No, but plenty of people still bought their products. The venues that are hard to forget: the giant saucer of the Olympic Stadium, but also the Orbit tower, the Aquatics Centre, the Basketball Arena and my favourite shape of all: the Velodrome. But as I lower my gaze and look at directly what's in front of me, I realise all of that is irrelevant without the single, most important thing in the Olympics: the spectators. The sheer range of faces, voices and costumes has been breathtaking. The whole world has been here. A high five of continents. Flags painted on their faces, butterflies on their cheeks, capes round their shoulders, anything to feel part of a bigger community. Some people have been less extravagant: sunglasses, shorts, handbags, t-shirts, hats and sandals have been enough for them but even they had a twinkle in their eye, a spring in their step or an expression of mild anticipation as they clutched a ticket and entered their Olympic ring of history. These people I will miss, because they are like me: Britain's quiet enthusiasts. I hope they find another outlet for their passions soon.

I glance over at Jessica, Sheena and Eric again. This time they are doing the Conga with two Australian hockey supporters, who are in great spirits after having won bronze in the Men's tournament by beating Great Britain 3-1. The Aussies are enjoying the sandwich: three Britons, one from Down Under. They take it in turns to rub in the point. Then another group of spectators pay homage to us by singing Prince's *Purple Rain* but with the words changed to Purple Red. It's strangely captivating and emotional. I watch this delicate spectacle and smile at a family walking past me. I approach them because I want to – time is ticking away. Dad is holding his daughter's hand and Mum is trying to keep watch on her (slightly more wayward) two sons.

'Hello, which event are you seeing?' I ask, crossing my hands in front of my waist. 'This is my last day and I really want to wish you the best.'

'Oh, that's nice of you,' says Daddy, looking down at this daughter. 'Chloe, do you want to shake the great Games Maker's hand? One day, you can say you were here…'

Chloe offers her hand and I almost have to close my eyes as I hold it because it's so supple and fragile.

'Thank you for everything you've done,' says Chloe. 'I saw your team on TV. Are you getting gold medals too?'

I laugh and bend down, with a bit of difficulty, to reach eye level with Chloe. 'We do have a shift system where we get bronze, silver and gold badges, yes, but I think you deserve a gold medal for being here today, don't you?'

'Yes, but not as much as Mo Farah, we're watching him now aren't we Daddy?'

Daddy looks at his watch. 'Not quite yet, darling, we've still got a few hours to go. We're going to have a browse around the Olympic Park.'

'Can we take this lady in?' she says, clutching my hand tight. 'I like her. She can tell me where Mo Farah is going to be. Does she know all the great Olympic people?'

'Of course, she does,' says Daddy, looking up at me. 'Come on, Chloe, let's go, I think this lovely lady has got work to do.'

'Oh not too much now,' I say, stroking Chloe's hair as she moves away. 'I saw Mo Farah last week in the Olympic Stadium and he won so let's hope he can do the same this evening.'

'Did you run with him?' she asks.

Dad and Mum laugh and start walking away with Chloe showing more reluctance. 'Sorry about that,' says Mum. 'She does come out with the strangest things.'

'No, it was one of the funniest things I've heard,' I say, getting upright again and straightening my tilted hat. 'I need to get back in shape anyway!'

'Anyway nice to talk to you,' says Mum. 'Say bye bye Chloe…'

Chloe waves and smiles. 'Bye bye and I hope I can see you on the track when it's night.'

'You will,' I say, raising my arm to wave.

I watch the family head towards the Olympic Stadium and breathe a marathon sigh. I look up into the sky and wish these feelings could last forever.

I think of the film *The Long Goodbye* as I carry out my own farewells – to staff, to team leaders, to spectators, and ultimately, to anyone who'll listen. Donald and I watched this film at a cinema in London and he was a big Elliot Gould fan after watching *MASH* a few years earlier and enjoying its absurd, satirical take on army life. I do not remember a single scene in *The Long Goodbye*, but do remember Donald's hand on mine on the arm rest. I never felt freer or happier. He had left the army in the late Sixties and got a full-time job at the library eight months later. This came mainly because he helped illiterate soldiers write letters to their wives during earlier campaigns – and even in some cases, poems and short stories. The thirst for education over service was too great and he chose to leave. Now, I was saying goodbye to a couple of young, fresh-faced soldiers from 2012. They had served the London Olympics so well that many people had forgotten about their contribution once the gold medals started to pile up and the British athletes (as well as us Games Makers) gained recognition. The two men, who can't be more 20 years old, have their picture taken with Jessica and me. So handsome, innocent and precise; like Donald was all those years ago. We wave goodbye as we head out of the Olympic Park for the last time, bags over our shoulders and a tinge of sadness in our hearts. Many spectators are still rushing in – Mo, Usain, Tom – are all still competing this evening so there's still a buzz of expectancy in the air. Jessica shakes her head and looks at me.

'Can't we just get a couple of sleeping bags and kip here tonight?' she says. 'Why would anyone want to leave this? It's like part of my soul has been left here.'

'Everything has to come to an end, but I know what you mean. I dread waking up in the morning. Did you say goodbye to Sheena and Rob?'

'They were a bit late in finishing their shift so I couldn't. We'll see them tomorrow though. What about Eric?'

'I think he just slipped out. He found the going tough in the last few days.'

'Is he coming?'

'I don't know. I did tell him about it – but he's got all these other volunteering commitments so I doubt it.'

We enter Stratford station and my mobile phone rings. I really don't want to answer it as my feet are hurting and I need a sit down before I can engage too deeply in conversation. But, with Jessica's news about Lawrence earlier in the day, I realise it might be important so reluctantly take it while trying to slalom through a mass crowd.

'Hello Frannie, it's Gillian. You're not going to believe this but my father's gone missing now too. I can't believe what's happening to me. I must be cursed…'

'Calm down Gillian,' I say, bending my ear right down into the phone to block out the noise. 'You say, your father's missing. How did that happen?'

'I don't know. I left him at home for less than an hour while I popped down to the supermarket for groceries and when I came back he wasn't there. William and Jack are out and, as you know, Lawrence hasn't been back since last evening after he visited your house. It's all falling apart, Frannie, I'm not sure I can take anymore of this…'

'Don't worry Gillian. We're on our way home now. Jessica is with me too. We'll come round straight away if you want. Might be a couple of hours though…'

'Oh will you? That'll be so kind. I'm not sure I'd be able to cope without you and Jessica. I'm thinking about calling the police but I might wait a bit longer now.'

'Do you think Lawrence took him?'

'What? It's never crossed my mind. Why would he want to do that?'

'No reason, it's just me thinking out loud. Your father wouldn't just walk out of the front door would he? I mean, he's ill but not that ill.'

'He's never done it before but, honestly, that kind of thing never crossed my mind. Lawrence is silly but surely he wouldn't go as far as to take Daddy out without my consent. They barely know each other.'

'That might be the point. Anyway, we're about to get on the Tube in a few minutes so we can talk about this when we get home…'

'Oh I'm so sorry, I nearly forgot: how was your last day at the Olympics? Must have been so emotional.'

'It was – and a bit more than that too…'

'You don't want it to stop do you?'

'No and nor does the country by the looks of things. But I'm not going to peep over my shoulder now just in case the tears start rolling down my cheeks. I'm going to look straight ahead at the Tube train and leave it all behind. It's the only way I can deal with things, really.'

'Donald would have been so proud of you now, Frannie, you do know that don't you? The bravery you showed by fronting up on those early dark mornings, saying hello to spectators even though you were hurting so much inside.'

'I know but even that's in the past now. I want to

look forward and see if I can make a big difference to people out there, not just inside the Olympic Park.'

'So you are joining the campaign next week?'

'Yes…'

'And you'll become a volunteer too? We might need three days a week from the start.'

'Can't wait.'

'Wonderful…'

She pauses and I think she's hung up.

'Gillian, are you still there?'

'Yes, I'm here it's just I feel so guilty about leaving him alone like that. I shouldn't have done it but you know how it is. I can't take him everywhere. I have to have some waking minutes to myself.'

'You didn't do anything wrong, don't beat yourself up about it. You never know he might turn up at the front door before we get back.'

'I wouldn't bet on it…'

'See you soon, then…'

'Bye – oh and give my best to Jessica.'

'I will.'

I end the call and look up at Jessica. I'm about to speak but she gets in first.

'Don't tell me her father's gone AWOL too…' she says.

'Looks like it…'

'And people said I was the unlucky one! If I marry into this family, they'll put a new curse on me every day!'

'You shouldn't laugh about it – this could be serious.'

'No, it isn't....'

'Why?' I say, slightly alarmed.

'Because Gillian's dad is with Lawrence. I got a text from William saying he'd spoken to his father and that the two men – that is Lawrence and his father-in-law – were eating at an Italian restaurant in another village. Lawrence had never taken him out before so he wanted to do it before it was too late.'

'But why didn't you tell me all this when I was speaking to Gillian? She's been worried sick.'

'I only got it a few minutes ago when we were saying our goodbyes. Gillian'll be fine. She's brought some of this upon herself.'

'What are you talking about?'

'I read a bit of her book and I felt she was doing too many things; trying to be a busybody, running campaigns, looking after her sick dad, it all felt a bit false to me.'

'It's not false, Jessica, she's genuine. She just tries to help as many people as she can. After all, isn't that what volunteering's about?'

'Yes, but there's a limit. You can't help some people...'

'Like you?' I say, with a long pause after saying the words. 'What would you have done if I hadn't have helped you in the first few days of the Olympics. Everybody needs support at some stage of their life.'

She offers a blank look and then breaks out into laughter. 'You're so good at getting me stumped, Frannie.' She puts her arm round my shoulder. 'You should stop doing that to me? I'm only a young lass.'

'Yes, a young lass with a lot to learn…'

'Well, a little…'

'No, a lot!'

'Okay a lot – but can you wish me up some luck too?'

We laugh and walk down to the platform. I take Jessica's arm and start singing *With a Little Bit of Luck* from My Fair Lady. The song has always been a favourite and I'm glad I have the confidence and initiative to start singing it, even if people are looking at me. Jessica eventually joins in and locks her arm into mine. She has been performing in the Olympic Park for two weeks; now it is my turn.

We are surprised, but not shocked, to see Lawrence opening his own front door. Jessica gives me a knowing glance as if she knew he'd come back with his tail between his legs. Lawrence smiles and opens the door extremely wide, almost wanting us to go in without saying a word. I step forward and go inside the house.

'Where's Gillian?' I ask, wiping my feet on the doormat even though it's unnecessary.

'Upstairs, I think,' he replies, rather abruptly.

'And your father-in-law?'

'In the living room, playing cards with me. Too many questions, Frannie, for Saturday tea-time. How was your Olympic day? Hope you went out with a bang…'

'Well, you nearly did, didn't you?'

He sighs and shakes his head. Jessica walks

318

in behind me and we both brush past him into the hallway.

'Did my apology not do anything for you ladies, yesterday? I thought we were back on terms.'

'Looks like your terms,' says Jessica, glancing at him as she walks past.

'Don't start. Gillian's upstairs if you want to see her. If you want to join us for some Black Jack or Poker then we're in the living room.'

'We've had enough of games, thanks,' says Jessica, starting to go up the stairs ahead of me. 'Two weeks of them...'

'You're pretty funny, do you know that? Hope some of it rubs off on William. He's not the sharpest of tools...'

Jessica sticks two fingers up but her back is turned to Lawrence so he can't see them. I grab her hand before she gets into trouble.

'Which room is she in, Lawrence?' I ask, feeling extremely tired as I go up the stairs.

'Our bedroom, of course. Please don't touch my beauty products please...'

We ignore him and get to the top of the stairs. I'm out of breath and Jessica looks at me.

'Are you okay?'

'Yes, but I knew we should have gone home first. I needed my coffee and half an hour sofa time before doing anything else strenuous. No problem though, we're here now, let's see it through.'

Jessica walks into the bedroom and I shuffle in behind her. Immediately, by the dressing table, we see

Gillian sitting on a chair, looking into a mirror. She bursts into tears as soon as she sees our reflection. We walk towards her and stop by her side.

'Oh Gillian, don't cry, it's over now,' I say, putting my hand on her shoulder and leaning my head onto hers. 'They're back now so there's nothing to worry about.'

'Fifteen minutes after I called you,' she says, continuing to sob. 'Fifteen bloody minutes! They came back almost immediately. Daddy couldn't eat any of the food Lawrence had bought for him so they came back. He hasn't got a clue. I hate him. I absolutely hate him.'

'Oh come on, don't talk like that...' I say, holding her tight. 'You need to forget about what happened now because they're both safe. Come on, let's go downstairs and we'll make you some tea and biscuits.' I glance at Jessica. 'We could do with some too, couldn't we?'

'Sure could. I'm hungry too.'

Gillian starts to wipe the tears away from her cheeks. 'I'm sorry about being so selfish. You two have had an extremely long day – and long fortnight – for that matter, so I've really got to end this charade.' She sniffs and takes a deep breath. She straightens her hair and gets up from the chair. 'Right, I will go downstairs and start making tea – and you two are staying. We're well stocked this evening because I've just been to the supermarket. Everything is on the menu.' She turns and looks at us. 'So what do you say girls?'

'I'm not sure,' I say, feeling as if I need to take my

trainers and socks off immediately otherwise my feet will overheat. 'I need my rest at home, Gillian. You know that. I'm very tired today.'

'No problem, Frannie,' says Gillian. 'Come on, sit on the bed and I'll take your shoes off. I know your ritual when you come home from work. It's essential for you, I'm not stupid. Then you can have a wash and lie on the bed while Jess and I make tea – or dinner – or whatever exotic thing we've got in mind. Come on, up you get.'

I reluctantly sit down on the bed and Gillian bends down and slips my trainers off my feet. She then takes my socks off. Strangely, I don't feel embarrassed at all. It's as if Gillian needed to do this after her father had disappeared. She needed the touch and warmth of an older person. She massages my feet for a couple of minutes and looks up at me.

'Now, is that a bit better?' she asks.

'You need to get behind the toes a bit more,' says Jessica. 'That soothes and releases the pressure in the head.'

Gillian looks up at Jessica. 'At least they're teaching you well on your Sports Science course.'

'William thinks it's all mumbo jumbo. Sleep, eat and burp is a good sign of health for him.'

'You need to work on him some more…'

'Where is he anyway?'

'He's been called in to work. They think they're going to be busier this evening.'

Jessica tuts and sighs. 'But he's handed his notice in. How can he go back?'

'They needed him and he agreed to do a last shift. Couldn't you do with the extra money? You are making a seismic move to the north of the country.'

'We'll get by.'

There is a short silence as Jessica watches me breathing deeply and, ultimately, feeling refreshed by Gillian's massage.

'So where did Lawrence go then?' asks Jessica.

'You mean with Daddy?'

'No, they went to an Italian restaurant, I'm up to date on that. I mean last night after he left us. So he wasn't missing after all then?'

Gillian takes her hands off my feet and looks up at Jessica. 'He said he stayed at a B&B out in the country somewhere although I'm not sure I believe him. He said he couldn't handle everything falling apart in his life.' She pauses and glances at me as I lie down on the bed. 'He also said he couldn't live without me.'

I rest my head on the pillow and enjoy it so much I am not sure I want to get up for the rest of the evening.

'I think that last part is true,' I say.

We finish dinner and walk back into the living room just in time to watch Mo Farah running in the 5000 metres. Jessica is on her feet throughout the race, cheering him on, while I offer mild encouragement when the bell rings for the final lap. The noise is deafening again but it's strange to feel it through a little box in the corner of the room rather than the stadium itself. This feels like helplessness; last week I felt as if I could almost touch Mo, make a difference and help him to the finishing line. Not this time. Gillian and Lawrence are quiet throughout the race. Her father, in his leather armchair, lets out a few grunts as the noise gets louder. Farah wins again and Jessica dances round the living room raising her fist in the air. Gillian and I both cheer, almost at the same time. Lawrence claps and then folds his arms almost immediately.

'Boy, can that man run,' he says, glancing across at Gillian. 'It's exactly what I've been doing lately. Long distance running...'

'No you've been hiding,' snaps Gillian.

'Oh come on, you two,' says Jessica, still with a massive smile on her face. 'Don't spoil it for everyone. This is a historic moment for Britain: a double Olympic champion. We should be celebrating not bickering.'

'Jessica's right,' says Gillian, raising her arm high in the air. 'All hail Mohammed Farah, King of England!'

'Hail to the King!' shouts Jessica, getting into the spirit. 'Well after Usain Bolt that is, who's er, the real king.'

'Who's the queen then?' asks Lawrence. 'Jessica Ennis?'

'Has to be,' says Jessica.

'And the Prince?'

'Oh I don't know, your wife started it...'

'Now, who's bickering?' says Gillian, with a smile. 'Let's not quarrel, we've got a long night. Who else is there to go, Jessica? Tom Daley?'

'Yes, Bolt in the relays, Tom Daley in the diving and Luke Campbell in the boxing.'

'Boxing?' says Lawrence. 'I thought they did all that during the day?'

'Not this one. Why, are you finally taking an interest in the Olympics after sixteen days? What took you so long?'

Lawrence looks at Gillian. 'And this is who you want for a daughter-in-law?'

'Might keep you in check, who knows?' replies Gillian. 'I need allies.'

Lawrence nods and leans back on the sofa. 'For your information, future princess, I've been following the boxing quite a bit throughout the Olympics: Anthony Joshua, Freddie Evans, those kind of fellas, even Nicola Adams…'

'Who did she beat to win Gold then?'

'I don't bloody know. Someone wearing red.'

Jessica and Gillian laugh. I suspect Gillian is pleased that Jessica is standing her ground in the back and forth bout with Lawrence. I am not swayed either way although I do get concerned from time to time that Jessica will push things too far. She must learn to show restraint sometimes. We are guests in this house.

'Who's coming tomorrow then, Francesca?' asks Lawrence, quickly trying to change the subject. 'Just a few select colleagues or a whole army of volunteers? I'm surprised you agreed to this. Do you think Donald would have approved?'

I can see Gillian already shaking her head at the tone of Lawrence's question.

'I think he would have approved because he loved the Olympics and what it stood for…'

'Your idea, was it?'

'Not originally, no. It was Jessica's.'

'Students do love their parties…'

'Can't you come up with a better cliché than that?' asks Jessica.

'Yes, how about 'Donald would be spinning in his grave'.'

'Lawrence, shut up!' says Gillian, looking extremely annoyed. 'Sorry about that Frannie…'

'It's okay, Gillian, we've got to get going anyway,' I say, getting up off the sofa. 'I need my rest and I'm not getting too much here. I'm just getting excited with all this success we're having. Come on, Jessica, let's go.'

'Oh no Frannie, come on, stay a bit longer. We were just starting to have a bit of fun.'

We head to the door and Jessica opens it. Gillian gets up and rushes behind us.

'I'm so sorry about his behaviour,' says Gillian. 'What I can do? I'll make sure he doesn't come tomorrow to spoil things…'

'I HEARD THAT. I WOULDN'T WANT TO FUCKING COME ANYWAY!'

I get out of the living room as fast as I can and head for the front door. I don't want a beautiful, glorious day to be tarnished at the finishing line. Gillian kisses me on the cheek. Jessica puts her arm round me. We head out into the street and I have to admit Lawrence has sown a seed of doubt. Would Donald want all those people in my house tomorrow? Maybe not, but he's not with us anymore; I make the decisions now. I want a full house after months of devastating silence. Is that so bad? If it is, I can take it because I've grown up so much in the last two weeks. It's like the timid, old Francesca that took baby steps into the Olympic Park never existed. For that, I can only be thankful.

DAY SEVENTEEN

I wake up just before 8am with a terrible pain in my back. Just my luck with all these visitors expected today. Is it anxiety or am I exhausted after the intensity and euphoria of a two-week spectacle? Neither, it feels as if Lawrence's return to aggressive behaviour has caused the pain; I had a dream a few hours earlier that he'd chased William all the way up the Yorkshire Moors and they had a duel at dawn in one of the fields, pistols at the ready, hats on and paces metronomically mapped out. They were wearing purple and red Games Maker uniforms. The only upside to this wild image is that I remember Gillian's medicine is still in my cabinet (I'd only used it once) so I get out of bed and go downstairs in the hope it will work its magic again. I pour some water and take two tablets. I think about the dream again. What happened when they were about to shoot each other? It's a hazy image but they actually end up exchanging t-shirts rather than firing bullets. It is an utterly stupid denouement (as Abigail would say after watching a terrible Hollywood film) but does have a certain logic to it.

I still feel tired and go back to bed. The drowsiness of the tablets puts me back to sleep. I wake up a couple of hours later and the pain is even greater now, a throbbing, searing discomfort in my lower back peppered by a glut of prickly muscle spasms. I think of home visits by the doctor and invasive investigations: scans, blood tests, pokes and prods. How would that go down with so many guests here? Everyone enjoying themselves while I'm bedridden, unable to tap into the nostalgia and feelgood factor. I get up again, annoyed that these thoughts are being allowed to seep into my head once more. If I hadn't gone to Lawrence's house last night, everything would have been fine. Jessica and I were happier than ever a couple of hours before that. I go downstairs and have breakfast; the warm coffee and buttery toast give me a lift. I write down the number of guests and the time they're expected to arrive. Only Deborah and Simon are expected by lunch – everyone else after 4pm. It would be great if none of them arrived until the Closing Ceremony which isn't expected to start until 9pm. That would give me time to have more pills – and be properly mobile.

Jessica wakes up just after noon, looking refreshed and relaxed, her cheeks glowing and her hair untied to make her look mature and graceful (with her London 2012 cap she looked at least 10 years younger). She puts the kettle on and turns on the radio. She changes the station from Radio Three to 6 Music, whatever that is. She prepares a hard-boiled egg, peanut butter on toast and peppermint tea and then comes down to sit at the breakfast table. She starts eating and then, finally, looks up at me.

'I don't want my parents to come,' she says,

rubbing a bit of butter off her fingers. 'I'm not sure this was a good idea after all…'

There is a moment of silence as I try to absorb Jessica's revelation with a mixture of astonishment and confusion.

'What are you on about?' I reply, trying not to exert myself as a bout of nerve pain had a habit of shooting down my back when I was under strain. 'You invited them all. How can you feel like that now?'

'I didn't invite them all…'

'Well, you know what I mean. If it was up to me, only your parents and Richard Krystal would come to the house.' I pick up the only letter I've opened from the stack of unopened mail lying in the centre of the breakfast table. 'This is from Abigail, my sister, who lives in Paris. Even she's congratulating us on a 'great Olympics'. Wonders will never cease.'

'Why didn't you invite her over?'

The mere raising of the question seems to increase the pain in my back. Jessica notices my discomfort.

'Okay maybe not. What's up anyway? Is it the back trouble? I saw some of those pills near the kettle.'

'Perceptive as ever,' I say, putting my hand on my lower back. 'I woke up with it this morning. The pain was excruciating.'

'Don't eat any more of those pills. We'll try something else after breakfast…'

'Like what?'

'Just trust me,' she says, taking a bite of her egg and following it up with a precise sip of peppermint tea. 'It's the lack of movement that causes it.'

'But I've been moving for the past two weeks. And besides, the pills have worked before.'

'You didn't have 30 people at your house that day. Or Lawrence's voice ringing in your ears…'

'Maybe you're right, maybe it is stress-related but if that's the case you're not exactly helping the cause. Why don't you want people to come? And particularly now, after we've been through all that trouble.'

She finishes off her egg and wipes her hands with a serviette. 'I'm worried Lawrence will have a barney with my Dad, that's the reason. If that happened in this house I would never forgive myself.'

'That's it?'

'Yes…'

'But that threat's been looming over us since you moved in here. And also when you started seeing William. What's changed now?'

She pauses and runs her finger round the rim of her teacup. 'It was last night, really. After his apology, I thought Lawrence would be a bit more respectful. If anything, he's gone the other way so it made me think a lot before I went to bed. I didn't sleep till about three…'

'But that's giving in to him. You've never been like that before. This is our house and we decide who we want here…'

'I know and I felt like that too but…' She folds her arms and leans back on the chair, '…he didn't let William come home last night after his shift so it's made me change my thoughts a little. He was locked out. William texted me at about 2am, asking if he could come here. I knew you were asleep so I said no; I didn't want to disturb you. It was bad enough, you dealing with Lawrence yesterday...'

'You should have just asked him to come round,' I say, tutting and shaking my head. 'I wouldn't have minded. I was fast asleep anyway. Where did he stay then? What happened?'

'He went to his landlord's house and he let him in and he slept on the sofa...'

I sigh and continue to shake my head. 'You should stop looking after me so much. I can handle it now. Poor William, Lord knows how he got through the night.'

'It wasn't too bad, they had a few drinks and watched DVDs...'

'I suppose he can't wait to leave home now...'

'He wanted to go this morning but I told him it was impossible.'

'And I'll tell you something else that is impossible...'

'What?'

'You telling anyone that they're not coming to my house. They are. And I'll be waiting for them.'

'But what if your back doesn't improve?'

'It will,' I say, with a smile. 'You just need to be true to your word. That still counts within these four walls.'

Jessica has some weird Bat for Lashes music playing in the living room as she demonstrates a yoga stretch while lying flat on her back on the carpet. She says this will cure my lower back pain. I watch, with no little anxiety, as she pulls up one leg to her chest and then does the same with the other. Then she raises one leg in the air, keeping her back still and straight, then the other. It looks quite strenuous and awkward for this time on a Sunday afternoon but I must admit I'm not in the mood to rule anything out as the pain in my lower back has actually got worse with medication not better. I thought Gillian said the pills worked every time? Not on this occasion. Jessica looks up at me from the carpet and tells me why I should follow her lead.

'When I played hockey, a few of my team-mates always had niggly back injuries,' she says, breathing deeply through her stomach. 'It's not surprising because we were bent over all the time with our hockey sticks sniffing around for the ball so our backs took a lot of strain. Anyway, this one girl did yoga and said it cured her back problems. I never had that problem but I still did the exercises because they're good for flexibility and movement...'

'I'm not sure Jessica,' I say, sitting down on the edge of the sofa with my hand on my chin. 'I don't want to make it worse.'

'It won't get worse, trust me. It can only help.'

'But I'm 68 years old! And I've never lay down on that carpet before. I'll almost be able to hear Donald's pounding boots if I did that.'

'All the more reason to do it then...' says, Jessica, now out of breath. 'Come on, you won't regret it.'

'But your mum and dad will be here soon…'

'Yes, and they won't want to see you suffer. Do you want to spend the whole day moping or being active? Two weeks of joy followed by one day of hell. You don't want it to end like that.'

I sigh and look around the room. It's as if there's a silent presence watching me from somewhere, waiting to laugh at me if I do something as silly this on my own carpet. But what have I got to lose? A bit of embarrassment is worth it if it reduces the pain. I reluctantly take off my shoes and lie down, awkwardly, next to Jessica. I look up at the high ceiling and wonder why Donald and I never replaced the patterned wallpaper we inherited. The globe-shaped light cover too. It all looked very old.

'Okay, close your eyes and relax first, Frannie,' she says, using her hand to demonstrate how to breathe deeply. 'Then we'll start moving the legs.'

I imagine Jessica could do a fine job as a yoga instructor: she's bossy enough, for a start! She asks me to grab hold of my left leg and raise it as high as I can past 90 degrees. I find it difficult, but the groans and the creaks seem to lessen as I raise the leg up and release it, doing the same motion again three times. I think of inspiring sportswomen and the way they move their bodies: Beth Tweddle, Jessica Ennis and Jayne Torvill; highly flexible and graceful. I gradually do more moves and find them oddly reassuring and soothing. For a while I even can't tell what Jessica is saying, as if I'm in some kind of zone. I imagine what it would be like if Simon and Deborah walked in now. I didn't care. Perhaps it was time for me to stop worrying about others people's perceptions and be bold. I look across at Jessica – her head all twisted and her hair all over the front of her face – and want to thank her for making me feel that way.

Jessica is in Donald's study browsing eBay on his old computer. She is seeing how much Olympic memorabilia is already up on the site – and what price it's selling for. She keeps shouting out these ridiculous prices and I do wonder if she's exaggerating.

'A basketball used in last night's men's final is going for more than three grand,' she says with more excitement than necessary. 'A maypole used in the opening ceremony; the asking price is £500. Those mascots too, what are they called?'

'Wenlock and Mandeville…'

'Should have put them in Stoke Mandeville. Anyway, there's sculptures of them going for £300 to begin with, I'm sure that'll increase. A Bradley Wiggins replica jersey: 600 smackers to begin with.'

'I thought people were a bit hard up…'

'They are – but everyone wants a piece of the best-tasting cake ever right now.'

The bell rings and I leave the bedroom to answer it.

'Oh, what about this…' she says. 'A Beth Tweddle gymnast outfit…'

'No…'

'Going for £150…'

'Funnily enough, I was just thinking about her…'

Jessica looks up at me. '…And that's why you feel better now, yes?'

I hold my back and open the door. 'A little – but there's still a bit to go.'

'You need a couple more sessions this evening…'

'You must be joking!'

I leave the room and walk downstairs to answer the door. A woman, who I don't recognise is in front of me, but I look over her shoulder and see Simon clearing the boot of his car so I realise it must be Deborah, Jessica's mum.

'Hello, Frannie, I'm so happy to be here,' she says, offering a firm handshake. 'What have you done with Jessica? You haven't locked her in the cellar have you? Wouldn't be surprised with her behaviour.'

'No, she's upstairs on the internet…'

Deborah rolls her eyes. 'Hope she cooked Sunday lunch for you?'

'We got up too late, really. I suppose we've skipped it. You're not hungry are you? We could still grab a late lunch.'

'No, we grabbed lunch at a crappy service station somewhere near Staffordshire.' She smiles and holds her stomach. 'I think it's still talking to me now!'

I laugh as she walks in. She is wearing a loose-fitting cardigan, dark jeans and trainers. Her light brown hair is very short and she has earrings in both ears. I notice a small tattoo on the side of the neck. She isn't the kind of dinnerlady I expected. I point the way to Donald's study, and she rushes up the stairs energetically. I continue to hold the door open for

Simon. He is taking his time. He has a case of wine, cans of beer, some carrier bags of groceries and even a colourful woman's dress on a coat hanger.

'Who is that for?' I shout, as he finally shuts the boot.

'For me, of course, don't you know I lead a double life!'

'I always knew you were a funny one…'

He laughs and walks towards the house. He comes in and I shut the door behind him.

'What about all that food and wine?' I ask. 'Who's going to drink that? Must have cost you a fortune.'

'I wanted to indulge a little to celebrate my new job, Frannie,' he says, dropping a couple of bags in the hallway and taking a breather. 'I've never felt happier after leaving that shithole bookies.'

'Do you have to swear?'

'No,' he says, with a grin. 'But it paints the picture a bit better, don't you think? You wouldn't want to get a job there.'

'I'd probably agree with that,' I say, picking up one of his bags and taking it into the kitchen. I am pleased that my back seems to be holding up.

'How's Jessica been anyway?' he asks, following me into the kitchen with his cases of wine. 'Behaving well, I hope.'

'She's been great…' I say, suddenly realising this *is* her last day in my house.

Simon expects me to elaborate but I don't.

'I sense a 'but' coming,' he says. 'She hasn't had

students coming round for all-night parties has she? The lass does like her music.'

'No, she's been fine,' I say, looking at Simon. 'It's just suddenly dawned on me that she'll be gone by midnight tonight – and I might not see her again for a long time.'

'Hey, come on it's a bit early to think that way,' he says, walking up to me and putting his arm round me. 'There'll be loads of visits after this. We'll all be going back and forth. Let's just think about today for now. This is your day – and we're going to top these wonderful Olympics off in style.'

I nod and he seems to acknowledge this as a green light to walk towards the case of wine and pull out a bottle. As if to pre-empt his thoughts, I point to the cupboard with the bottle opener and he pulls it out. He uncorks the bottle and reaches for two glasses. He pours two glasses of white wine – and I do not stop him even though it's very early in the day for me. He offers me the glass of wine and I take it, hesitating as I inch it towards my lips. I take a drink and then break out into a very slow, deliberate smile.

'CHEERS!' he says, touching my glass with his.

'Cheers…'

'To Frannie, I thank you from the bottom of my heart for looking after my beautiful, beautiful daughter. She is my life and my soul – and, from today, you are too…'

Simon and Jessica are watching British boxer Anthony Joshua on TV as he fights for the gold medal.

Deborah and I are chatting on the sofa, discussing the differences in volunteering skills in the two parts of the country. The front door bell rings thick and fast during this period. Sheena, her husband Gary, and their three childen: Theo, Jack and Nicola, all come in to make it a packed living room. Eric arrives soon after, looking resplendent in a dark blue blazer, grey trousers and a Union flag dicky-bow tie. Is he overdressed? Probably, but he mentions that as a bachelor if he can't get noticed by the way he dresses how is he going to get attention? Richard Krystal and his girlfriend Melissa arrive about 15 minutes later, with a couple of homemade cards, made by Melissa's two daughters. They show five wonky, but colourful, Olympic rings with the letters T-H-A-N-K written in each of the rings and then a 'U' underneath them. It's curiously uplifting. By this time, Anthony Joshua has won gold in the super heavyweight final – and everyone's mood is boisterous and upbeat. I go into the kitchen and start preparing dinner – but Deborah and Sheena are adamant they want me out of the kitchen this evening because I shouldn't have 'to lift a finger tonight'. I show them where everything is and off they go, preparing the steak, washing the salad and peeling the potatoes. I go back into the living room and end up sitting near Gary who smiles at me but doesn't say anything. He reaches into his pocket and starts fiddling with his mobile phone.

'Hope you're not bored already?' I say, feeling guilty that there doesn't seem to be enough activity to entertain him. 'Your children seemed to be enjoying themselves though. They're out in the garden with Melissa's daughters. Do you want a drink?'

'I'm fine, thanks,' he says, glancing up at me. 'I'm just getting over Chelsea's result today. They lost 3-2 to City. That's why I might look a bit frazzled.' He takes a deep breath and blows out some air. 'Right, I'm better now. Only takes me a few seconds to get over a bad result.'

'So has the season started then? Seems a bit non-stop to me.'

'Sort of. The Premier League starts next week. Today was the Community Shield.'

'Used to be called the Charity Shield didn't it?'

'Yes…'

'Do you know why they changed the name?'

'Haven't the foggiest…'

'Hmm, charity and community: maybe they thought charity was a dirty word. Community sounds much better.' I pause and look at the TV as competitors take part in the modern pentathlon. 'I suppose it's a bit like Games Makers. That sounds much better than volunteers. Sounds like we did something. Volunteers feels empty even though it's nothing like that.'

'I was telling Sheena earlier, have you noticed how these politicians are getting on the bandwagon now with all this Games Makers talk? They can't wait to be photographed with you now. They weren't around much at the beginning.'

'They like success, don't they?'

He nods and agrees so I decide it's the right time to take the plunge.

'You were cynical too though, weren't you?' I ask, looking at him directly for the first time. 'Sheena said you didn't want her to be a volunteer.'

'Well yeah,' he says, sounding a bit defensive. 'But that was because we had three kids to look after and we were stretched. Cash was also tight, so we had to weigh up a lot of things.' He puts his mobile in his pocket and straightens a collar on his polo t-shirt. 'But we made the right decision in the end. I'm proud of her that she saw it through but I also feel satisfied that I mucked in and looked after the kids for a couple of weeks. It was bloody hard though, there's no denying that.'

'Had you looked after them before?'

'Couple of days, yeah, but not for so long.' He smiles and looks at me. 'In the end, I was desperate for Sheena to come back. Fact is, I don't have the bond that Sheena has with her children – and I'm not ashamed to admit it. Every time I picked our youngest up, or changed his nappy, I found that my hands weren't soft enough for that kind of life. I just don't have the patience or the subtlety. I need to feel the harder things in life: a glass of ale, a tyre or an oil-stained engine. I know it sounds stupid but that's just how it is. I just couldn't get close enough to the kids. They wanted Mummy back.'

'Well, they've got her back now…'

Gary nods but then looks horrified as Theo comes into the living room, crying and bawling. The toddler runs over to Gary and his father can tell, with a sniff of his nostrils, that his nappy needs changing.

'You're going to need those soft hands, Gary,' I say, with a smile.

'Where's Sheena anyway, can't she do it?'

'She's preparing dinner so she's tied up.'

Gary pauses and looks at me, with the kind of pleading eyes I never thought he possessed. His face resembles a little child's more than Theo's does.

'Can't you do it, Frannie?' he asks. 'We've got all the gear in the hallway. Wipes and everything...'

I want to say no but Theo starts screaming. I look into the little boy's face – and realise that I must not miss this opportunity. To be a mother for a few seconds is worth it.

I get a call from Rob – he can't make it this evening. I am slightly disappointed, mainly because I won't get to meet his daughters or his wife, but when he fills me in about an emergency that he has to deal with, I completely understand his predicament.

'It's that tall boy I took along with me to the Olympic Park; Jamie,' he says, completely out of breath and unable to get his words out fast enough. 'He got quite ill this afternoon and because I live nearby, his parents asked me to drive him to the hospital. They haven't got transport, you see, and not too much money either so I wanted to help them out. I hope you don't mind, Frannie, as I really wanted to come.'

'Don't be silly, that boy is more important. Do they know what might be wrong with him?'

'Might be meningitis but we don't know. I just hope he gets better. He's wonderful to have around.

The Olympics changed him. He made so many friends and got his confidence up. He even thinks he could drive the van instead of me!' Rob pauses and sighs. 'But it's his parents I'm thinking about, I have to be there for them. I must do my bit.'

'Of course, I understand Rob. You've done enough for me anyway.'

'Maybe I can visit before the Paralympics start? I'll be doing some heavy shifts then too so perhaps I can pop up then and have a chinwag?'

'You do too much, Rob…'

'Such is the volunteer's life, Frannie. People rely on us round the clock and we have to be there for them. I do find it strange that we're letting our hair down today and yet our work has got in the way again. It's the curse of our trade, I'm afraid.'

'I wouldn't call it a curse…'

'It is if you can't have fun on nights like this,' he says, with a smile. 'Hope to see your picture on Facebook dancing the night away…'

'You must be joking…'

'Or doing the Mobot?'

'I've tried, my arms ache too much…'

Rob laughs hysterically. 'God, I'm going to miss this. Anyway, look I've got to go now so give everyone my Sunday best and hope you have a rollicking time.'

'Goodbye Rob…'

'Blow the Olympic flame out for me…'

'I will.'

* * *

We have all had dinner and the Closing Ceremony is about to start. Jessica has asked everyone to come into living room and I wonder why. The guests have been scattered all over the house in the past few hours – the garden, the bedrooms, the kitchen – that I fear they actually won't all squeeze into our main room. But squash in they do and I'm starting to get nervous that Jessica is up to her tricks again. After a few minutes of waiting, she walks in carrying a strange-looking podium, shaped like a mountain. She plonks it in the centre of the room and then stretches out the palms of her hands, looking at me as if to say I should come and stand on it. What on earth for? She goes back into the kitchen and comes back moments later with a megaphone, starting to look like the Games Maker I saw striding across the Olympic Park. She turns the megaphone on as everyone packed into the living room starts to cheer.

'Ladies and Gents, I'm going to keep this short as Big Ben's already chiming and I don't want you to miss the start of the Closing Ceremony but I want to put it on record that, without this lady to my right, I wouldn't have got through these Olympics in one piece. She looked after me, she gave me a bed to sleep in, she listened to me and, most of all, she was a great, great friend. I pay tribute to her this evening. She is a true Olympic champion, so I'd like you to welcome her onto the Pennine Podium this evening…'

'The Pennine Podium!' I say. 'What's that?'

Everyone laughs and then they all urge me to walk up to the podium.

'It's a northern version of the nice white ones you see at the Olympics,' says Jessica, speaking away from the megaphone. 'Times are hard, you know that.'

'Don't make a mountain out of a molehill, Frannie!' shouts Richard Krystal.

'You're our golden girl!' says Sheena. 'Come on, get up there…'

I reluctantly get up and walk to the podium. The applause is so loud I worry that the neighbours will be around any second to complain. I step up on the podium and then Jessica pulls out what looks like a gold medal from her pocket.

'What on earth is that?' I ask, looking sheepish as everyone stares at me. 'You're embarrassing me now.'

She then walks over to the TV and turns the sound down. She pulls out her mobile phone and fiddles around with it a little before a song starts to play. It's Petula Clark's *Downtown*. She puts the mobile down on the table and turns the volume right up. She walks back towards me and puts the gold medal (or is it?) round my neck.

'Where did you get that?' I ask. 'Is it real?'

'It's from the London Games of 1948. We had to search far and wide. It's real all right.'

She goes back into the kitchen and returns with a bouquet of flowers. She hands them to me and then turns on the megaphone.

'Ladies and gents, our Gold medal Games Maker, give her a round of applause…'

The applause is even louder than last time, with whistles, whooping and screams from the kids adding to the raucous, rowdy atmosphere. Jessica puts the megaphone down and kisses me on both cheeks. She stops after the second peck and looks me straight in the eyes for a few seconds. The chorus of *Downtown* is about to erupt. I think of what could have been for a few seconds but Jessica's gentle face melts it all away. She moves away from me and starts singing and dancing to the song right in the centre of the room. A few others join her as the song's chorus digs deep into my soul. A tear escapes from my eye – but I did it, I went down town and had the time of my life.

The Closing Ceremony is in full swing when Gillian and William arrive. The Pet Shop Boys are cycling into the Olympic stadium in their colourful pointy hats and Deborah thinks this means we're in for a much more eccentric show than Danny Boyle's first night. There's a lot more music: Emeli Sandè, Ray Davies, Madness, Elbow but what strikes me is the mood and atmosphere in the Olympic stadium. Do I detect a hint of sadness that it's call coming to an end? A tinge of melancholia? There are still cheers and shouts, of course, but perhaps British people sense the post-Olympic gloom of a Monday morning and don't like it; work has always felt something of a burden. I drink wine and chat to Deborah while all this is going on. Jessica has gone upstairs, with her journalist friend from the magazine (who finally arrives after missing his train) to do a short interview about her time as a Games Maker. She wants to do it now as she feels the London media won't care about her once she's back home. I'm not sure about that but at least she's representing us – the Games Makers – in the best light. Deborah, though, wants to know where she is. I tell her she's in Donald's study talking to a man from a lifestyle magazine. Deborah is surprised but happy that her daughter is learning more about the 'dark arts' of the media as she puts it.

'She's probably getting tips from the journalist about the blog her and William are setting up,' she says, stroking her earring.

'I thought that was just William,' I say. 'Are they doing something together then?'

'Yes, they're trying to set up a business relating to sports memorabilia. William's got the business and IT expertise and Jessica's got the sports background so they're hopeful it can do something. Sport is such a big business these days: the Olympics, World Cups, the Ashes...'

'The Ashes? I bet William came up with that one. He used to go with Donald when he was a boy.'

'Well, at least he's put it to good use then...'

I pause and take the gold medal (from earlier in the evening) off my neck. I'd forgotten it was even there.

'Do you think they'll make a good couple then?' I ask. 'Maybe get married, have kids?'

'Yes, but only if William can settle down in the north. I think he's a bit naive about how easy it will be.'

The door opens and Gillian walks into the room.

She politely smiles at both of us and sits next to Deborah.

'Where's William?' asks Deborah.

'Oh, he's in with Jessica and that ghastly journalist in Donald's study,' says Gillian. 'He asks so many questions I want to cuff him one.'

Deborah and I laugh. Gillian picks up a glass of wine and takes a sip.

'You shouldn't have let him in there, Frannie, I thought that place was sacred.'

'It's the only place free, really. We've got kids roaming about all over the place so most of the rooms are taken.'

'Hmm, so when are you leaving then Deborah?' asks Gillian, finishing off her drink alarmingly quickly.

'Probably about eleven, but definitely before the ceremony ends. We've both got work in the morning so, even though we'd like to stay, it's not possible.' Deborah leans back on the sofa and folds her arms. 'So where's Lawrence then? Why isn't he here?'

'Do we have to talk about him?'

'No.'

'Good…'

Gillian doesn't say anything else and refills her glass with some more wine. I think of saying something but the touch of friction I feel in the air seems to stop me from making a contribution. Instead, we watch more of the ceremony with George Michael singing *White Light* on stage. Finally, Deborah says something about George Michael having pneumonia and this song was about him saying thank you to the doctors for saving his life. I listen closer to the lyrics. What it about these songs tonight? They seem to be speaking directly to me. Yes, I'm alive – and this mini-house party was the best thing I ever did.

By 11pm, people start to leave and I'm annoyed I haven't been able to speak to some of them in depth. Richard Krystal stops me on the landing after taking Melissa's four-year-old daughter to the toilet. He says he's enjoyed the night so much even though he spent most of time chasing after the kids to ensure they didn't break anything or have quarrels with Sheena's children.

'I've just seen the Spice Girls in the Closing Ceremony pulling out of black cabs so that's more than enough for me,' he says, bending down to do up a loose button on Sarah's trousers. 'I start at ten tomorrow morning so we've got to get on. Pity I won't see the fireworks.'

'I'm sorry we didn't have a chance to talk, Richard. I've been so busy with everyone else. It's been a bit overwhelming really.'

'Policemen shouldn't get too close anyway,' he says, offering his hand. 'A bit of distance is good for us. It keeps us sharp and on our toes.'

I shake his hand but it all feels too formal and awkward.

'Maybe next time, eh?' he says. 'Who knows I could be back at the end of the Paralympics. One of my colleagues is competing – so I'm going to watch him.'

'Was he injured on duty?'

'Yes, a speedy car pursuit. He was chasing a hit and run driver. They both smashed into a bus coming the other way. Lost both his legs.'

'Oh, that's quite sad...'

'At least he'll have a chance to compete in the Olympic Stadium though. I'm proud of him.'

There is a moment of silence and then Richard smiles and grabs hold of Sarah's hand. He starts walking down the stairs but then the front door bell rings which startles Sarah – and she begins to cry. He tries to soothe her but she gets quite irritated. I follow them down the stairs and peer down at the front door as Jessica goes to open it. Who could it be at this time? Lawrence walks into the house a few seconds later. He looks up at me on the stairs.

'Hello Frannie, I know it's late,' he says, crossing his hands in front of his waist. 'But I want you to know that I'm here for you just like everyone else. I'm sorry about yesterday but that's history now. I will see my son off as it's a father's duty to do so. I have to be there for him.' He walks forward towards the living room door. 'Now, where are we at with this Olympic jamboree? Is the darned thing not over yet?'

Jessica rolls her eyes and looks at me. I nod in acknowledgement – but am determined that he won't spoil this night for anyone in this house. If he does, Richard is just a few paces away and can be relied on to take some notes.

Within the next hour most of the guests leave and, just after midnight as the fireworks from the Closing

Ceremony pop and crackle, Simon and Deborah are also packed and ready to go home. William and Jessica are in and out of the house like yo-yo's, glancing at the TV, picking up bags and, generally, forgetting there might be neighbours sleeping at this time of night. Jessica is still singing Take That's *Rule the World* under her breath (even though she isn't a fan) while she carries out these menial tasks. She puts her head on William's shoulder as the Olympic flame goes out. She does not make eye contact with me until all the packing is done – and the car boot has been closed for the last time. Once they are all outside – and there is only Gillian and Lawrence left in the house with me – they all hug me one by one and get in the car. William and Gillian embrace too. William is annoyed that his father hasn't come to the door (he is inside watching the last rites of the ceremony). He gets in the back of the car as Simon and Deborah get in the front. Jessica walks up to me and stops a few inches away. She looks down on the ground.

'Didn't we just share something incredible?' she says, finally looking up at me.

'I think we did. But we have to make sure it goes on…'

'When are you going to visit?'

'Come on, we've just had two weeks together. You'll get sick of the sight of me!'

She shakes her head and grabs me in the tightest embrace I can remember. She is in tears and tilts her head so I can feel her moist cheeks on the side of her forehead. I smile and clasp my hands round her back.

'Come on, your mum and dad are waiting,'

I say, finally letting go. 'They've got work in the morning…'

She wipes the tears away from her cheeks and moves away very quickly. She rushes towards the back door of the car and opens it. She gets in and Deborah starts the car. Simon winds down his passenger side window and waves.

'Goodbye Frannie,' he says, turning his wave into a salute. 'Thanks for everything you've done.'

William and Deborah also wave. Jessica doesn't and looks straight ahead. The car moves off and she finally glances at me unable to keep the tears at bay. The car goes down to the end of the street and then disappears into the night-time mist. I wait at the door for a few seconds, the sound of the engine and Petula Clark's voice lingering in my head as if they were one and the same thing. It's as if I am in a trance, but if I am, Gillian quickly jolts me out of it.

'I'm going home now, Frannie,' she says, tapping me on the shoulder. 'Jack's been with my father all night so I need to make sure they're doing okay. And besides, I'm not sure I want to spend any more time with *him* …'

I almost forgot Lawrence was still inside my house – the only person left.

'Oh come on, Gillian, just a few more minutes…'

'No, honestly I can't. How about we talk tomorrow at the library? I can tell you about your new volunteering role and what your duties will be. What do you say?'

'Well yes but…' I lower my voice. 'He's still inside.'

'But he respects you more than me, so you can deal with it better,' she says, stroking my arm and then beginning to walk away. 'See you tomorrow.'

I offer a limp wave but don't say anything. She walks through the gate and down the street. I walk back inside the house and let out an almighty sigh. I walk into the living room and see Lawrence sitting there in silence with the TV turned off. There is something on his lap. I recognise it as Gillian's book about her relationship with her father.

'This was lying on top of your radio,' he says, raising the book in his hand. 'I've never seen it before. I understand Gillian wrote it.'

'You knew nothing about it?'

'No-one tells me anything, Frannie, you know that.' He looks down at the book and nods. 'I read the first few pages. I must say it was incredibly moving. Can I borrow it to read?'

'Can Gillian not give you a copy?'

'I'll be lucky to get a biscuit from her right now.' He taps the book in his hands and stands up. 'So, what do you say? I will bring it back immediately.'

'Yes, no problem. I've read it all anyway.'

He straightens his belt and then walks to the door. 'My wife's an author, eh? I didn't expect that. Maybe if she didn't do all these things in secret we could have a future together.'

'And have you?'

'What?'

'Got a future together?'

He pauses and turns the book over in his hands, looking at the blurb on the back.

'As far as I'm concerned, absolutely. Seeing Jessica and William together like that has made me think again. I'm going to give it my best shot.'

'It'll have to be better than it has been so far…'

'This…' he says, tapping the book on his thigh, '… might be the missing link.'

I nod and there is a moment of acknowledgment between us. He opens the door and walks out. I hear his footsteps down the hallway and then the front door open and close. I breathe another sigh of relief and slump down on the sofa. I look around the empty room and it seems to be still vibrating with the noise of music, people, gossip and children. I get up and go to the kitchen. I make myself a cup of coffee and head upstairs to my bedroom. I get changed and sit down on my bed for a few minutes. I get off the bed and head to Donald's study. I walk in and sit on his old office chair. The silence is all around me again. A house full of people and now just me again, all on my own. I look at Donald's old bed and decide to snuggle up inside it. This time there will be no loneliness, no despair and no sadness. I put my head on the pillow and delight in the fortnight of memories I've just experienced. Golden days that may never come again. I think about Jessica – and her voice that kept me awake for all those nights. She is with me now – and so are all the other people I laughed with, cried with, and told jokes with at London 2012. We are one. Nothing can ever change that.

ACKNOWLEDGEMENTS

A massive thank you to all the London 2012 Games Makers who spoke to me before I wrote this novel – but a bigger thanks to five people in particular.

Suzette Woodward
John Fuller
Claire Wynarczyk
Amy Wharton
Claire Nash

Thanks for your patience, understanding and recollections.

Also a big thanks to the other voluntary organisations who, perhaps weren't involved in London 2012, but still took their time out to speak to me.

A final thanks to the team at Troubador, athletes, journalists and other sporting figures for their suggestions and observations.

This may have been the most pleasurable novel I'll ever write – but that's down to the contributions of everyone already mentioned.

They volunteered a bit of their time…

…and for that I'm grateful.